ALWAYS IN MY MIND

ALWAYS
IN MY MIND

Lilian
Roberts Finlay

COLLINS
8 Grafton Street, London W1
1988

William Collins Sons & Co Ltd
London · Glasgow · Sydney · Auckland
Toronto · Johannesburg

The author wishes to thank A. P. Watt
Ltd., on behalf of Michael B. Yeats
and Macmillan London Ltd., for
permission to quote from 'Cap and Bells'
and 'A Poet to His Beloved' in *The Wind Among
the Reeds* by William Butler Yeats, published
by Macmillan in 1950.

First published in great Britain by Collins 1988
Copyright © 1988 by Lilian Roberts Finlay
ISBN 0 00 223924

Made and printed in Great Britain by
William Collins Sons & Co. Ltd, Glasgow

For you, my love.

'If all else perished, and he remained, I should still continue to be . . . he's always, always in my mind – not as a pleasure, any more than I am always a pleasure to myself – but as my own being.'

WUTHERING HEIGHTS Emily Bronte

Chapter One

Mama had been in London for almost three weeks and now she was home. She had presents for everyone: for me and for Gran and for our maid, Phyllis, and for the shop girl, Daisy Emm. But most of all for me, lots and lots of presents for me: dolls and storybooks and frilly dresses and an exciting bangle in a velvet box.

'The shops in London are so magnificent, Mother,' she told Gran and Phyllis and me. 'Things you would never see in Dublin. Will wouldn't stop buying presents for Lia! Every day there was something in the shops that he must get for Lia. Something new and different every day!'

Gran held up the little bracelet. 'But, Marie, is it right to buy a golden bracelet for such a tiny girl?'

Mama laughed happily. She looked so pretty, her blue eyes were sparkling, the lamplight caught her fluffy fair hair coiled around her head. I could see Phyllis gazing at Mama with fervent adoration. Mama was Phyllis's ideal of all a woman should be. And wasn't it strange that I considered, even then, that Phyllis Daly's Ma was exactly right for a mother, fat and floury and surrounded by lovable little Dalys in rags and tatters? Mrs Daly was a great Ma for hugging and kissing her little ones while wiping their noses with a corner of her blouse. 'The poor childher,' she called them. Mama sometimes kissed me very gently on the forehead, a little absent-mindedly I thought. I longed to kiss her and sit on her knee and whisper that I loved her. Ah, perhaps she was too young, too elegant to have a

9

bothersome child. Or perhaps I knew that her thoughts of love were always with my father, her darling Will, fighting for his country in a land called France far across the sea. For his furlough from the Front, she went to London to be with him. Gran said it was like a second honeymoon every time; and Marie came back looking, Gran said, like a bride again. Even when she was expecting *me*, Gran said, she went to Will. They were sure I was going to be a boy, and Gran told me I would have been named William. When I turned into a girl, Gran said that Dada told Mama to give me a piece of his name anyway and that he was glad I was not a boy who would have to go to War. I understood this mystery of a piece of his name only when I began to learn how to spell.

With much tut-tutting, Gran fastened the gold bracelet on my wrist. 'Well, I never!' she tutted. 'Gold!'

'A gold bracelet!' Mama laughed. 'If it were studded with diamonds and rubies and emeralds, it still would not be precious enough for his little daughter that he has never yet seen. He treasures her little photographs but he is longing for the day when she will run into his arms. He dreams of seeing her. He talks of such a wonderful homecoming when the War is over!'

'Will that be soon, Ma'am?' asked Phyllis.

'I am sure it will,' Mama said, smiling, 'very soon.'

Mama handed over Phyllis's present in a big dress box. I knew it would be a coat and a blouse and a skirt. It was always the same present because Mama knew that, each time, Phyllis had to hand on her present clothes to the next sister. Phyllis had told me that clothes from London were like a gift from Heaven. I knew she would be choked with thanks and joy and the anticipation of queening up and down the South Lotts Road next Sunday.

'And something extra this time, Phyllis.' Mama looked at Phyllis affectionately. 'Ever since Lia was born you have been my right hand. My husband chose this.'

Phyllis took the necklace in her hands. Her eyes filled to

cry with gratitude as she gazed on the heavy amber beads. I saw it was the very sort of necklace she was always admiring in jewellery shops.

'You're never done giving me things, Ma'am,' she mumbled and her tear-filled eyes told Mama that she would treasure this gift forever.

Gran was fitting on the gloves and admiring the handbag that were her presents from London. There was a little frown of worry above her eyebrows.

'Marie, isn't it a bit . . . a bit . . . extravagant to be spending all this money every time you go over to Will in London?'

Nothing could quench Mama's gaiety. 'Will is not short of money on furlough, Mother. He has no way of spending it at the Front, you know.'

Evidently this kind of talk did not please Gran, who had four of her sons, as she often said, 'out there'. Now she was sharp with Mama.

'Marie, don't talk of the Front as if it were the front wall! They could all be shot, you know. Others don't take it as lightly as you do. I am not very fond of my daughter-in-law, Julia, as you know, but I must say I have to admire the way she is saving Johnny's money. She stashes away every penny of it. She and Johnny are going to start a guesthouse down in Bray when Johnny gets home from the Front. Of course, Julia's *from* Bray, her mother keeps lodgers. But Julia will have a *guesthouse* when the War is over.' Gran crossed herself piously the way Phyllis always did, and added, 'God help the guests.'

'A guesthouse!' echoed Phyllis, who had never heard of such a place.

'Everyone in Bray will have a guesthouse soon,' Mama said disdainfully.

'Well,' answered Gran, 'it *is* the new place for holidays and the nearest seaside resort to Kingstown. When the War is over, the English people will come flocking in droves – twelve and six return on the Mail Boat from Holyhead.'

11

'*We* have this place *with* the licence,' retorted Mama proudly, 'and Will is going to turn it into a singing pub.'

Phyllis and I exchanged secret glances. A Singing Pub? What was that?

Mama tossed aside the importance of Julia and Johnny's miserly savings. 'Will took me to every theatre in London, Mother!' her sparkle returned, 'and out to dinner every night! We stayed in a gorgeous hotel near the Marble Arch – all red plush!'

'Ah sure Will is a grand man,' said Gran generously, 'and how is he getting on at all in that awful War?'

Mama's face was beautiful. 'He looks so handsome! His uniform is so splendid! We danced in a ballroom, and when we were dancing, he sang into my ear (softly-like, very softly) all the songs they are singing in London. Oh Phyllis, I nearly forgot that I brought you back the sheet music with the words from the London shows.'

Phyllis took the papers with reverence. She was forever singing at her work. I thought she probably was the best singer in the world. She could rattle out the tunes on our piano, pressing her foot on the pedal so that great thumping chords echoed around our rooms over the shop. Phyllis was, in her own words, as proud as punch whenever Mama invited her 'to give us a tune.'

Now Phyllis was figuring out the words on the sheet music:

> *If I should plant a tiny seed of love*
> *In the garden of your heart*
> *would it grow to be a great big tree some day*
> *Or would it wither and . . .*

'I know this air, Ma'am, but I didn't know –' And then, ever dutiful, she checked herself. 'Hadn't I better be bringing the tea up now for yourself and Missus B?' Come on now, lovey, you can give Phyllis a hand with the tray . . .'

There was a winding flight of stairs down to the kitchen.

Here at the foot of the stairs was a hall and a hall-door. That door was never opened as everyone came into our house through the shop, and anyway the hall was always packed up with bags of sugar and boxes of butter. It was cold in this hall because a further winding stair led down to the cellar from which came an icy breeze through a creaky door. On this door Daisy Emm, the shop girl, had pasted a lurid picture of Hell. There were hundreds of horned devils with tails and red eyes, dragging old men in nightshirts down, down into everlasting flames. Daisy Emm said it was not only old men in nightshirts who went down into Hell. Oh no, little girls like Lia got consumed in those Flames of Hell if they ever went down those cellar steps. It wasn't just wine and spirits racked up down there, Daisy Emm said, there were strange things in sacks that floated in the water, filthy blood-coloured water that came up into the lower cellar at high-tide on the Dodder. The Dodder was the river that went into Dublin Bay at the Ringsend Basin.

'And those sacks can split open,' Daisy Emm warned me, 'can split wide open! So never forget, Miss, it was curiosity that killed the cat. Look at the picture of Hell on the door and let that remind you!'

I always held Phyllis's hand tightly when we went through from the shop to the kitchen. Upstairs I was not so afraid, as Hell must be downwards. Phyllis never contradicted Daisy Emm, so there must have been truth in Daisy Emm's warning. Maybe Phyllis was afraid too, although Gran had told me that Phyllis was twelve years older than me. She had started to work for Mama when she was twelve years of age.

There were eleven Dalys, Gran told me, 'like steps of stairs . . . but who am I to talk? I had the same, and more power to Ma Daly, she hasn't lost any yet.' Gran often mourned her four children who had died in infancy, all within a short few weeks, of some awful sickness called 'diphtheria'. 'No cure for that disease,' Gran would sigh, 'little children choked to death.'

13

Life seemed a very sad sort of story at times and it seemed we lived in a sad sort of place as soon as we stepped out of our own comfortable house. Except for Mama who owned the shop and employed Phyllis and Daisy Emm and an old man who did the heavy lifting work (and attended to the dreaded cellar), everyone else in Ringsend was poor. All the women had big families, 'and husbands who drank the wages' as they told Mama when they came on Fridays with their 'little books' to settle their weekly debt. Mama sat in her glass-panelled office, overlooking the shop, and she totted up the sums of money due for the groceries of the past week. I was allowed to perch beside Mama and listen, and sometimes clean the nibs of her pens – always provided I did not fidget or ask questions.

'Listen to Phyllis, lovey. Don't put your spoke in where it's not wanted. Mama will get upset. And you will be sent to the kitchen. Now remember, lovey – it's Phyllis's only day off in the week.'

Being sent to the kitchen for punishment meant passing the awful threatening picture of Hell, me alone and unguarded. That fear kept me silent and motionless on 'settling day'.

In the big kitchen with Phyllis, all sadness disappeared. Often Gran was there too, teaching Phyllis to cook. Gran had been taught by her Aunt Hannah, in Philadelphia, where Gran had lived when she was a young girl; 'an exile', 'an emigrant' was what Gran called herself. And Aunt Hannah, Gran said, was a true professional cook in a great hotel.

'I declare to my God, you're a natural born cook!' Gran often said to Phyllis. 'I never have to tell you anything twice! Do you write it down or what?'

I knew, because Phyllis had told me, that cooking was like music in her head. When once she knew the air, and learned the words, she never forgot either of them. She made a song out of everything, she said, and fixed it with the right tune:

14

'seven ounces of flour and half that of butter break two eggs and beat them well . . .' had an airy rhythm quite different from the measured beat of 'a pound of the best skirt steak two carrots and a Spanish onion . . .' accompanied by the regular thump—thump of the chopping knife on the wooden board.

'I love cooking and I love the pianna,' Phyllis confided to me regularly, 'what do you love best, lovey?'

I loved best being in Gran's little house in the city. I loved Gran best in the whole world. But I didn't say because I knew, in Phyllis's opinion, I should answer 'Mama'.

Phyllis and Daisy Emm and I had our meals in the kitchen. Mama's tray was carried upstairs to our sitting-room where the piano was. There was a lovely fireplace in this room, all marble and gilt with a big clock that came from Dada's home. Mama always drew a visitor's attention to this fireplace, telling how this shop was a tavern in the old coaching times. The attached house had been part of the hostelry; now that house was a run-down tenement in which lived two poor families who paid rent to Mama – when they were able. There were stables for the coaching horses out in the back courtyard. The stables were let to a man who made and repaired wooden wheels. He always paid his rent.

This sitting-room, 'Mama's room' Phyllis called it, was spacious and comfortable in the late Victorian style of that time. There were many china cabinets, flower-stands, side-tables, chiffoniers, and what-nots that Phyllis called 'dust-traps'. There were many comfortable armchairs, and two uncomfortable sofas. The big window looking out over the courtyard held a view of the distant Dublin mountains, Ticknock and Kilmashogue – one of the many uncles had told me these names. The other window looked up Ringsend Road to the Tram Stables, and Boland's Mills and the Hanover Basin where the trams had to wait for the iron bridge to open and close. This was an exciting adventure for me and Phyllis to watch if it happened on our daily walk. Sometimes bold boys 'scutted' on the moving metal and were roundly and loudly abused by Phyllis who said they were bloody buggers and blaggards. These kinds of words were sacred to Phyllis and Daisy Emm . . . children never used them for fear of upsetting Mama.

The Daly family were on our walk route, so we called in for a small chat. Mr Daly played the piano in the pit of the AZEM Picture House in Sandymount, so he was usually there during the day. He was a lovely tubby man who, as Mrs Daly said frequently, 'could turn his hand to anything, apart from the music altogether, he'd help a neighbour without thought of reward to fix a bit of wallpaper or paint a door.' I used to think that she forgot she had said the same praise yesterday, but he smiled without objection. He was never too busy to get down on his knees to ask me how I was and how was Mama and when was Dada expected home. Every day he, too, said the same questions and I said the same answers. I loved it. I told Phyllis she should be glad to have such a lovely father and she agreed 'only for the one every year regular.' She would not explain this, 'Not for little ears,' she said. 'You are always lookin' for information! Gettin' notions that would only upset Mama if she heard of them.'

For four or five years life, even when it seemed sad, followed a regular pattern in our house and shop. In the shop, people went on endlessly about the Nineteen-Sixteen Rebellion, but always glancing over their shoulder to see who was listening. Friend or foe? There were those who talked of the Sunburst of Freedom for Eire. Women crossed themselves with great piety when they whispered the Names of The Dead Heroes, and Patrick Pearse, and the Shedding of Fenian Blood. Then there seemed to be a lull between the Sunburst of Freedom and the departure of the 'Old Conqueror'. I asked questions of everyone, but somehow it was not easy to get answers.

'What are people afraid of?' I pestered Gran.

'They know damn well that the English won't give in that easily,' Gran told me in the privacy of her little house, 'and the half of them want the English to stay, they don't trust the gunrunners. But the English are in the middle of their own War with the Germans and they aren't sending proper soldiery over here to put manners on the Irish. They'll send somebody though, they won't be bested, they'll get the rebels into jails.'

The next time that Gran heard me asking questions, she called me out of the shop and took me firmly by the shoulder up to our sitting-room.

'Now child,' Gran said sternly, 'it is best for you to stop asking questions. You understand nothing and that's how it ought to be. But since I know you are all ears and full of curiosity, listen to this,' and she lowered her voice cautiously as everyone did then, 'though your Mama is a true blue patriotic Irishwoman (and why wouldn't she be, wasn't she born and bred in the city of Dublin?) all the same, isn't she married to an Englishman? (Well, a Welshman then, sure what's the difference? – Lia, don't interrupt me, like a good child) and you know, child, Will has risen very high in the British Army. Marie (your Mama) is the wife of a British Officer. Did you know she met him first at a Regimental Dance in Arbor Hill Barracks? Did you know that? Oh lovely she was that night, eighteen years of age, all dressed in a white muslin dress that I brought back from America for my poor sister, Kitty, who died of the consumption. Kitty never got to wear it. Layers and layers of muslin trimmed with gimpy lace. It took hours and hours to iron it even though it had lain in a box all those years. But Marie loved it and it was just her fit although you would have thought it was long out of fashion, but sure ball gowns never go out of fashion. Poor Kitty never got to go to a Ball!'

'But Gran, you were going to tell me about the British Army?'

Gran dried her eyes. She often thought back to Kitty and other sisters who had been 'wiped out,' she said, by the terrible disease of galloping consumption.

'Oh yes,' she said, 'you and your questions. You are upsetting Mama. Mama is the wife of a British Officer and some of the crowd around here have called her a renegade. What? No, Lia child, I don't know what it means. All I know is that she has to go very quiet in the shop when the Ringsend firebrands start their fireworks!'

I drew close to Gran. These words evoked a terrifying spectacle. She put her arms around me, and whispered in an even softer voice, 'They say the English have been here for seven hundred years and they are leaving tomorrow!'

'Will *we* see them going?' I breathed. The English! I wondered what they looked like. I remembered that Phyllis always hurried me past the Protestant church because all Protestants, she said, were English. If I could find out who were the Protestants, I would sneak up near that church and watch the English departing. Was the 'Old Conqueror' English?

'Gran, are we Protestants if Dada is a British Officer?'

'No, child, there are thousands and thousands of Irishmen in the English Army fighting in France, like your Uncle Johnny and your Uncle Jim and your Uncle Michael. And all those Irishmen can't be all Protestants because in Ireland nearly all the people are Catholic and they all have dozens of kids, that's their religion. The Protestants have what is known as a "Protestant Pair", usually a boy and a girl. So the Protestants are dwindling away, and the Catholics have the . . . have the . . . What's the word?'

I was puzzled. 'But we don't go to Mass like Phyllis does on a Sunday, Gran?'

Gran's cheeks went very pink, 'Well, we may be a bit lax,' she said. 'It was your Grandfather's fault! He wouldn't let a

18

priest of any colour past the door! He was a hard man – a good man, of course.' Gran mopped her eyes again, and then she added firmly, 'But Will said *you* were to be baptized, and you were. Marie has the certificate somewhere, I am sure. It cost five shillings!'

'And what about you, Gran?'

'When I was young,' replied Gran, 'we had the Band of Hope, and we had tea and bread – sandwiches at Sunday School. And that's enough, Lia, you would go on all day with your "what happened then?". Remember – no more quizzing in the shop.'

The shop and the house were always full of people who were full of laughter and song. Phyllis and Daisy Emm were always going dancing in the Marigold Ballroom with exciting young men on whose knees they sat in our kitchen, and sometimes Daisy Emm would go down the cellar steps with her young man, totally unmindful of the terrors of the picture of Hell.

Mama got free tickets for the Tivoli Theatre, and the Queen's Theatre in Brunswick Street. The posters with detailed programmes were pasted around the shop and, since Mama had to take me with her, I would have the programmes read to me endlessly in advance so I could anticipate the delights ahead. The Tivoli had jugglers and singers and dancers of every nationality under the sun, even from faraway Japan. Mama had favourite singers, especially one who sang the song which made her cry:

> *'Somewhere the sun is shining,*
> *Somewhere a little rain.*
> *Somewhere a heart is pining,*
> *Pining for love in vain . . .'*

'I know Dada must come home soon,' she would whisper to me, 'I long for him so . . .'

The Tivoli was on Burgh Quay. It had a very posh vestibule with great polished brass railings which Phyllis told me were solid gold. I liked going to the Queen's. The tram stopped right at the door of the Upper Circle and we were able to hurry up the stone stairs with our free passes and secure a seat in the front row. The Queen's was the home of melodrama. 'East Lynn', 'The Colleen Bawn', 'The Shaughraun', 'The Lord Mayor of Dublin', and every week another. Singers of sad songs were all very well in their own way, but I loved the very real stories of the melodrama. At Christmas, Mama gave the free passes to Phyllis and all the little Dalys came to the Pantomime. They loved to eat liquorice snakes all during the performance, and that was a wonderful secret delight. Mama never permitted eating in the theatre. That was for 'gurriers'. The tone of ladylike disgust in Mama's voice when she used the word 'gurriers' told me what it meant. They were the poor, shawl-clad, shoeless, foul-mouthed, unschooled, jobless tenement-dwellers – in fact the most of the people who lived in Ringsend and Brunswick Street and Townsend Street and even as far south of the Liffey as Irishtown. Beyond Irishtown, Mama told me there were wonderful affluent areas like Sandymount and Merrion and Blackrock and a beautiful seaside beach called Seapoint to which she was always promising to take me on the train in the summer.

When the Uncles, Johnny and Jim and Michael, were home on furlough or on sick leave, all the families assembled in Mama's house. Picnics were planned weeks in advance. Hundreds of sandwiches of ham and eggs were made by Gran and Phyllis and packed in wicker hampers. Gran made her special cakes, for each one of her sons had a particular fancy in the variety of Gran's cakes, although the caraway was always included because no one made caraway like Gran did, they said. Uncle Jim, who loved to roll on the grass with his fat wife, said the caraway had 'special properties'. Neither Phyllis nor I really knew what Uncle Jim had in mind, but Phyllis learned to make the caraway cake exactly as Gran did, and ever after when she took the caraway cake out of the oven, she would cross herself piously and say, 'God rest his poor old soul! Wasn't he the dangerous flirt?'

The 'Strawberry Beds' was the favourite picnic place. We hired three hansom cabs from Ringsend to Chapelizod. We were taken through the city and along the Quays to the Conyngham Road at a good trot. At Chapelizod, the men went into Caulfield's public house leaving the women and children in the cabs to proceed slowly to the foot of Knockmaroon Hill. Now we all got out and the cabmen led the horses up the hill. Here we waited for the men to catch up on us. We were all city children, my cousins and I, and it was exciting to feel we were miles away from Dublin. Uncle Michael, who was a great reader with an amount of book-learning of which I knew Gran was very proud, always instructed us to look down into the valley ahead. 'There's your River Liffey, the same one that flows into the sea at the end of your Gran's street. And look across there to your right, to the big iron gates with the nice stone lodge where the keeper lives, there's your Phoenix Park, the biggest park in Europe, like they say Sackville Street is the widest street in Europe.'

Mama always whispered to me that she had seen streets in London much wider, but no one ever contradicted Uncle Michael because he had had an injury in the War and felt, Gran said, 'his head at him in a dispute.' He always told us the story of Chapelizod when we sat on the benches eating our picnic and watching the River Liffey glinting in the sunlight. The other Uncles and their wives took their picnic inside the Strawberry Beds, which was a very popular tavern. Gran loved a glass of porter and Mama brought it to her where she had spread a rug on the grass, on which she would have a little snooze before the afternoon was over.

As Uncle Michael told the story, Chapelizod really meant the chapel of Isolde. In the Irish language, which he said was still spoken in the West of Ireland, the words were 'seipeal Isolda'. Isolde was a beautiful Irish Princess, the daughter of a wicked chieftain who lived up the Liffey somewhere. There were English chieftains who came adventuring to Ireland from a place called Cornwall. They sailed up the Liffey and they attacked the wicked Irish chieftain in his castle, and they captured the Princess Isolde. She mustn't have worried about being captured because she fell in love with the English chieftain's son who was, of course, a Prince as well. His name was Tristan. So a great war was begun for the return of the lovely Isolde. Uncle Michael was not sure who won the war, but Tristan and Isolde sailed away together and were lovers. The sad thing that almost spoiled every picnic at the 'Strawberry Beds' was that the lovers' boat ran into a terrible storm and it sank. Uncle Michael said for a solemn fact that their wonderful boat with silken sails is to be seen on moonlit nights coasting along the black rocks of Cornwall. Phyllis loved that story every time I told it to her.

We went once on a picnic to the waterfall at a place called Powerscourt. My cousin Percy climbed up the waterfall rocks while we all stood shouting at him to come down. He fell down and had to be taken to a hospital where the doctor put seventeen stitches in his head. The next picnic we went back to the Liffey and the Strawberry Beds. Percy fell into the river on one picnic, but he did not drown which Aunt Julia said was a pity. But then Aunt Julia never had any children to worry about, as Gran said.

I was always taken by Phyllis to make the arrangements for the hansom cabs. Mr Heiton owned the business and he lived in Thorncastle Street in Ringsend. Mr Heiton had a huge big wife of his own, but he liked to tickle Phyllis inside her blouse to find out, he said, how was she shaping up. She struggled, of course, in a weak attempt to fend him off.

'Well?' she would demand, rearranging her blouse.

'You're not makin' enough butther! You need a bit a help!' he always replied, winking in a leery way.

22

Phyllis would act offended, and flounce away. Out of sight, she would begin to giggle that infectious giggle with which everyone had to join in.

'What kind of help do you need?' I asked her after one of these encounters.

She screamed with laughter. 'A rub of his old relic, I suppose!'

I knew what a relic was. It was a scrap of a Saint's clothing, and it could cure illness.

'Perhaps Father Union could give you an old relic,' I suggested.

This so convulsed Phyllis that she had to tell it to Daisy Emm when we got home.

Father Union was the much-feared Parish Priest of Ringsend.

'Will I tell Mama, to make her laugh?' I asked as they fell around the kitchen, shrieking over and over again, 'God protect us from all harm!' But they warned me not to breathe a word about Mr Heiton, for Mama would be upset. And indeed I never breathed a word, nor about a thousand other things they constantly swore would upset Mama.

There was one thing that really did upset Mama, and vexed my grandmother, too.

'You will have to get that child up to bed at a proper hour, Marie. It's disgraceful.'

'Oh I know, I know, I know. Don't begin that all over again. It's not my fault, Mother. I do my best.'

'Don't start that silly weeping! Of course it is your fault. When she comes to my house, I have her in bed at eight o'clock, and asleep too. And she always looks the better for it.'

'It's the shop, Mother. When I'm down in the shop on the girls' night off –'

'*And* the nights you take her to the Tivoli! Taking a child to the Tivoli! Anyway, why do you let the girls off on the same night?'

'Ah sure they like to go together! I couldn't say no.'

'Time you learned! You've no guts! How can you hope to get on if you let people run you around the way you do? Think of the child.'

And my mother always promised that when times got more settled, she would make better arrangements for me.

Despite my grandmother's fears, I must have been very well protected indeed during those years. For that time in Dublin was a time of Insurrection, followed soon by Civil War.

As the wife of a British Officer, my mother's status lacked security. She was sent to jail in Mountjoy Prison, for fourteen days, for receiving a bag of sugar intended for the beleaguered garrison in Boland's Mills. It was said that the shop was a halfway house for their supplies. Gran took me to see her in a cell in Mountjoy. Was the pillow made of stone, or did she say it was as hard as stone? The blow to her pride was enormous. She was treated as a petty thief, not as a patriotic Irishwoman.

When Mama came home from jail, she was listless and pale. She never talked now of the promised homecoming. Gran said not to worry her, no one knew when the wretched War would be over. Every evening, Mama sat in her low chair by the window that looked up Ringsend Road. She was forever reading the letters that she kept in the carved box which was Dada's first present to her.

Although I could not read, I knew all about these letters, Dada's love letters from the Prisoner-of-War Camp in Germany. Sometimes, in response to my pleading, she read some pages, descriptions telling how they had to fight-up for poor legless soldiers who could not help themselves. And sometimes he wrote out little verses for Lia who would soon, very soon he hoped, be seeing someone who was longing to see her:

> *Be good, sweet maid, and let who will be clever.*
> *Do noble deeds, not dream them all day long*
> *And so make life, and death, that vast forever*
> *One grand, sweet song.'*

He did not claim to have composed the verses, but of course Mama believed he was a romantic poet as well as a brave soldier. And I shared her love and belief without the power to put the childish passion into words. I confided this to Gran on the day in the week I spent in her little house. She only shook her head sadly. 'It comes to us all. I hope to my God that Will comes home safe or I don't know what will become of her. Look at Julia, and all the years she denied herself to save for the guesthouse, and Johnny will never see it. All she has is a letter to say he died for King and Country. I never could see what he saw in her, but there is no doubt she will be able to soldier on. She's one of the world's workers. Poor Marie, she could never manage without a man, but we must stop worrying because Dada is safe enough in a Camp. Well, safer than in a battlefield. He was long enough in that.'

Johnny had been killed in battle in July and in August the word came that Jim too was gone, blown up in a land mine. In November, the War ended and the great and wonderful news came that all prisoners-of-war would be coming home.

Mama was radiantly beautiful. She was running to the mirror, she was re-arranging her long fair hair in different styles. She had a favourite shop in Dublin, Walpoles in Suffolk Street, and we were in there every day spending hours in the fitting room. Phyllis was given unrestricted use of the piano, and Mama sang along many of her cherished melodies, pouring out her heart to the one who would be coming to claim it:

> 'Love thee, dearest, love thee
> Yes, that star is not more true
> When my vows deceive thee,
> He will wander too
> Tho' too oft dim with tears like him
> Like him my light will shine . . .'

And Phyllis would press down hard on the pedal so the very ceiling would shake and we would all dissolve in laughter.

'Oh what a merry Christmas we are going to have, after all!' Mama sang out many times.

Mama and Gran took me into town to Moore Street where Gran said she knew the huckster who sold the best Christmas decorations in Dublin, and the cheapest, which was always a consideration with Gran. It was very exciting to see all the stalls along the sides of the street loaded down with red-berried holly and coloured balloons and monkeys-on-sticks and Christmas trees twined about with gold and silver tinsel and toy trams that could be wound up to run along and chains of necklaces that Phyllis would love to be wearing. I could have stayed there until midnight.

Going home on the tram we had dozens of bulky parcels. A man stood up to give Mama a seat, and she took me to sit on her knee. Her lovely, flawless face was close to mine. There was a misty perfume from the fur collar of her coat. For one whole half-hour I knew this was Paradise, and for many years it was the nearest I ever came to ecstasy.

Chapter Two

A few days before Christmas the telegram came. In the train, en route for the Channel steamer, my Dada had died of a terrible sickness called 'Spanish 'Flu'. He, and hundreds of other soldiers returning home after years of war, had died, and were buried in Holland.

In a lifetime, I have never forgotten the sound of my mother's tears.

Over and over, Gran appealed to her, 'Marie, Marie, for God's sake, give over. You'll drive yourself mad.'

Perhaps she did.

She sat on the low chair beside the window.

Close to her breast, she held the carved box. It was all she had of her dead hero. Through the day and through the night, she sat holding the box. I sat on the floor but she was never aware of me. She no longer had use for me. I wanted to talk to her, to cry with her, to kiss her tears away. Most of all, I wanted to tell her my heart was bursting with love for her.

'I am going to be six,' I told her when Phyllis brought me in to say goodnight, 'I am going to be a big girl and I am going to be your friend . . .'

Her wild eyes and sad distracted face awed me into silence.

It was only when Phyllis had tucked me into bed that I remembered all the kind things I had been going to say. Then I cried and cried, but into my pillow because Mama would be upset. I was sure I was just as lonely in my little bed as she was in her big bed. I longed to creep into her room, and creep into her bed. Some unnamed fear held me back. Perhaps I did not want to know, finally and forever, that she did not need me any more. Time quickly proved my childish instinct was right.

At first, she gave herself to the business of minding the shop. Daisy Emm was sent home, and Phyllis's hours were irregular and mainly in the house.

'Mother, will you take the child? She should be starting school soon – isn't there a nice convent school near you in Henrietta Street, or is it Dominic Street?' The request was repeated many times in the months following that awful telegram. My grandmother loved me dearly, the more because Mama did not, but she was adamant in her refusal to take me into her home as a little paying guest. I could come for little holidays, she said, but my place was with my mother.

'Time heals everything, Marie. Yes – everything. I lost my man too, remember. The child is more to you than the shop. You keep your child. You will never regret it.'

It was always the same answer, but I knew I would not be kept.

Mama had ceased to put her arms about me in the gentle, graceful way she had always done, lifting my face with her fingertips, and pressing her warm lips against my forehead. She used my full name if she called me, never the petname she had invented. In the evenings now, she did not open the carved box, the letters remained unread. She put rouge on her cheeks, and went down to the shop.

Phyllis Daly's last duty was to put me to bed before she went home. She was always kind, and more than kind. She knew no bedtime stories, but she would sing and dance in a very comical way, and if my tears of laughter turned to tears of loneliness, she would try tickling me as a last resort.

She was seventeen now and she was 'madly in love,' she claimed, with two different fellows. 'As different,' she told me every night, 'as chalk and cheese. You wouldn't believe the difference! Cheese is a howl! Makes me die laughin'. Up to all the dodges! But Chalk is an awful eejit. Yew'd have to tell him where to put it or he'd be stirring his tea with it!' Even I knew that Phyllis Daly repeated Daisy Emm's vulgar, funny and offensive sayings, but in all innocence. The difference was that Phyllis's infectious giggle would make me laugh so uproariously that Mama would come to say that I was to go to sleep and let Phyllis go down to the shop.

There was another reason for my resentful loneliness. The big detective from Dublin Castle to whom Mama had appealed for help when she was sent to Mountjoy Prison, and who had helped her (she said) by having her sentence reduced to fourteen days instead of six months, this detective had become a regular caller.

At first he came only to the shop to buy cigars and wine, but as the months passed after the awful telegram of Dada's death, he was admitted to our house. A cup of tea in the kitchen gradually turned into a visit at night in our sitting-room and Phyllis carrying up a tray with sherry and glasses. On those nights, Daisy Emm was brought back and she was the one who had to face down to the cellar if 'yer man (as they called him) fancied a drop of the hard stuff.' I was never sure if that was the same as 'a ball of malt' which he appeared to fancy on other nights. On those nights I was confined to the kitchen with Phyllis.

'Ah no fear, Ma'am, I'll look after her. Sure Lovey wouldn't run up those stairs at night to save her little life. Gallopin' horses wouldn't get her past the kitchen door to be stared at by that picture – the divils' eyes in it follow her halfway up the stairs . . . Ah, no, Ma'am, rest easy, I'll see you won't be disturbed. And we'll go to bed nice and quiet, won't we, Lovey?'

All Phyllis wanted for Mama was an end of bitter tears. If a little harmless flirtation with a big handsome man would make her beloved mistress happy, then Phyllis would play her part faithfully. I knew always and always that Phyllis loved me and was endlessly patient and kind. But there was never any doubt that Mama came first.

This detective seemed to me like a Black Shadow who came swiftly through the shop and up the winding stair. This Shadow came between me and the precious hour that Mama had shared with me every day. Instead of a loving Dada who had been promised to me for all my life, this evil Shadow had been sent. I refused ever to look at him. I did not want to know his face. I wanted to feel hatred. In my imagination, I made up stories about this lying, thieving Black Shadow. I cried myself to sleep to prove to myself that I was desperately unhappy.

'You are a bold, bad girl, Lia,' Mama scolded. 'Burton has been a good friend to us. You are acting like a little gurrier.' That was her lowest condemnation.

'I hate him,' I shouted at her, although I knew Phyllis would sulk at me for a week for upsetting Mama. 'And I don't care!'

'You stop that snivelling! You have to be friends with him. I say so.'

The next time Burton was expected, Phyllis was instructed to do a thorough job on me in the big tin bath in front of the kitchen fire. I was dressed in one of the frilly frocks that had come from Dada. Phyllis brushed my hair until I begged for mercy. Then Mama came and tied it back with a satin bow.

'Bring her up, Phyllis,' Mama said, 'when I call from the landing. Now, Lia, be sure you have your manners.' She said it nicely to coax me.

'Oh she will, Ma'am, she will. I've been drillin' her! And I have the room a treat, and there's a grand fire, should last the night!'

And so I was brought up to our sitting-room, and offered to Burton.

Mama put me sitting beside her on the ottoman to one

side of the much-admired fireplace. Burton was stretched comfortably in the big armchair which Mama used to say would be Dada's special-chair-by-the-fire-in-wintertime-when-the-War-was-over.

'Look up, Lia, don't hang your head down so! Lia!'

I could smell the cigar smoke. I could see his well-polished shoes. I had never seen shoes like that: so leathery, so confidently, so negligently placed on our hearth rug. I climbed onto Mama's knee, and for once she permitted me to stay.

'A very beautiful picture you make,' Burton said, 'the two of you.'

Traitorously, I liked his voice – so different from the Ringsend voices. It reminded me of the clover honey that Gran dropped slowly from the spoon on fresh hot scones. Although his voice was very deep, there were no blurry notes in it. Like the golden honey, you could see the light shining through.

Slowly, slowly, I raised my eyes until I found his face. His dark brown eyes were twinkling, his teeth beneath a heavy moustache were smiling. It was a smile I would learn to know, a smile he always smiled for me. It was a tender smile full of complicity. His smile said, and his smile would always say, we understand each other.

'Come and sit on my knee,' Burton invited.

'Go on, Lia,' Mama urged, 'be agreeable.' She lifted me up and Burton took me on his knee.

He smelled warmer and nicer than anyone I had known. Was it some aromatic soap he used, some fragrant oil on his hair or on his moustache, was that the faintest breath of port wine, did he use some secret perfume on his hands or on his cheeks? In that first moment he was full of a mysterious essence which seemed to convey the idea of masculinity to the mind of a small girl whose Dada had never held her in his arms . . . whose Dada had never seen her.

I lay back and gazed at him. This Black Shadow was

31

actually a very real man who sat in Dada's chair and smiled this intimate smile, a man who could have been Lia's Dada.

Very quickly I struggled down, but only because I wanted so much to stay there. I wanted to pretend to be the little girl whose Dada exhaled the perfume of roses. Running out to the landing, I cried to Phyllis to come from the kitchen for me. Once there, I threw myself into her arms and cried and cried, saying again and again, 'It's not fair! It's not fair!'

After Phyllis put me to bed, she went down to the shop to help Mama. Because the shop was licensed, it was seldom closed before midnight. On the nights when Mama was with Burton, Phyllis had to hurry down to help Daisy Emm. I tried every night to keep Phyllis as long as I could, and she, who was the kindest-natured girl in the world, would try to make me laugh and be happy before, at last, she had to run down the winding stair, shouting on every step, 'Be good now, Lovey, and go to sleep!'

When Phyllis was gone, the night stretched ahead like a black eternity. Maybe I fell asleep quickly some nights but there were nights I stole down to the crowded shop, my bedraggled nightgown wet with tears, sobbing and pleading to be let have a little bed under the counter, near people, near company, near Mama.

Loneliness was what was hurting me. Boldness was my mother's name for it. And at last I too was sent away. I was bold, I was a disgrace.

Now I saw my mother only at intervals. No more on her free night did she take me to the Tivoli, or the Queen's. She had the company of Burton. An old woman in Hastings Street, off Ringsend Road, was paid seven shillings a week to board me at her house, for sleeping and a cup of tea.

Hastings Street was a long narrow street of poor houses. Downstairs there was a living-room, a small kitchen and a lavatory in a tiny walled yard. Upstairs there was a mean front bedroom and a very mean back bedroom. Hastings Street and Little's Terrace were locked back to back by the walls of each others' miserable yards.

The time had come for me to leave the comfortable rooms in our house. Every night at half past seven, Phyllis took me across the South Lotts Road as far as the door in Hastings Street.

The first night she thought to settle me in comfortably and make sure I would be all right. Crossing the streets and holding my hand as she always did, she told me that next week I would be starting to go to school. Mama had found a school run by two old ladies in Queen's Square.

'These oul wans used to be actresses,' Phyllis said. 'Me Da says that Queen's Square is full of lodgings for theatre people that come to Dublin.'

'To play in the Queen's or the Gaiety or the Tivoli?' I enquired knowledgeably. Phyllis said she'd ask her Da.

I was going to be six, she said, on the twenty-first of February. Does everyone always remember the first time she hears the date of her own birthday? The coldness and the darkness of that evening and the feel of Phyllis's woollen glove come back to me with the word 'birthday', and I remember again the small parcelled chamber pot that I was clutching to my chest.

Mrs Mayne would not permit Phyllis to pass through the front door.

'You can go now, Phyllis Daly, if you please,' said the old woman in her cracked voice, 'I must shut my door.'

'I'll put her things away!' roared Phyllis.

'Move off now sharp,' repeated the old woman, 'she can put her own things on the box in the room.'

'I want to settle her in for the night!' Phyllis bellowed.

'Settle her in?' Mrs Mayne cackled. 'Is it a lady's maid you are or what?'

'She's only a baby!' Phyllis screamed, close to tears.

'She's not a baby,' the old woman was getting very angry,

33

'her mother told me that she is going to start school and I am to have her up at eight o'clock in the morning, so now, Phyllis Daly!'

'Let me put her suitcase up in the room, can't ya?' shouted Phyllis even more loudly and moving as if to knock the old woman down, or like to anyway.

'And have a sly look around?' sneered Mrs Mayne, suddenly exerting her strength and pushing Phyllis out into the street, slamming the door with a tremendous bang. I heard Phyllis shouting her favourite condemnation for anything, and she shouted it three times: 'Pure bloody buggery!' Then I heard her thumping step going back up the street.

The old woman lit a candle and dragged my case up the stairs. I stumbled after her, clutching the chamber pot.

She put the case on a box, and opened it.

'Take out what you want, and then shut it. It'll keep the dust off your things. Did you bring the chamber? God, it's freezin' up here. Hurry in and then blow out the light.'

I listened to her footsteps on the stairs. A heavy door banged below. By stretching out my arms I could almost touch each wall. My candlelit shadow was trembling like a giant on the low ceiling. I had never undressed myself before. I had never brushed my hair. Where would I wash my face and hands? If I got my clothes off, how would I get them on in the morning? There was a bodice with a lot of tiny buttons up the back.

My coat came off easily enough but I did not know what to do with it. There was no hook to hang it, and anyway I felt cold so I put it on again. I looked for my brush. My hair felt full of tangles and the brush hurt. Perhaps Phyllis had gone back to tell Mama how horrible the old woman was. Then I remembered. Phyllis was going back to mind the shop for Mama's night out with Burton. No more than I would dare, would she dare to upset Mama.

I had lost Mama and now I had lost Phyllis. My refuge

was always tears. Now these began to fall. The old woman would come and I would melt her heart with my tears. Unbelievably she did not come. Perhaps she had gone out. Fear was added now to desolation. I filled the air with big gulping sobs. I opened the door but I was afraid of the darkness on the stairs. Something scurried across the crack of candlelight so I shut the door and sat down on the bed to cry as loud and as hard as I could.

Through the noise I was making, there was something tapping at the window. I buried my face on the bed, so that I could hear only myself. Then the window was pushed up, and shut again. I was petrified with terror – I had heard of 'Black and Tans'! I was lifted gently off the bed, I was being soothed in someone's arms, someone was trying to dry my face. I peeped through my fingers. This was not a 'gurrier' from Ringsend, the voice was not honeyed like Burton's, but it had an accent, a cadence, of someone who spoke English, but with reluctance.

A gentle voice was asking, 'Are you going to yell all night – I've got to study, you know. Come on now, little one, dry those tears. There, there, stop crying!'

With a quick response to affection, I was soon babbling out all my troubles – not only the immediate problem of undressing, but all the sorrows that had heaped up on me since that day of the telegram, making me an orphan like in a story. And now today the final disaster. Gran had gone to England to help the widow of the uncle killed in the last days of the war. Even to remember the jolly uncles of the picnic days started off my tears again; and Phyllis, I told him, had read in the paper that this is the War to end all War, only that's too late for them.

My new friend was very patient. He listened, smiling a little. He patted my hands, until I had quite calmed down.

I knew him of course. I had recognized him when I peered through my fingers as he lifted me off the bed. His mother came into the shop with her 'little book', there was a sister too. I knew they lived in Little's Terrace, he had heard the yelling, and crossed the narrow walls connecting the houses.

'Your mother teaches the piano,' I told him brightly, 'and your sister sings too. I heard her in the Ierne Hall. She won a prize, and Phyllis didn't, but I think Phyllis was the best. I would have given her the prize!'

He showed a lot of big white teeth when he smiled. 'But then you love Phyllis, don't you?' I saw that point but I also loved the way Phyllis sang. 'All flashing eyes and heaving diddies, that's the way to sing,' Phyllis had often told me.

'Yes, but your sister stands too still,' I objected. 'Look at me, now!'

I jumped up, and showed him how his sister stood, drooping like a flower out of water. Then Phyllis. 'She pumps up and down, and waves her arms, and her head goes, look, like this, and her eyes roll ooh and ooh!'

He laughed and clapped, and then he said very seriously, 'Yes, she was very funny.'

I was triumphant, 'There, you see!'

'But the song was one of heartbreak and exile,' he said. 'Laelia interpreted the song. Do you understand? A forsaken woman far away from the country for which her hero sacrificed his young life?'

I never had any trouble understanding words. I knew at once what he meant.

'That is why she won the prize?' I asked, using the new word very carefully. 'Interpretation?'

'That,' he said gravely, 'and the beauty of her voice.'

Suddenly, I remembered the old woman and I clung to him again. 'She will hear us,' I whispered close to his ear.

'Don't worry about Mrs Mayne,' he said cheerfully. 'She is stone deaf and she sleeps downstairs anyway, because there is a hole in the front roof. Now how about going to bed, and letting me go back to my books? Come on now, I'll help you.'

36

His hands were warm and gentle as he took my clothes off. He found a nightie and a towel in the little suitcase on the box. There was no jug of water, nor basin in the room.

'Lick that,' he smiled, 'I must get the tears off your face. Shall I brush your hair, such long hair for such a little girl. Now into bed. Here are your clothes on the end of the bed. In the morning turn the buttons all to the front. Don't forget that, it's important.'

When he bent down to say goodbye, I put my arms quickly around his neck. 'I love you,' I whispered, 'will you marry me?'

'But of course,' he answered, 'if you can only wait about twenty years.'

'Oh I don't mind that,' I assured him, 'will you come tomorrow night?'

He laughed again as he went through the window. 'I love your teeth, too,' I called after him.

It was only when he was gone that I thought to tell him how cold my feet were.

Of course, I had to tell Phyllis all about my new friend as she was taking me to school next morning. She looked aghast, and she tightened her grip on my hand.

'Pure bloody buggery!' she ejaculated. 'God protect us from all harm. Do you know what they are? Those Vashinskys? They're Jews, that's what they are!'

'Juice!' I echoed. 'What do you mean?'

'Jew-es! Jew-es!' Phyllis repeated, looking as scandalized as she used to at Mr Heiton. 'I wouldn't let a Jew into me bedroom for love or money! D'ya hear that? Love or money!'

'What's wrong with them?' I asked.

'Dirty, that's what they are. Dirty!'

'Not *my* friend!' I felt very loyal and I pulled my hand away from Phyllis. She grabbed my arm, 'Now we don't want to upset Mama, do we? I mean, young fellas in a little girl's bedroom! I mean, he's not just a little boy, he must be about fifteen. He got some sort of a scholarship or some-thing and I heard his mother telling your Mama that he's going to study for a doctor next year or sometime. He's supposed to be clever!' she added grudgingly.

I remembered that Laelia had taken the prize from Phyllis. 'You're just jealous, Phyllis!' and then I was sorry for saying that. I threw my arms around her and pressed my face against her skirt. 'I was so lonely,' I sobbed, 'and he was so kind to me about the bodice and all.'

Phyllis knelt down on the ground to comfort me. She cried with me and I knew she cried for me although she did not know the pain of loneliness because in her house there were ten of them, and she slept in a bed with two small sisters. How I envied them for that! Phyllis at the top and them at the bottom all mixed up with Phyllis's big legs.

'Don't tell Mama,' I begged her. 'I will be good. I pro-mise. I promise. I will do exactly what you tell me. Only don't tell on me, please.'

Every night when Phyllis brought me over to Mrs Mayne's house, she extracted a promise at the door.

'No funny carry-on now. Promise Phyllis. Cross your heart and swear to die, if this night you tell a lie! You'll go into bed like a lamb. Never again! Faithful promise!'

I nodded solemnly many times but behind my back I crossed two fingers and then uncrossed them. This was a sign of absolving one's conscience from a lie. A girl in the new school had shown me this and I regarded it as a very useful piece of knowledge.

And almost every night Tadek came across the wall. He undressed me, rubbed me gently with the towel, especially my feet 'for the circulation' he said, and the very word was warm. Then he put on my nightie, buttoning it up and smoothing it right down to my toes. I sat up in bed and he brushed my hair. I told him many times how much I loved him for it seemed as if loving him grew big enough to fill the world. Secretly I made plans for our future together, the kind of house we would have with a big red fire and a glowing lamp; the number of children we would have – at least ten so they would never be lonely. When he bent to say goodnight, I always asked him to kiss me on the mouth (Daisy Emm had told Phyllis that was 'The Ultimate') but he never would – 'Someday! Someday!'

When the winter nights began to shorten, Tadek had to wait for darkness before crossing the wall. I learned to get my clothes off and to fold them neatly. I was careful never to adjust my nightgown quite correctly, getting a sleeve tangled, or the frill of the collar pushed into a buttonhole. Tadek accepted the ruse. The smoothing-down-to-my-heels of the nightie was a lovely ritual that I never wanted to give up. When he came very late, he stayed a little longer to make up for my waiting, and because he had finished his study that much earlier. As he brushed my hair, I asked many questions about what he learned. He was too young by a year to take his Pre-Med exam in the College of Surgeons, he told me. He had a whole year to fill and he filled it with study. I felt he must be the wisest boy in the world, with the greatest brain and the nicest teeth. I watched his teeth with so much concentration as he answered my questions that I scarcely listened.

'You know you ask me that every night.'

'Do I? Well, tell me again.'

'No, it's away over your head. You tell me something instead. How's school?'

School was never good and because Tadek was sympathetic I made it sound even worse. 'I was a dunce. I was put standing at the wall. I was slapped with a cane, so hard that I cried every day.'

'Show me your hand,' and Tadek would hold my small hand to the candlelight and examine it carefully. 'I see no mark of the cane. You are a little exaggerator.' He would kiss the palm of my hand very tenderly because he read my need and responded to it as far as he thought suitable.

39

I had need of help in other ways. I longed to read yet seemed unable to recognize the simplest words twice in succession. I had not progressed beyond 'Hooks' in writing. Tadek took the matter in hand. When I could repeat the alphabet from memory, beginning at any letter and returning to it, he named a letter for me to write down, copying from the large alphabet he had printed thickly on a piece of cardboard. By degrees he would call out two, then three, letters. Then we went back to the beginning. Each letter, now totally familiar, had a special sound of its own, he told me, some letters had three or more sounds, sharp and soft, similar and different.

I do not remember how many weeks passed before I could grasp this. It was a great victory for him when I told him that, instead of staring at the ceiling and longing for him to come, I had been practising little words. 'I got "nun" and "none",' I greeted him excitedly. His wonderful smile would have rewarded torture.

I began to understand how difficult it was for him to bring pencils and copybooks to me. In a time when nearly everyone in Ringsend was poor, Tadek's parents were very poor. His father had been a lens-maker, his sight had failed and he was dependent on the charity of the small Jewish community. His mother taught piano to a few poor pupils. To allow their son to study instead of seeking a job, was a supreme sacrifice.

Tadek never found it easy to talk about himself, or his family circumstances. When he came across the wall at night, and of course it could not be every night, he escaped from the very real poverty and misery of his home into a kind of pretend poverty in Mrs Mayne's back bedroom. Everyone in Ringsend knew that Mama was wealthy. Because I was so miserable notwithstanding her money, Tadek had to invent a kind of happy fairytale land for me. So he seldom referred to his family's diminishing means, or to his father's blindness. He loved his parents with a fiercely protective love. Just now and then, he would tell me that he would lead them out of the Wilderness. I understood what he meant by this, he knew that I understood and when he had something that was bitterly pressing on his heart, I understood even without words. He was the one person in my little world who was always patient with my endless questions.

Because Ringsend was a small place where neighbours knew all about each other, I knew from listening in the shop everything (which was little enough) there was to know about the Vashinskys. There was a Pogrom in their native land. I understood this to mean that people of their religion were banished and their riches taken from them. I did not know why. The Vashinskys were trying to get to America and they ended in Dublin. I did not know why.

There was one thing I did know, young and silly as I was. The time before Tadek was like a night and a day. Tadek's coming was the whole of my childhood. I saw him only for a little while most nights in the dingy bedroom in Hastings Street, yet he informed every hour of my day. He was my friend, my brother, my father, my family. I told him a million times that I loved him. He would shake his head, smiling to show that he liked being loved, but had no response to make.

Chapter Three

'I thought I would find you tonight rolled up in the blanket, having a good sob,' was Tadek's greeting to me one night when he found me struggling with a homemade card on which I was printing 'Happy Anniversery to my dear Tadek'. We had known each other a whole year, so I thought he was teasing me. Tadek took the card, and examined it with evident admiration. 'You are most artistic,' he said, 'but there are two "A"s in anniversary. It is a very big word for a little girl.' Then he sat down on the bed beside me, and taking the pencil, he circled the wrong spelling.

'Don't get upset, Lia,' he said.

'I'm not upset,' I answered. 'It is only an old word!'

'It is a lovely word,' Tadek murmured, 'but that is not what I meant when I said not to get upset, Lia.'

'Can't you stay tonight?' That always upset me.

'They have not told you?' asked Tadek. 'Laelia heard it in the shop when she went to buy candles.'

I shook my head. 'Told me what?' I asked.

'About your Mama getting married?'

No one had told me. I knew at once that they would have put Phyllis under a solemn promise not to tell, and with Phyllis the important thing was still 'We mustn't upset Mama'. The hurt of not being told, of being left out, of being rejected from Mama's life, of Mama waiting until Gran was away in Torquay with Uncle Michael on a little holiday. The hurt, the hurt. I stared at Tadek. The hurt was unbelievable. The hurt was winding in my stomach like a corkscrew winding into a wine bottle. I was still staring at Tadek, seeing him perhaps for the very first time, his eyes are so dark they are black, his hair is so dark it is black and curls down on his neck, and his nose is not small but it is a perfect shape, his eyebrows are curved like arrows, he is thin there are hollows in his cheeks he must be hungry.

Tadek took a white handkerchief from his pocket. He let me cry and cry and cry. 'Funny little thing,' he murmured, 'crying is the only thing that helps you.'

The next night, Phyllis took me to sleep at her house. I shared a bed with her two little sisters and Phyllis slept on their couch. I was to stay in Daly's for the three weeks of Mama's honeymoon with Burton. There was no big wedding with flowers the way I had pictured it when I was feeling rejected. Phyllis said they had gone off secretly on the mail boat from Kingstown to Holyhead and Burton had told Mama, who had told Phyllis, that he had it all arranged for a Civil Ceremony in London. Phyllis kept on crossing herself and hoping that 'Civil was the same binding until death do us part as the Church was'. She didn't, she confided in the deepest secrecy, feel that Mama should trust herself so completely to that Burton. She predicted that there would be Holy Hell let loose when Gran came back from her holiday.

It was great fun staying in Phyllis's house and the Dalys were very pleased with the money Mama had left for my keep. I missed Tadek at night but sometimes I saw him in the distance during the day. Unfortunately, one of the little sisters had the measles and I picked up the infection. The little sister got better but my measles developed into something called Scarlet Fever. An ambulance came for me and I was put in isolation in Clonskeagh Fever Hospital.

I was not to see the row of massive proportions which Gran created on being told of Mama's marriage. Nor did I see the desolation into which Mama was thrown when she returned to find me in a fever hospital. Phyllis expatiated on both, but that is not the same thing as being on the spot and then telling other people.

It seemed an age before the old routine of Mrs Mayne's bed-and-tea, for seven shillings a week, was at last resumed.

Tadek hugged me.

'You are as thin as a sparrow,' he said, 'you look awful! They must have starved you in that Fever Hospital. That can't be right. You could end up suffering from malnutrition. That must be wrong, to lose so much weight in a hospital.'

Every night for a long time he used to bring something for me to eat. Very often it was a thin pancake rolled around a little cheese. Sometimes it was a tiny puffy pastry that had been fried in oil. Tadek said that was 'mandeln' and he was very fond of it. Another of his favourites he called 'latkes'. They tasted of cinnamon, and were like the potato cakes Gran cooked on Fridays. When he stopped bringing little treats, it was not because I had grown fat. It was because the Vashinskys were growing poorer. Despite Tadek's endless study, and the fact that he won a scholarship into the college, his parents were finding it harder to pay their rent and feed their two children. Now it was Tadek who was thin.

Phyllis Daly still brought me to school each morning, and one morning she said: 'Do you remember the young fella that climbed into your window? Well, I heard his aul fella is going to be put out for not paying the rent.'

'Wouldn't their friends pay it for them?' I asked.

'What do you mean, their friends!' scoffed Phyllis who, while thoroughly kind-hearted, nevertheless took a keen delight in tragedy and misfortune. 'Oh well of course if you mean the Jews over on the South Circular, I did hear they were paying for Laelia Vashinsky to go to the College of Music in Westland Row. Not,' she added airily, 'that it will do her much good. She might be able to sing eventually, but she has no looks. All black eyes and big teeth.'

Wisely, I said nothing about that. 'Would Mama pay their rent for them?' I asked. 'I am sure she would if she knew.'

'You must be coddin',' laughed Phyllis, 'sure lately they had to ask your Mama for credit for bread – and you know where that ends up – on the "Kathleen Mavourneen". "It may be for weeks and it may be forever",' she sang a few bars of the old song that was one of Gran's favourite melodies. 'And next stop James's Street – that is if Jews are let in to the Catholics' Poor House.'

'But if you were to tell Mama,' I pressed, 'how nice they are, how hard they work, and all those things . . .'

Phyllis was looking at me suspiciously. 'What do you know about them? Come on, tell Phyllis. Did that young fella ever . . ?'

'Oh no,' I said virtuously. I lowered my eyelids, frantically crossed and uncrossed my fingers behind my back. 'You know I wouldn't tell you a lie, Phyllis, he never came back – not even once!'

She heaved a great sigh of relief. She took being in charge of me very seriously indeed.

'Pure bloody buggery climbing in through a window! A Jew! Wouldn't you know it!'

'But I am very sorry for poor people,' I continued the impressive virtuous act, 'couldn't you ask Mama?'

'Looka, we don't want to upset Mama, do we? She has enougha worry as it is. That Burton would drink Guinness's Brewery. And there's the other thing which is worse again. About the shop being condemned. Worrying over Jews! That's a laugh!'

I asked Tadek what condemning a shop was all about.

'Hadn't you noticed the big girders pushed up into the walls of the shop? The Dublin Corporation men came out and condemned it. They put up a notice, 'not fit for human habitation'. I suppose it is because of the big cracks in the walls. Maybe they got worse lately.'

'Mama says the cracks are because of the damp. Water

45

comes into the cellar when the high tide comes up the Dodder.'

'We get damp in our place too. I think all around here is built on a swamp. I hate it. It must be the ugliest place on earth.'

I did not know any other place. I stared at him in astonishment. I remembered the picnics.

'I was at Powerscourt Waterfall,' I said, 'but it was in the middle of the country. It would be lonely.'

'Lonely! That is what is inside you, not inside a waterfall. But I don't mean the country. You don't even know Dublin, Lia. There are magnificent squares surrounded by Georgian houses. There is Trinity with Elizabethan architecture and a crescent curve of genius surmounted with classic ironwork. There are sixteenth-century streets to make you think you are back in the Middle Ages. But Ringsend is a poor, mean place with houses made for pygmies. Dublin was the second city of the Empire. Did you know that, little one?'

I did not like such talk. It crystallized for me the feeling that my cosy life could not go on for ever. I had nothing against Ringsend. I did not notice the things Tadek noticed. The few people I knew were easy-going, like the Dalys. I feared that just beyond Tadek's shadow in the candlelight – as close as that – were people who would take him away. Talking of other lovely places foretold discontent with what we had.

That Tadek should succeed in all his ambitions had become the subject of daily prayer. When the teacher in school told us to pray for 'Special Intentions' I covered my face with my hands and whispered 'Tadek' into the hollow made by my fingers. When the teacher told us to make little sacrifices, as the Saints did, for our Special Intentions, I once gave two sweets to the girl beside me, but really I found it easier to put a little stone in my shoe, a penance practised by some Saint. Tadek must surely succeed if it depended on my prayers and penances. I dared not ask, I could only hope, that he included me essentially in his future. Rent not paid, shop condemned, were threatening forces that had to be kept at bay in our time together. And they were. The candlelight in the dark room reflected only playful tenderness and a happy security, totally unfounded, yet never later equalled.

When I was eight the rooms over the shop had to be closed. The roof had suffered from the cracked walls. The shop was fortified with great wooden beams, the ground floor alone was in use.

During the years that I was bundled off each night to Hastings Street, I had seen Burton scarcely at all. He was never at home during the day, and I was never there at night. Phyllis said he had his car for his job, and could use it himself as well. He took Mama away almost every weekend, and if they were not away I was sent to stay with Gran.

But I knew every move because Phyllis loved to talk about Mama, and I never stopped asking questions. 'Miss Why Though' was Daisy Emm's name for me, and Daisy Emm was now in charge of the shop. I was not so scared of Daisy Emm now because Burton had torn down the picture of Hell and the creaky door had been mended so I never imagined ghostly voices in the hallway any more.

Phyllis told me that Burton had bought a house on the Strand Road in Sandymount. He hated Ringsend, she said, 'as if *we* all had the plague.'

On her day off, at Mama's suggestion, she brought me on the top of the tram to Sandymount. As soon as we had passed Irishtown, I noticed the houses had gardens and brightly-painted hall doors. This must be the entrance into what Mama had called 'the affluent suburbs'.

'We won't get off the tram in the village on the way there,' said Phyllis, 'because we will have a great view of it from up here. Mama sez it's a very nice village with a park in it. We'll go into it on the way back, won't we, Lovey? Sure couldn't it be our walk for today? No, Lovey, you're not gettin' too big for walks! Walks is good for you. And I could buy you an ice-cream wafer in the village. Mama gave me the money, so now!'

47

We admired the village from the top of the tram. The little park was full of flowering trees. Then the tram swung off to the left, and suddenly we were out on the Strand Road. I had not imagined any place so vastly open. There was an endless stretch of sand going off off off to a mountain in the distance.

'I thought there was going to be sea! Where is the sea?' I asked.

'So did I,' said Phyllis. 'I'll ask the tram conductor when he comes up the stairs the next time.' And she did.

'The tide is out, Miss!' he answered jovially, giving her a big wink. 'Tides go out and tides come in!'

'Once a week, like?' I queried civilly.

'Every day, Miss, maybe twice!'

Phyllis may have thought this rather dangerous, so she asked him very cautiously, 'When the tide is in, can we paddle out to the mountain?'

'The mountain? You mean the Hill of Howth?' Evidently this was very funny, 'You'd want to tuck your stockin's up into your knickers!'

Phyllis went red in the face and I knew she wanted to laugh. We got off at the next stop. When we sat on the low sea wall, she fulminated against tram conductors who had no respect for little ears. Then she went off into one of her fits of giggles, and after a while we walked happily on.

'That big stone tower is Sandymount Tower,' Mama had told Phyllis. 'They call it a Martello tower because it was built for some war or other, and the house that Burton has bought is this side of the tower. Looka, I have the keys and we are allowed to go in and walk around but there is no furniture in it yet.'

We crossed the road and gazed up at the house, number one hundred and nineteen, the middle one of three big houses.

'My Geez!' gasped Phyllis. 'It's an enormous big bugger of a place. There'll be some elbow-grease required to keep that place in order!'

But I liked it. The rooms were elegantly proportioned, and some had stained-glass doors and windows like you would see in pictures of churches.

'Burton had a regular gang of painters and carpenters in here for weeks past,' Phyllis had heard Mama saying. 'But, speakin' personal-like, I can't say I admire his taste. All that white paint! Bright but monotonous! Mama said to look out for a room on the return landing which will be your room, Lovey.'

In that moment, I knew the meaning of the foreboding knot in my stomach. I liked the look of the house, but sleeping in it was something I thought safely postponed for ever. Mama had Burton, and to me they were almost strangers.

'I don't mind sleeping in Mrs Mayne's,' I said to Phyllis and I knew there was a question in my voice.

'That dump!' said Phyllis, almost spitting. 'Burton has been agitating to have you out of there these months and months past. Mama thinks you sleep better away from the shop. But when they move, you'll be moving up here, Lovey! Oh, here's the room on the return, the one for you. Well, thanks be to the livin' God, there's a bit of wallpaper on this room.'

The wallpaper was a design of pale woodland greenery hiding little houses, and a dado of trailing ivy leaves. There was a wide recessed window which had a deep window seat. I would have a garden view from this window. The Dublin mountains seemed nearer and bluer than the ones we could see from Ringsend. It was all so sad, unbearably sad.

'How many miles are we from Ringsend, Phyllis?'

'I'll chance two,' she answered, 'but I really don't have a notion.'

'Is a mile long?' I begged.'Please tell me how many hours it would take to walk a mile?'

'I don't have a notion, lovey,' called back Phyllis, who was climbing steeply up a narrow staircase to the attics. 'There's a room here for me, too, but I'll probably go home to Ringsend most nights.'

With all my heart, I envied Phyllis.

'You could set up a hotel here,' panted Phyllis, 'there must be four bedrooms and three big parlours and a great big kitchen – and there's another kitchen in the basement with a coal range in it and more rooms down there, but Mama's not goin' to be usin' them rooms. And Burton got in another lavatory! Two lavatories! Along of a bathroom!'

'And a garden back and front,' I added sadly.

'And all that sand out there,' said Phyllis, who liked to have the last word, 'and a tide that goes in and out!'

Mama told everyone that she adored this big house in Sandymount. It seemed to fulfil all her dreams of how a lady should live.

'And why don't you go and live in it, Marie?' asked Gran. 'Retire! Give up Ringsend.'

'The shop is valuable, Mother, with the licence.'

'Well, sell the licence,' retorted Gran. 'Hogan over on my street got a great sum for his licence and the place was even worse run-down than Ringsend.'

Mama always liked to appear submissive to Gran. 'I'll think about it, Mother, when we finish furnishing all the rooms.'

'This running up and down will kill you. You will ruin your health – live down in Ringsend until you move up for good and all.' I could see that Gran really worried about Mama's health.

'But the morning is the best up there,' Mama's voice was dreamy, 'I see the sun rising every morning, Mother, when we are getting up. I never knew the sun came up over the edge the way it does, like it was the edge of the world. We have the big bedroom in the front, and Burton says it faces to the East. First the sun comes slowly and then quicker and quicker. Lia, when you move up to us, I will show you some morning. *Your* room looks out over the back garden – it is

50

not furnished yet. Burton has ordered white furniture from Arnott's shop in Henry Street. But I will show you how the strand fills with light first, then Kingstown, then the Pigeon House to the Lighthouse, and then sun falls on the City itself.'

Mama was not given to long speeches, or not to me anyway. I was almost reconciled to leaving Ringsend if the first light of every day could always make her eyes shine down on me.

'I am naming the house "Sunrise",' she added, 'and John Daly will paint the name on the pier gates tomorrow.'

'And what about Lia's school if you move her up to Sandymount?' Gran asked, and my heart jumped up, not reconciled at all. 'It is a long way on the tram from Sandymount to Queen's Square on a winter's morning!'

'That was a useless school, Burton said. . . . He has found another school, much more go-ahead, on St John's Road, and she won't have to go on the tram, it is near.'

'How do you feel about that, childy?' asked Gran. 'New house and new school!'

'I don't want to leave my school!' I told them vehemently, suddenly feeling a fierce loyalty to the two Miss Audleys although I was always telling Tadek how boring they were. There were six pupils and we passed the day just like the old ladies themselves: having the odd cup of tea with an arrowroot biscuit, and warming our hands at the fire; learning to knit from Miss Allie while listening to stories being read aloud from comics. *Chick's Own* had divided syllables making it easy to learn reading and, maybe, spelling. *Tiger Tim's Weekly* had better stories. Miss Betty Audley loved reading from *The School Friend*, and guessing how the mystery serials would go the next week: who stole the scarab ring, or was the ghost haunting the old ruin really a ghost at all? The two old ladies also took in *Peg's Paper*, and *Home Notes*. I decided that I would truly miss the Miss Audleys.

I began to cry sorrowfully, so Mama would pity me. She flounced out of the room. Gran put her arms around me, she knew there was something I would miss. 'There, there, child, nothing lasts for ever.'

The summer was coming. It was decided to let me finish out the term in Queen's Square by which time, they said, my room with the woodland wallpaper would be completely ready.

Phyllis still took me to school on the tram. She still prepared meals in the big kitchen behind the shop. She still took me, each night, to Hastings Street, and when she returned to the shop Mama went to Sandymount, to her beloved 'Sunrise'. Phyllis helped Daisy Emm until they closed the shop.

It looked like the old routine could go on and on and maybe for ever, but I knew each night brought doom nearer and nearer. Daylight lasted a little longer each day, and I had to sit on my bed waiting and waiting for Tadek. If he lit the candle in his room, I knew for certain he would be coming. If no light appeared, there was some reason he could not come, and twenty-four hours stretched ahead like a year.

The night came that was to be my last in that cold dark room. That night, Tadek came. He stayed a long time. He found it hard to comfort me.

'You will have a lovely bright room in a lovely bright house with a lovely bright view from every window and, moreover, with a lovely bright bathroom. Do you realize the glory of a lovely bright bathroom in a house? Lia, do not cry . . . think of the bright side. Bright bright bright! What is there to cry for?'

But I knew that Tadek knew what there was to cry for. I knew by the way he held me against his jacket.

'Sandymount is nice,' he said. 'All that open sky and the sea coming in every day. There's a big lough of water called the Cockle Lake, and a place called the Shelly Banks. You

52

are going to love it. You are lucky, that's what you are.' He knew I was not lucky because shelly banks and bathrooms were nothing compared to what I had had, in love and company.

'How will I see you?' I begged desolately.

'We'll find a way,' he smiled. 'You'll see. The summer is coming and I'll go up along the strand and we'll meet. We will dig up cockles! I will bring two little spades.' Now, he was laughing.

'But you won't be able in the summer,' I reminded him, 'because you will be in that hospital.'

Tadek, as a second-year medical student, had secured a job in the casualty ward of a city hospital. The money was very small yet the promise of it had stayed the landlord's hand. 'I won't be in the hospital all the time,' he smiled. But I was filled with foreboding. The previous summer he had had a job helping on a laundry dray and I remembered how tired he used to be. Yet after he went back each night across the wall I used to see in his window the dim light of the candle and I would know he had his precious books out even though he must be half-asleep.

That last night our candle had guttered out before Tadek went home. When there was nothing left to say and even my sobs were silent, he sat on the bed rocking me. I remembered for ever how warm his hands were through my nightdress, how warm his cheeks were against mine. I am sure now that, in spite of my tears, we were filled with optimism for the continuation of our close friendship. Optimism for the distant future is scarcely imaginable in a child of nine years. I thought only of the coming summer. But Tadek? He was eighteen then, there is no doubt he was sensitive and perceptive. Is it possible that he knew then that all my security had been vested in him, and his in me? We may think of affection as an unending flood, renewing itself with each new contact, widening with each new reciprocation. It takes a lifetime to learn that affection has no perennial source. The well-spring of love is touched once, the same miracle is never repeated. Lucky is the person to whom the miracle is given, neither too soon nor too late.

The miracle was between my mother and my father. She was trying to recreate it between herself and Burton. When I came to live in 'Sunrise', I noticed the hours she spent in front of the mirror. She was using many more beauty aids than the occasional dab of rouge. Her high-boned blouses had given way to ever lower necklines – what Phyllis called 'the glad neck'.

A sewing machine was bought and the little dressmaker from Ringsend was continuously fitting and making. In his position Burton attended many social functions. Often at the end of a day in the shop she had to hurry home to Sandymount, attire herself in a ballgown and be ready to dance the night away. Burton would be already home, striding from the bedroom to the bathroom, shouting for Phyllis to clean his dancing pumps, bring him a glass, get this get that. Phyllis was afraid of him, and more afraid that if she were impertinent he would in anger attack Mama.

When Mama arrived from the shop, the noise would grow in volume although Mama would plead for quiet. He had recently bought a gramophone and on these occasions it was my task to keep winding it up while 'the music got him into the right spirit.' 'The spirits out of the bottle aren't enough,' Phyllis would mutter through the din. He prided himself on being musical – classical he claimed – so while the March from 'Aida' thumped forth, his baritone voice would flow along with it as he carried his glass from room to room.

When he was in a different room, Mama would glide quickly into the drawing-room where I was attending to the gramophone, and she would snatch a few drinks from a bottle. I always pretended not to notice because I was ashamed. It looked so furtive. Gran took a drink with great heartiness. In fact Gran occasionally got, as she giggled, 'a bit tiddly! Keeps your heart up!' Mama got something but it was not 'tiddly'. She got foolishly sentimental towards me, and provocative towards Burton. Her hair fell down and she would cajole him 'to come and get me' while she fell over chairs in her efforts to flit like a fairy.

I used to run out into the garden, choking with wounded pride. Sometimes I ran over to the strand, running, running to get away from the sound of my mother's crazy titter and Burton's vulgar remarks. Hoping, always hoping that this would be the day Tadek would come to the strand to look for me. I would search with my eyes on the wide sandy stretches. If I saw a figure, I would hurry in that direction. Checked, I would search again. Tadek never came, or he never came when I was there. I cherished this faint doubt to stave off bitterness. Mama, having rescued us from Ringsend and established us in a lovely house in Sandymount, had forbidden me to go down to Ringsend again.

'You must never,' she said, 'mix with the gurriers again.'

I could have gone. There were many hours after school, and during holidays, that I was left to my own devices. I could have gone down in the tram. I often had the necessary few pence. I often thought of doing so in the hope of meeting Tadek unexpectedly as he came out on the street. But I never went. I knew I would not see him hanging about the street. That was not Tadek's style. Moreover, I would be seen by some old neighbour; the fear of upsetting Mama dominated me. It was the only form of loving her that I knew.

Gran came during the summer to stay for short spells in 'Sunrise'. She too loved the house, and its situation. We walked for miles and miles along the strand and she told me the story of her life. I could never get enough of Gran's life story.

Dubliners do not emigrate to America, it is country people who do that, she told me, but in the years after the Famine everyone emigrated. Gran's mother had sent Gran to Philadelphia in 1870 to an aunt who was reputed to be wealthy . . . 'When I was a little girl the same age as you are now, able to write my name but not much else, she packed me off with a label on me!'

She went out to America in a ship that took many weeks, met many storms, and many people died. She was all alone among those desperate people, a small girl who could hardly read or write, but somehow she survived to be my Gran.

'Aunt Hannah claimed me off Ellis Island. She had to carry me onto a boat, and onto a train. She told me often afterwards that I was as 'wake as wather'. Aunt Hannah had been all her life in the States, Gran said, but to hear her talk you would think she never left Narramore in the county of Carlow. 'Ah, but she was a kind-hearted loving woman. As big as a man, she was, and the courage of a Turk. She never married. She used to say I was her child. And indeed she was a mother to me, more considerate for my happiness than my own mother ever was.'

When Gran was nineteen, Aunt Hannah paid her fare home to Ireland. It was time for a visit to the mother who had not seen her for ten years. More important, Gran was to ask her mother's consent and blessing for marriage to her young man in Philadelphia. Aunt Hannah had investigated this young man, Gran said, and found him thoroughly to her liking. To Gran ever afterwards he remained the unattainable figure of romantic love, for her mother did not give her consent. The harsh refusal was stamped on Gran's memory.

'Your place is here at home. Do you think I can live for ever? A daughter's duty is by a mother's side. Marry a foreigner! If they were so well off in Poland, why didn't they stay there?'

For Gran had claimed that her beloved Georgio came from a highborn, landed family, who had emigrated to better themselves in the New World. Of course, it was stupid of Gran's mother to belittle emigrants, many of her own relatives emigrated. 'She was a selfish old woman,' I always burst out at this point in the story, Georgio's family history becoming involved and confused with Tadek's family history to the point of tears.

'Ah no,' Gran would reply. 'She saw so many go in those years who never came back. She was frightened I would return to Philadelphia, marry, and get lost in a world she would never know. She was lonely too, although she had started up this little shop in the Coombe, and it was doing well.'

There was more than one heart broken by my great-grandmother when she refused to allow her daughter to return and marry Georgio. Aunt Hannah's heart was broken. I have read the old yellow letters in which she pleads for the return of her darling Delia, offering indeed to send money for her sister, Gran's mother, to come out to the States with Delia, and offering as a last inducement 'the greater part of my nest egg' in compensation. Hannah died a few years afterwards, and the nest egg came anyway. Her darling Delia saw very little of the money. Her mother got married again to a self-styled boot-and-shoe manufacturer ('that always sounded better than a cobbler,' remarked Gran). This gentleman's name was Tossy Wade. Nest eggs to him were quickly expendable for he had a passion for the races, and not much luck in winning.

Great-grandma Wade, and Tossy, were still living in the Coombe shop when we bought 'Sunrise'. There was a suggestion that they would come and live in the garden-level rooms. I thought that would be a delightful arrangement. The garden-level rooms were never used, because Mama had transferred all the kitchen arrangements to the big sunny room at the end of the hall, the third reception room. I remember telling Phyllis how Tossy and the old great-granny would be like two friendly gnomes sheltering from the garden.

'Haven't I enough to do without looking after two aul gnomes?' she asked.

'But they'd be there all the time,' I answered craftily, 'and so

57

you could go out with Chalk or Cheese instead of having to stay in to mind me.'

'Sure it's more gas having one of them in here when your Mama's out.' Phyllis had an answer for everything but all the same I trusted her. When Chalk or Cheese came in, it was a noisy party. Phyllis loved to sing and Chalk, or was it Cheese, rattled out an accompaniment on the mouth organ. Phyllis let me come down out of bed and sit on the table and join in the fun. She was a great one for fending off amorous advances that she was plainly inviting. It was as funny as a night at the Tivoli.

There were nights she had no boy in. She had to wash her hair, or do the ironing. She sang lustily right through either of those chores while I lay up in bed happy to let sleep steal over me while I listened, joining in softly in the bits I knew. 'If I Were the Only Girl in the World', a great favourite of hers, conjured up for me a stupendous picture of Phyllis with her yellow hair blowing in the wind, away out in the vastness of Sandymount Strand.

Every day in summer, Gran and I walked barefoot on the strand, early or late as the tide permitted. I have never forgotten those lovely walks and those lovely talks. I often asked her if Georgio's heart was broken because she never went back. She always denied this, but a little reluctantly.

'When you are young the heart mends easily. But I did hear,' she was careful to add, 'I did hear, years afterwards, that he never married. He gave up his life to getting money. I did hear that he was a terribly rich man.'

'How did he get rich when they were all so poor, like you told me, all those children and the poor mother having to sew nearly all night?' I loved these details of family life. Gran was sure it was this very industriousness that had set Georgio to pursue wealth.

'They mended watches and clocks,' she told me, 'that was the father's business. They understood jewellery, the value of it. Georgio understood everything mechanical and how to mend it and other things like cameras and doctors' instruments. It seemed a poor way then of scratching a living, or so my mother said at the time.'

'Would you like to be one of the rich ladies of America, Gran?' I asked her.

She looked at me, and her very blue eyes were shining. 'I would love it,' she whispered, 'but don't tell anyone I ever told you that. I would love silk dresses and perfume and gold earrings and money in my purse. Just think,' she laughed softly, 'I could take you on a holiday to London and we could stay in a posh hotel.'

It sounded heavenly to go on a trip with Gran. 'But why am I not to tell anyone?' I asked.

Gran put her arm around my shoulder as we walked across the sand towards 'Sunrise'. She was very sad and very solemn. 'Because those are wicked thoughts. You never get to Heaven unless you settle to what the Lord has put in your path. Not just settle to it, but be happy with it and make other people happy. If you go through life moaning about what you might have had, you won't earn your just reward, will you?'

'But,' I persisted, 'you would have liked to marry Georgio and be rich. You would have been happy that way too.'

'That's enough about it for today,' she always finished firmly. 'Maybe the Lord didn't want me to have that life, maybe he knows best. We don't make our own lives, you know.'

The sadness in her face was enough for me. I knew she carried a broken heart all through her life. For her too the miracle had happened too soon. We do not make our own lives, she had said. I used to think she was wrong, a little weak perhaps. I thought I would make my own life. As I grew older I thought I could see people determinedly resisting the buffeting fate of circumstance, fashioning events their way. I wonder now, can anyone do that? At the moment of decision, am I blind to decision's necessity? Am

59

I so close up to the blank wall of necessity that the distant view is hidden from my perception?

What was it that made Gran submit? She had rebellion in her heart, but she had not the return fare in her pocket. She had love for Georgio, but also she had love for her mother. She was not very long at home before a new suitor appeared. This was a cousin, bearing the same name as herself, Brabazon. He was a fine-looking man of thirty-five, lately retired from the British Army in India, on a pension that was considered princely for those times. The match was made by plotting relations. Did Aunt Hannah tell Georgio's family of this? Did she pass around the wedding group pictures taken by Mr Lafayette in Westmoreland Street, in which Gran looks small and daunted and Grandfather looks too masculine for comfort? And if she did, how did Georgio feel? Did he think of Gran as faithless and heartless? Oh, she wasn't!

She wasn't! She settled to life, as was her philosophy. She bore fifteen children, not all of whom lived to be grown up. My mother was the youngest. Gran became a wonderful cook. She cooked dinners for the gentry, she often told me, to help her buy clothes for the children. She loved cooking, but at times it had been heavy work with one child at her skirt, and another waiting to be born. She made many friends in life, and she bore many hardships. In a sense, she never grew old. In a sense, her life remained at the emotional point it reached on her wedding day when she relinquished Georgio for ever, and settled to a married life into which love never came.

I have often wondered, was my own life made by Fate, or by potent example?

Gran's thoughts urged her towards a certain horizon of memory when she talked to me as a little girl. She had not gone beyond that horizon when I listened to her gentle meandering words years afterwards.

Chapter Four

When Mama became ill the first time, it seemed quite natural that I should go to stay with Gran. Daisy Emm was brought back to the shop, and Phyllis went back and forth between the shop and 'Sunrise'.

Gran was worried because I missed so much school. She had a very healthy respect for well-educated people; without education, she said, you get pushed to the wall. She was worried, too, about Burton's drinking. She referred to it darkly as 'street angel house devil' which seemed bewildering and mysterious. Yet another worry was the street in which she lived. It was quite close to the city centre and in Gran's opinion, 'it had gone down.' I was under the strictest orders not to look out of the windows at night-time. She explained to me that she and I could go to 'Sunrise' but for Burton – she was afraid of him, so I was too, although he had always been very pleasant to me. Very fatherly, I used to think, because I wanted a father. He took me up on his knee, and cuddled me, and kissed me, constantly. He made me feel rich with all the money he gave me. I knew well when Mama tried to make him jealous by fussing over me to make him feel left out. I was sorry for her because behind her back he made winks and kisses at me. Sometimes they tugged me from one to the other. He always won.

He would run upstairs with me in his arms, throw me on the big double bed and tickle me inside my knickers while he lay panting and laughing beside me. My mother would stand there calling to him to stop until he reached out a strong arm to pull her down as well. Then I would be given money, and told to run off to the Tower shop. I usually met some of the other children from around at the shop. I knew instinctively to stay out as long as I could – sometimes until dark. Even so, when I came back to the house, they were usually still locked into the bedroom. I would find something to eat and, lonely again, climb into bed. I never went to sleep without saying prayers for Tadek and longing for a glimpse of his smile.

I did not tell Gran about Burton's kisses, or the money he gave me – sometimes a half-sovereign of which he seemed to have a supply. I never spent the half-sovereigns, I put them away in a little box intending some day to have a bracelet made for Phyllis. I had seen her admire those bracelets. I loved Phyllis so much. She got little or nothing for herself by the time she helped her mother and her sisters. I just did not say all this to Gran because when I was with Gran, all my life was different.

In her little house, we lived together like two little nuns. Talk of Burton was not to be encouraged. She was a great one for a definite routine. We rose at the same time quite early, worked at our tasks together and went to bed at the hour of nine. Gran undressed underneath a big tent of a nightgown, while I went behind her Chinese screen where the commode was kept. We shared the same big bed with a pillow always placed between us. It pleased me without my knowing why that Gran and I treated each other with modest reserve where the physical was in question; our intimacy lay elsewhere. It was more than pleasing, it was happiness whose essential reason remained a mystery.

All the work of the house was done by ten o'clock each morning. That included the preparation of food for the day. Then we tidied ourselves, and set out for town. On fine days we dawdled about the shops. Gran loved Grafton Street and Stephens Green. She always had a little money for coffee in Roberts Cafe. I was nervously apprehensive when she produced her own little cakes from her capacious bag. Luckily we were never asked to leave the cafe, although it was clearly printed on the menu 'customers are asked to avail of the cafe-food only'. Gran assured me that was only 'to keep out the wrong element'. She clearly did not include us in the wrong element even if she followed the wrong rule.

On wet, or very cold days, we went to the National Gallery to see the pictures, or to the Natural History Museum to see the animals and butterflies in their glass cases. Sometimes we went to a little picture gallery in Harcourt Street which had all the charm of a gentleman's residence. Gran knew the door porter there and we were put sitting while he chatted over old times. It was always the identical conversation.

Opposite Gran's house in the narrow street lived Mrs Dunne. They were not friends, exactly, but Gran was very sorry for Mrs Dunne who had been left a widow at twenty-four years of age. Mrs Dunne's daughter was in Grangegorman, the Lunatic Asylum for the city of Dublin. Mrs Dunne was always distraught about her daughter and was wanting to take her out and keep her at home. Gran said Mrs Dunne felt guilty about the daughter but she was a foolish woman. How could she go out to work (she scrubbed floors in a hospital), with the daughter at home to be minded? The doctor at the Asylum was against the idea, and Mrs Dunne frequently asked Gran to accompany her up to the Asylum to plead for the daughter's release. The neighbours in that narrow street often asked Gran to do things for them. They had great respect and regard for her. Her years in America had given her a certain dignity and, by nature, she was resourceful.

In a soft moment, Gran agreed to go along with Mrs Dunne. The doctor must have been impressed. It was agreed that Biddy Dunne be allowed home for a four-day holiday in the summer. Gran arranged with Mrs Dunne to help her in the hiring of a hansom cab, to take us to the

Asylum and bring Biddy home. I was left sitting in the cab while the two women went into the big gloomy building. Gran had all the papers for Mrs Dunne to sign in return for Biddy's release. I was shaky with fright when I saw Gran and Mrs Dunne dragging and struggling and shouting until at last they pushed Biddy into the hansom cab.

Biddy did not look any worse than moonfaced. It was the smell she brought into the cab, like oniony stew, that was awful. She laughed a lot, very loudly, the smell came out of her mouth as well as from her clothes. Her hands were everywhere at once, poking at our hair and our bodies, pulling at the faded tassles on the armrests. Mrs Dunne's face had lost its usual hunted look. She seemed pleased with Biddy. She kept on talking to her about a nice cup of tea, and even a nice bath. I knew Mrs Dunne had no bathroom. I wanted to ask Gran if Mrs Dunne would put Biddy in the big tub at the fire. This was how Gran and I bathed, with the shelter of the Chinese screen. I wondered how Biddy would fit. She had loads of hanging fat, I was squashed into the corner of the cab. Gran pressed my hand against her skirt to tell me to quit the questioning.

At last we got back to the narrow street. With much screeching and poking, Mrs Dunne got Biddy into their house and slammed the door. When Gran had paid the cabman, and we were safely inside our house, Gran said (as I knew she would) that we would take off all our garments which must go out into the washhouse. She fetched the Chinese screen. We each had a bowl of cool water to wash ourselves all over. The big tin of talcum powder, taken down on very special occasions, was used to dust us down and make us fragrant as roses. I did not like to tell Gran that the smell of Biddy was still in my nose. I have never quite forgotten it. Gran decided we would rest in our night-robes, take some cocoa, and retire early. She was quite exhausted and full of fear, she said, for the future. How in Heaven's name would Mrs Dunne manage? Mrs Dunne, Gran said, had neither the strength nor the speed of a spider!

I was awakened by loud screeching. I knew at once it was

Biddy. By Gran's clock on the wardrobe it was almost six o'clock. Biddy was calling Gran.

'Looka, Mrs Brabazon, looka!'

I crept over Gran's sleeping body to get quickly over to the window. When I raised the blind, light flooded into the room. Gran was up and beside me in a flash, then she was pushing me away from the window. But I had seen it. Biddy was hanging out of their window dangling a hacked-off bloody leg. She was covered in blood, her face and her hair. She was screeching and laughing and called: 'Looka! Looka!'

For weeks and weeks afterwards, back in my own bedroom in 'Sunrise', I woke out of sleep tearfully pleading with Biddy not to cut off her leg. Eventually it was Burton who, despite Mama's forbidding it, told me that the stupid bitch had chopped up her own old lady, spent the night at it, while the people in the next house listened through the wall. 'Your Gran,' he added, 'wants her brain examined. Went over there in her night-clothes and took the flaming hatchet off the madwoman. Might well have met her death.' My mother accused him of gloating over everything filthy. They started another of the rows that usually ended in the locked bedroom. This time, it ended by his striking her across the mouth. He then stormed out while she screamed at him to go and get drunk. Then she went to the shop and I was left alone in the big house. That was a pattern to which I had grown accustomed.

What, I wonder, was I doing while Gran went over to poor Mrs Dunne? I remember nothing about the hatchet. Nor do I remember Gran bringing me home to Sandymount. I can still see as clearly as if it happened yesterday, the bloodied face of Biddy and her fearful bloodied burden.

Gran had been dispatched off to England to have a holiday with one of the surviving Uncles who had settled in Torquay. She was gone for many months. It seemed to have

65

been decided by Mama that Gran was no longer fit to be left to mind a child, the constant phrase was, 'It is all too much for her . . . she is getting old.'

Phyllis was installed as permanent housekeeper and childminder in 'Sunrise'. Mama was fulltime in the shop with Daisy Emm as assistant. The shop was still condemned as unfit for habitation but not apparently unfit for a shop. While Mama's health held out, while she kept out of hospital anyway, this arrangement jogged along.

I was very close to Phyllis. I loved her almost as much as I loved Gran. In a way, there were extra pleasures in life when Phyllis was around. She never scolded, nothing was that important. She sang all day at her work, expecting everyone else to sing along. She always went home on her halfday, bringing her money to her mother and helping out.

They lived around the corner from Tadek's house. When there was no school, Phyllis had to take me with her. I knew the best I could hope for was to see Tadek, even a glimpse from the Dalys' window. My lovely friendship with Tadek was a secret. I did not need to be told that to reveal what had happened between us would be to bring down the wrath of God, or even worse, to upset Mama.

I did not know then that it was a friendship of supreme innocence.

When a child is going to be punished if found out, then the child is ridden with guilt. So I sat demurely by the Dalys' window with a book in my hands. I missed nothing that went up or down on the path outside. As often as not, I saw Tadek. I noted how he looked, what he wore, his hair always seemed blacker, crisper in sunlight. Once he had spotted me at the window, he always looked for me. He did not dare to smile, nor openly acknowledge a greeting. All the same, he made a gesture of some sort, usually running his fingers through his hair. The glow of bliss inside me secured my life for another week until Phyllis's day off brought another visit to Ringsend.

There was a great day we spent in the Dalys' when Gladys, the eldest sister, got married. It was a summer's day so hot that the big downstairs window was open and the children were sitting on the sills. Looking in at the grown-ups drinking and singing, I saw Phyllis sitting on the couch with Eileen, her sister, and the good-looking bridegroom sitting between them. He had one hand inside Phyllis's blouse cupping her diddy, always Phyllis's word, and the other hand cupping the diddy of Eileen, inside her blouse. It seemed a cosy and intimate way to sit. The two girls appeared to be in the very deepest enjoyment. Strangely, when I asked Phyllis if it was nice, she smiled hugely but remembered nothing at all about it. I assured her that I had especially noticed that her mother went out into the back kitchen at the time, and she said she was glad of that, but where was her Da? This set her off laughing again. She said it reminded her of old Heiton in Thorncastle Street.

With Phyllis all intimacy was light-hearted and completely innocent fun. She steered clear of Burton, though he often made a pretence of pawing her when he had drink taken. I supposed that 'we mustn't upset Mama' was the guiding rule, but perhaps fear played a big part.

I was afraid of Burton in one way, afraid of incurring his anger. He had a quick and ferocious temper, when he let fly with his fists. I had seen him unbuckling his belt to Mama, I had always run out of the room and out of the house before he could use it.

'He is kind at heart,' she used to say, 'quite soft-hearted really, he would cry over a puppy.'

That was true. He adored dogs, a characteristic which I found very attractive because I did too. I remember forever with a catch in my throat, a King Charles spaniel that he bought for my ninth birthday. She had a long pedigree and a long pedigree name, we called her 'Silky'. With meticulous care Burton showed me the exact right way to feed a puppy, bed her, walk her, brush her, train her so that she could have the run of the house. When she grew into a beautiful young animal ready to produce a litter, he brought us, Silky and me, to the dog breeder's house along the Strand Road. He explained to Silky, as we went along, exactly what was going to happen to her. I understood, although I must have been little more than ten, that the explanation was for my ears. I asked questions on Silky's behalf. It was quite a game hearing the facts of life. Burton was in his element.

When he was like that, a handsome smiling man, warm brown eyes and a quizzical smile, I felt drawn to him in a peculiarly strong tingling way. He knew that too, because he would bend and kiss me. The pressure of my hand in his was thoroughly satisfying. While we were friends together, real pals as he said, he filled my world. No one else was safe from him, but I was.

I see now that to Gran, to all the Aunts and Uncles who were Mama's family, to Phyllis, who had been with Mama before his coming, even to Mama who had loved before, he was still a stranger, an interloper. Only I accepted him unquestioningly – he had been in my life as long as I could remember. I accepted him, at times, with the magic acceptance of mutual attraction. Otherwise, I should surely have kicked and screamed when he scooped me out of my small bed, and had me sleep with him in the big double bed, his arms enveloping me, his hard body pressed against mine. That occurred often enough to become the pattern when neither Phyllis nor Mama was in the house. The money he gave me was a strong reason for silence, the urgent need for his warmth was even stronger.

Gran was never allowed to take me home with her now – the street was dangerous, they said.

By the time I was twelve, Tadek had become almost as distant as the stars. If he had any lingering regard for me, it never drove him up to the Strand which I searched for him every day.

Mama never kissed or hugged me. She was often ill with a

68

dreadful headache. When she and Burton had a row, she did not come home, sleeping in the room behind the shop. Phyllis worried about Mama, often going down to look after her and coming back to 'Sunrise' on an early tram to get me to school.

Burton, an elegant dresser himself, took a pride in my appearance, buying my clothes and shoes. When Phyllis stayed away, he bathed me and cooked delicious breakfasts. He helped, too, with my schoolwork – quick ways of doing sums were his speciality.

I became aware that a really big row had started up, and was dragging along, between Mama and Burton. This time I was the focus of it. My education, no less.

Burton had influence with the Freemasons. He had succeeded in obtaining a place for me in the Freemason Boarding School in Ballsbridge. He was genuinely thunderstruck when Mama, who never went to Mass nor to the Sacraments, nor to any church, insisted that her daughter was to have a Roman Catholic education. To Burton, the Irish Catholics were peasants, he had never heard of the Roman variety, he said – but he was capable of saying anything to annoy her, 'teasing' he called it.

I had often been to Mass with Phyllis. I had seen children going up to receive Communion. I was envious of their involvement in the ritual. I could not go because, as Phyllis explained, I had not made my Communion. Apparently, I had been baptized a Roman Catholic at three days old in the hospital in which I was born because Dada had told Mama that was proper. My mother was convinced that I was therefore committed to a certain religion whether we liked it or not. Nothing could shake her conviction. Phyllis agreed with her, nodding her head wisely at the deep theology of it all. 'It would bring down the wrath of God,' she repeated piously.

Burton was drinking very heavily now. Mama stayed at night in the shop, to escape a beating, I suppose, for the

69

argument went on. Burton had ordered the uniform for the Masonic school. Mama had no idea what was the right school for a Catholic child who had not progressed beyond baptism. Gran did not practise any religion, she talked vaguely about being in the Band of Hope in her early days, she remembered a few bars of a hymn:

> 'Open your hole, open your hole
> Open your holy Bible
> Come on Sal, come on Sal
> Come on Salvation.'

Phyllis found this an exhilarating hymn and was heard singing it with loud guffaws while she polished the stairs. Gran thought a little more reverence would be in order, but Phyllis always preferred gusto, Gran said.

When Burton was very drunk he stayed out later than ever, going straight to his bed when he had slammed the door enough to shake the hinges. Slamming doors was a sign of heavy drinking. Normally he was a careful man with his own property. On the nights I was alone in the house and I heard the slamming, I would turn happily on my side to go to sleep. His mood, I knew then, would be long past the maudlin lovey-dovey sentimentality he displayed for me when he was only half-drunk. If he slammed hard, he went to bed without a goodnight kiss.

There came the night when it did not work that way. He was slamming doors and lumbered into my bedroom carrying the lamp from the landing. For the first time, I was really frightened. His eyes were not brown but red. His moustache was glistening. Setting down the lamp, he began to unbuckle his belt.

I began to cry loudly, imploring him not to beat me. I was terrified, truly terrified. He laid the heavy leather belt on the rail of my bed and stooped over me. Choking with dread, I burrowed my head down into the pillow. He grabbed my head and forced me to look upwards.

'Open your eyes. Open your eyes,' he repeated hoarsely. He threw down the bedclothes and, holding me with one big hand, he drew the belt down on my legs. My furious yelling turned to tears of real pain. Suddenly he was on his knees beside the bed, he was covering me with kisses. I was trying to struggle, I was weak. I felt his enormous hulk moving down down down on top of me as if a black pit had opened and closed over my head.

I have no clear recollection of the sequence of events after that and, in truth, my mind has never set itself to recollect. The sheer horror I felt must have spurred me to act as I did. I must suppose that Burton was too drunk to be aware of my escape from the room. When he was drunk enough he slept like a dead man. I must have walked, or run, clad only in a sodden nightdress, along the back strand to Ringsend – a distance of more than a mile. I must have knocked on the shop, calling to Mama and Phyllis, and got no answer. I must have gone to Tadek's door, and found refuge. Maybe I ran from 'Sunrise' to look on the strand for Tadek, as I did so often. Maybe instinct led me on to Tadek's house, maybe in my plight I felt forsaken by Mama and Phyllis.

I became conscious of the fact that I was in a strange bed, a strange room, but Tadek and Laelia were there. Their concerned and anxious faces were bent over me, my hand was in Tadek's hand. If I had been struck blind, I should have known it was Tadek's hand. It was enough to have come out of the nightmare, I kept falling asleep each time I saw their faces. I did not know then that I had been lying in Laelia's bed for days and nights before consciousness returned.

My mother had been sent for. Poor Mama, her distress must have been great. Apparently I had been babbling out the sordid story as I was knocking on the Vashinskys' door, repeating the details many times, crying for help, begging for pity. Tadek had been able to get a doctor friend very quickly from the hospital to which he was attached. This

71

doctor made whatever examination he deemed necessary. I remember nothing about the examination. The doctor came several times afterwards to see me, he was a kindly elderly man. Tadek told me eventually that I had suffered no harm, but the shock had been severe.

'You must take care to rationalize that shock,' he said.

I had not the faintest idea what he meant about rationalizing but of course, always pretending to be equal to Tadek, I did not ask questions about that. Because the shock had been caused by Burton, perhaps the shock was not the same as if the assailant had been a stranger. At that time, Burton had taken care of my life in a kindly way. He pleased my imagination in many ways, he occupied a large part of my active affection – a far larger part than Mama did. He himself was full of affection; and full of information about animals and birds and nature, the sort of things children love to ask questions about.

When Tadek asked about monthly periods, I could not conceal my lack of knowledge. Burton had not mentioned monthly periods, but I did know all about bitches in heat. Was that the same thing? Tadek did not know whether to laugh or scold (I knew his look), so he frowned politely.

'You really are a neglected child,' he said.

'So, tell me,' I said, 'begin at the beginning.'

Despite all his book learning, Tadek was too shy to go any further. He taught me, instead, how to play chess. But that was weeks after I had come.

It had been decided by someone, the doctor I suppose, that I was to stay at the Vashinskys until Mama had plans for me. Daisy Emm brought money and boxes of groceries every few days. I remember I longed to be up and about, but I thought it expedient to drag out the convalescence.

Gran came to see me, glancing dubiously around the little room I shared with Laelia. I would have liked to go to Gran, equally, I loved her dearly. I heard her downstairs explaining angrily to Mrs Vashinsky that Burton had already looked for me in her house, so I wouldn't be safe there.

Phyllis, who came every day and was in the unhappy position of not being able to forgive herself for her absence on that night, and who knew Burton perhaps more nefariously than Mama did, had managed to whisper to me that, 'Yer man denies everything – no recollection, he says, never happened, he says – load of rubbish, he says.'

For a long while when Mama came, she wept. She did not hold me in her arms and kiss the tip of my nose like Gran did, but she wept so bitterly that I knew it was shame. I cried too, not speaking, only fondling her hands to make sure she knew I loved her. The real feeling of loving her never came, so neither did the words.

Chapter Five

That time in Tadek's house was a time of pure happiness. There were guilty moments when I knew I owed this blissful joy to Burton, whose name was never mentioned.

Tadek was gone all day to the hospital, and Laelia was at the Jewish school. Mr Vashinsky was now quite blind. He sat by the fireside, sometimes he chanted remembered verses in a low musical voice. Often he told me stories of his childhood in Zamość, a town near the Russian border. At first they were wealthy and lived in a fine house. He described their pictures, their furniture, their great family gatherings. Then came their oppressors, their homes were burned, in the night they fled leaving their valuable possessions heaped up in the street, where they had tried to save them from the fires. They became wanderers across Europe. Their money dwindled away. Many died by the waysides. It was heartbreaking to them to have to leave their beloved dead in unknown soil, unmarked so they were never found again.

It had become Mr Vashinsky's dearest wish that he should go home to die in Zamość, and take his resting place beside his parents in the Jewish cemetery, on the bank of the river. Over his parents' grave was a magnificent headstone, sheltered by a cedar of Lebanon. Always Tadek and Laelia listened to this account of their ancestors' grave with loving respect. Always they promised to fulfil their father's wishes in the matter of his burial.

Tadek was especially close to his father. They conversed together in Hebrew. On their Sabbath, Tadek read to him from a great book, a book of gilded pages and coloured ribbons. This book, and a balalaika, were among the few items they had managed to save. Tadek strummed on the balalaika sometimes, old folk-tunes that his mother liked to sing. Laelia did not sing at home. She had a scholarship to the College of Music in Westland Row, she saved her voice for using it there.

Phyllis made constant enquiries about Laelia's singing. She seemed not to believe me when I said I never heard her singing now. 'Grown out of it,' said Phyllis hopefully. Phyllis had recovered a lot of her high good humour as the weeks went by, so I supposed she was singing at her work as she always did.

There were times I missed being with Phyllis. She could always make me laugh. Gran came frequently to see me. She struck up a great friendship with Mr and Mrs Vashinsky. She always brought a box of homemade walnut toffee for Mister V., as she called him, and he liked to suck it. She was adept at making toffee and sweets of all sorts.

The Vashinskys loved to hear of her years in Philadelphia. That place had been their goal until Mr Vashinsky's brother was killed there in a street accident. This brother was going to sponsor them in America and send the fare for them to cross the Atlantic. To Gran, this story was told so often that she felt she had witnessed that very accident as she swept the steps of her employer's house one snowy morning. She entered into their family history as if it were a part of her own life. The brother who had suffered the street-accident death became identified in her memory as Georgio's brother, he had been trapped in the snow, and he was a dealer in clocks and instruments just like Mr V.'s brother. Just like Georgio. To hear Gran tell of Philadelphia, I knew her heart was still there. She made the streets live, naming the owners of the different shops, some with names not unlike Vashinsky.

There was no concealing the fact that I was quite over the shock, but they let me go on basking in their atmosphere of cosy domesticity. I loved each day with its promise of Tadek at evening. He made such a fuss of me with his enquiries when he came in from the hospital, almost as if he were practising his bedside manner on an heiress. I adored play-acting, responding with fluttering eyelashes and babyish pouts; Laelia, who was of a serious disposition, had to laugh at this performance. Her manner to me was always affectionate, and sisterly.

She praised me every day. 'You have the nicest hair I ever saw,' she would say, 'it is so easy to fix it in all different ways. Now, look in the mirror! Shall I put the bow up on the top, or like this, to one side? No, I will brush it back and tie the bow like those eighteenth-century beauties in the Gallery pictures. Look at me? Did you know you are very pretty? You have your mother's eyes – and such long eyelashes! But you don't brush your teeth with toothpaste – promise me you will! Every day? Yes. I know Phyllis says soot is the best for your teeth but I don't believe her. She just happens to have teeth like a horse – well, I mean, very strong. And so have you, so you must take care of them. Promise me! Faithfully!'

She did a lot of little things for me because, I thought, she was proud and independent and must repay the easier circumstances my being there had brought to the house. I basked in her flattery, it was so comforting. Tadek never mentioned my hair or my eyes, but he was always laughing. It was a time of rare happiness except for sometimes when unwanted thoughts came and I was unable to accept, or reject them.

Then, as always, there were secrets that a person had to keep so that other people could form impressions uninfluenced by inner knowledge. It was an instinctive reaction which I came to recognize in myself only gradually as time passed. It was to take years to understand that my initial response to Burton, when he took me on his knee in Mama's room in Ringsend, had set up an emotional chain for him, towards him; it was set so deep that it never found words, yet it could surface swiftly, as the breaking of a great wave can engulf the breakwater.

I wanted to explain to Tadek that sometimes unhappy thoughts were tangled up with Burton.

'Lia, what are you dreaming about now? You look so puzzled. What is it? Come on,' Tadek said, 'I'll listen.'

I did not tell him, I could not, that while I was completely happy to be with him and with Laelia, I was missing Burton. Tadek and Laelia had never seen Burton. To them I think he was the Black Shadow he had been to me in the beginning. I had not told Burton about Tadek, I had not told anyone about Tadek because Tadek had forbidden me ever to mention our friendship. He had explained, so far as I was able to understand, that the ethics of a doctor were the highest ethics anyone could have. All he had ever done was to comfort a child with words and innocent actions. But who would believe him? Worse still, he said, who would believe a Jewish boy in this country of militant Catholics?

I wanted to explain to Tadek (who had forbidden anyone to mention the name of Burton to me) how I felt about Burton. I wanted to talk it all out, to cry and to be comforted. The psychology Tadek knew then seemed bound up in the word 'rationalize'. Rationalize was the magic charm that dealt with all emotional frustrations. There was an austerity in Tadek that I worshipped, and resented a very little.

Only as a child is aware, was I aware that Burton had given me more of himself than Mama had given me. His giving was totally different from Tadek's giving. He was always there when I needed to be petted, and hugged, and made much of. He was the fragrantly masculine warmth of a father in a small girl's life. I was not at all aware that his intimate relationship with this child went further than propriety permitted. I had accepted his intimacy without question, without fear, without thought.

And I missed him the more when it was tacitly made known that he had not done any physical harm to me.

I missed his presence in my life and there was no one to fulfil this need of nature when they took Burton away. No one knew that the frenzied escape from the drunken Burton was the overwhelming fear of the sudden unknown. No one knew that there was also a momentary longing to stay. I did not recognize this as a sinful desire because I had never heard of sin.

Burton gave me the sort of male love a small daughter understands. He did not comply with the unwritten rules. If he had, he would have taken away from me far more than he gave. Loving Tadek faithfully without hope of return; longing vaguely, guiltily, for the return of Burton, were to become the irreconcilables in a heart that longed for familial love.

Then, one day, Mama came with her plans, and all my lovely life came to an end.

I was to be sent away to a boarding school. Mama had found the right school.

'These nuns are French nuns,' Mama said, 'they are quite broad-minded about a child not being instructed in any religion. The Sister told me that, in their Mission work, they have to deal with pagan children, so they are accustomed to that.'

'Am I a pagan child?' I enquired. It sounded interesting.

'I suppose so,' Mama answered reluctantly. 'I suppose so but it is not my fault, I did my best.' She always said that.

'Do you think I will be making my First Communion, like Phyllis's little sister? She had a lovely dress.' Which I knew Mama had supplied.

'The Sisters will tell you all that, and whatever dress they think suitable.' Mama was losing interest. 'I must speak to Mrs Vashinsky about the clothes.'

So Mrs Vashinksy received delivery of the uniform from Kelletts of George's Street. She took up, and took in, to make sure that I looked neat and tidy and still allow for when I would at last start to grow, being small for my nearly twelve years, they all agreed. Gran took me into town to buy shoes and hockey boots and a tennis racquet. Gran felt, she said, 'as if we are really going up in the world! A tennis racquet, if you don't mind! A proper Lady Burst-the-Bucket!' She had got that from Phyllis, whose funny remarks always made Gran laugh.

Burton was taking Mama on a cruise holiday in the hope, Gran said, that it would improve her health.

'God knows he is trying to make up,' sighed Gran, 'although he denies everything. You know, child, that he is staying in England after the holiday? He is either changing his job out of Dublin Castle into a similar job in England – he never warmed to the change of government here (ah well, you couldn't blame him for that, natural he would prefer the English), or he is leaving the Service altogether and going for some other thing. Ah, he's a young man yet!'

'And what about Mama?' I asked.

'When she comes back, she has promised me to get rid of that awful shop, no matter how much money it makes at night! The licence is worth a lot of money and, when she sells, Burton is to get that money for what he is after putting into "Sunrise". Then she can live there – that's the deal, childy.'

'How will they live in "Sunrise" if he is in England?'

'They have ideas of travelling back and forth,' Gran answered, 'but if you ask me, after what happened, he will be afraid to show his face around here again!'

I was not very convinced that Burton would ever be afraid of anything. I knew now that I was believed to be the injured, innocent victim of a drunken attack. If the name of Burton was mentioned, I tried to be busily occupied in 'rationalizing'.

'Will we have "Sunrise" for this summer, Gran?'

'We will,' she said. 'I am to caretake. If you want to stay with Laelia, you can, child. But Mama said if she wants to stay in "Sunrise" with you, she can.'

Gran had the happy facility of arranging her ideas to the

79

best advantage. Resolutely she held to the opinion that Laelia was a very suitable friend for Lia. Tadek was not mentioned.

So that lovely summer came that was to be the last summer of childhood. There would be a few more summer holidays with Tadek and Laelia, when they were grown up and I would pretend to be.

The summer before boarding school was the perfect sun-lit summer now sewn into the tapestry of memory. In Ireland we say a heatwave summer comes every fifth year. That one was a fifth year.

Now there were four of us. Tadek and Laelia; Tadek's friend and fellow student, Max, and I, Lia. Max was much bigger and stronger than Tadek – but not kinder or nicer, equally kind and nice. He and I had, immediately, an enormous interest in common. I had Silky and he had Toozy, both King Charles spaniels. Silky had the perfect mix of brown and white Blenheim colouring while Toozy had more white than brown.

I commented on this. 'But all the same,' I said, 'your Toozy has a lovely coat. Just look at her big furry ruff!'

'That is because he is not a her!' Max laughed at me, 'The males always have better coats than the females! Didn't you know that?'

'Like peacocks!' added Laelia.

'I am very worried now,' I told Max. 'What will I do if Silky becomes a mother, and I am in the boarding school?'

'I give you my word on Toozy's behalf,' Max laughed, 'there is no need to worry. Our Toozy has been to see the vet! Toozy is not in his first youth any more.'

So there were six of us. Silky and Toozy were part of all our outings except when Tadek took me off on the bar of his bicycle. There was a special ride out past the Pigeon House to the Half Moon Swimming Club from where we walked the rest of the way out to the Lighthouse . . . Tadek holding my hand tightly for fear the wind would blow me away, so open is that place. Then at the Half Moon, Tadek swam on the deep side and I was sent to paddle in the Shelly Banks. We gathered fan-shells for Mrs Vashinsky. She stuck them on the grim walls of the backyard in a pattern of stars.

Mostly we spent our days all together on the hard-packed strand in Sandymount. For hours and hours we played a sort of cricket-baseball game. Other days we played at making sand castles in competition with each other, sand houses, sand forts, or all together making a gigantic castle with battlements and turrets. When the tide came in to wash our castle away, we were ready in our togs to dash into the water and splash madly. Unless we waded out and out to Howth on the horizon, there was no depth. Neither Laelia nor I knew how to swim anyway.

In the late afternoon, Gran came over to the sea wall to ring an old bell. Mama stayed down in Ringsend in the shop until after eleven at night with Phyllis to help her. Burton had never come back from England. So Gran felt free to cook little feasts and have us all over to picnic under the apple trees in the back garden.

'That's a strapping fine young lad,' Gran would remark of Max, 'and such lovely manners.'

'But Tadek is nice too!' I would insist.

'Oh yes, no doubt, no doubt,' Gran would agree, 'but very fine-drawn. Delicate, perhaps?'

'He is as strong as a horse!' I would insist. 'He can carry me on the handlebar of his bike!'

Gran would laugh at me. 'Look at you! You are as heavy as a full-grown mouse!'

Some days we walked to Merrion Gates all along the Strand Road. There we waited for a tram to take us as far as Kingstown Baths. These trams were nicer than the Ringsend trams, being covered in on top. Tadek and I sat together, and Laelia sat with Max. They found plenty to chat about to each other.

'Don't you think they make a lovely couple?' I would whisper to Tadek.

'Where do you get these ideas?' he would reply. I was always hoping he would say in return: 'Don't *we* make a lovely couple?'

One day when I made this remark about Laelia and Max, he turned to look at me, smiling a very little. 'Some day,' he whispered, 'you, Lia, will probably grow up, and I shall probably be sorry.'

There were days we went to Blackrock, not to bathe but to sit in the park and listen to the band. On those days, Laelia and Tadek sat at the band stand and listened to the music. Max and I walked our dogs around and around the pond. It seemed as if we could talk for ever about our dogs, and about dogs we had heard about or read about.

'I thought at first I would go on for veterinary,' Max told me, 'but I talked it over with my father. He thinks medicine suits a Jew better. I think now he is right.'

I asked him one day, 'Don't you think Laelia is lovely?' I gazed back towards the band stand, seeing Laelia's exquisite, attentive face. 'Don't you?'

He followed my gaze in some surprise, and then he said slowly, 'Yes, I suppose so . . . I had not noticed her much.'

Max always had money, and he treated us to ice cream. Several times he took us all to the pictures. We went twice to the same picture, 'The Sheik of Araby', because that was Laelia's favourite. Sometimes Tadek let me slip my hand into his if the picture had frightening bits, like in 'The Count of Monte Cristo'. I knew that dry, thin hand so well. Nearer to Heaven I could not be when Tadek's hand touched mine.

At the end of the summer, I had a big worry. Since Burton had not come back and I would be in the boarding school, there would be no one to look after Silky. In a way that defied 'rationalization', she was my precious link with Burton. I could not say this. I confided my worry to Max.

'Would you let Silky come and live with Toozy, Lia?' Max asked. 'They are going to miss each other after these weeks together. She can come back to you when you want her.'

So Silky went to live in Max's house in a place called Terenure, a place I had never seen. Tadek said it was near the city. I felt I was lucky to have acquired a friend like Max.

It seemed as if it had been the whole summer: day after day, and all day long, that we had played and laughed and delighted in each other. It seemed like that because I was still a child, but of course it was not. It was a series of days that spanned that lovely summer, a few in June, a few more in July, most in August. They came when they could spare the time, to please a child. Tadek and Laelia never had money for amusement, they were content with the fun of the strand. And Max? He was Tadek's friend so he fitted in.

'You should be very thankful to them for coming up here to cheer you up,' Gran always reminded me to show gratitude and never to use people, 'after all, they likely enough have more important things to do.'

And I was thankful, so thankful. All life through, I have never forgotten.

Mama was away when the day came for me to go to school. Gran had ordered one of Mr Heiton's taxi cabs from Ringsend. Tadek and Laelia were coming too, Mr Heiton would bring them home afterwards and then bring Gran back to 'Sunrise'.

Phyllis came in floods of tears to say goodbye with great promises to come and see me. In fact, she could not come. In those days, tram fares were a big item in her few shillings, she walked everywhere. Cluny Convent was just too far to walk.

'You are in for a big surprise, Lia,' Gran said when we were all settled into Mr Heiton's taxi for the journey to the boarding school.

'I love surprises, Gran! Oh, please tell me!'

'Telling you would be no surprise,' Tadek said.

'Oh, do you know?' I asked him. 'Oh please tell . . .'

'No, Lia, he doesn't know,' put in Gran, thoroughly

delighted with herself. 'This is a guessing what-the-surprise-is kind of a game.' I settled myself into my corner. Gran was set on distracting me so I abandoned the idea of tears which had been just below the surface all the morning. No one had mentioned Mama's absence, and it would be mean to be hurt. As Tadek had pointed out to me, a boarding school must be costing Mama a lot of money; what Tadek said was, 'Think of the sacrifices being made for you.' He would not think well of me if I said, 'I am being got rid of,' so it seemed best to accept the sacrifices as Tadek said, 'with a good grace, and no self-pity.' He had gone on for several sentences about self-pity (I knew he was telling me about myself and inside me I was full of new resolutions for the future when he would not be there to comfort me). 'Remember, Lia, self-pity is the most corroding of all emotions. No, I won't explain, just remember.'

Going along Brunswick Street, around College Green, into Westmoreland Street, across O'Connell Bridge, up Sackville Street as far as Nelson's Pillar, Gran kept on asking me, 'Where are we now, Lia?' and I knew each time. As soon as we left Nelson's Pillar behind, I was lost. Laelia did not know Dublin very well either, so Tadek began to answer for me. Parnell Square, North Frederick Street, Berkeley Road, Phibsboro, along the North Circular and into the Phoenix Park.

'Now, child, do you remember?' asked Gran.

'But I was never here before in this Park.' I was emphatic. Tadek was smiling. Laelia was as puzzled as I was.

'The Phoenix Park?' prompted Gran, chuckling. 'You were here before . . . remember?'

I looked out of Mr Heiton's taxi at all the tree-lined roads.

Gran was laughing now. 'We never came *through* the Park before, because there wouldn't have been enough watering holes for your poor Uncle Jim, God rest him this day.'

Tadek knew what a watering hole was. 'Oh, Mrs B., you went by a way with a few pubs on it?'

'We did, son!' laughed Gran triumphantly. 'We went by way of Chapelizod to the Strawberry Beds.'

'The picnics!' shouted Laelia and Tadek together. I had told them all about the picnics when I was living in their house – acting out the story of Tristan and Isolde for them. Laelia had known some music that was made about the lovers, and she hummed along with the story. I tried to catch Tadek's eye because we had talked about how Tristan had sailed away with Isolde, but Tadek had fixed his gaze on the trees; and after that, he hardly spoke.

'And is that where the Convent is, Mrs B.?' asked Laelia. 'At the Strawberry Beds?'

'Ah no, darlin',' Gran replied, 'but Marie told me it is the top of Knockmaroon, high up overlooking the valley of the Liffey.'

'It sounds lovely,' murmured Laelia.

Soon after that, we were waving goodbye.

I did not cry. I was so excited at the thought of all the new clothes in the big trunk, the thought of a bright new life in an expensive school, the new friends especially.

And yet, I should have shed tears. The nun led me away and I waved goodbye to Gran and Tadek and Laelia – even to Mr Heiton. All unknown to me, it was goodbye to the love and security that had been enriching my life that summer. I believed then, and for a long time afterwards, that life must forever propel itself towards new happiness. Gradually I found out that the very particular brand of happiness which had filled my being with contentment had withdrawn onto a peak which grew more distant with each passing year.

I knew then that I would love Tadek for ever and ever. He dwelt in that part of me that was good and worthy. He was my sacred shrine. There was a reverence in my heart for him. But as the weeks went on into months, I became aware that an element had been ripped out of my life. When I tried to go to sleep each night in the narrow bed in the cubicle, some part of me waited for the slamming of the heavy hall door. Burton was in, he would be coming for his kiss. I was forgiving and forgetting, longing and anticipating all in one big sigh.

Burton, whose body was always fragrant with roses and port wine and cigars, Burton was the essential element of warmth in my childhood. Burton was the one my loneliness craved. Night after night, against this tall cliff I crashed in a sea of tears.

Chapter Six

Cluny Convent was lovely. It was a country mansion set well back among ancient chestnut trees on the edge of the Phoenix Park.

The Park, by use and custom, had become an extension of the Convent grounds. We first-years took our crocodile walks there. We played crazy cricket, and mad hockey in the level clearings, guarded always by two nuns pacing sedately among the trees.

The senior girls had proper playing fields and tennis-courts and croquet lawns within the Convent walls. When a girl entered senior classes at fifteen, the Park was rigorously out of bounds. Some danger, unspecified but greatly dreaded, lurked beneath the brambly overgrowth in the Furry Glen.

Every year, around the eerily magical time of Hallow Eve (or Spira Gira as we called it then), a whisper started going about, the half-rumours on each girl's trembling lips, about a schoolgirl, only sixteen and very beautiful, who had been lured into the Glen by a black-robed figure, mysteriously assaulted and battered to death.

Her pitiful ghost was to be seen, on All Souls' Night, drooping humbly at the Chapel door, begging forgiveness.

Of course she could not be allowed into the Chapel. Not forever!

She was unclean. Her soul was damned for all eternity.

Our souls were nourished on this belief that a sin against purity was the unspeakable sin. If there were other sins, they were not given much attention. Yet the sins against purity were of a nature about which no nun cared to be explicit. It was, however, hinted that such sins took many forms.

As we grew older, our minds on the subject of dark sin became deeply confused. It was dangerous and sinful to ask questions. Questions, we were told, displayed a prurient curiosity. It was hard on a born questioner like me, and even harder to keep all my secrets to myself when I began to have friends. But Tadek had warned me when I said I would write to him every week from the boarding school.

'Write to my mother, Lia, always to my mother. I can read between the lines what there is for me. And remember to be silent about our friendship,' he smiled that marvellous smile, 'we said twenty years, remember?'

Perhaps I could have told Berny a little about Tadek. But I never did. And to whom could I speak about Burton? To no one, ever. In time, I could almost forget him for weeks. The Prayer for Purity must have helped.

I fell in love with Cluny on the very first day. I had new clothes, new possessions, new books, and most important of all, the chance to make friends. When the places were given in the Refectory, I had the great luck to find myself between Berny and Lucille.

I turned to each of them when the nun had said Grace Before Meals (which I had never heard before but which I thought was like a spell over the food), and held out a hand to each.

'I'm Lia,' I said. 'Can we be friends?'

They both thought this funny and began to laugh, but they responded.

'I'm Berny. I'm from Belfast, where are you from?'

'From Ringsend,' I told them. They had never heard of it, which was surprising, I thought that everyone knew Ringsend. Lucille was from County Kildare, her father had a stud farm, she told us. She loved horses and, if girls could be vets, she would be one. She hoped to be a show-jumper, and to be in the Royal Dublin.

If she had said she came from Katmandu, I could not have been more astonished. A dozen questions came to mind, but I just could not bear to display my total ignorance.

'My Dad is a doctor,' Berny said. 'Most years we go down to Dublin for the Horse Show.'

In Dublin? A Horse Show? No one had told me. I wondered, did Phyllis know?

'Wouldn't it be gifty,' Lucille said, 'if we could get our cubicles together in the dorm?'

'You know, of course, that girls must be friends in threes, never in twos?' Berny asked us.

'How do you know that?' I asked her.

'My mother was here at school,' Berny answered. 'And it is *the* strictest rule. You could be expelled for breaking it!'

Expelled! Another new word. My blood ran cold at the very thought. I could picture Mama's upset.

'Could we three be it, then?' I asked in trepidation.

'Are we all twelve?' asked Lucille.

We are the same age to a month or so, I was the youngest and Lucille was the eldest, but all within a month.

'Suppose,' said Berny cautiously, 'we give our threedom a trial?' And Lucille said, 'Why not?'

We got our cubicles in line together, with Berny in the middle. When the nun bade us kneel down that night at the foot of each bed for our night prayers, I had never said prayers before, but I offered praise and thanks for finding friends. Then I whispered Tadek's name into the hollow of my fingers, over and over, for his success in life.

On the other side of my place in the dorm, there was a girl named Helen. She did not find it amusing when I spoke to her.

'I am Lia,' I said to her when we were sorting out our possessions into the two drawers in our night-tables, and I added, to make her smile, 'Isn't this a funny big jug and basin, and full of cold water! What's your name?'

'Mind your own business!' She turned her back to me.

89

I asked Berny, 'Did I do wrong to speak to Helen?'

I always asked Berny about the puzzling things because her mother had been to school in Cluny, and this indicated a long traditional knowledge about boarding schools and , about education. I kept the knowledge to myself that Mama had finished school at twelve years, as had Phyllis, and Gran had never gone to school at all because her mother had sent her to Philadelphia: 'Scrubbing doorsteps at nine years of age,' Gran used to tell me. In the long-ago days when Mama read the letters in the carved box, she had talked a little about when she was at school.

'I had to wear a white pinafore to school in the Model Schools in Marlborough Street. That's right in the centre of Dublin city. The Archbishop ordered that, so all the children had a clean appearance. We were so poor, you know, in those days. I think the nuns in some convent made the pinafores, but our mothers had to keep them white. The children who came in, in dirty pinafores, they got the leather on the hand six times.'

'Did that ever happen to you, Mama?' I held her little hand in mine. It was white and pink and soft and she wore pretty rings.

'Oh no,' she smiled down at her hands, 'I was the youngest in our family, the only girl after all the boys. If *they* had to do it themselves, *they* made sure that my pinafore was shining white, and starched, every Monday morning, and I made sure to take it off after school, not like some bold children who went out in the streets to play in their pinafores – maybe swinging on lamp posts and jagging them!'

'What did you learn in school, Mama?'

'You know,' she mused, 'I don't really remember. I must have learned how to count money because I never make mistakes in counting. But your Dada laughs at me,' and she was smiling tenderly as she always smiled when she said his name, 'because I do not know the rivers and towns of all the countries. He knows everything, he is so interesting. All about the history of the world!'

Ah, how lovely it was in the days before Burton.

'But, you know what I am going to tell you, Lia . . . your Dada thinks I write good writing. I was able to tell him that in the Model Schools in Marlborough Street, there is a frame hanging on the wall with a sample of my writing! When I was twelve, I got the prize!'

'Was it a gold medal, Mama?'

'Silly billy!' she laughed at me. 'I got six new pennies . . . it was considered a lot,' she added defensively.

I treasured all this knowledge about Mama. It was the sum total of her education and it was precious but it did not leave me much to build on – unlike Berny.

Berny was considering me with that wise little purse of the lips of hers. 'Be absolutely truthful, Lia, do you not know why Helen Doyle feels like ticking you off when she sees you – and especially when you patronize her by beaming at her?'

I must have looked so completely dumbfounded that Berny took pity on me. 'All right,' she said, 'now when I tell you, and I tell you only because I think you are dumb on that score . . . sort of dumb, like innocent . . . you are not to question me. Agreed? The thing we cannot forget for a moment is the word "expel". You and I should not be talking alone even now – so, I'll tell you if you promise to forget I spoke.'

This was utterly bewildering, but I nodded excitedly, 'I promise! I promise!'

Berny leaned over to me and, with a quick look around, she whispered in my ear. Then she headed for the stairs, and clattered down, calling back, 'Come on and we will find Lucille.'

I followed, but very slowly. Another burden. I had so many things to live up to. I had so many things to hide. And this was unexpected. Could Gran have warned me, or could Phyllis, or Tadek? What had Laelia said that I had taken for loving flattery, and instantly forgotten? Berny had whispered: 'It is because you are so pretty . . . your hair . . . your teeth . . . everything . . . especially your eyes . . . I don't think you know.'

So, until the day I left school, Helen Doyle slept in the next bed. We never, ever, exchanged a single word.

Our cubicles had white curtains which we drew for privacy. I loved that, it reminded me always of Gran and her Chinese screen. And I didn't love it, because often I was wide awake and longed to whisper to Berny. I knew from the very first night when the Rules of the School were read to us, that to speak when the curtains were drawn was one of *the* dark sins, risking expulsion.

Very quickly I found my way about the school and into the daily routine. Starting the day with Mass in the small Chapel, and ending the day there with night prayers, brought all of us together like a family. There were seventy girls, all boarders, divided into six classes and ranging in age from twelve to eighteen.

It was not long before I was sufficiently instructed to make my First Holy Communion, which would take place before the Christmas Holidays. Before First Communion there was First Confession.

Mère Ann-Thérèse took me every day for lessons in the Ten Commandments. Since she spoke only in French, and since I knew very little French in my first term, perhaps I may be forgiven for wondering many times if that First Confession was an adequate one.

The Chaplain, during my first two years in Cluny, was young and gentle.

'So, are you very pleased you have come at last to the Holy House of God?'

'Oh yes, Father.'

'And this is the very first time you have come to confess your sins?'

'Yes, Father, the very first.' I was trembling with the exciting joy of it all. I was counting the days until I would be wearing the Spanish lace mantilla which Mama had sent for me.

'So, join your hands and begin: "Bless me, Father, for I have sinned".'

I joined my hands as Mère Anne-Thérèse had shown me,

together and with the tips of the fingers touching my chin, and I repeated the words with fervour.

Then there was a silence.

'So begin, child.'

'What shall I say, Father?'

'Now tell your sins and beg for forgiveness.'

So far as I could understand Mère Ann-Thérèse's instruction, I was unlikely to have committed sins against most of the Ten Commandments, maybe what were called venial sins of a trivial sort, but one should not take up a priest's valuable time with stupidities. The exception was the sixth, Mère Ann-Thérèse said. One must be very exacting about the sixth, but she left it at that.

There was another silence.

'Have you something to hide?' the priest enquired.

'Oh no, Father.' But had I? Within the sixth Commandment, 'Thou shalt not commit adultery', was there a compulsion to tell this priest about Tadek? Should I say that underneath my warm acceptance of the everyday life of Cluny, a separate life of loving Tadek went steadily on? Or should I leave Tadek and his careful guarded affection out of this Confession, and rather should I give the priest the facts about Burton? Should I tell this priest, who was patiently waiting for me to confess, that the unbidden thought of Burton could flood my nature with a pulsing, guilty longing?

'Let me help you then, child, by taking you through the Ten Commandments. The first two refer to the honouring of God in our daily lives. In the future, always remember that. The third enjoins on you the obligation of Mass on Sundays and Holy Days, which, after today, will be obligatory on you. The fourth is very important: "Honour thy father and thy mother". Do you honour your parents, child?'

'Oh yes, Father, I love Gran and Mama and my Dada who is dead.'

'And the fifth Commandment: Do you tell lies?'

This was a knotty one. I seemed, always, to have so much to hide.

'Father, only when I have to, I tell a lie.'

The priest seemed to smile. 'Well, that is honest. But try to love the truth.'

Now here it comes, I thought – the dreaded sixth.

'The sixth Commandment, then,' said the priest. 'I am sure you have not had the occasion to commit adultery. The sixth, however, covers many sins against the virtue of purity. Do you wish to tell me of any sin now?'

Another silence in which I wrestled with a deep puzzlement.

'Have you gone out with boys?' the priest asked.

'No, Father.'

'Or done impure acts with girls?'

'No, Father.'

'Or committed sins of self-abuse?'

'Oh no, Father.' Whatever that meant, it sounded repulsive, and I was certain I would hate it.

'I think you are a good child,' the priest said. 'Say an Act of Contrition now, truly ask God's pardon, make a firm purpose to stay with the truth in your dealings with others.'

He murmured the words of the Absolution in Latin while I, with tears of very real sorrow, said the Act of Contrition.

'Go in peace, child. If there are any sins which you may have overlooked through ignorance or forgetfulness, they are absolved. For your Penance, say three Hail Marys. And remember me in your prayers, child, when you come to the altar for your First Communion.'

'Oh I will, Father, I will!'

I was so grateful to be absolved of those problematic questions. There was a wonderful feeling of light-headedness when I knelt in the Chapel to say the three Hail Marys.

When that gentle priest went away on the Foreign Missions, he was replaced by Père Rancier. This French priest had a dour and forbidding aspect. When I confessed to him in the routine weekly Confession, I was very careful to leave the unresolved sins of childhood behind the barrier of that First Confession.

'Did you know, Lia, what Napoleon told his mother about his First Holy Communion?' Lucille was full of odd bits of information.

'Who was Napoleon?' I loved odd bits of information.

'He was an emperor,' she said. 'I think they had a French Revolution and he won all the battles. He told his mother that the day of his First Holy Communion was the happiest day of his whole life!'

I understood very well how Napoleon felt. I wore the lovely veil. I was the most important girl in the school for one whole day. It was a marvellous day to be important for all the right reasons, a marvellous day to have all the nuns smile at me, to receive holy pictures from each girl in my class. The Reverend Mother, usually a distant figure, gave me a pearly rosary on a silver chain; Berny gave me flowered notepaper with her holy picture, and from Lucille I got a lace handkerchief . . . always a hoarder, these gifts are in their little boxes among my keepsakes.

My mother sent an enormous iced cake, so big that everyone had some. Gran sent her homemade walnut toffee and American fudge which everyone agreed was scrumptious.

The feeling of inner radiance lasted a long, long time. When Confirmation came a year later, I was only one among hundreds in the local parish church. Sadly, it was something of an anticlimax.

Thanks to Tadek and Laelia, who had been coaching me when they had had an odd moment during the summer, the initiation into classes was not a great problem as I had feared.

Laelia had a flair for languages, and of course for music. She had given me a grasp of spoken French in simple phrases. As the nuns in Cluny were all French-speaking, this was an enormous help. Laelia had shown me how to read tonic solfa, so I was able to pick out the hymns. Hymns were a large part of all our activities then, in and out of the Chapel.

Tadek's early contribution to my education was by far the

more important. He had taught me to read with a love of the words and their sounds. He had stressed the importance of loving, actually loving, the words.

'Dwell on that word, Lia,' he would say, 'listen to it, compare it with a sound that is not meaningful. When you are reading, read aloud to yourself. Books are full of sounds. Don't just let your eye travel along the line as if your eye is an empty tram on a track. You will miss so much.'

He knew, none better, that the love of books would bring an enthusiasm for knowledge.

And so, because of Tadek and through Tadek, there was one day in every week that stood out for me as the high point of all the week. On Thursdays, Mr Frank Fay came out to Cluny from the Abbey Theatre in Dublin to give Elocution classes.

The nuns called it Elocution, but Mr Fay called it 'Living'. 'Voices could, and should, and must, be used to the best advantage,' was the way he started each class. 'Not every person is given a voice that other persons want to listen to, and not every person is given an ear. The ear is all-important. With both present in one head, a voice capable of moving mountains can be achieved. They will tell you in this Convent that Faith can move mountains. Have faith in your voice, and pray for an ear.'

'There is a voice for every emotion, mood, act. A man who is hungry, or angry, or loving, asks for his breakfast in a hungry, or angry, or loving voice. Now you, miss, give me that voice. No? Well then, you, miss.'

He used his voice for us, over and over again. To my amazement, many of the girls were bored. Would it have surprised them to know, and of course not one of us knew then, that Mr Fay was probably the greatest teacher of his art in the world?

I had never heard of the Abbey Theatre. The Tivoli was the theatre favoured by Gran and Mama, and by Phyllis who had often acted out the entire Tivoli performance for my benefit –

singing, dancing, mimicry, juggling hilariously . . . while accompanying herself on the piano. And I, in turn, had acted out the melodrama from the Queen's for her; she would soft-pedal the sad parts of the drama and thump out jubilant chords for what I told her was 'undying love triumphant' – or so it said on the programme.

Mr Frank Fay was small, delicate, shabby – or so he seemed to me who was accustomed to the magnificence of Burton. His face had a pinched, sensitive look. To us schoolgirls he looked old.

Since he was the only man who came among us, perhaps to some feminine souls he was a disappointment. Not to me. I recognized right from the beginning that the fire in him spoke to the fire in me. When he told us about the founding of the Abbey Theatre, the Irish Literary Renaissance, the new plays they were putting on – different, real, poetic, totally unlike the melodrama of the Queen's which was now, he said, slipping into the past; when he recited a few lines from 'The Land of Youth', my eyes never left his face. When he intoned (like a litany in Chapel) the names of the new writers: the poet Yeats, John Millington Synge, Sean O'Casey, Lady Augusta Gregory, my ears drank in his words. He dropped these names like seeds into my waiting mind to take root for ever.

In my bed at night I rearranged my future. I would give a few years to the Abbey Theatre before I concentrated on life's real objective which had not altered in the least since the very first night Tadek had smoothed my nightie down to my toes . . . Tadek and the little house with the glowing fire and the rosy lamp and the ten children. That was the dream of security for the future, but perhaps not immediately on leaving school. The twenty years of waiting would be up when I was twenty-five – and twenty-five seemed like old age. Sometimes I wavered about the Abbey Theatre. Suppose Tadek was ready to get married?

'Berny, what would you think about acting as a career after school?'

'I would hate it!' Berny replied.

Lucille was very disappointed in me. 'I thought you and I were going to breed King Charles spaniels? Have you changed your mind on that?'

I looked at Lucille in dismay. I loved everything about Lucille. She was my idea of pretty: merry eyes, snub nose, carroty curls. We were never done talking about animals, especially dogs and horses. I had Silky still living at Max's house; and she had four dogs, all collies; and she had a horse of her own called 'Plucky' of whom she talked fondly and constantly and missed terribly.

'Lucille, don't be miffed at me. I thought we could do that as well as a lot of other things.'

'What other things?' Lucille demanded.

'Well, like acting . . . or getting married.'

'Getting married!' Lucille burst out laughing. 'You get funnier every day!'

Berny, who always walked in the middle of the threedom, patted my arm in a warning gesture. 'Lia, keep this new fancy to yourself.'

From the first day, I had always listened to Berny's warnings, but I simply had to ask why I should not mention acting. After all, Frank Fay . . .

'Yes, I know that you and Mr Fay idolize each other. And maybe some day you can get together. But not now. The nuns would say that the stage is not the place for a Catholic convent-reared girl. They would expel you for spreading unsavoury notions, or they would dismiss him. Which would you prefer, Lia?'

'Neither,' I replied, almost in tears.

'So, remember. Anyway, we will be lucky if the nuns let him put on a play for our parents at the end of the year . . . They want Elocution, not play-acting.'

'*A play!*' I had not dreamed of such a possibility.

'They always did in my mother's time,' Berny said. 'Only they didn't have Frank Fay then, but some music master called Vianni. They put on some play called "The Gipsy Baron" with songs in it, and another thing called "Floradora". Mummy said it is a great opportunity for "clicking".'

'Clicking?' repeated Lucille and I.

'You know,' Berny said a little impatiently, 'clicking with other girls' brothers on the night of the play. The nuns give supper in the Concert Hall, and everyone mills around. That is the thing *I* will be looking forward to *if* they let your darling Frank put on a play.'

Lucille and I had often to suspend our talk of dogs to give time to Berny to talk of boys. She had had two fiercely passionate love affairs, she told us, the previous summer on holiday in Portrush. The first one the first fortnight and the second one the second fortnight. The second one was still going on, and she was trying to find a way to write to her beloved who was a boarder in Portora.

'I know a way to do invisible writing,' Lucille had told her. 'You fill a fountain pen with water. You place thin paper on a marble slab, write the letter, dry slowly – not with blotting paper of course. When he gets the letter, he must hold it up to the light and read it.'

'Where do I find a marble slab?' Berny wanted to know.

I always wanted to know where Lucille found all the odd hints of the hitherto unknown. Blotting paper came into a lot of her treasure-trove of information.

'Did you ever feel like taking a day in bed, Lia?' she asked me one day when I was having problems with a geography essay.

'You have to go to Sister Agnes to get your temperature taken to see if you are sick,' I answered. 'Berny said so.'

'Not if you faint in the Chapel,' Lucille told me in the low voice we used for secrets. 'Here is what you do: bring a wad of blotting paper up to bed with you. Let it soak in cold water overnight. Place a pad of it in each shoe in the morning. You won't be ten minutes in the Chapel before you will go off in a dead faint! Honest!'

And one wintry morning, Lucille went off in a dead faint

during Mass. I was almost overcome with a fierce fit of the giggles which I had to turn into a fit of coughing. Sister Agnes and a senior girl carried Lucille out of the Chapel.

In the Ref, each time I took a sip of tea I began to laugh again. Berny had been sent up to the dorm with a cup of tea for Lucille. When she sat down beside me, I asked, grinning and winking, 'Is the poor patient quite blotted out, then?'

Berny glanced at me slightingly. 'It won't be so funny when you have it!'

'I'll never have it!' I was still grinning, thinking of the blotting paper.

'Oh yes, you will, Smartie. We all get it. It is even in our poetry book: "The curse has come upon me, said the Lady of Shalott".'

Some things we figure out for ourselves. I remembered Tadek's question about the monthly period. I felt I would quite like to be borne on high from whatever was going to happen to me. I would adore the drama of it . . . Tennyson-like.

During the Christmas and Easter holidays, I stayed in Gran's house in the narrow street that ran from the centre of Dublin down to the quayside of the River Liffey. Her little routine for her days had never altered and I slipped happily backwards in time. I was reading a lot now, and I read aloud to her each night. I gave the characters in the books the sort of voices, moods, and accents of which Mr Fay would surely approve. I enjoyed it as much as she did.

'Childy, you are as good as a pantomime!' she said when we were having our bedtime cup of tea and piece of cake. Gran always put a spoonful of whiskey in her tea. It made her sleep, she said.

Mama had left strict orders that I was not to be permitted to go across to Ringsend, and 'Sunrise' was locked up. Phyllis, however, walked from Ringsend to join us as often as she was able. She and Daisy Emm were in charge of the shop. Mama was spending Christmas with Burton in London. At Easter, Mama was in hospital, and visitors were not allowed.

On the first Sunday after Easter, we returned to school.

Reverend Mother called a meeting of all the girls in the Senior Study Hall. She made the usual announcements, calling attention to standards of politeness and neatness, and an ever-stricter adherence to the Rules of the School. Then she said:

'After much thought, we have decided that Mr Fay will be allowed to present a play for your parents on the last Saturday in May. Summer holidays will commence on the second day of June.

'Now, pay close attention, *mes enfants*. No girl over the age of fourteen years will expect a rôle in the play. There are certain girls who play the piano, or the violin, acceptably enough. They will not ask for a rôle in this play. They may be allowed solo performances on their chosen instruments if Mère Mathilde sees fit. Those among the senior girls who sing in the choir in the Chapel will contribute a choral number to the evening's programme. Those seniors who do not sing may assist with the *maquillage*. Others of them may assist with the supper.'

I noticed a great rustle of interest when the supper was mentioned.

'As to the play,' the Reverend Mother continued in a sterner voice, 'it is a play of mixed characters, male and female. Any girl who makes use of this occasion to initiate unseemly gestures – I repeat, unseemly gestures – will lose her rôle in the play. And she will be disciplined in the manner of custom.'

Reverend Mother had spoken in French and it had been translated into English by Mother Reine so no girl could pretend not to understand. I knew what 'disciplined in the manner of custom' meant. Berny had told us that, while her mother did not know exactly what happened to the girl being

101

disciplined, it was known then, and it was known now, as the Spanish Inquisition. Those words struck terror into the hardiest of us.

On Thursday, Mr Fay gave us the background of the play. The title of the play was '*Sagart Aroon*'.

'The title is Irish. Do any of you know how to speak Irish?'

Irish was not then a compulsory subject for exams. In a year or two, it became so.

Helen Doyle held up her hand. Mr Fay surveyed her, lowering his glasses and gazing over them. She was a tall girl, rosy-cheeked and stout. She had clipped, dark hair worn in a fringe.

'Excellent!' said Mr Fay. 'You will play the manservant in the Desmond Castle. He has a fair few lines, as old family retainers always have, and he speaks only Gaelic.'

Mr Fay had a way of taking off his glasses and directing a glance here and there at us. It was a good gesture for drawing our erring attention back to him.

'The play is set in the early seventeenth century when the Irish people all spoke Irish – the Gaelic tongue. The nobility, who were mostly Norman or Anglo-Norman, also knew English, and French, and they travelled to the Continent of Europe a great deal . . . visiting their great-aunts, I suppose!'

We guessed this was a witticism and we all smiled.

'*Sagart* means a priest. *Aroon* may mean well-loved, precious. It may also refer to a secret, a mysterious plot, a vengeful deceit. The title therefore is double-meaning.

'In the early seventeenth century, the Penal Laws had followed on the sixteenth-century Reformation. The great sport of the English redcoats was priest-hunting.' He paused for a moment. 'You young ladies have been told that Saint Patrick brought the Faith to Ireland, and banished the old pagan ways along with the snakes? You have? Yes, well, the Normans re-inforced it. They brought with them from Mediaeval Europe a very superior Faith full of monks and monasteries and abbeys and castles. They consolidated them-

102

selves in Ireland by intermarriage with the ancient families of the old Gaelic aristocracy. . . .' He paused reflectively, looking around . . . 'they had beautiful daughters for marriage then as now. . . .

'This is the first time that I have had your undivided attention, young ladies. Perhaps I should be teaching my version of history?'

We gave the subdued girlish titter considered appropriate when a teacher made a joke.

'Very well. The Reformation aimed at the Dissolution of the Catholic Faith; in Ireland the Penal Laws stamped out the Faith and the Gaelic language.

'Does anyone want me to repeat that introduction?'

We all shook our heads. His very voice made all things clear.

'So. The officers of the English Crown were given the work of priest-hunting. On every priest's head was a price. Caught alive he might be worth a hundred golden guineas. The unfortunate priest could then be tortured on the rack to reveal where he had hidden the marvellous vessels of the altar, wrought in gold and embossed with precious jewels. That find would be a further bounty for the priest-hunter.'

Mr Fay sat down. He opened his big book of notes.

'The scene is set throughout in the Great Hall of the Desmond Castle (now remember the history of the century, the Penal Laws), the home of a powerful Norman family with close ties to the English Crown. The principal characters in the play will be:

'The Earl and Countess of Desmond.
Their son, Justin, a newly-ordained priest fresh from his studies in Louvain after ten years.
Their daughter, a beautiful maiden known as the Fair Geraldine.
Sir Gervaise: the handsome Captain of the Redcoats with whom Geraldine is passionately in love, and he

with her. She does not know that the gallant Captain is a notorious priest-hunter and bounty-seeker, by which means he has become immensely rich.

In their love-making, the Fair Geraldine reveals to Sir Gervaise the hidden presence of her brother, the priest.'

Mr Fay scanned all the faces in the classroom. I am sure we were all craning forward, our eyes wide with anticipation.

'I will leave you all to guess at the development of the climax.' He smiled at our long-drawn 'Aaah!' of disappointment. 'However,' he added, 'I am giving each of you four assorted pages of lines, and next Thursday we will audition.'

Trooping down the stairs, Berny chuckled, 'He'll never get that past Mère Ann-Thérèse! Passionately in love, if you don't mind!'

I was too excited to speak, I was almost tripping over the steps, but Lucille gave Berny a poke in the back.

'You'd be great in that part with all the "passionate", Ber! With your experience!' Lucille was constantly teasing Berny about her love affairs. 'I can't imagine what she sees in boys!' she would moan aloud when Berny went on and on about the boy in Portora, captain of the cricket team, devastatingly good-looking. 'Honestly,' Lucille told us, 'I have three older brothers and you should come and live with them! They hog everything! And such meanies!

'Eh, Berny, would you like the part of the gallant Captain?' Lucille asked.

'I don't want any part,' Berny answered. 'I will be helping with the supper.'

Lucille and I exchanged a glance. The 'clicking'!

'My extremely handsome excamabious brothers will be coming if Mammy can get their heads out of the slurry pit!' said Lucille in the very serious tone she used when she was dying to burst into guffaws of mocking laughter. But Berny was always able to take a joke. Serenely secure in her life, her family, her future, she never took offence, she never sulked. She had a smooth, candid face with wide-apart grey eyes. 'Make sure Mammy washes the dung out of their hair,' she smiled, 'and I promise to look them over!'

When Thursday came and we were all auditioned, I was given the rôle of the Fair Geraldine. I all but died of excitement. I wanted to jump up and down and wave my lines in the air. I entered immediately into the spirited rôle: tossing my hair, walking tall with disdain as befitted the daughter of an Earl, glancing haughtily with each word I spoke in class or in the Refectory.

Berny warned me, 'Don't be such a dodo, Lia! The formation of our personalities while we are in Cluny is the direct opposite to the way you are going on. Mère Ann-Thérèse has her beady eye on you! No need to be so uproariously full of yourself! You need to learn a bit of deception, Lia!'

If only she knew the tons of tender longing I had to bury every day.

Each girl was given a splendid invitation card for four of her family to come to the great night. It was all set out on the card: there would be a concert, followed by an interval. Then the play, '*Sagart Aroon*', and after that: the supper.

We were told that for the supper, all the chairs would be grouped for families. The girls who had not taken part in the concert, or play, would then appear all spruced-up carrying trays and teapots.

The Concert Hall was the big hall, a new wing of the old country house, in which we had weekly lessons in physical education (known to us as 'drill'); weekly classes in ballroom and classical dancing; mid-term examinations; and forty minutes every night of recreation during which we could dance, or talk, or play games of ludo or draughts. So the Concert Hall was in daily use. However, for the great night which took place once only in each year, the walls would be painted; the floor would be sanded; potted palms and flowering tubs from the Convent conservatory would be used for decoration.

The thought of it made me hold my breath . . . the glory of it for my family to see!

Despite Berny's cooling touch, I was seething with expectation. Mama was out of hospital again, so she and Gran and Tadek and Laelia would come in Mr Heiton's taxi on the great night. Tadek. Tadek.

His beloved name was almost on the tip of my tongue as the rehearsals progressed week by week.

If Mr Fay expected love to be spoken in accents of love, then he should have it done by me in full measure.

Breda Culligan was tall and slim and nice-looking. She was the gallant Captain. When she took my hand to draw me towards her, for me it was like going into Tadek's arms, touching Tadek's hair, holding up my face for Tadek's gentle kiss, breathing his name in accents of muted passion. Tadek used always to murmur: 'little play-actor' and laugh at me.

Breda Culligan's face went scarlet with embarrassment during these rehearsals. The nuns frowned on such immodest blushing. Rehearsals were to be considerably cooled down as much when I displayed ardent desirous love for the Captain as when I flew madly at him, denouncing his treachery, snatching his sword, and running him to the ground. The two French nuns, who guarded all our activities, complained daily to Mère Ann-Thérèse that I was *'sans gêne'*, even *'honteuse, un peu'*. Mr Fay assured Mére Ann-Thérèse that I was merely enthusiastic, trying hard to please.

I promised myself that there would be feeling, real feeling on the night, the great night. I had a little note from Gran to say that Mama was in good form, that I should send the invitation in good time so Tadek and Laelia would be free, and Mr Heiton's taxi would be ordered as I had asked.

I kissed the envelope and put it with all the others on the tray for Mère Madeleine to inspect, and stamp, and post.

Then Mère Madeleine sent for me to appear in her office. She was not one of the nuns who favoured me. When she wished not to understand anyone, her English became obscure. Our letters both incoming and outgoing were read by Mère Madeleine.

'*Qui est ce que ce* Tadek?' she enquired in her sugary voice.

'*Il est mon* . . .' inevitably I hesitated.

'*Oui*?'

'*Il est mon cousin.*' I knew she detected the lie.

'*Son père est le frère de Mama*?'

'*Non, non, Soeur. Il est* . . . *sa mère est* . . .'

She pounced on me, '*Pas ton frère! La nuit est pour les parents; la famille! Allez!*'

I produced tears immediately. Most of the nuns were kind-hearted, they did not like to see their pupils distressed, but not Mère Madeleine. In the years ahead, I was to find out that she quite enjoyed children's tears. Now she opened the door, and pushed me out onto the corridor.

'*Frères, seulement! Allez!*'

My letter for the week went this time to Mrs Vashinsky. I told her all about the play, how excited I was, how I looked forward to seeing Laelia. I stressed how sad it was that Tadek could not come because only girls' brothers and fathers were allowed, I repeated at length how brilliant I was in the play, what a pity he would not see me, but as Mère Madeleine had said, it was only brothers who could come on Parents Day. In this pathetic little letter the most amateur detective could have read a direct appeal to Tadek. I was lucky Mère Madeleine accepted my submissive obedience at its face value. The letter was sent.

Even the fact that Tadek would not be there to see me as the lovely Geraldine, who of course dies in the end of the play (who could live on after betraying a priest?), even that did not dim my delight in being the centre of the stage, the focus of attention. I knew Laelia would describe me to him in every detail. I was utterly secure in their devotion to me. I would miss him with all my heart but he would hear that I was trying to forge ahead, and not giving in to self-pity.

Tadek read my letter to his mother correctly. Apparently

he knew all about the Abbey Theatre. He went to see Frank Fay. In some magical manner he persuaded Mr Fay to enrol him as an assistant props man for the night. The bribe may have been Mr Heiton's taxi-cab, paid for by Mama. Mr Fay, on his weekly visits to Cluny, had to take the tram out from Dublin to Chapelizod and climb Knockmaroon Hill to the Park, a good mile. Mr Heiton's taxi-cab bowled out through the main road of the Park in great comfort, and style. Mr Fay would be glad to be carried out in comfort, and home at the end of the night.

We children who were in the concert did not visit before-hand in the parlour with our parents. The first I saw of Tadek was on the stage, placing a wooden bench under Mr Fay's direction. He gave me that wonderful gleaming smile. Before I could speak, he said quickly, 'I am the props man, Ted!' He hurried over to Mr Fay, who needed help.

I must have been gazing in open-mouthed adoration at him, I must have been whispering his name. He cast a stern, admonishing glance over his shoulder, 'Ssh – Lia!'

There was tremendous excitement among the cast, and a fierce temptation to fall into fits of giggles . . . when the girls noted the curly black hair and dark eyes of the props man. Mr Fay looked even older and more desiccated compared to the youthful splendour of Tadek, or Ted, as they all quickly called him. Of course, we had to be careful. The usual two guarding nuns were ensconced among the side drops to make sure we behaved ourselves as proper young ladies.

Tadek was able, very cleverly, to speak a few words of warning. 'I got here,' he said, 'now don't overdo it.'

But I had to reply, 'I love you,' in a tiny whisper. And he held my elbow only for a second to breathe, 'Me, too.'

It seemed my life was suddenly in full swing again. The play was really a success. Mr Fay was seen to relax and smile. The audience was wonderfully enthusiastic, clapping hard at the end of each act. I had spotted Gran and Mama. I felt Mama must be proud of me at last. I knew Gran was happy for me because she was waving her umbrella at the very end. Laelia told me, during the supper, that Mama had a hanky to her eyes during my big scenes. I was sure that meant I was good, I had moved her to tears. When I introduced Berny and Lucille to Mama, she smiled in a tragically beautiful way. They thought she was like an actress you would see in a cinema. I liked that.

Mr Fay and Tadek stood off to one side during the supper. They were surrounded by nuns, plying them with sandwiches, and tea. I continued my play-acting, occasionally fluttering my painted eyelashes in Tadek's direction, but being extremely demure, conscious of Mère Madeleine nearby. Mr Fay had been greatly taken with Mama, who looked very fashionable in a long sand-coloured coat trimmed with fur. She was always the quiet one, leaving the talk to others. Nevertheless, she had managed to convey to Mr Fay her great interest in the Abbey, and they had arranged to meet there in the week following. Laelia, too, had aroused Mr Fay's interest, as she was to arouse the interest of everyone, in and out of the theatre, in the years ahead.

All too soon, the night was nearly over. There was a wonderful feeling of light-headed happiness until I brought up the subject of the long holidays ahead.

'Shall I be in the Vashinskys'?' I asked Mama.

She looked slightly horrified. 'In Ringsend?' she replied. 'Oh no, not any more. I have arranged for you to spend the summer in Bray with Aunt Julia.'

With Mama, I did not argue. It had been ingrained into me by Phyllis that Mama must not be upset. I had begun to understand that there was a good reason for that.

Gran, always watchful for me, put in a cheery word. 'I'll be down there for my holiday during July. Julia has asked me every year, but I'll go this year!'

I knew Gran was not too keen on her widowed daughter-in-law, Julia. She was of the opinion that Julia was stingy. I found out that she was right.

I had managed to write a long letter to Phyllis in between the pages of a copy-book, telling her how I missed her and telling her all about the play which I promised I would act out for her during the summer if I could be in Ringsend with her. I gave her full descriptions of my two friends and I told her all about the blotting paper faint. I knew she would go into fits of her giggles when she read that. I ended the letter with loads and loads of love. That kind of letter would never pass Mère Madeleine's censorship. I slipped it into Gran's capacious handbag along with her umbrella. She nodded in that lovely conspiratorial way we all had of 'not upsetting Mama'.

Just at the last, I got a quick chance of telling Tadek about Bray.

'You are not going into exile,' he whispered back, smiling down at me. 'Bray is a grand place, even nicer than Sandymount – more sea! We'll come down on the train – it is only sixpence. Dry the tears now, Lia – I have great news for you – Max's father gave him a car for his twenty-first birthday!'

'A car! For his birthday!'

'It's a second hand two-seater, but it goes like the hammers of hell! We'll have great fun! Now smile for me, Lia . . .' For a second, he held my hand and then they were all getting into Mr Heiton's taxi with Mr Fay and Mama still chatting away . . . and the nuns out on the front steps shushing us back into the school now that our visitors had gone.

It had been a night of unbridled excitement. Lucille, who always knew something appropriate for any occasion, began to chant in a very low monotone:

> 'The holidays at last are here, hooray for the summer
>   holidays!
> The happiest time of all the year, shout hooray for
>   holidays!
> Break up tables, break up chairs, throw the teachers down
>   the stairs!
> Kick up –'

'Lucille O'Nolan!' It was the scandalized voice of Mère

110

Madeleine. 'Bring me one hundred lines at ten o'clock tomorrow morning: "The disobedient child is selfish".'

Lucille had perfected a trick of writing lines with two pens tied together. It was a good trick, but I could never get it to work for me. I was glad Lucille was so resourceful because she must have got thousands of lines from Mère Madeleine.

Chapter Seven

There were so many joyful events in that first summer holiday in Bray. The very first, and very joyful, was my reunion with Silky. I was so fearful that she would have completely forgotten me as I stood out on the steps of Aunt Julia's Guesthouse that I kept on running my fingers through my hair in case it was different from what Silky would remember. Usen't it to be always mussy before I went away to school?

Then, suddenly, Max pulled in to the kerb in his car. It was open, with no roof, and I saw the two dogs sitting in state on the seat beside him.

I took Silky in my arms. She began to lick my face, reflectively, tenderly. She remembered me.

'She is licking your tears, Lia.' Max was very amused.

'She knows me,' I hugged the little dog, 'she knows me, doesn't she, Max?'

'How could she forget you, Lia? I told her, day in day out, not to forget little Lia!'

'Did you really, Max?' I wanted to believe him, but he was smiling so much I thought he was just teasing.

'And Toozy, too! Look, he remembers me as well.'

'Don't leave *me* out!' Max laughed. 'I remember you, too. Look, I brought you a bag of your favourite ice-cream caramels!'

'Oh yummy! How did you remember that I adored these sweets? Oh Max, your car is gorgeous! Can we go for a drive?'

'Sure we can, but you had better get permission from your Aunt – what's her name?'

'Julia,' I whispered to him, 'and she is a desperate meany!'

At that moment, Aunt Julia came out of her front door.

'Whose dogs are those?' she demanded.

'This is my friend, Max,' I said. 'This is Aunt Julia. And this is Silky, and this is Toozy.'

'So long as you don't bring them into the house,' she said sharply, ignoring Max's outstretched hand.

'But Silky is going to live with me for the whole summer,' I said pleadingly.

'In my house? Not likely!' retorted Aunt Julia.

'Mama agreed it!' I jumped at her. 'And she said she would pay extra for it! So now!'

I saw Max's eyebrows lifting. He had not guessed I could be cheeky.

Aunt Julia put her hands on her hips. 'Your Mama did not say that Silky was a dog!'

I was almost in tears. 'Well, she meant to,' I besought her. 'Please let Silky stay and I'll sleep in the attic and you can give my good bedroom to your guests. Please!'

'And have a dog barking all night? Disturbing my household? Keeping my guests awake on their holidays?'

I was hugging Silky. 'Silky never barks when she is sleeping on my bed!'

Aunt Julia was aghast with displeasure. 'A dog sleeping on a bed! Do you think this is the zoo?'

Max's voice was full of laughter when he spoke. 'She is a very well-behaved little dog, Ma'am. Very clean.'

'We'll see if we believe that!' said Aunt Julia. 'One false move and you, young man, can come and take it back.'

'I should like to take Lia for a drive in my car,' Max said.

'Have you her Mama's permission? You certainly haven't mine.'

'Oh he has! He has!' I burst out quickly. 'Mama said he could!'

I never minded telling a lie when it was absolutely necessary.

113

Aunt Julia hesitated. 'Lia must be in at six o'clock for her high tea.'

Max was equal to that. 'I am going to give her high tea in a hotel down on the sea-front! he said quickly. 'And I will have her back before eight.'

'Hotel!' said Aunt Julia witheringly. 'Look at her! Did she ever learn anything in that school? How to use a comb, for instance?'

'She's grand,' called Max, pushing me and the dogs into the car. ''Bye for now!'

When he had driven down the road and round a corner, Max pulled in. He was smiling hugely, 'Do you think this is the zoo?' he mimicked. We laughed so much that the dogs began to bark.

'Barking is forbidden!' Max told them sternly, and we began to laugh all over again.

'The first thing we must do,' Max said, turning the car back towards the main street, 'we must buy a nice lead for Silky so you can take her with you everywhere. I have her basket and a couple of small blankets in the boot.'

I turned around and looked at Max. He was such a big burly fellow with horn-rimmed glasses that I had been a little in awe of him until now. Even the previous summer, I was not sure if he liked me, I was such a hanger-on when Tadek had other friends. And then, Tadek had told me several times that Max was a brilliant student. He was considered, Tadek said, to be a very brainy fellow indeed.

'You are very nice,' I said to him. He did not glance away from the road, but he smiled and said, 'Good.'

That was the first day. After that, Tadek and Max came together. Sometimes Tadek and Laelia came down from Ringsend in the train. I think they chose sunny days to come because I do not remember a wet or a cold day.

Tadek had bought a secondhand Brownie box camera. He went quite crazy on the idea of pictures of all of us on every possible occasion. There we are: perched up on rocks,

114

picnicking in the sand dunes; washed over with waves at the edge of the sea; playing rounders; all piled into the Citroën with Gran and the dogs.

The pictures don't bear looking at too often, tears come tumbling down. Yet, faded as they are, they portray an amazing happiness enjoyed by people who had little else but that happiness. Laelia is so lovely in these old pictures. Her hair falls on her shoulders, she looks far away across the sea, dreaming of a wondrous future. She is like a biblical princess of centuries ago.

That summer I learned to swim at Greystones. Here Max said the water was twice as clean which Tadek said was rubbish – Max just liked to drive further! Tadek taught me. I prolonged the lessons to last all the summer. 'I was,' I told them seriously, 'rather nervous of the sea.' Tadek, as he always did, accepted my artful deceptions, and played along. Max offered to give me extra tuition.

'A big reckless fellow like you!' said Tadek. 'You would drown the poor child!'

Gran came on her holiday as she had promised. Being with Gran was to know contentment. Her concern was always for the wellbeing of others. Max took us for several drives out to Kilmacanogue and up the Rocky Valley, and sometimes we brought a picnic. Gran had a great eye for scenery, she would sit and admire the golden blaze of gorse on Carraig Una. She had a fancy for Max, something about him appealed to her, she said.

'He drives so sedately,' she always observed. But I knew that was just for her, just to hear her purr with pleasure. Tadek had told me that Max would push the little car up to seventy miles an hour when only he and Max were out on a main road. Highways and dual carriageways had not been heard of in Ireland then.

When Gran sat in front with Max, I sat in the fold-up 'dicky-seat' in the boot, clutching the two dogs. If Tadek came along, and Gran as well, he joined me on the fold-up seat with his two arms tightly around me and the dogs as we all bounced along. I loved that.

Days when no one came down from Dublin to Bray, I was so pleased to have Silky. She walked beautifully on the lead. But then, Burton had taught her to walk when she was a tiny puppy. Alone with Silky, grooming her, talking to her, brought back the poignant memory of being with Burton in the early days in 'Sunrise'. . . . The day of my birthday when he had come early to sit on the edge of my bed, the teeny-weeny puppy in the hollow of his hands: 'Your birthday present, Lia!' Oh, how I loved him in that moment. I had been longing for a puppy, and just that very kind of puppy, a King Charles. I remembered what he said: 'A very very special little doggy for my own very very special little girly,' and he kissed me lingeringly. It was beautiful to be kissed by Burton with the puppy snuggling between us. If only it had not been wrong.

I had had a whole year now of Religious Instruction. I could not claim a pagan innocence. I was made aware that I had a conscience which told me right from wrong. Burton was a wrongdoer. I should never, never admit him into my thoughts.

Holding Silky on my lap, ruffling her feathery curls, I could not but remember the affectionate side of Burton, and the unique perfume of his presence.

I tried and tried, but it was so hard to banish him for ever.

On the very last day, Tadek suggested a walk for just the two of us. We went up Bray Head, around the cliff path high up over the sea.

'Is it true,' I asked, 'that on a clear day, you could see the Welsh Mountains from here?'

'Where do you get all this useless information, Lia?' Tadek was smiling down at me. 'It would want to be very clear! It is over sixty miles away!'

We walked on in silence. I was always full of questions but I knew, with Tadek, when to keep quiet. We never went

116

off walking on our own like this. I would have liked to, but that was not Tadek's way. I knew he had something to tell me. I hoped it was not going to be a little lecture about being grateful for all the chances I was being given in life.

I was beginning to long for the day when I would not be a child to Tadek. I was not sure what the next stage would be. I was only sure of the end with the rosy lamp and the glowing fire. Some of the twenty years of waiting had passed by now. I looked up to Tadek so. I admired him so. And I loved him so. I could wait.

'You know, Lia, I have told you that Max and I are qualified in the autumn?'

'Um, I know. It is very exciting! And you will get marvellous jobs in Dublin in the big hospitals!'

'Well . . .' Tadek hesitated, '. . . not just straightaway. Max is going to study psychology. His father is sending him to Vienna. They have family relations there. His father is a very rich man. I think I told you about his father, didn't I? He is an art dealer in Dublin – I think he is a collector also – anyway, he travels the world. He is a very fine man. My father knew his brother . . . they were boys together in Zamość . . . they were of an age. Max's father was the youngest of a big family.'

There was a long pause. We had stopped walking. Tadek was staring down at the sea breaking on the rocks far below.

Tadek's low tone was full of painful emotion when he said, reflectively, 'Max's father has been very good to my family in the past couple of years, and to me since Max became my friend . . . Jews are slow to press assistance on Jews. We like to walk alone.'

This was all about Max and Max's father. That was not what he had come around this lonely path to say.

I waited for a while, and then I tugged his hand.

'It's about you, isn't it, Tadek?'

He took the tugging hand and held it between his own two hands.

117

'Such a little hand! Yes, Lia, it is about me. Please promise me you won't cry. Please . . . You have so much now in your life to make you –'

I interrupted him. I could not listen to a lecture now.

'I promise. I promise not to cry if you promise me something, when you have said the bad thing.'

Still holding my hand, he said slowly, 'I have secured a post in a hospital in Bournemouth – that's a place in the South of England.'

'For a little while?' I asked eagerly.

'For two years. I need the experience, and I need to earn the money.'

Two years seemed like for ever. 'I shall miss you,' I said bravely, and I blinked hard at the sea that stretched for all of sixty miles away to England.

'Now let us turn back towards the seafront,' he said briskly.

We walked and I fought hard to keep the tears from spilling down. At last I said, 'You made your promise if I didn't cry?'

We stopped again.

'What is it, Lia?'

'Will you promise to go on loving me like always even when you are sixty miles away?'

The tears were threatening again.

Very swiftly, Tadek bent and kissed my forehead. 'Always always always,' he whispered. Straightening as swiftly, he started off to run – 'Race you to the ice-cream stand,' he called back to me.

The second year in Cluny was not a carbon copy of the first year, but almost so.

In that second year, we began to grow up.

In September, I was very happy to meet up with my friends again. Lucille and Berny and I were back together in the dorm and in the Ref.

We had a million confidences to exchange about our

summer holidays. I talked a lot about Silky and Laelia and Max and Gran. I made them laugh when I imitated Aunt Julia.

I never made any mention of Tadek. For one thing, he did not wish it. And for another, his memory generated so much tender emotion that my eyes would fill with tears.

Lucille gave us full accounts of all the local horse shows – she dignified them as Equestrian Events so proud of them was she. Her dad had yearlings which had to be walked every day, and with extreme care, not allowed to put their hooves in ruts. He would be selling these young horses in England. He had promised Lucille a really magnificent wristlet watch out of his profitable sales. Lucille's eyes glowed when she talked of her dad and his horses; and of her own special horse, Plucky, who had carried her to victory and to the acquisition of much-prized rosettes in the gymkhanas.

Berny had manoeuvred a meeting with last year's boy, the captain of the cricket team in Portora Royal. He would be in Queen's University in October. Closer acquaintance had not increased her erstwhile passion, although it appeared to have increased his, Berny told us with great certainty. Unfortunately for his hopes, he had been supplanted by an English boy on holiday in Donegal with his uncle, the Earl of something. In Berny's ever-ready romantic heart, this new hero was beyond description, superb. He was leader of the choices, so far. A senior in some famous English college, he had followed her holidaying family to Weston-Super-Mare ('which place,' she said, 'was not exactly his cup of tea') and, so sophisticated was he that he had taken Berny out to dinner in a Grand Hotel several times, and, listen to this you kids, to a *thé dansant* every afternoon in a different Grand Hotel!

'What did your mother say?' demanded Lucille. 'You aren't fourteen yet.'

'Oh, Mummy liked him,' Berny answered, quite calm in the face of Lucille's astonishment. 'And everyone thinks I look at least sixteen.'

'But you're not!' Lucille felt that Berny could be led astray.

119

'My mother says you have to be very careful with boys. My mother says they are not the same as girls!'

Berny laughed delightedly. 'I wonder, is that because they have bigger ears?'

Lucille flushed but she would not let her mother be defeated. 'No,' she said, 'bigger feelings!'

'Bigger what?' asked Berny lightly.

Afterwards, I would remember the quipping of my two friends. I took it all lightheartedly, as they did. It never came near to any of the thoughts I had to be careful to hide.

Dimly, wordlessly, I concluded that Lucille's mother would guard Lucille from all harm. Berny's mother would know how to keep Berny's world spinning correctly on its axis.

Even more dimly, it was to be borne in on my consciousness that (always allowing for the benefits of Religious Instruction) my safe conduct through these unspecified perils had been left to chance.

'Let's enjoy this year,' Berny said one day when we had been arguing about something of no importance. 'Next year we will be seniors. Mummy says it is altogether different!'

Mr Fay came every Thursday. I worshipped him. I lived from week to week for his classes.

He and Tadek had remained firm friends. Sometimes we had secret conversations under cover of Living Dialogue:

'Our dark-haired friend, loaded with academic honours, Will set sail before the time of the moon!'

'You speak of the one who goes forth to heal the sick?'

Again please, with a touch of eager interest, young lady.

'And the other one, the Semite, May the mighty wind not deal roughly with that one!'

'Nor the large waves sink the ship!'

Try that again with anguish. 'There are many tales to impart. . . .'

There was less and less to impart as time passed.

Every third Sunday, Gran came for a visit with me in the nuns' parlour.

'No, I don't mind,' she always answered to my enquiries. 'I get the tram to the North Circular Gate. Then I go into Lonergan's shop for the bag of sweets for you to share with your nice friends. I have a chat about old times with Mrs Lonergan, a decent Dublin woman. Then I set off across the Park. I don't mind the walk at all, childy, so stop worrying. I go back by the road because that way is downhill from Knockmaroon. The Lucan tram takes me from Chapelizod into the City for four pence. So, no more questions about my poor old feet. They're grand!'

Like it always was with Gran, we had much the same conversations each time. Like Phyllis's mother long ago. To me, this was warmly reassuring. I did not want change. I asked first about Mama. Sometimes she was in London. That meant she was with Burton. I was careful never to mention his name. I knew Gran hated the very sound of it. Sometimes Mama was in the hospital. Mostly she was in the shop working away to make money.

'She promised me she would give up that shop, but she never will. It is killing her. Now she has to put the money up for your education, Lia. She thinks only of your welfare. She works Sunday to let the girls off.'

Coming near the summer again, I wanted to be sure that Mama and Gran would come to the play that we were rehearsing with Mr Fay.

'The nuns insisted on Shakespeare this time, Gran, and I have a lovely part.'

'Oh, the last play was wonderful! And you were wonderful in it, childy!'

'Will Mama come?'

'Well, if she can't come, would you like me to bring Mrs Vashinsky? I visit them every week. They are lonely now with the boy and Laelia both gone. You know, he sent the money for Laelia to go to Italy?'

My heart swelled with pride in Tadek so I could hardly speak.

'Will I invite her, if Mama is away?'

'Oh I would love her to come!' I cried. 'She loves Shakespeare.'

'Shakespeare you say? Usen't they to have that on in the Queen's? I never was at it. What is it about, Lia?'

I felt very important telling Gran the story of 'The Tempest' in which I would play Ariel.

Perhaps 'The Tempest' is not the easiest of Shakespeare's plays to explain. Gran's brows were knotted in bewilderment at the idea of a Duke called Prospero being exiled on an island with his young daughter for fourteen years while his wicked brother ruled at home and, strangely, this exiled Duke was able to call in magic help from his elf, Ariel, and every other kind of help from his ugly slave, Caliban.

'Now Gran, listen: by the magic, Prospero makes a shipwreck . . .'

'Wait now,' Gran pleaded, 'I am getting a bit lost!'

'Ariel has some lovely little songs, Gran, and I am able to sing them. Here's one you will like, Gran:

> *"Full fathom five thy father lies;*
> *Of his bones are coral made;*
> *Those are pearls that were his eyes:*
> *Nothing of him that doth fade,*
> *But doth suffer a sea-change*
> *Into something rich and strange." '*

'Did his father get drowned?' asked Gran. 'But whose father?'

'Ferdinand's father!' I answered. 'Ferdinand was the son to the King of Naples.'

'Oh dear!' Gran said sadly. 'I think you had best begin the story again, childy.'

'I'll sing you another little song, Gran. This is a really lovely one:

122

"Where the bee sucks, there suck I:
In a cowslip's bell I lie;
There I couch when owls do cry.
On a bat's back I do fly . . ."'

'She must have been very small,' Gran interrupted.

'She was only a little elf, Gran, but I think Prospero really loved her. He calls her his "tricksy spirit".'

'What happened in the end?' asked Gran.

'Prospero set her free, but you know, Gran, he was going to be lonely without her.'

'And what happened to the daughter you said in the beginning of the story?'

'Oh, she got Ferdinand!' I said with enthusiasm.

'Well, well, well,' Gran did not commit herself further. 'I wonder, now, will Mrs Vashinsky understand it?'

'You explain it to her, Gran.'

'I can only do my best.' She smiled doubtfully as we were walking to the side gate to say goodbye.

She gave me a big hug and a kiss. 'You are as good as a pantomime, childy! Did you give me the letter for Phyllis?'

'It is in your handbag, Gran.'

'She'll be over tonight before she goes home. If I haven't got the letter from you, she'll be very disappointed.'

'I didn't know she went home? I thought she slept in Ringsend to keep Mama company?'

'Oh well,' Gran said reluctantly, 'Marie goes up to "Sunrise" this last week. He is back there now.' She tightened her shawl around her shoulders, preparatory to setting off down the hill. 'Temporary, Marie says.'

It had been decided that this summer holiday, I would be sent to the Gaeltacht in Galway, to an Irish college.

'Mama's one thought is to further your education, Lia child,' Gran told me when she brought the news out to

Cluny. 'She read in the paper that the Irish will be a compulsory subject. You have to take that subject in the Government Exams now in future.'

'I know, Gran, it will be starting here next September with a special teacher.'

'But, don't you see, childy, she wants you to be one step ahead?'

I told Berny and Lucille. They were not very impressed.

Berny's parents had decided that, in senior class, she must choose subjects suitable for going on for medicine. . . . The same as her doctor-father, of whom she was very proud. Latin was more likely to be required than Irish.

Lucille's eldest brother had been in an Irish college the previous summer.

'He had great gas altogether,' Lucille told us. 'They were smoking cigarettes and drinking every night. And one night, they took out a boat and went for a midnight swim, two girls and three fellows!'

'Were they caught?' we asked.

'Something happened!' Lucille said. 'Daddy got a letter from the principal! Shane won't be let go this year, Daddy says, after Rory disgracing the family last year. Daddy says those Irish colleges are only courting colleges! Mammy says she would never let me go to one of them!'

Gran had told me that Mrs V., as she called her, expected Laelia and Tadek home in the month of August when I would be in Aunt Julia's guesthouse. At that time, Mama and Burton were going on a cruise in the Mediterranean.

'I think,' Gran said carefully, 'that they are trying to make a reconciliation. He was insisting that you were to be included in that holiday – that cruise. That awful row went on and on for weeks. Marie would not give in.' Gran looked at me. 'No, Lia, that's right – I didn't think you would want to go!'

I do not know how she read that in my face.

*

The Irish College was a long distance out on the sea coast beyond Galway. There were about forty of us, boys and girls, on the bus from the train station. I was happy to look out at this wild scenery.

'Is that sea the Atlantic Ocean?' I asked a boy beside me.

'Well, it is still Galway Bay,' he answered, 'but as we go further west, we get to the Atlantic.'

I looked at the boy. He had a nice tanned face and quiffed-back blond hair. I liked him.

'I am Lia,' I said. 'What's your name?'

'James Mulhern,' he answered. He had a nice smile. 'But you should call me Seamus. We are not allowed to use a word of the *Béarla* here in Carraroe.'

'What's the *Béarla*?' I asked.

'That's Irish for English. Don't you know any Irish? *Cúpla focal* is a couple of words – have you *cúpla focal*?'

'We are going to start it in September for the Intermediate Exam. We are getting a new teacher.'

'If you are heard speaking English in Carraroe,' he said solemnly, 'you will be sent home.'

I was not sure where home would be until August. Gran was having a holiday with the widow in Torquay of whom she was fond.

'Seamus, will you be my friend and speak for me when I get stuck?'

He looked me over appraisingly. 'I suppose I could – you're a bit young!'

'I am not young!' I said indignantly. But I was relieved I would not be sent home on the next bus.

'I was here last year,' Seamus told me. 'There was a girl here last year, Áine Rice. I thought you were her when I sat down beside you, the same kind of hair, but you're not. We were both mad on the Ceilidh – that's Irish dancing, you know, jigs and reels and the Walls of Limerick, and the *Rince Mór* which is like a barn dance. We have the Ceilidh every night in the hall in the village. It's great!'

'I love dancing,' I told him.

'It's the schelp after the Ceilidh,' he gave me a knowing wink.

'It sounds great fun!' Whatever schelp is?

When we were taking down our suitcases from the rack, Seamus was helping me. He said with some decision, 'We'll go out together for the month, then.'

There was a huge big concrete quadrangle in a space that was once a field on top of a cliff. At the edges of the quadrangle, the gorse and the furze grew thickly. Paths had been trodden through the gorse to the village and to the sea and to the harbour.

Down the middle of the great concrete square, was a low single-storey building of classrooms. That was the Irish College.

Similar buildings down opposite sides were the students' dormitories, girls on one side and boys the other. The teachers boarded in the local houses and cottages. The dormitories were very plain with washbasins and latrines at each end.

The girl in the next bed to mine came over and sat on my bed when I arrived dragging my suitcase. She was a good-looking girl, with a dark cloud of hair and very blue eyes.

'What's your name?' she asked. 'Mine's Rhona O'Dare. Do you smoke? This place is like joining the French Foreign Legion.'

'Do you know a lot of Irish?' I asked. I was positive that everyone but me would be fluent.

'Nanny is a native speaker. We have had it pushed down our necks with our milk. Daddy is in the Government. My sister is on the other side of me. She doesn't mind it, but I hate it!'

'We are speaking English,' I reminded her.

She let out a string of what sounded like imprecations with a lot of blethers and mushas . . . it was a habit she had.

'It is such a blinding bore here!' she moaned. 'They won't let you sunbathe! They won't let you swim! They won't let you sail! You have to wait for nightfall to have a bit of fun! Have you got a fella?'

I supposed I had Seamus? I nodded slightly.

'No need to look guilty,' she laughed. 'I came back this year because I have an absolutely fierce pashy crush on one of the teachers. I can'never see him in Dublin – he has a wife and two kids. She doesn't come down here. I had to come anyway, Daddy insisted. But if Séan Brua isn't here this year, I'll go mad! I'll throw myself off the stupid cliff!'

Lucille had told me that her mother had told her that there was a new type of girl now: the one who used to be a 'flapper' was now 'fast'. I would tell Lucille I had seen one sitting on my bed.

Her Séan Brua, tall and handsome and very popular, was there all right. Rhona had a month of perfect bliss, she said so every night when we were getting ready for the Ceilidh. She never returned to the dormitory for hours and hours after the dancing finished. She woke us all up by falling and crashing and mouthing the strings of swear-words, finally collapsing on her bed and staying there until lunchtime next day. All the same, she was very likeable. I seem to have heard that she followed in her daddy's footsteps, ending in a Government of the day.

Getting back to the dormitory after the Ceilidh was not easy for anyone. If you didn't hang around for a lot of slobbery kissing, you were shouted at for a spoil-sport, or a *lán de sásta*, which meant 'full of yourself', a stuck-up Biddy.

I loved the classes. I set my mind to learn as much as I possibly could. I forced myself to speak in Irish even when I knew that I had the cases and genders and tenses and conjugations all skew-ways. I filled notebooks with idiomatic phrases that the teachers assured were the *fíor-gael*, the real true talk of the natives out on the wild western coasts. I was secretly very proud of my progress.

But more and more I dreaded the ending of the Ceilidh every night. Having danced all night with Seamus Mulhern and enjoyed it thoroughly, it seemed only manners to walk back to the College with him. Everyone walked home in couples.

A lot of the bolder, more daring spirits walked first to the harbour. Here they lit up cigarettes and passed a few bottles

127

around from hand to hand. Someone always started a reel on a mouth organ, and off we flew on an impromptu dance with everyone swinging in and out and thumping on the wooden slats.

That was all good fun until the first *'oidhche inhaith agus póg, ma' shé do thoil'*. No boy was satisfied with one 'goodnight and a kiss, please'. There had to be seconds, and thirds, and finals, and chases along the harbour wall with bloodthirsty shouts and female shrieks: *Stad, stad! Anois ta mise ag tuitim san fairrge!* And sometimes, a giddy girl did fall in, and had to be rescued from drowning.

I would find myself pinned against the wall of the big boathouse while Seamus flattened my face with wet kisses. My pushing and kicking and resisting seemed to encourage him to get rougher and rougher.

I began to dislike Seamus, even in daylight. His nightly attentions were too high a price for the amount of Irish he knew. I learned faster and faster. I never missed a class.

In the third week, I felt strong enough to speak for myself and walk out on my own. When the Ceilidh ended and we were standing to sing the National Anthem, I took his arm from my shoulder. I said *'Oidhche Mhaith!'* in a loud, clear voice and I walked rapidly away.

He caught up with me outside the hall, he gripped my arm. 'What's the matter with you, Lia?'

'Let go my arm. I am going straight back to the College.'

'Why? What have I done?'

'I don't want to go out with you any more.'

'Why?' He was really hurting my arm.

'That's why!' I felt like being inconsequential.

He pushed me against the sidewall of a cottage, away from the stream of couples strolling down from the hall.

'Let me go. . . .' I tried to say but his mouth was hard pressed down on mine, and his body was flattened against mine.

Instantly I knew the fear and terror that had riven into me

on the nightmare time I had run out onto the strand away from "Sunrise". With a rage of horror I felt his hand tearing at my dress, pulling it upwards to get at my body. I was screaming soundlessly: this must not happen, and then I heard my voice. Sheer panic had wrenched my mouth from under his mouth. I was yelling, yelling, and I could not stop. There was never a louder, more terrified screaming and it was coming from someone who had scarcely been touched, much less hurt.

The boy fell over backwards, got to his feet in the same movement, and fled down the hill, and I still yelled and shouted in mad hysteria.

Some people came and brought me to the dormitory. The *Fear Mór* was sent for. He fussed around for a few minutes. Someone brought a hot drink. I was very quiet and ready to go to sleep. Then they all went away. But I did not sleep.

I think James Mulhern was sent home the next day. I never saw him again. But I lay awake for nights thinking of him with deep regret. The thought tormented me that there was a situation in life which I could not deal with, although all the girls around me felt no fear. I had let myself in for that situation, and led James Mulhern into a kind of trap he had never suspected. How could he?

He was a nice enough boy, a likeable boy, just doing what boys do. He would have been justified if he thought I was leading him on – after all, I asked for his friendship, didn't I? I spent nights trying to do what Tadek always told me to do: trying to rationalize.

I wished he had not had to be punished. He had to face his parents at home. I remembered he had talked a bit about his mother one day, and I thought he was fond of her. I regretted my reaction, I felt ashamed.

Night after night, I was unable to drop off to sleep because I had discovered within myself a terrifying morbid fear. There was a haunting terror that lived in the depths of me.

Knowing where that terror stemmed from was no help at all.

I had grown up another bit learning how to be fluent in Irish. I wondered sometimes if Mama had only known what forced growth had taken place in a month of Irish College, might she have thought that life in the Vashinskys, adjacent to the Ringsend gurriers, would have been safer?

She never knew, and she never would have suspected.

Education, Mama thought, was a built-in protection. It was a safeguard in life that she had never had, but which she would work to provide for Lia.

For Lia, who would infinitely have preferred the everyday sight of Mama's lovely face, and who longed for Mama's quiet presence in her life.

August came at last. Laelia shared my room in Aunt Julia's, and Mama paid the extra. It was her way of trying to repay the Vashinskys' care of me. Silky slept on the end of our bed. She was the best little doggy once again.

Tadek and Max and Toozy came down almost every day. Now Max had a bigger car, and we all fitted inside.

Tadek usually sat in the front with Max. Sometimes Max let Tadek drive. He drove very well. He had got a licence and he expected to have a car in his next job. Max had asked his father to include Tadek on the insurance.

But sometimes Tadek sat in the back of the car with me and the dogs. Every now and then, we exchanged our special look.

'There is no need to tell our happiness,' I had told Tadek, 'just so long as we two know.' Tadek smiled down at me, that gleaming smile I loved so much.

They all asked a lot of questions about my month in the Irish College.

To them I was still a child, although Gran thought that I had, as she put it: 'taken a stretch.'

So I said nothing about Seamus, nor about Rhona O'Dare. Perhaps I would tell Berny and Lucille – but, perhaps not. I was unable to put away the guilt complex, and the complex was compounded by the mental picture of James Mulhern's nice friendly face the day he talked of his mother. I hoped with all my heart that his parents did not punish him for having been sent home in disgrace. I prayed in my night prayers every night that he had understanding parents. I regretted so much that screaming hysterical outburst. How could I prevent such a thing ever happening again? I wanted to tell Tadek this problem. In the end, I said nothing.

I answered the questions about Carraroe by chattering 'fluently' in Irish about the weather, the dogs, the seashore, the fish in the sea, the nice new motorcar: endless simple phrases that I had memorized. To my delight, my friends were overcome with admiration for my cleverality. . . .

'What about some Irish dancing, Lia?' I would be prompted by Laelia.

Always a little show-off, I was prepared to demonstrate: the Fairy Reel, the Irish Washerwoman's Jig, any number of invented, stepping-out hornpipes. Max and Tadek kept the rhythm with what they called 'authentic gob music', and Laelia would keep time by clapping.

I was still their child that summer. I knew it. I was content. I hated and feared change. They indulged me, and I loved them for it. They knew I was fourteen. I did not mention the fact, and I was all the time aware of it, that in September I would be a senior.

That summer, in Max's comfortable car, we really discovered and explored Wicklow . . . the Garden of Ireland. There are high mountain ranges, from Lugnaquilla to Douce to the long ranges of the Glen of Imaal. There are pastoral valleys: Laragh, Clara, Glendalough. There are great inland lakes in the mountains. And there are the miles and miles of rock-strewn shore opening out into silver-sand coves, and stretches of golden sand with sheltering dunes.

The day we discovered Brittas Bay, seven miles down off the main road, Tadek said he felt like,

'Stout Cortez . . . Silent, upon a peak in Darien.'

131

Tadek quoted poetry quite often, just a line or two that had got stuck, he said, in his memory.

We went many times picnicking in Brittas Bay. From the height of the sand dunes, we raced each other down into the blue sea. Laelia and I could both swim very well now. We had a big red beach ball and we played some sea-game we had invented.

On weekdays, there was never a crowd in Brittas Bay. Mostly we had the whole place entirely to ourselves. We walked along the shore for miles, looking for driftwood of odd shapes. Laelia often started a song, maybe a popular catchy tune, and we would all sing along – running and jumping from one song into another as if the music came beating up from our toes.

On Sundays when there might be crowds of children on 'our' beach, we climbed mountains. The Big Sugar Loaf was the favourite because it was the nearest and easiest. Three miles out of Bray, up a mile of the Rocky Valley, and leave the car. We start climbing gently upwards over the turfy sward until we reach the big dark boulders near the top.

There seemed to be a little more money that year. Every day, Max brought with him a big bag of two-penny packets of Jacob's Biscuits, and bottles of 'Vimto'. Oh, the unforgettable taste of 'Vimto' on the tongue near the top of the Big Sugar Loaf!

'Max, I am worried about Toozy. Look at us, we are all panting and we are big and strong! His poor old tongue is hanging out and his poor old tummy is almost on the ground!'

I was kissing the top of Toozy's head. 'Maybe, Max, he is getting O-L-D.' I spelled out the word for fear of hurting Toozy's feelings.

'He is, poor old boy, and he has a bit of a liver condition. We should have left you in the car, Toozer, old son, but you know yourself you hate to be left behind.'

'How O-L-D is he, Max?'

'Let me think . . . he was my eleventh birthday present – or was it twelfth?'

'He must be twice as old as Silky, then. She is six.'

'And isn't it funny,' said Max, 'how devoted they are to each other? At home, Silky never lets him out of her sight!'

I reached up on my tiptoes and gave Max a little kiss on the cheek, 'Thank you for being so kind to Silky,' I said to him.

Only in the last few days of August did we mention such a thing as a future. This time, I would be saying goodbye to my friends for a long, long time.

Max would be returning to Vienna and this time he would stay for three years. His father would visit him and they would holiday together.

Laelia had won a scholarship to Milan for a year, and it might be extended to two.

Tadek was returning to the South of England. He had been given a chance to specialize. From there, he would look for work in America.

'Why not Paris?' Max asked. 'We have a house there.'

'Thank you,' Tadek said. 'We'll see.'

I guessed that Tadek was thinking of his parents when he said to Max: 'We'll see.' Gran had told me that Mr V., as she called him, had had a few bad turns. . . . 'He is only holding his own,' was what she said about someone whose death she might reasonably expect, and she said that about Mr V.

Max left it to the very last possible moment to take Silky into the car for her journey back to Max's house in Terenure.

It was always sad saying goodbye to Silky and imploring her not to forget me.

'My father always reminds me that you are welcome to visit with Silky any time – except the Sabbath.'

Silky fixed her prominent brown eyes on me and wagged her tail to every word I said. It got harder each time to let her go. At last, I put her into the back seat beside Toozy.

'Oh Max, just look at the way she snuggles up to him. She just loves him! Look, Max, Toozy is licking Silky.'

'Run in, Lia! The rain is getting very heavy.'

The car began to move off. I waved. ''Bye, Max, thank you a million for everything! 'Bye Silky! 'Bye Toozy!'

Chapter Eight

In September I was very proud to become a senior. I would sit for my first Government Examination in the following June, the Intermediate, now replacing the old Middle Grade.

Many girls would leave school after the Inter. Some would take commercial courses, or domestic economy courses, or perhaps sit for lower grade Civil Service Examinations. Most of the girls who would leave after the Inter would return home to wait for Mr Right to arrive and marry them. At that time, if a girl did not enter the Convent, her vocation was marriage. The word 'career', referring to girls, had yet to be heard.

I was positively puffed up with pride to know that I, and my special friends, would be going forward together to the Leaving Certificate with the possibility of going on to the University.

That Berny and Lucille were still my friends made me utterly contented. All three of us knew, and liked, all the other girls in our class. We noticed that they drifted into threes and fives, interchanging, never for long the same. We three held fast.

Being a senior brought a new sense of responsibility. Each girl was closely watched on matters of ethical deportment. This included religious duties, general standards such as honesty, courtesy, consideration. Social niceties, friendliness, the ability to walk, talk, dance with due elegance, these were all important. Being first in class did not bring much praise, such a one was merely clever. Tennis courts, hockey pitches, croquet lawns were all available and well kept. Games, while played as a recreation, were not accounted as worth too much bother. Those who wished to play did so, others passed recreation hours in their own way.

The big important thing in Senior School was the rooting-out of Particular Friendship. This was the heinous sin, this Particular Friendship. Threes was the rule. Fives were permitted too, but regarded as ostentatious. To be ostentatious was vulgar. Exuberant sneezing or coughing was vulgar. Any act which attracted attention to the individual was a vulgar act, the attention it drew was an immodest attention. Particular Friendship was worse than vulgar, it was sinful. It was a Cause for Confession. If confessed, as I found out, the penitent drew down on herself punishment known to us girls as the Spanish Inquisition. A victim could claim – with a little judicious exaggeration – that she had experienced torture.

I was almost fifteen, in the middle of my first senior year, when I had the misfortune to fall crazily in love with a Senior Prefect. Her name was Bonny Kelarr.

I had noticed that she was very amused by me. During night recreation, she often called me over to where she sat with the other Senior Prefects. She had me repeat mimicries, or toss off phrases in my particular brand of bog-Irish. I was happy to oblige. I was one who needed notice taken of me without realizing that acute need. Deep, deep down I lived another life always conscious of loves I could not have, could not express, could not even be sure of, but longed for . . . at times, overwhelmingly.

Bonny Kelarr was a beautiful girl, tall and amply built. Her colouring was red-gold with burnished skin to match. Her bosom quivered when she walked.

One night, on the dimly-lit staircase, she put her hands on my chest and kissed my mouth. Her kiss was hot and went into my pelvic region with the force of a torpedo. From that moment, I wanted to live within her orbit.

In the Chapel, in the Refectory, anywhere, I could not take my eyes off her. Berny warned me, 'Lia, it is time you learned. Keep it sub rosa.'

'Sub rosa?' I questioned.

'It means after dark, you ninny.'

Bonny Kelarr, being a Prefect, was above suspicion. She was able to manoeuvre events as she pleased. She chose to make me miserable by hard looks and niggling punishments in the dormitory. Then, when I was reduced to frantic misery and ready to lick her shoes, she would smile at me most radiantly, and say:

'Thank you, Lia, you are a perfect pet!'

The Prefects' cubicles were strategically placed among the other cubicles, no doubt for supervision. The Prefects flicked along the white cubicles to make sure each girl was safely tucked up in bed, and then they turned off the lamps.

Bonny Kelarr's cubicle was separated from mine by Helen Doyle's cubicle.

Reckless of what I was doing, I adored her with my eyes. Each night I waited just inside my cubicle for her flick of the curtain. Occasionally, she gave me that stinging hot kiss. More often, her questing hand promised delights to come.

Worshipping a wonderful girl, the most beautiful girl in the school, had to be good because it felt, so perfectly, a lovely part of my life. Besides, lots of other girls had 'affairs'. It was part of boarding-school ethos, accepted without question. Affairs were the order of the night, the more varied the better. Thereby, one could gain a reputation for being 'sophisticated'.

To be part of this forbidden pleasure, to risk the dark sin of Particular Friendship, was actually the heart of the excitement. The zest was the being in the running, no longer an innocent outsider.

She kept me waiting for weeks, trying my affections most painfully. Then at last she let me know that I was to have the transporting ecstasy of going into her bed.

In a state of suppressed excitement, I lay in my cubicle waiting for the deep even breathing of Helen Doyle to commence. That was the signal. Then I crept behind Helen's washstand, behind her bed, behind Bonny's washstand, and I climbed up into Bonny's bed.

It was like going into a meadow of summer grasses. Her undulating body filled the narrow bed so there was a constant movement as of flowers receiving a fragrant breeze. She was not wearing her nightgown, and mine rode up around my shoulders. She took my hands, guiding them to her breasts, moving my fingers to pleasure her. She drew my lips with her lips in that strange kiss, stinging and hot.

Did the encounter last five minutes? Ten minutes . . . scarcely. I had no feeling that my turn to be loved (pleasured?) would ever come. Suddenly, I was eased out on to the cold floor to sneak back to my lonely bed.

How much I would have learned, how deeply I might have entered into Bonny Kelarr's forbidden night-world, I never got the chance to find out. There were some I knew who began on that path and, like Eurydice going down into the Underworld, they never came back.

As for me, the following day I was called to the office of Mère Madeleine.

Was there a conscientious tale-bearer in the bed by which I stole on that ill-fated adventure? A tale-bearer who lay straight and correct in her dim cubicle, breathing evenly and happily in a sleep of innocence?

Mère Madeleine had the Chaplain, Père Rancier, in her office. Standing by the window was Bonny Kelarr.

Then I knew why I was there. I was terrified. It would be the Spanish Inquisition. My legs and hands began to shake.

With desperate hope I turned towards Bonny. She was eighteen and a Prefect. I was nothing and not quite fifteen. She averted her eyes in a pained fashion.

The interview was conducted in French. The nun's tone was one of utter contempt.

'*La voilà, la belle petite comédienne qui voudrait nous faire croire qu'elle est l'égale de la grande Bernhardt! Elle veut jouer la tentatrice, faisant de notre école son théâtre, n'est-ce pas vrai – et les bonnes élèves les victimes de son esprit débauché! Regardez-la, qui ose me lever ces yeux pleins d'interrogation! Regardez-la qui joue à l'innocente à présent!*'

Turning to Bonny Kelarr, the nun continued in a different tone: caring, considerate, sugary.

'*Et cette malheureuse fille, ma pauvre* Bonny, *elle vous avait importunée de ses baisers, n'est-ce pas?*' Père Rancier, who must have heard this startling revelation before they sent for me, he gripped the big ferule on the table as if he would belabour me immediately.

Bonny's gaze was fixed on the trees beyond the window. '*Oui, ma Mère,*' she replied in a low, embarrassed voice. Reluctantly, piously, as if in distress she withdrew her gaze from the trees and lowered her eyelids. Then she bravely spoke again:

'*Et plus que de ses baisers . . . de ses . . . ses . . .*' Bonny now put her hands over her beautiful face as if with shame at what she was about to reveal. I was quaking with abject dread.

'*Oui, continuez, ma pauvre fille,*' rapped Père Rancier and I could see his knuckles taut on the ferule.

Bonny Kelarr looked directly at me as if to quell any contradiction that might arise from my lips.

She need not have worried. I was gripping my hands to stop shaking and now I was almost petrified with fear.

In a voice full of disgust, she slowly came out with the words: '*Sa nudité . . . elle m'expose son corps . . . elle est . . . depravée. Ma mère, elle est vraiment depravée!*'

Even in that moment of degradation, I recognized the lie. She was the one who lay naked on the coverlet of her bed when I climbed up to kiss her goodnight. She was the one who had taken my fingers to the big buds on her breasts . . . the imagery of meadow flowers was slow to fade.

She was the one who had initiated the 'affair'. I was not totally innocent, but I knew I was not depraved.

'*Ma chère Bonny, cet entretien est terminé maintenant. Retirez-vous, s'il vous plaît.*'

Now I saw Bonny Kelarr as a large, heavy young woman closing the door, deliberate insolence on a face that was no longer the beautiful face of a dream. I began to sob bitterly.

Mère Madeleine pushed me roughly, contemptuously, to the floor.

'*Silence, s'il vous plaît,*' she hissed at me.

Mère Madeleine handed a prayer book to Père Rancier. He read a long invocation imploring God to look in mercy on this pitiful sinner. I knelt, shaking, on the flagged floor. He did not raise his hand in the blessing of Absolution. This was not a Confession, then? I was not yet forgiven.

Mère Madeline rasped out some words, repeating herself because I was slow to understand:

'*Levez-vous! Mettez-vous debout!*'

I stumbled to my feet. Their faces wavered in front of me. I was half-blind with tears.

'*Levez-vous, Mademoiselle! Déshabillez-vous. La chemise aussi. Et les sous-vêtements. Baissez les bras! Ne cherchez pas à vous cacher – baissez les bras, je vous dis!*'

There cannot be a more horrible humiliation. And even more humiliating was to lack the courage to disobey. When my upper body was naked, Mère Madeleine detached the thin leather *lanière* from her belt, handing it to the grim priest.

With neat precise strokes, he flashed the thong repeatedly on my shoulders, my arms, and across my meagre bosom, while he continued to intone from the book.

This was a ritual, a penance, a sentence of punishment without a sound of protest from the victim. The fear was even worse than the pain. The thong stung like a flame. For weeks afterwards, my upper body was tattooed with a criss-cross of blue weals.

Imprisoned in pain, I was made to kneel and confess my

sin. God alone knows what I mumbled and God alone knows what effect that unwilling Confession had on my puny faith. What was the lesson I was to learn that day? I have often wondered.

I was sent to the Infirmary to sleep. I must be separated. I was unclean. I would pollute the other children.

The Infirmary was a lonely, cold place. I was given no food. Fasting, Mère Madeleine said, would clear the mind, and give me time to think about my sin. There had been no Absolution to my Confession. The punishment was only beginning.

I knew dimly that I was seeking always for a return warm and fulfilling. It did not have to be a sexual encounter. I feared and respected the sixth Commandment, and indeed we were never let forget it.

Why had I not learned from the summer college? Bonny Kelarr was not different from a boy – it was all in the sixth Commandment.

I cried until the tears dried up.

This time there was no losing consciousness. There was no escaping to the comfort of the Vashinskys' little house. The effects of the thong were worse and longer-lasting than Burton's attempted assault. I was older, aware of meaning. From then onward, the seeking avenues of my imagination often became blocked tunnels. Venturings were suspect, people could be untrustworthy. The road that led backward in time, and forward to my promised future, was very hard to discern and believe in when I lay shivering that one long night in the School Infirmary.

Until the day she died, and perhaps after that too, there was a perfect telepathic communication between me and Gran.

The very day after I had spent the night in the Infirmary, Gran arrived out to Cluny. She had news, bad news, and although random visiting was not allowed, she insisted on seeing me.

140

My tears, when she folded her arms around me, were as much of joy for her coming as of pain for the tunic pressing on the thong marks.

Remembering the Chinese screen, and all Gran's example of modesty, there was no possibility of telling her about my punishment. I could imagine her denouncing the thong, and threatening a High Court action on the nuns; but I could also imagine her secret grief that I would involve myself with another girl in immodest behaviour. I stayed silent.

Gran's news was truly bad. Mama had been taken into hospital again. Gran glanced around the nuns' parlour – this news was not for their ears, holy women and all as they were.

'This time is the worst,' Gran told me gently, still keeping her arm about me. 'The doctors say the treatment will be long and slow. Lia child, poor Marie's mind is going. Sure, the truth is she has never been the same since the night she got the telegram about that awful Spanish 'flu. If Will had only been spared to her! Ah, God in Heaven what a lovely life they would have had! Your Dada was a darlin' man, and you know, childy, they were made for each other! Ah, the plans they had, God love them!'

Gran dried her eyes. 'If poor Will had only been spared! Marie is such a loving, defenceless poor thing! She needs a good man to take care of her. But that Burton! May God forgive me when I tell you that I would swing on the end of a rope for him.'

Burton was not at hand to take his share of the worry. He had had himself transferred to Bradford for the next six months.

'He said it was for six months, but if you ask me – he's gone for good and left your poor Mama to battle on as best she can. It was all over that old Masonic school. He was set on that place for you where he has influence and could keep an eye on you – the school is up at the top of Sandymount Avenue – and where you would get it all free through some funds he has access to. But Marie wouldn't give in, no matter what it cost

141

to have you here in Cluny. She wanted you to have the religion as well as the education. That was another row — about nuns.' (Gran lowered her voice, glancing around even more cautiously.) 'He said awful things about nuns and priests — he used to make Marie cry the things he said. Not that any of us ever had any dealings with nuns or priests, but the arguments were most bitter.'

I had a bright idea. 'Wouldn't it settle everything, Gran, if I left here and went to the other place?' I spoke very earnestly out of the very real pain of the inflicted *lanière*.

'No, childy, it would solve nothing now. Burton's gone. The change of Government finished him. He never wanted to work under this lot! There was a new law brought out that all the detectives in the Castle, even the topnotchers, were to learn to speak Irish, if you don't mind — and that is the language for their daily business. Ridiculous, isn't it? That set him back on the whiskey with a vengeance! Phyllis hinted to me that enough whiskey makes him violent to poor Marie!'

The sight of Gran in tears was heartbreaking.

'And a few days after he went, your Mama had a visit from Montgomery the Solicitor who told her that Burton had made her a present of the title deeds of "Sunrise". You would think she would be delighted. But what does she do? She has a complete collapse, God love her.'

Usually the nuns sent the portress with a tray of tea and biscuits to a visitor. Today no one came. I felt guilty.

'Of course,' Gran added, 'poor Marie has to think now of the rates and the upkeep. It's a big place, and the garden as well. I have to stay in "Sunrise" now to caretake. It's a big barracks of a place to be looking after.'

'I'll come and help you,' I offered.

'Ah no, childy, you are happy here.' Then she looked at me closely. 'Have you been crying lately? You look very peaky. What's that dark mark on your neck?'

'Probably a pencil mark,' I replied, 'but I cannot eat much, and I cannot sleep at all.'

Gran looked at me doubtfully. I hid my face against her neck, every cowardly instinct in me longed for the comfort of 'Sunrise' and Phyllis and Gran.

'Well,' she said slowly, 'I don't like interfering with your education, Lia, but perhaps under the circumstances of Mama's sickness, maybe I should see the nun in charge, and take you home with me for a few days.

In her kindness, she had let me offer to come with her. She felt that my place should be at home at this time, but she would never insist until the necessity was urgent. She could not know how I had passed the endless night longing for her and home. I had so often told her that I really loved Cluny, I was happy there. Up to now.

There was no difficulty in leaving. Mère Madeleine may have been in a mood to have me expelled. I took only an overnight bag, so all my other possessions would signify my return. Surely the nuns' hearts would soften? I could bear to leave, but not to be expelled.

Soon Gran and I, arm in arm, were going down through the Furry Glen to get the tram at the Chapelizod Gate. Phyllis was in 'Sunrise' waiting tea for Gran. She had baked little scones. I remember always the lovely cooking smells wherever Phyllis was. I suffered her hugs as best I could, but there was no deceiving Phyllis. When I was in bed at last, she demanded to know what was ailing me.

I pushed back the neck of my nightdress. 'Jeez!' she breathed, bending over me. 'What happened? Were you burned? Show me. Is it a new disease?'

I began to tell her about the thong. She began to bawl her usual endearing epithets.

'Pure bloody buggery. The bitch! The bloody bitch. The aul hoor. The filthy hoor! Jeez, if I ever get me hands on that wan! Was it for missin' yer lessons, was it?'

Phyllis went on and on, but she lowered her voice for fear Gran would hear . . . Everything Phyllis said was balm to my ear. Even had I told her about Bonny Kelarr (and I made sure not to sully my image with Phyllis), even if I had spelled out the entire episode, Phyllis would have had no difficulty in seeing it my way. I was her child, she would have defended me against wolves.

Phyllis knew, better than I, that Mama was close to death. Mama, who had no regard for money-pinching, had kept Phyllis's family going through very hard times. Clothes, perfumes, jewellery, all went to Phyllis as soon as Mama tired of them, quickly, often after an hour's use. Apart from all the little bonuses, Phyllis adored Mama. Mama was her ideal of a lady: fragile, fashionable, and to the end so lovely. Phyllis was constantly trying to inculcate affection for Mama into me. She could not really credit that a child would not love its mother, but she suspected me of some shortfall in that direction. Mama was held up as an example in all things ladylike, and that went on long after Mama had been dead for many years.

It was arranged that Gran would take me into the hospital to see Mama on Easter Sunday. In Gran's world, children were always brought to the deathbed farewell. Phyllis went every night to see Mama, crying for hours when she came home. She assured me that I need not be afraid to go, poor Mama was only like a lamb, as quiet as a lamb, only sinking slowly like a lamb. I never expected Phyllis to be eloquent, I understood her.

I was very frightened of being taken to see Mama in the Mental Hospital. I had begun to believe that my wickedness had brought Mama's death upon us.

'Phyllis, could a great sin bring about Mama's death?'

Phyllis was very indignant. 'She never done a sin in her whole life. Mistakes she made, poor lady. She may not have gone down to the church, but she always gave me the money to put on the plate. Me Da says your Mama was more Christian than forty Catholics.'

'Could someone else's sin cause her death?' I knew by the reluctant way she was looking at me that she thought I was referring to Burton. Some innate delicacy would not allow her to discuss him in relation to Mama.

'Now, Lovey, you don't look all that well, but we'll wrap you up in your school coat, and put on a scarf, and we will go down to the hospital in the mornin'. All your talk will only vex your Gran, and God knows she's been through enough.'

In the morning, we all three went on the tram to the hospital. I felt sick at the thought of my guilt, and frightened at what we might see ... not Mama but the awful Grangegorman which I now knew was the same horrible place to which we had gone to take out Biddy. And Biddy had never completely left my nightmare dreams.

I could hardly make myself lift my feet up the wide stone steps of the hospital.

In the reception area Gran gave in our names. The porter consulted with a nurse in the office.

'Burton?' he said to Gran. 'That patient passed away at 4 a.m.'

Gran almost collapsed. Phyllis led her to a bench. Mama was dead. Remorse choked my throat and I huddled up to Gran. I could not remember when had I last seen Mama. Now I knew why they were so insistent on my coming here. I should have said goodbye to Mama. Maybe thanked her? I could have told her I loved her. Now I could only remember all the times I didn't love her. Didn't I owe her everything, all the education, and the friends, and now she would never know I appreciated all she tried to do for me.

'Childy, childy, don't take on so. Your Mama always meant for the best.' Gran was drying my eyes and her own and Phyllis's.

Poor Phyllis. Now I tried to comfort her.

The porter was handing a card to Gran. 'Here, missus, if you give this to the man on the mortuary, you can view the body.'

My Gran was the bravest little woman that ever was.

'Sit down on that bench, childy,' she said to me, 'you're

going to no mortuary. Keep an eye on that child,' she said to the porter, 'I'll hold you responsible.'

Gran hugged me and kissed me. Phyllis was sobbing aloud. Her bright face was all red and glistening. She gave me an agonized glance as she went after Gran down a gloomy passage.

I sat, as they had told me, in the cold hall. There seemed to be no days or months or years between this desolate place and the loving intimate days and years we spent in the big room over the shop, reading Dada's letters, and the little poems: '*Be good, sweet maid* . . .' Oh Mama, Mama, if only I had been good, you would not have died.

There must have been days and years in between but there had not been time to tell her . . .

Gran and Phyllis came back. They did not say what they had seen, and I was afraid to ask.

Gran took my arm and tucked it under hers.

'Look back on the good times, childy. Look back on the time before . . . before . . . Well, think of going to the Tivoli and the . . .' Gran held me against her, and Phyllis put her arms around both of us. In the shelter of the hospital gate, we wept for Mama.

I could not convince myself that it was Mama in the big oak coffin. She had gone away, so often had she gone away, and if I waited long enough in the past she had always come back. The coffin seemed massive for so dainty a little lady as Mama. All the sorrows of her life would have room to weigh down that huge box.

Phyllis handed me a clean white handkerchief in the Funeral Parlour. She expected a display of grief. Mr Fay would have been proud of my performance, but I could not convince myself. Not in that Funeral Parlour decorated with artificial roses.

'We are not going to be allowed to bring poor Marie into

the church – the priest told Phyllis when she went down,' Gran was telling Aunt Julia and I was listening. 'I had them all baptized but none of them ever practised.'

'And of course you don't yourself, Mrs B.,' said Aunt Julia smartly. 'A great pity! If only for the good example to "you know who".' Me, I supposed.

'On the other hand,' said Gran, unwilling to be put down by Aunt Julia, 'I was never baptized. We practised a different brand of religion.' More than that she would not divulge despite Aunt Julia's queries.

Phyllis tried to comfort Gran and me, although she felt it keenly that Mama should be shut out of the Catholic Church.

'If poor Mama isn't let into the Catholic Church, just to lie in it for the night, how she will get into Heaven is the mystery?' Phyllis repeated this dreadful worry over and over. 'I know it is a mortal sin to be married in the Protestant Church, so it could be worse than mortal to go to the civil ceremony with Burton. The priest said she could not go into consecrated ground,' Phyllis blessed herself, 'and that is the reason we can't go to the chapel, Lovey.' And poor Phyllis began to cry again.

Burton had been sent for. He used his influence, and Mama was buried in a Protestant plot.

All the Catholic relations, and some old friends and neighbours like the Dalys, stood in silence against the railings of the Protestant plot.

I struggled to go in with Gran, but Aunt Julia held my arm in a vice-like grip.

'Cross that barrier,' she threatened me, 'and you will be excommunicated.'

Phyllis gasped with horror. She seemed to understand the awe-inspiring word 'excommunicated'. 'Oh, Lovey,' she whispered, 'them nuns would not let you back into the school!'

I still tried to pull my arm from Aunt Julia. 'Let me go! Let me go!' But I had to stay.

There was no priest or vicar. The undertaker was Mr Heiton, and his assistant held a wreath of flowers. The mourners at the grave were Burton, a magnificent figure of a man, and poor little Gran. No law of any Church would have kept Gran from that graveside.

Burton held the door of the funeral coach for Gran, but she brushed past him. He halted the car at the railings. His sombre brown eyes examined the faces one by one. He was searching for a certain face. I had hidden behind Aunt Julia, my forehead pressed low against her heavy coat. The car went on.

Mrs Vashinsky had been standing shyly behind the knot of people, now she put her arms around me. 'Liddel love, liddel love,' she whispered and I was consoled. Gran and Phyllis and Aunt Julia hurried me into the taxi. When I looked for her, Mrs Vashinsky had disappeared.

Gran's little face was blotched with tears. She held my hand tightly. Her voice was hoarse and broken . . . 'Childy, childy, poor little orphan. And tomorrow will be Marie's birthday. She will be thirty-seven tomorrow.'

Chapter Nine

According to Gran, always a great one for unconscious humour, graveyards and funerals gave people fearful colds. You'd get your death at funerals was what she used to say. After my mother's funeral, I went down with pleural pneumonia. I thought it began the night I spent in the Infirmary in a state of shock, afraid to be heard crying, afraid to ask for a blanket or a drink. How had I ever chosen to ignore the dire punishment inflicted for the sin of Particular Friendship? Had Gran not taken me home the next day, I should have had to endure further humiliations until my sin was expiated.

These were the thoughts that repeated themselves in my mind during the endless weeks I lay sick in 'Sunrise'. As events turned out, I missed the last term of that year. For a long time I was very ill. Gran did not know if I would ever be going back – financially speaking. She was finding it difficult to manage the running of the shop, although Phyllis was an enormous help there. But without Phyllis, Gran was over-worked in 'Sunrise'.

'D'you know what I found out today?' demanded Gran one morning as she puffed in with a breakfast tray. 'Such a coincidence! There are sixty steps in this house from the back door to the attic, and I'll be sixty my next birthday. If the good Lord spares me!' She liked to add pious things like that, the sort of thing Phyllis said.

She took a letter from the tray. 'And this came this morning, it's a bill for the rates. What am I going to do? It's a good job the fine weather is coming, we're very low for coal, although Daisy Emm says it was ordered but she don't know if it was paid for. She says your Mama kept household receipts up here in some box.'

I thought suddenly about the carved box in which Mama kept the letters from the Front. I wondered where it was. In her room, I supposed. I thought I would be afraid to go in there on my own. Mama might be haunting it. She might be wandering around in that lace nightdress through which you could see the shadows of her body. I put the idea of the carved box firmly out of my mind. 'What about Montgomery the Solicitor?' I asked Gran. 'Mama took me into his office at Christmas. I could show you where the office is. She talked about money to him .'

Gran took another letter from the tray.

'A letter for you, childy,' she said, 'from foreign parts by the look of it.'

My heart leaped with joy. Tadek! Tadek had written at last, and never at a better moment!

'It is not writing I know,' and I could not keep the disappointment out of my voice. 'Sit down, Gran, and I'll read it out loud. It must be from Laelia, maybe they heard of Mama . . .'

The letter was from Max in Vienna:

'My dear Lia, I am a very poor letter-writer, and now when I write, it is bad news. Please forgive me. I am quite out of touch with our mutual friends for the past six months, so nothing to report on them.

'My father writes to say that our poor old Toozy finally succumbed to that old liver complaint. He was fourteen years of age. He would have gone long ago but for Silky. They lived for each other. I am sorry to have to tell you, Lia, that Silky just died of her loneliness. Her little heart broke when Toozy was no more. I am truly sorry, Lia.

150

'My father has had made a little plot in the garden for them, he tells me, and there is a headstone with their names. He loved them, too.

'I am not sure if there is occasional postal censorship on foreigners, so I will say nothing about the strange things that are happening here.

'Always your friend, Max.'

'Don't cry, childy, don't cry. You know, someone once said there is a heaven for dogs.'

Burton always said that. He described it as a Happy Hunting Ground. It was so easy to cry and cry for Silky when my feelings of grief for Mama were so tangled with remorse.

As soon as I was better, we went to the Solicitor's office. Gran explained all her difficulties before Mr Montgomery got time to open his mouth, and even when he finally began to speak, she kept on adding more worries: school fees, summer holidays, down to the fact that I had taken a stretch, and was growing out of my clothes!

It seemed my mother had thought of everything. There was a fund set aside to take care of my fees at Cluny and into University, if that should be decided, an ample amount lodged in Kelletts to cover clothing for Cluny. She owned the goodwill and stock of the shop, she now owned the substantial house, 'Sunrise'. My father, it was now revealed, had set up a trust which would mature when I was twenty-eight. He had also left to her stocks and shares which should come to me in due course.

I stole a look at Gran's comely face. She was beaming with pride. Knowing her fondness for romantic tales of chivalry and highborn maidens, I guessed she was now viewing me in the light of a beautiful heiress. No doubt in due course there would be a queue of suitors. Then her face fell. Mr Montgomery had finally silenced her.

'Most of these provisions we laid down in the will which

she made at Christmas,' he said. 'As you are no doubt aware, that will must pass through the Probate Courts. And Probate is being opposed by Mr Burton, the step-father of this child.'

Gran looked blank.

'I thought he was in England?' she asked.

'He is now,' replied the Solicitor, 'but I am in touch with his Solicitors. He himself called here after the funeral. He is fully entitled to know the terms of his wife's will, you know.'

'But he left her,' said Gran tearfully, 'high and dry he left her.'

The Solicitor looked pained and surprised at this phrase. 'On the contrary, Mrs Brabazon, he went away on business, giving her a present of the deeds of a very substantial house. A house which he himself bought, which he feels is, in the circumstances, his.'

'Circumstances?' queried Gran, now quite perplexed at the turn of the conversation.

'The circumstances of my client's sudden death,' replied Mr Montgomery briskly. 'The husband is greatly concerned about the welfare of his step-daughter, he has quite other ideas for her education. He is indeed concerned, moreover, that he receives no mention in my client's will. No mention whatever. Myself, I found that strange. I protested to my client about it, a small bequest would have sufficed. But no mention – she was adamant. On this grounds, Mr Burton may very well have a case in Probate, his legal adviser has told him. It is his opinion, sorrowfully as he admits, that his wife was mentally deranged when making this will. They were, he assures me, a most devoted couple. Indeed, I myself do not know of any other husband who presents his wife with the deeds of a house – certainly not a house like "Sunrise".'

Almost before he had said the last word, Gran had risen, gathering me in against her. 'You're a Judas!' she said scornfully. She marched us out of his office with a great show of bravado which I knew she was far from feeling. I suppose she had to retract her hasty words later when she briefed

Montgomery, despite her distrust of him, to fight Burton over the will.

Gran was determined that Burton would never get the care of me. For many months, the case dragged on.

The rest of the story is easily told.

My pretty little mother left very little when all the court battles were over, and the legal costs paid.

Burton won back 'Sunrise'. He made a deal with a friend of his to take the condemned shop off his hands for the price of the famous lease and the well-stocked cellar.

He was not awarded custody of the child. He held to the Masonic idea, and the Judge held that a change at this stage of the child's education and religious training would not be good. It took weeks to argue that point, Gran told me. On Gran's insistence, Montgomery employed Senior Counsel.

The funds for my education, and general 'keep' to the age of eighteen, were somehow rescued and put aside. My father's provisions for me were safeguarded until I would be twenty-eight years of age.

'Will I be poor until I will be twenty-eight?' I asked Gran in despair.

'Sure that is only twelve years or so, childy!' answered Gran in astonishment.

Twelve years was a lifetime. All my chances would have flashed by while I was poor!

Finally, I was made a Ward of Court until I would be twenty-one.

'And what does that mean, a Ward of Court?' I asked Gran when she came out to see me in Cluny. I was back at school a long time before the court case was over.

'I am not too certain of the ins and outs of it,' Gran said, 'but I think that decisions will be made through Montgomery, about money and further education if that is to be decided.'

'Do I have a say in it?' I asked.

Gran looked at me speculatively. She always had that look when she was assessing a suitable reply.

'Well, Lia, we will cross that bridge when we come to it.'

'What will Phyllis do?'

'Montgomery sent a letter that "Sunrise" is to be taken care of until Burton knows what he is going to do with it. There is wages for both of us. Phyllis has the place shining. She says she sees Marie everywhere.'

I gave Gran a big kiss. I knew she could do with the extra bit of money. I knew she missed all Mama's help.

I was so glad that it had been afforded for me to go back to Cluny. This would be my second-last year.

I worried right up to the very last minute, would Berny and Lucille have me back into the threedom. I knew I had disgraced myself and I was covered with shame.

I saw them first in the Convent Hall. I hung back. They would have to make the first move – and they did.

'Lia! Lia! Lia! We were afraid you were never going to come back! We heard you were very ill! Are you all right? One night at night prayers, Mère Ann-Thérèse made us all say a decade of the rosary for your Happy Death! Lucille was in floods of tears! So were you, Berny Frayne! Oh, I am so glad you are back! We missed you something awful! How is Silky? We got a Doberman and I have two little Shetland ponies of my own! Oh Lia, I have just got to tell you about an Italian in our hotel in Sorrento! Italians are absolutely the most . . . I think he is of a noble line! He is twenty! Twenty! Oh, I swoon when I think of him! I have got pictures of the ponies – just wait 'til you see. . . .'

It was a blissfully happy reunion and it was followed by a blissfully happy year. There was never a cloud in the sky.

I had missed the Inter but it was agreed that I would be able to take the Leaving Certificate if I really worked this year. I could do the Matriculation at the end of this year, but I would still be too young for College.

Once only was the unhappy event of the year before referred to.

'Lia,' Berny asked me one day, 'did you ever hear the word "set-up", did you?'

'What does it mean?' It was a new word to me.

'It is what was done to you last year – you were set up.' She pursed her lips in a little quirk that made her look wise beyond her years.

'What happened last year, I let myself in for.' I knew, I had had plenty of time to think of my stupidity.

'I warned you,' Berny said, 'but you were not the only one that was acting the maggot. Half the dorm was at it. You were set up. There were two of *them* – it was done through jealousy. Remember? I told you to watch out!'

Bonny Kelarr had done the Leaving Certificate and had left Cluny. Mère Madeleine had been 'posted' to their Mission in the Seychelle Islands. Mr Fay had retired from teaching. Père Rancier's hard-lined face was the one we saw at the altar for morning Mass. He made earnest piety difficult for me, but I fought the idea of his implacable cruelty by refusing to dwell on the thought. Nobody had asked me to do what I did, and I should have known the consequences. I clung to this resolution.

Gran came out to Cluny in Mr Heiton's taxi to take me home for the summer.

'I declare to my God,' she exclaimed when I presented myself in the Convent Hall, 'you've taken a stretch at last. Look at the tunic! It is way above your knees. Last year's summer dresses will never fit you!'

'They are very childish, anyway!' I informed her.

'Childish is it now?' said Gran in genuine astonishment. It had just dawned on her that I was about to grow up. It took a few minutes for her to like the idea.

'I'm taller than you now, Gran.'

We measured against each other. I must have grown a couple of inches in a year.

Gran chuckled, 'Sure *I* am growing down like the cow's tail! Well, it is into Montgomery we must go on Monday, you will have to have new clothes.'

'He is so stingy with the money, Gran – he will never give us enough for nice things.'

'What we'll do is this,' said Gran with relish. 'We will make out all your needs, and then we will treble the amount of money!'

Even Mr Heiton seemed to see a difference. He doffed his hat to me as he handed us into his taxi.

On the way to Sandymount, Gran told me that Max and Tadek were still away. In Germany, she thought. Mr V. was not well at all. Only holding his own, poor man. Phyllis had a bit of a job in Fusco's Fish and Chips, but she was running up and down to 'Sunrise' as well.

'Killed she is,' said Gran, 'but sure what else can we do to keep the place in order?'

Gran and I settled into 'Sunrise', with Phyllis coming up from Ringsend almost every day.

Phyllis had a way of 'putting her hand over the place,' as she said. Gran swore that Phyllis had a secret, some sort of magic spell, for getting a house to look shining and orderly in a special way that no other person ever had. And she could cook too, maybe even better than Gran. And as for singing and playing the piano . . . Gran said she was as good as a pantomime.

Gran and I walked on the strand every day, and I listened again and again to Gran's story of her life from the emigrant ship right up to the present day.

Every week we went down to Ringsend to visit the Vashinskys. Mr V. was now confined to bed. Tadek's little mother seemed smaller and very tired.

'I think they are very hard up,' Gran said each time, 'they cannot afford the medicine for Mr V. I wonder now do their children realize their poverty.'

Gran always brought little cakes she had made, and some

eggs for making egg-flips for the invalid. She was afraid of offending their independence.

'I saw Tadek's writing on an envelope on their mantelpiece,' I told Gran, 'and it was a registered envelope.' I felt very proud of Tadek.

Then one day into our easy-going life in the big comfortable house with the windows open to the sea breeze, a letter came from Montgomery.

'They are putting the house on the market,' Gran was reading the letter, 'Burton wants to sell it – empty.' She handed the letter to me and she said very sadly, 'I never thought it would come to this. I thought he would soften his heart for Marie's poor orphan.'

I read the letter. 'We have to pack all that belongs to us, and where will we go?'

'Where else but over to my place,' answered Gran, 'sure there will only be the two of us, and this place is too big for us anyway.'

'But we will miss the strand, Gran, won't we?'

I knew Tadek was far, far away but if I stayed near the strand, there was a chance that some day he would come looking for me there.

Burton came on the last day of the clearing-out.

Gran and Phyllis had gone in the tram, laden with all the bits and pieces of personal luggage that Gran thought she could possibly fit into her little house in the narrow street.

Earlier they had taken similar stuff to Phyllis's mother's house: all Mama's clothes, shoes, and hats that had been packed in tissue paper after Mama's death; endless boxes of trinkets, talc, perfume, even books that Phyllis had seen Mama reading.

I had gathered into two suitcases what I thought were personal to me like letters and snapshots and some books that Burton had given me through the years. I could not bear to part with the big coloured books of children's stories, and the dog books.

I had found the precious carved box, and now it was carefully placed on my suitcases. All the drawers were empty now, and the wardrobes, and the presses. All the furniture was considered to be Burton's, he was sending it to an auction room on Ellis Quay.

I had pulled my mother's green easy chair to the window, and I was gazing across the great empty sands for the last time. I was a lonely orphan, dramatizing my situation a little, but sad nonetheless. Then I saw Burton at the pier gates. I wonder, was he reading the name 'Sunrise' that my mother had had painted in such high hopes ten years before?

He saw me, and he lifted his hand in a cheery salute. He guessed I was alone, there was something in the way he hastened up the path. He came straight over to my chair, drew me up and kissed me most affectionately.

Of course, I should have resented him and for a hundred good reasons. The very look of him, the very size of him, dispelled resentment.

I recognized a marvellous warmth in him that I needed, the way a drooping flower needs the sun. Cigar smoke, port wine, some musky perfumes, all evoke Burton even now, making my heart beat faster. That day, his silver-grey suit fitted his large frame superbly, his moustaches caught up the touch of silver, his brown eyes were filled with that twinkle I knew so well. When he released my shoulders, I swayed against him so that he must hold me again, and this time more firmly.

'You have grown tall,' he murmured against my hair. 'Quite the young lady.'

'Only another year of school,' I told him primly.

'And then what will you do?' he asked with that warm depth of interest which was his special gift.

'I was thinking of a school of acting.' I was quite confident he would approve. He adored the theatre.

'Not in Dublin, I hope — not the Abbey — turf-fire brown-bread comedy. London! That's the place. The Royal

158

Academy of Dramatic Art. That's the ticket for you! That's your style. . . .' He pressed me against him, briefly.

'Oh, but Mr Fay said –' I began to interrupt him.

'Blast Mr Fay – whoever he is! Forget all that stuff about the nuns. You come to London, like I say. You don't have to worry about money, or anything else. I'll look after you. I'll put you through.'

Across his shoulder, I saw Gran tiredly shuffling through the gate. My awful treachery suddenly struck me. I sat down, and broke into tears.

From the door, Gran began to screech at him.

'Get out, Get out! There are your keys,' she flung them at him. 'We'll bang the door when we are leaving. Send your men in the morning. Get out!'

Burton did not lose his dignity for a second. He bent to retrieve his keys where they had fallen beside my suitcases. As he rose up, he turned his back on me, in an instant he was gone. It was when I heard his car zooming away from the gate that I realized Mama's carved box had gone with him.

As a Ward of Court, would I have been released into Burton's custody to go to London? If so, would I have made the grade in the R.A.D.A.? What would Burton have wanted from me then? What would I have been prepared to give then?

There is some poison in guilt that frets at the nerves. Back at school again for my last year, the thought of Burton's offer sometimes woke me up in the middle of the night. I would lie awake for an hour planning the route via Burton's backing to the Royal Academy of Dramatic Art in London. I would see Burton as a kindly, paternal figure – the person he was when I was a child, the person I could make him be, because of course I was different from Mama. With me, my youth, my vivacity, he would not need to drink.

At night, in the dorm in my narrow iron bed, I accepted

159

Burton totally. In the morning, at Mass in the Convent Chapel, I recoiled with horror. I had learned a few new words here and there. Burton was a child molester, even more hideously he was a lecher. Of course, I did not actually believe these words about Burton; rather, in some part of me, I treasured the image of myself as an irresistible temptation to a virile man like Burton. Irresistible, so one must suspend judgement. He was a Jekyll-and-Hyde; his personality, essentially affectionate, changed under the influence of drink to naked bestiality – another new and horrific word.

When I had read *The Strange Case of Dr Jekyll and Mr Hyde*, I had told Gran the story of the book. She loved having me give her short versions of my reading, acting out the rôles that appealed to me; 'You are as good as a pantomime!' she would laugh. She was very intrigued by *Jekyll and Hyde*, one of the truest stories she ever heard.

'It is what I have always found,' she told me. 'Everyone is two people – one good and one bad, damn bad. The bad is always damn bad. A house angel and a street devil – though it is usually the other way around! Most folk think they can do what the hell they like at home – they have to behave themselves in public.'

Gran could use strong language when she felt strongly, not when she was angry. She was not two people, despite her theory. She was the same at home or abroad, the dearest person in the whole world. That day when Burton held me in his arms in 'Sunrise', and I enjoyed again his fragrant ambience, if he had asked me to choose between Gran and himself . . . whom would I have chosen?

In September, our choices were made for our future livelihoods.

Berny must get at least three honours in her Leaving, because she was going to be a doctor like her Dad.

Lucille's mother had decided that Lucille would go to

Atholl Crescent in Edinburgh to become a domestic economy instructress, and not a vet as Lucille had dreamed.

Berny had warned me again not to mention 'going on the stage', so I was merely working for a good Leaving.

We gave up all recreation to huddle together over the books. We heard each other recite reams of poetry, pages of literary criticism, all in the four languages of Latin, English, French and Irish. Berny had extra science, Lucille had domestic and physical hygiene, and I had art history. We all got tuition in mathematics, since we were to take an honours paper.

The Convent grounds at Cluny were always beautiful. An old French lay-sister, Soeur Norbert, worked from early morning until dusk on her flowerbeds.

Those flowerbeds! Never since have there been such lovely colours in tulips and roses. There were grass-edged walks among the many sweet-scented flowerbeds. Books in hands, Berny and Lucille and I went round and round during recreation, happily filled with a righteous sense of learning well.

One special day, I had a most extraordinary thought. It was borne into my mind on the perfume of an exquisite full pink rose, suddenly flaking away into many petals as if it had given up its life in ecstasy.

'I don't want ever to leave here,' I was thinking. 'I am safe here, pure, intact, known, accepted. The dangers of the world cannot touch me here. Next year, I will walk again among these roses. I shall be dressed as a postulant. I have proven in these last months that I respect discipline, that I can work with dedication.'

Quite suddenly the sunlit Convent garden became my whole world. Who was there outside who cared for me? My mother was dead, and soon Gran too would be gone.

Tadek was wrapped away in a life of which I knew nothing, no doubt he had forgotten me. Laelia too. I had seen a report in a newspaper of her success in a concert, and now she was in

161

Vienna on another scholarship. I supposed she would meet up with Max in Vienna, perhaps they would marry, certainly they would forget the scrubby kid who used to sit in the fold-up seat.

Burton was one of the dangers of the world. He was a 'sinful thought' which perhaps I should confess to Père Rancier.

My eyes surely filled with tears at the picture of the orphan dependent now on the stern nuns whose child she had become.

At night recreation, as we paced up and down, I told Berny and Lucille that I had decided to 'enter'. That 'enter' was a word I began to use with a poignant note of feeling in my voice that would have made Mr Fay proud of me. They were both astounded that I should have such an idea, and frankly incredulous.

Lucille said, 'You'd make a lovely nun! All the girls would want you for a "Particular" – you'd get a million holy pictures!'

But Berny, always wise and gentle, said after a little while, 'Please don't make up your mind just yet. Maybe we could make a novena about it? Please don't be in a hurry. I think it is a hard, lonely life.'

So I added 'hard' and 'lonely' to my new sense of self-immolation. I talked of nothing but 'entering', telling everybody. I invested the idea with a mystery and exultation that seemed to me quite mediaeval. Daily I recited long prayers from a 'Child of Mary' manual, although I had not been elected to the Children of Mary. The prayers were designed to invoke the help of Our Lady in the Choice of a Vocation. The manual stressed the importance of having a Real Vocation. I believed I had.

That rose, falling in the sunshine, had been a special sign. After all, how often does a rose fall apart just as one's eye rests on it? All the sincerity of which I was capable was foremost in my desires and aspirations.

Meanwhile, I continued to study and pray with complete

and tireless concentration. With an irony of which I was unconscious, I continued to pray as always for Tadek's success and safe-keeping; and to remember, dimly and remotely, the masterful figure of Burton.

At the end of May, a week before the Examination, I was told to appear in the office. It was not Mère Madeleine now, but it might as well have been. Père Rancier was standing by the window, where Bonny Kelarr had stood on that unforgettable day. I had thought it might be news from Gran, or about Gran, until I saw him. The nun spoke in English, as was becoming the custom, many of the old French nuns being now inactive.

'It has come to my notice, Miss, that you are going about the school announcing to the other children that you will be entering the Order in September.'

The contemptuous tone of her voice warned me not to look up in expectant joy. Since she had paused, I nodded my head. 'Typical!' she said. 'Our Order did not give you leave to pre-empt its acceptance of you.'

I must have looked at her in wonder.

'You may well stare, Miss. I have examined your record in this school. I would not recommend your entry application should you be impertinent enough to make one. Beyond me you are, therefore, unable to go. I do not have to give reasons, but I will inform you for your own good. It is distasteful to me to speak of your chastisement in this room, and of which Père Rancier has informed me fully. There is moreover a further reason. We understand your mother lived in sin, was married outside the Catholic Church, and had to be interred in unconsecrated ground. There are also other reasons. You may go now.'

As I fumbled blindly at the door, her cutting voice delivered another short speech. 'There *are* Penitential Orders which might possibly consider an application such as yours. Be warned, your dossier from here will follow you.'

I was heartbroken. And this time, it was genuine. So

ashamed was I of what the nun had said in the office that I did not tell Berny and Lucille a single word. Years afterwards, I did tell Berny that the nuns would not have me, and why. Years afterwards. Then, a week before the Exam, I put my head down to the books all day, and cried under the blanket at night. No one really noticed, the big exam was all that mattered.

As it happened, and for what it was ever worth, I got six honours and higher marks in several subjects than anyone else in the country. That result did not come out until the end of August. The summer that came in between was to take another piece of my old life away.

Chapter Ten

When I went home after the exam, I went in Mr Heiton's taxi. This time to Gran's for a few days. All the clothes and books and hockey sticks and racquets and souvenirs of six years had to be got together and taken from Cluny. Gran had made a space for them in her little house, now fairly cluttered with the odds and ends she had brought from 'Sunrise'.

There was no point in telling Gran that I had been thinking of becoming a nun. It would have seemed like a bizarre idea to her, and it was all over now. As we settled down to have our supper, I asked her if she would go in to see Montgomery the Solicitor. I wanted to go to the Abbey School of Acting. I knew there was an audition, but they would hardly refuse me as I had certificates from Mr Fay.

So Gran went in to Mr Montgomery. It would take time, he said, and he bade Gran to bring me in to the office on a date in July. Until then Gran and I went down to Aunt Julia's.

Even though I had no hope of seeing Tadek during that summer, Bray was a good place. I was accustomed to Aunt Julia's vagaries, seldom heeding her. I had grown very fond of the seafront, the cliff path around the Head, the souvenir shops on Albert Walk: 'Bangles, Baubles and Beads'. Although Gran was beginning to feel her age, and seemed to be getting smaller every year, she was still a tireless walker. She paddled her feet while I had a daily 'dip'. We never bothered with Aunt Julia's dinners, preferring to buy shellfish from a stall. This we ate with some brown bread which Gran bought in a 'home-made' shop. An apple or an orange was a good dessert. I think perhaps we managed on very little money.

The interview with the Solicitor was nearly due. We went back to Gran's house on the train. There were two letters on the mat, one was from Montgomery to confirm the appointment date, the other had no stamp, and had been delivered personally. I knew at once it was Laelia's handwriting, she used to write to me when I first went to school.

Little's Terrace
Ringsend

Dear Mrs Brabazon

My poor father is very low in his illness. You would cheer us by a little visit, if you would. I must go away soon.

Your affectionate friend
Laelia Vashinsky

Tadek opened the hall door. I stood, unable to move over the threshold, barely conscious that Gran had hurried up the hall to Mrs Vashinsky. Tadek was incredibly handsome. He was not the slender boy of my heart's image. He was a man out of a Renaissance painting. His tinted face was offset by the darkness of his eyes, his brows, his black hair and . . . was it possible? a moustache.

He was staring at me. I took an uncertain step and I held up my face for a kiss, closing my eyes as I always did for this longed-for kiss, fleeting but warm.

There was no kiss. I opened my eyes, Tadek was still staring at me in a kind of wonder.

My voice came in a murmur, 'Are you disappointed because I have grown up?' I wanted to assure him that inside I was the very same. Grown up but not grown independent. I tried to put all my loving him into my eyes. Maybe I succeeded, he lowered his gaze.

He drew me in and he closed the hall door.

'Forgive me, Lia, my memory slipped a notch somewhere,' he gave me a gleaming smile, 'I was expecting your Gran to have you by the hand.'

Tadek was not going to let our past overtake us and become our present in which we would indulge in rhapsodies. Such a thought would not come to him. His total concern now would be for his sick father.

Instinctively I knew this. With Tadek I accepted withdrawal, non-communication, a cool covering of emotion. By different roads we had come to this moment, and a moment was all it would be.

Instinct works faster than thought. Like a flash of lightning, it illuminates. Our time had not yet come.

Mr Vashinsky was dying. Poor little Mrs Vashinsky was worn out. She had nursed him devotedly night and day for many weeks before she had sent for Tadek and Laelia, and now she was on the verge of collapse.

'Get your mother up to bed for a few hours,' Gran said to Tadek, 'let you sit with your father. I have something here for a bit of dinner so I'll take charge of the kitchen. Yes, yes, it is kosher – I understand, I have helped your mother often. Ah, Laelia, there you are. Lia, you help Laelia.'

Down through the years, I have never seen a woman so wondrously lovely as Laelia. Every feature of her face was harmonious. Now she had acquired a sophistication in the way she wore her hair, her clothes. Her hands were so elegant when she stretched out her arms to embrace me.

I had been secretly hoping that they would find me improved, greatly improved, even 'fetching'. Beside her, I was still the skinny little girl who used to play races with the dogs on Sandymount strand while she and Max applauded wildly and Tadek held a pretend stopwatch.

'Do you see Max in Vienna?' I asked her.

'Once or twice I saw him,' Laelia said, 'our times for being free are never the same, and we live on opposite sides of a very big city. But he did make a point of arranging a day when I went there in the beginning. He brought me to the wonderful Palace of Schönbrunn. It is like a palace from a fairy-tale.'

'I used to make up a fairy-tale about you and Max,' I said to Laelia. 'You would both be rich and famous, and the whole world would come to your wedding!'

I remember the gentle way she answered me, 'Lia, Lia, our little romantic! The Prince and Cinderella! Just because people liked each other when they were children does not mean they grow up to marry each other.'

'But it does not mean they will not marry, does it?' I needed urgent reassurance.

'Of course not,' Laelia smiled, 'some do, some don't! I might as well say that *you* will marry Max – he is always talking about you and how you make him laugh!'

I knew the one I intended to marry, but I did not tell Laelia.

Mr Vashinsky still lived, Laelia lingered, reluctant to leave the family before the end. She had already endangered her career by waiting another day and another day. We all spoke now in whispers. Gran attended to the household tasks and the Vashinskys sat by the old man's bed. Tadek read sometimes from the Hebrew book, and sometimes Laelia sang very softly. At last, it was decided that she must bid goodbye to her father, and return to Vienna.

Tadek hired a car from Mr Heiton to drive Laelia to the mail boat for Holyhead. From Holyhead the train would take her to London. When Tadek put the car in the car park, we joined the long queue of people waiting to board the boat.

Just ahead of us in the queue, I saw a tall familiar figure. It was Burton. He was wearing a fur-collared sheepskin coat, the first of that kind I had ever seen. He looked tanned and handsome when he turned to look around at the queue. He saw me immediately and came back.

Neither Tadek nor Laelia had ever actually seen Burton.

168

They never referred to him; his very existence must be, in their view, a remembrance of hurt for me. So when this handsome stranger joined us, some instinct of shame buried his name in my throat. I heard myself introducing Tadek and Laelia to Mr . . . Mr . . .

'Mr Jack,' he supplied charmingly. 'Are we all travelling?'

The situation was explained to him. Tadek seemed pleased, or at any rate relieved that Laelia would have friendly company. When our part of the queue reached the ticket-gate, Burton took Laelia's case from Tadek. They went forward together. Laelia turned several times to wave back to us. Her lovely face was sad. One almost felt Burton's protective sympathy for her and her response to it, so expressive were their bodies' attitudes. I know I was overwhelmed with guilt before Tadek. I had acted out a lie that no power on earth was going to make me retract. We walked back to the car park.

Tadek looked at me, then at his watch, and again at me. 'You seem downcast,' he said. 'Not enough fresh air. I think we could give ourselves an hour. Were you ever up on the Vico? Come on, hop in. We'll go and see Killiney.'

The first time anyone sees Killiney Bay from the Vico must be one of life's experiences. Tadek said that day that people had compared it to the Bay of Naples, 'See Naples and die.' I had not seen Naples nor anywhere else. That evening, with Tadek's arm around my shoulders, I wanted to die of the beauty of it. That view is so exactly placed, it fills the sea and the sky with colour as a great oil painting fills a frame. The place, the deepening twilight, the moment, all were exactly right to tell Tadek that I loved him, I always had, I always would.

We sat on the wall. I absorbed the view as I knew he expected me to do, in reverent silence.

'Tadek, I love you so much,' I whispered, and even as I whispered I hoped with all my heart that he would never find out that I had omitted the name of Burton from that introduction.

Tadek lifted me off the wall. 'Come on down and I will show you White Rock Strand. Max and I often came here for a swim.'

We climbed down towards the beach, clambering up the big white rocks until we were overhanging a rocky pool full of clear, green water. We sat there looking out across the bay while the last light drained slowly out of the sky.

'This scenery would go to your head,' Tadek said, giving me a little hug as I leaned against him.

'Tadek, I wish you would give me long, long passionate kisses like in the films.' I used my best pathetic pleading voice.

'Sit up, you little hussy,' he laughed at me.

'Oh Tadek, please, please, I really mean it. I miss you so fearfully when you are far away. Tadek, I . . .'

Suddenly he was serious. He took his arm from around my shoulder. Too late, I remembered his dying father. This was not the moment after all. I scrambled to my feet.

'I'm sorry,' I said, 'I am truly sorry.'

Without a word, we climbed back up the cliff. It was almost dark as we got into the car. In twenty minutes we were passing along Sandymount Strand and nearly home. Tadek pulled in at the seawall, he switched off the engine.

'We had better talk,' he said, 'and the only reason we are talking now, and not in five years' time, or any other time, is because I shall be gone in a day or two and I do not know when I shall be back. I intend to come back. That goes without saying. Nevertheless, it may not be immediately, it may not be soon. I may be able to work in Germany, I have letters of introduction. The field is overcrowded here. That is *my* side of it. There is yours. We believe in your talent for the theatre. You must work that out of your system, or you must prove yourself. You have not begun yet. You are still full of make believe. Remember, if you do not work at your talent, you do not deserve your reward. The talent must be used fully.'

My reward. I wondered did he mean himself, that my

170

reward would be what I had most wanted all these years? No, I suppose he was talking of some sort of fulfilment.

'But,' Tadek continued, laying stress on the word, 'there is a more important aspect of our lives which does not occur to you. Well, you are still a child. I am a Jew. Jews are set apart.'

'Couldn't I be a Jew?' I asked.

'No,' Tadek answered shortly. 'Jews are born Jews.'

Dimly, I had known this thing about Jews was some sort of a block. I remembered Phyllis's scandalized tone, 'They are Jew-es, that's what they are!'

'Tadek,' I asked humbly, 'what exactly am I?'

'You are an Irish Catholic,' he answered, 'it is just as limiting as being a Jew.'

He had been staring out through the windscreen, now he turned to look at me for the first time. His face was half in darkness, but I could see the whiteness of his teeth.

'Why are you smiling,' I asked, 'when everything is so sad?'

Tadek took my hand in his.

'In a way, it is sad,' he said, 'because I feel that when I take my eye off you, you will do something stupid, well, silly then. Take this business of "kisses like in the picture-house".' Now he was smiling. 'Suppose I start in with passionate kisses, what do I do for an encore?'

'Oh, they don't do anything else,' I assured him, 'just kisses, going on for minutes and minutes.'

'I am sure you had better think that over,' Tadek said very seriously. 'Be careful whose kisses you invite. They are the prologue, not the entire story.'

He started up the car, and we moved off from the seawall. He had made no promises for a happy-ever-after future. He was not the Tadek who had said, 'If you don't mind waiting twenty years.'

He was a Tadek who, with firm indifference, had just disengaged himself from my lifelong adoration. He must know he was cruel. I could feel the tears stinging my eyelids. If I just relaxed a muscle, a deluge of tears would come

171

pouring down . . . Like in Mrs Mayne's bedroom long ago. He could not resist then. I stole a little look at his face. It was closed, set, obdurate. I would not cry for him, I hated him.

We drew up at Little's Terrace.

'You go in, and fetch Gran. I'll run the two of you up to the bridge before I bring the car back to Heiton.'

He caught my hand, as I was opening the car door. 'Look,' he said, 'we both know the things we want. Sometimes it does not seem easy to get them. But there is always hope.'

Love came flooding back into my heart, and with it happiness. Tadek was back on his pedestal, right in the centre of my being. There was always hope, he had said. Sure it was as good as a promise.

That was the last time we were alone. Mr Vashinsky passed away a few days afterwards. All the arrangements had been made with an undertaker. Max's father was to accompany Tadek and the coffin as far as Paris. From there Max would go with Tadek to Zamość, where Max had made the final preparations for the burial under the cedar of Lebanon.

Mr Heiton was a man of many callings. He held a little auction of the Vashinskys' worldly goods. Out of the proceeds, he supplied a taxi to take Mrs Vashinsky, Gran and me to Gran's little house. Mrs Vashinsky held the Hebrew book on her knee, and I held the balalaika.

Gran's house was not unlike the house in Little's Terrace, having much the same shape and accommodation. Mrs Vashinsky was made comfortable in a little room that had been mine, and I slept again in Gran's room as when I was a small child. The Chinese screen ritual was once again used when necessary.

The interview with Montgomery the Solicitor was only a week away.

The interview was short. The Solicitor had ascertained that the Abbey School would take me as a pupil. Their hours of teaching each day were five to seven. My fees would be paid by the Court, but not my keep. It was their suggestion that I sit for a Civil Service Examination, take a good well-paid pensionable job, thus supporting myself. I was to look on the theatre as a pleasant pastime, a hobby.

That night I lay very still beside Gran, very still for fear she would hear my restless thoughts. I was thinking of Burton. I knew I could get in touch with him through Dublin Castle, where he had worked, maybe still worked. I set my mind to thinking of him in a practical, clear light – simply as a helpmate, a stepping stone. He would not want me to waste my time in the Civil Service when I could be carving out a great future on the stage. He, too, was a practical man, and a worshipper of theatre.

I was able to go a certain distance with those thoughts, then in imagination a cloud gathered about Burton's image. All the sin words the nuns had imprinted on my mind went floating through the cloud: promiscuous, lascivious, fornication, deviation, molestation, bestiality, sexuality, immodesty, impurity, adultery, hellfire beyond redemption. After a few nights of such thoughts, I found myself applying for the examination entrance papers, and starting once again to concentrate on study.

On the first day of September, I entered the Civil Service. On the first day of October I started the School of Acting course. A new life had begun.

I had plenty of time to dream of the theatre in the Land Commission. The work I was given to do never at any time measured up to the study which had gone into the Entrance Examination. Nor would the work ever have exercised any natural ability. Pen-pusher was a word very exactly coined. When I had been there about a month, I was given rent receipts to fill in and put in envelopes for sending to the farmers of the country who were buying their lands under a Land Purchase Scheme. The pay was less than two pounds a week, so it was a fair equation.

On the first day, a girl a little older than I gave me some sheets of paper, a ruler and a pencil.

'I'm Chersy Cotter,' she smiled at me, 'look as if you are working until you get used to being here!'

Chersy was tall and blonde and always very groomed. Although she was full of fun and the most light-hearted person, there was a quality in her that drew the respect of all about her. Her work in the Land Commission had the same impeccable neatness as had her appearance. I have been so lucky in the friends sent to me by a kindly providence. Chersy took me under her wing on that first day, and she has remained a caring friend through life.

The days slipped by easily. Each clerk's desk had a pencil sharpener operated by a tiny wheel. It was a way of passing a few minutes in every hour to sharpen the pencil. Everyone did it with funny comments at which everyone else laughed dutifully.

Girls in offices were still something of a novelty to the older men. Mr Reeve, the elderly Higher Executive, had his little daily joke when he announced with grave solemnity that he would be coming to inspect the girls' drawers, so everything must be on view! He was a very patient and kindly man.

There were tea-breaks. The last one in made the tea in the strongroom, and ran out to O'Neill's Pub on Merrion Row for luscious cheese sandwiches, and to the D.B.C. for jam doughnuts.

Surely those big, fresh sandwiches were more than four pence? And the doughnuts only a penny halfpenny? That is the price recorded in a little notebook in which I laid out my expenses amounting to one pound including the few shillings I managed to save hopefully.

To my great joy, Montgomery the Solicitor had ordained that I was to live at Gran's. He did not approve of the district, but as he said, who else would keep me for a pound a week? Also there were no tram-fares as it was only a ten-minute walk to the office.

Gran and Mrs Vashinsky were very happy together. Going home each night to the two old ladies in the narrow street had strengthened my sense of security for the long-awaited future. That Tadek's mother was with us was like having a hostage against Tadek's return to me.

I could not say this to Gran, nor ever to anyone. Sometimes I enclosed a little note to Tadek with his mother's letter – on his birthday or at Christmas. Mostly I was conscious of waiting, simply waiting. Waiting for the in-between years to pass. Waiting for the not being a Jew to seem unimportant. Waiting for the reward which would be given for talent used, and proven – hadn't he said that? The waiting for Tadek was the backdrop to my life, the deep unchanging centre.

Tadek's letters were sometimes gloomy in a way Mrs Vashinsky could not understand when she read them aloud to us. Germany, he wrote, was going through a very queer time. He did not know if it would be called Nationalism, or a resurgence of militarism. He just hoped nothing worse was going to happen before he finished his three-year contract in the hospital.

I felt Tadek wrote less than he actually thought. But I did not worry. There was a solemn side to Tadek's character which I accepted without thinking that it was any more important than the cheery side.

Laelia's letters were cheery enough. Italy was wonderful in all sorts of ways. She was surrounded by friends. There was a rosy optimism for the future in every word. She had offers to sing in London in the coming year and, if she were to believe her teacher, perhaps in the Metropolitan in New York – wouldn't that be wonderful?

Gran and Mrs Vashinsky were joined every Thursday by Phyllis. She was working in the kitchen in Jammet's Restaurant in Nassau Street. She loved her work. She was learning a great deal about cooking which she had always enjoyed next to playing the piano – 'Queezeen, Lovey, not

175

just plain cooking' – and usually on a Thursday she made a special treat for us. Always full of energy (and because she knew she was saving me, although she would never admit that), she tackled all the cleaning in that magical way she had. That little house shone like silver in every corner.

From October on, real life began for me at five o'clock each evening from Monday to Saturday.

At five o'clock I was like a bird prepared for flight. I flew down all the flights of stairs in the Land Commission and across a few streets to the Abbey Theatre. To the side and half underneath the Abbey is the Peacock which was considered the experimental part of the Abbey. The Peacock was painted in peacock blue. This is where the Abbey School met for classes, and for rehearsals as the work progressed.

There were twenty pupils in the School, some as young as I and some considerably older: young men and women, older women and men.

The poet Yeats and his friend, Lady Augusta Gregory, took a deep interest in the School. I, who had been instructed by Mr Frank Fay, was fully aware that Mr Yeats was a poet among poets and a man among men. I went fully, consciously, into that wonderful presence, careful to open the door for him with my eyes lowered, so in awe was I. I would never have spoken to him. No one did. We listened to him when he recited his poetry in that deep, toneless, chanting voice that came from remote mountain chasms, and we knew we were privileged beyond riches.

Not only were we privileged to be in the company of Mr Yeats and our teachers, Mr Lennox Robinson and Miss Ria Mooney, we were there when the Abbey was in full flower. There were actors and actresses whose names have been enshrined in a gallery of fame: F. J. McCormack, Barry Fitzgerald, Arthur Shields, Cyril Cusack, Maureen Delaney, Sheila Richards, Eileen Crowe, M. J. Dolan.

The men and women who were acting then have never been surpassed. Many, even now, recall the art of those old

Abbey actors. It would be easy to fill pages describing each one in his original rôle. For the playwrights were new too, and writing for the very people who would portray the parts, knowing the particular strengths and charms of their rôle-creators.

The poet Yeats had written plays for the beauteous Maud Gonne, whose 'hair was a folded flower, and the quiet of love in her feet'. It is a great glory to know that we, who were young then, walked the streets of Dublin town with the poet whose marvellous words were being written out of the very air we breathed:

> *'I bring you with reverent hands*
> *The books of my numberless dreams,*
> *White woman that passion has worn*
> *As the tide wears the dove-grey sands. . . .'*

Ah, poetry that grows grander as the years roll on.

Lennox Robinson was one of our teachers. A man of immense dedication to the theatre, he was the oddest, loveliest, kindest creature I ever met or knew. People said he was a hard drinker but I never saw any aspect of his character that was ungentle. He looked like a tall schoolboy and he was loved by the students. And so was Ria Mooney, our other teacher. Besides being a wonderful teacher she was a powerful actress. I have never forgotten her 'Kitty O'Shea' to F. J. McCormack's 'Parnell'. The play itself was little more than documentary, but their portrayals carried it to a revelation of passion seldom seen now. Ria Mooney achieved international fame, returning always to the Abbey. All of us in the School worshipped Miss Mooney.

There were special occasions when Lennox Robinson invited the students out to his villa on the cliffs at the Vico (the famous view beloved of Tadek). Here we would sit around the floor and Robinson would read to us, and talk to us, about European drama.

Sometimes in the summer, Ria Mooney invited us all out to her cottage at Annamoe in the Wicklow mountains. We hitched lifts or went on bicycles. She let us help her to white-wash the cottage and dig in the garden. We all contributed to the picnic, because we knew that money in the theatre was hopeless in Dublin. Gran loaded me up with bags of sandwiches and cakes and her walnut toffee. Charades were the big fun of the evening, sometimes under the moonlight in the long summer nights.

We set off for Dublin when the sun was coming up over the Wicklow mountains. We all had jobs to go to at nine a.m. Inevitably someone would start singing that old lovesong, and we would all join in:

> *Like sunrise on the Wicklow Hills*
> *So dawned my love for you, machree. . . .'*

It is a plaintive air to bring tears to the eyes: not then but now.

There were two other girls about my age, Francesca and Gladys, and we were friends. They did not take the place of Berny and Lucille, though, with whom I exchanged regular letters and occasional visits. Berny had started in the College of Surgeons and was swamped by study, she said.

The real dream of my future, when Tadek and I would belong together in some place as yet unknown, I held cherished and silent deep within. The rest of life, bounded by Gran's little house and the dreary Land Commission on one side of the River Liffey, and the Abbey School of Acting on the other side, that rest of life was an enchanted world in which time was very happily and swiftly passing.

Chapter 11

Just like in Mr Fay's classes, the end of the year came after Easter. Three plays out of the Abbey repertoire were prepared, two one-act plays and a three-acter. The plays were chosen with a view to giving all the pupils a fair chance of displaying themselves. On their showing, certificates were awarded. No longer did I get the plum parts as at school, Francesca was ahead of me. All the same, looking at the old programmes now, I was given plenty of space to distinguish myself.

The plays were put on for two nights, Thursday and Friday. The excitement was marvellous, although we pretended to be very blasé, considering ourselves pure professionals.

On the first night, members of the Board of Directors of the Abbey honoured us, and we were allowed to invite our own friends.

I invited everyone I knew, determined that people would think I was quite a quality actress. Gran and Mrs Vashinsky and Phyllis came, also Berny, who was coming to the end of her first year in Medical School, and Chersy from the office. Aunt Julia made the trip from Bray, although 'strictly speaking she did not approve of young girls going on the stage, and what would the nuns think she would like to know.'

Unexpectedly, Max's father turned up. After the show, he took all of us to supper in the Shelbourne Hotel. I was very proud that night, and grateful to Max for having such a lovely father.

Chersy was very impressed, my stock soared. Next day in the office she told all the Section how good an actress I was, so that night they all came to the Peacock. Again I was brought out to supper, this time by one person.

Now there comes a pause in the setting-down of this story. A new element, all unknowing, entered my life that night in the guise of a supper-date.

My life had all the ingredients necessary for security. I knew what they were. Of course I knew. I should not have allowed a single trace of the unknown to creep in – and certainly not the unknown in the shape of an amazingly handsome young man.

In defence, I was still very much a schoolgirl despite my longing for Tadek. In moments of intense loneliness which came when I thought of him as perhaps being gone forever, the unwanted vision of a splendid all-powerful Burton would overcloud all other feelings.

The heartbreaking need for a very Particular Friendship had never gone away. I had been punished by the nuns, but not cured. The need, I discovered, was still there.

Having someone now to reassure me, admire me, even love me awhile, that was all very necessary. I was sure it was necessary. So I went out to supper with Tony Lloyd, a Higher Executive Officer in the Land Commission. I had acquired a Boyfriend. In those days, a girl's status was determined by the height, breadth, and excellence of her Boyfriend. A girl's natural ambition then was to be married. I saw it all about me in the Land Commission.

There were several sorts of young people in the Land Commission. There were the new arrivals from the country places into the city. Boys and girls who had done well in their exams now filled junior positions in the Irish Civil Service. The new Irish Government had taken over the Civil Service from the British and was making many changes. These young country people led frugal lives because the pay was small.

Dubliners and suburban Dubliners, because they lived at home, managed rather better. They looked down on their country cousins, referring to them as 'the culchies'.

And there were the Ascendancy types, those who were in high office under the English regime. They despised both the culchies and the native Dubliners. They belonged to golf and rugby clubs, took holidays in England, and lived on the south side of the city. They had motorcars when cars were a sign of upper middle-class wealth.

Tony Lloyd was the Ascendancy type. He had the special accented voice of his class, and he was outstandingly handsome.

It was flattering to be seen with him. He had been educated at an exclusive college of which he talked constantly. He had achieved fame in sport. He had been capped twice for Ireland in rugby and had played cricket for the Gentlemen of Ireland. Either of these feats was on the tip of his tongue in every conversation.

He was a very well-known man-about-town in the city of Dublin. With him I entered a public house for the first time. His idea of an evening out was a night in a pub. He had his favourite pub where there were bound to be other drinking pals with whom he had played rugby or been to college, and where he knew and approved of the owner who seemed to be a close confidential friend. He had certain shops for buying clothes, shops to which his father had introduced him, shops where the resident tailor would know to a fraction of an inch if his measurements had changed. Such an intimate knowledge of his stylish person delighted Tony.

'I like the kind of clothes you wear, Lia,' he said. 'Do you have a little dressmaker around the corner?'

'Not around the corner, Tony. She lives in our house, with my Gran.'

Mrs Vashinsky was a gifted needlewoman. Materials were cheap in those days. If Mrs Vashinsky had been born into the world of fashion, she would have become a top designer.

'When are you going to take me to meet this famous Gran?'

'Oh someday, Tony, someday!' I always answered airily. But I knew I would not. Neither would I consent to going with Tony to meet his mother in their mansion in Foxrock. 'Someday' was the answer to that request also.

For several years, Tony was on the fringe of a life that held idyllic weekends in Annamoe, and long cultural discussions in Mr Robinson's villa on the Vico. After the School in the evening, it had become the habit to go off to other theatrical activities with Francesca and Gladys. We belonged to a little theatre club on Stephen's Green, and a film society in Rathmines.

'There's your faithful boyfriend in his gorgeous car!' the others would say as we came out of the Peacock, and as often as not, they would go off without me. I would have preferred to go with them, but Tony was overwhelmingly (and flatteringly) persistent.

Now we were offered parts in the Abbey itself. Gladys and I got bit parts in crowds, perhaps neighbouring women. Francesca had begun to be noticed. She had a perfect malleable face for stage-work, and a certain mysterious aura about the way she acted. One felt there were depths beyond depths in her personality while she was on stage. Off stage, one lost that feeling. Very often she did not understand what a play was about, satire or irony were meaningless words. Her comedy could fall flat, the cadence of poetic drama could elude her. Once a fault was carefully explained, she was able to overcome her lack. Her driving force was ambition. I could see in Francesca a power I had not got. Francesca should have been a potent example to me to tread warily and to tread alone. Having a boyfriend was beguiling and confusing and leading me in a direction contrary to my innermost desires. . . . All of this I could not see because I had not that essential power.

Since Tony Lloyd insisted on taking me with him everywhere, he undertook to educate me in the business of drinking . . . very gradually, of course. There were things like shandies at first which were, he said, mostly lemonade. How long it took him to get me on to a mixture of port and brandy I have forgotten. After three of those mixtures, I was able to see Tony as very interesting, his handsome flushed face full of power and knowledge.

It never for a moment occurred to me that Tony Lloyd was anything more than a passing part of my life, flattering to my feminine sense of achievement mainly because I sensed that I was envied by other girls in the office.

When he told me, as he did occasionally, that some other female had taken my place at his side in the favourite pub, I felt no great disturbance. Within me was a shrine to another love of which Tony was not even aware. When Tony went off on his rugby weekends, it was vaguely hinted that accommodating young women ministered to his every need in a way of which, apparently, I was too young to know.

I told Chersy about this.

Her answer was always derisive. 'Big boaster! Do you think he'd tell you if there was any truth in it? If he got anything, he had to pay for it. I hope it cost him plenty! You just watch out when he gets a load of the jar. Swear an oath now!'

The dangers of the world, as foretold by the nuns in Cluny, were both repelling and alluring! Only half-aware of what I was swearing I always promised to be careful.

Then Tony's father died. Their house was let. The mother moved to Tunbridge Wells, whence she had come originally. For the rest of her life she aimed to live there with her sister, who was unmarried. For a while there was much upheaval. Tony, after weeks of consultation, took a small flat in Fitzwilliam Square which his mother furnished with suitable pieces from their old home. It was in quiet good taste, Tony was very proud of it. It became another of his conversation topics when he planned a wonderful house-warming party.

Phyllis came one night with the great news that she was to

be married. The chef in Jammet's had been 'taken' with Phyllis almost from the first day she went to work in the kitchen. How could he resist her? She was a big girl, splendidly built in good proportion. Her skin and hair and eyes were always shining. Cleanliness was an ideal which she spent her life in achieving. Not only her person was clean, but any area she occupied, any utensil she used. The work involved in all this cleanliness never stopped Phyllis from singing and laughing and taking interest in other people. She was utterly devoted to her own family, to me, and now to Jacques. Luckily she had not to choose between any of us, but I knew I had a very special place.

'But, Phyllis,' Gran asked, 'isn't he French?'

'Of course,' said Phyllis. 'Mr Jammet brought him over from Paris six years ago. His mother and father and all his brothers and sisters are in the business the old Jammets have over there.'

I was remembering how Burton used to be a regular diner in Jammet's – the best in Dublin, in his expert opinion.

'But French,' said Gran. 'I remember when you went there, you told us he doesn't know a word of English! How do you talk to him, or have you learned French?'

'Not a word,' laughed Phyllis, 'sure Madame does it all for us. He said it to her, about getting married I mean, and she said it to me. She told me all the advantages, him being a good chef, and single and all.'

'And did you agree to marry him straightaway?' asked Gran.

'Well,' replied Phyllis, 'I said I would tell me Mam, and see what she said.'

This was really exciting.

'What happened then?' we both asked.

'Well! What happened then, was this,' replied Phyllis, entering into the shared joy of a story, 'me Mam told me Dad, and he said to bring out the fella and they would look him over. So we gave the house a big clean-up, and me Mam cooked a nice meal. Madame told Jacques, the day was fixed,

184

all the family was assembled – that made nearly thirty, including the kids. Me Dad knew a few words of French from the Great World War, he was in the Battle of Ypres don't you know – he remembered a few words like "napoo", and Mademoiselle from Armenteers "parlez-vous". Oh they got on famous, him and Jacques. He got Jacques rightly tanked up. You shoulda seen the two of them. Jacques brought me a few bottles of wine chosen special by Missoo Jammet and they mixed that with me Dad's porter. Me Mam played the old piano and we all sang. Of course, I did all me specials, like I used to do in the Ierne Hall, do you remember, Lovey? "She is Far from the Land" and "Danny Boy".'

Oh, I could just picture it all in the Dalys' big kitchen. Phyllis with flashing eyes and heaving diddies and loads and loads of gusto. And her sister's husband getting his hands into the younger sisters' jumpers.

'I was wearing the silk lace blouse your Mama gave me, God rest her soul,' continued Phyllis, 'and the narrow black skirt. It is a bit tight for me now but it is so ladylike. If only Mama could have been there to tell her. . . .'

Phyllis's eyes had filled with tears. I put my arms around her. Mama's daughter had almost forgotten Mama, while Mama's faithful servant always remembered.

Madame Jammet took care of the wedding arrangements. Gran and I were invited. When I saw the bridegroom I knew just how voluptuous and irresistible Phyllis must seem to him. He was tall and sallow, a plain quiet man. I could understand his being tongue-tied with the language difficulty, but singularly unsmiling worried me. Would Phyllis be able to coax smiles out of him on the honeymoon?

'What did you make of Jacques apart from how dumb he appeared?' I asked Gran when we got home.

Gran considered the question. 'He will make a good husband,' she said.

'Oh but Gran, wouldn't you have liked someone better-looking for Phyllis? He seems so lugubrious.'

185

But Gran shook her head. 'Lia, I think you put too much store by good looks! Handsome is as handsome does, the old saying goes, and remember that when you go to choose! Fellows are one thing, husbands are another. By all accounts he is a great chap at his work. When you are looking at him, you are seeing him, all there is. I wouldn't say lugubrious, quiet perhaps, thoughtful, even considerate. You mustn't have seen his eyes soften up when he turned to Phyllis at the altar. And the same religion – she was always a great little one for the religious duties. Her mother is the same. I'd say that must have kept those Dalys together. They are very united in spite of hard times.'

'But Gran, Phyllis is so full of life. Won't he be a real damper? And not a word of English!'

'Not at all,' said Gran judiciously. 'You don't need words for everything. He'll be the right husband for her. A little rein here and there is what she needs – for a help, not a hindrance.'

When we were talking of Phyllis, Tadek's mother was sitting, quietly listening. She had grown quieter as the months slipped away. After we had had a little supper, she and Gran prepared for bed. Usually, I read for a little while by candlelight, then I too crept into bed. If I had been out with Tony, or late in the Abbey, the old ladies were fast asleep when I came in.

This night, Gran crept softly down again. She had wrapped a woolly shawl over her nightdress, now she closed the door on the end of the stairs. She sat down beside me.

'I am worried about Mrs V.,' she whispered. 'She is not herself at all.'

'Yes,' I answered because I had been thinking just that, 'she is so quiet.'

'It is worse than quiet,' said Gran sadly, 'she is losing interest. She hasn't the appetite of a bird. She is upset too because she has not heard from the son.'

I had not thought of this. It did not seem so long since Tadek's last letter. I did not always get to read his mother's

186

letters on the day they arrived, sometimes I let a week or two pass without seeming to remember to ask for the latest news.

'I think a month has passed without a word,' whispered Gran, 'but maybe more, it could be two months.'

'And Laelia?' I enquired, to which Gran gave a guess that Mrs V. had not heard from Laelia since Christmas. Soon it would be summer.

'Will you write to them?' Gran was searching in the drawer of her little chiffonier. 'Here are the two last letters she got from them, she always keeps them handy here, and reads them several times a day.'

I took the letters. I had read this one from Tadek, there was a reference to the introduction of the Nuremberg Law into Hungary. I had no idea what this meant, I wondered, did Mrs V. know? Was there, in this, something to worry about? Tadek had a hospital address in Budapest. I noted this address. Turning to Laelia's letter was heartlifting. She was rehearsing for opera in London. The rehearsals would take many months, and the pay was very small, a mere token. She was lucky to have found accommodation with a friend. I wrote down this address also, it was an apartment in Kensington.

Before I went to bed, I wrote the two letters telling Tadek and Laelia that their mother was not in the best of health, that Gran and I felt it would be wonderful for her to have a little visit from them if they could manage it at all. In as indirect a way as I could, I assured them that we were grand financially, and that indeed I did not think there was any immediate danger. And not to worry as we would take every care of their mother. Next morning on the way to work I posted the letters.

Tony Lloyd now had an office all to himself. It seemed to be a part of his official duties to read all the daily newspapers. Certainly that is what he did, so he should be well informed.

The next time we were seated in his favourite pub, I asked: 'Tony, what are the Nuremberg Laws?'

Tony liked being asked questions to which he knew the answer; if he did not know the answer he changed the conversation immediately. Now he knew, at least he knew a little on which he could elaborate. So he took out his pipe, going through the pipe-cleaning and filling formula. This was an unhurried performance, denoting that he was giving the question due consideration. When at last he spoke, my heart turned over.

'They are mainly anti-Jewish laws which have been introduced in Germany. This fellow, Hitler, does not seem too fond of the Jews. For example, the number of Jewish employees cannot exceed twenty percent in any firm, nor can the proportion of salaries and wages exceed that amount. Automatically thousands of Jews have become idle, without work, or means of subsistence.'

'Is that only in Germany?' I asked fearfully.

'Or anywhere this Hitler has influence, I suppose,' answered Tony cheerfully.

'But of course he doesn't have any in, say, a place like Hungary?'

But Tony was up-to-date in his newspaper reading.

'I wouldn't put it past him,' he answered, 'now that he has marched into Austria, and the Third Reich has become Hungary's next-door neighbour. There are bound to be, in Hungary, fellows who would like to get rid of the Jews. There are some fairly well-known Hungarian Jews, you know – especially among the arts. That play I took you to in the Gate, "Liliom", that's written by a Hungarian Jew, Ferenc Molnar.'

Tony knew he had my admiring and respectful attention when he displayed this kind of knowledge. He could go on all night when he had an avid listener, he usually ended by becoming a bore. But not this time. Among the other things he told me was one that held my heart in an icy grip.

'Jews in Hungary are not allowed to serve in the army. They can't do their military service. Jewish writers, skilled technicians, doctors, professional men like lawyers, must dig trenches in labour camps. Crazy, isn't it?'

'But, Tony, if those Jews, like doctors, just happen to be there, in Hungary, I mean – if they really belong somewhere else – if they don't have to do military service and so don't get put in those labour camps – they would be all right, wouldn't they?'

Tony seemed very sure that if any chap in any country not his own had his passport in good order, then he could get out and go home to his own place.

Well, that was reassuring. Tadek had his Irish passport. Quite suddenly I realized that I did not know what passport Tadek had, maybe it was a Polish passport. I seemed to remember a conversation long ago about passports, and Max, who was the first to go away, showing his Irish passport. Max was still in Vienna, I thought.

'Tony, forget about Hungary for a moment. What about Austria?'

'Like I told you, Hitler is all over Austria. If you are still talking about the Jews, they wouldn't stand a snowball's chance in hell in Austria. It's the concentration camp for the Jews in Austria.'

I watched anxiously every day for a letter from Tadek. After a fortnight, a little note on dainty flowered paper came from Laelia. She was full of concern for her mother, and so grateful to me for letting her know. She sent money and a promise to come for a long holiday in September. It was not possible for her to come before that, just not possible.

I watched Mrs V. turn the pretty missive over and over in her hands. She was glad, so glad, to hear from her daughter, yet she was puzzled. Without knowing why, she looked helpless. She had grown very much thinner. Gran had accompanied her to the doctor. A tonic for the blood was all he had given her.

I thought the anxiety was beginning to tell on Gran. We no

189

longer had Phyllis to help us. She had her own place now, and indeed she kept it like a little palace. She still worked in the kitchen of Jammet's with Jacques, although Gran and I often wondered what way they chatted. Naturally her half-day was spent with her husband. I decided to go over to Dalys to seek help from one of the younger girls a few hours a week. This was arranged. The Abbey was paying a small wage now for the small parts and I was able to afford help for my two old ladies.

It was strange to me that Tony Lloyd seemed to regard me as an essential part of his daily routine. He sulked if I had other things to do when he issued his frequent invitations. Birthdays, his and mine, Christmas, Easter, holidays, all warranted a present, a night at the theatre, the cinema, a visit to the seaside or to the zoo. He had a car, he expected to enjoy what he called a 'bit of a coort' afterwards. Speaking in his upper-crust accent turned 'coort', instead of 'court' into a bit of fun for him! The 'coort' was not objectionable. Tony prided himself on having a wholesome respect for a lady; as he put it, 'Anyone who was not a lady could look out for herself.'

The 'coort' showed a warmer, needing, trusting side of his nature, except when he had too much drink when in his words, in apology afterwards, 'He lost the run of himself.' He was so outrageously handsome, and not unlovable, that he was easy to forgive. I had grown used to him, yet never for a moment did I see him as the handsome husband in my future. That position was booked, or it would remain empty. He did not use words of love any more than I did. He did not refer to marriage as a plan, nor even as a possibility. In his most boozily ardent moments, he never proposed.

Chersy, now engaged to a most eligible young barrister, often cross-questioned me about my evenings with Tony.

'Kisses!' she would echo incredulously. 'And what else?'

Ought I mention that he had told me he liked my hand stroking his bare back as we lay on the beach after swimming?

'Well, not much really,' I would reply.

'Are you telling the truth?' Chersy would demand. 'Does he not put his hand . . . ?'

But I would also interrupt her, 'Oh no no no, Tony is not like that!'

'All those kisses, and then he goes tamely home,' Chersy was sadly puzzled. 'Or does he go down to Mabbot Street? Or worse still, is there something wrong with him?'

'Of course there's nothing wrong with him,' I would reply loyally. 'What on earth could be wrong with him?'

Chersy was always certain he was, 'Getting it somewhere. You just watch it, he's up to something,' she insisted.

So I was very pleased to be able to announce to Chersy that Tony was giving a party in his flat for his thirtieth birthday. Moreover he had told me that it was going to be a very special night, a *very* special night. I was to invite Chersy and her fiancé, Gladys and her fiancé, and Francesca, who disdained boyfriends but for whom an escort would be provided. Tony was ordering all the food, pre-packed from the D.B.C., and all sorts of drink from O'Neill's.

'A very special night!' mused Chersy for days before the party. 'A very special night.'

She went over all the possibilities. Had Tony come into money? Was he resigning and going off to Australia, or America, or maybe to Canada? Was it a farewell party of some sort? Was he giving up, and entering the priesthood? Fellows did that from time to time, got remorse of the old conscience. 'You swear to me that he hasn't proposed, are you telling the truth? Is it that kind of a "do", like the one my Mum gave when I got engaged?

'Tony often has little dinner parties in the flat,' I told her. 'He makes a big "do" out of nothing – you know Tony. It always ends up in a big long repetition of the time he played for Ireland when they beat Wales. The only different thing this time is that I have promised to stay the night, and spend the next day with him. He is going out to see the place they lived –'

'Stay the night!' Chersy was aghast. 'Stay the night! So that's it. A proper orgy he wants, and God knows what when we all go home. Is he mad? He has another guess coming. Don't say a word. We'll enjoy his party, but when we leave, you are coming with us. Not a word now. And stop laughing.'

It was to be a long, long time before I knew what was going to be so special about Tony's thirtieth birthday party, the night, or the next day.

On the very afternoon of that so special day, I had a 'phone call from a neighbour of Gran's. Mrs Vashinsky had dropped dead, and would I come home at once. Immediately, I decided to take my full holiday leave and handed in the Leave Docket to the Higher Executive Officer. I tried to see Tony. His office was empty. He was busy somewhere with his party preparations. Chersy also was missing. She had time off to go to the hairdresser.

I raced over to Fitzwilliam Square. There was no answer to the bell. I had lost time looking for him, suddenly he was not in the least important. I forgot to give a 'phone message for him. I ran across the town to the narrow street where all I had left was Gran.

Chapter Twelve

Gran had sent for the doctor who had most recently seen Mrs Vashinsky. He had brought in another doctor, there was talk of a postmortem. At last the doctors decided that poor Mrs Vashinsky had just faded away. They questioned Gran about Mrs V.'s circumstances. Gran had to admit that indeed her poor friend had fretted unceasingly because she had no letter from her son, and no money for a long time. Gran thought it was because of the money that Mrs V. had eaten less and less.

The doctors enquired if we had money for a funeral, and strongly advised that we send urgent telegrams to the son and daughter. I went to the post office as soon as the doctors had gone. It cost quite a bit to send the wires, I did not like to be abrupt.

Two women had come in to lay out the poor dead body, tiny as a child in the small white bed. They had to be paid. When that was done, little as it was, we did not know if we would have enough for immediate expenses, let alone a funeral. And where would she be buried? We went through her few personal belongings, but there were no grave papers.

'Could you go the the Jews?' Gran asked.

'I would not know exactly where to go,' I said, 'but do you remember Max's father? The one who took us to the Shelbourne? I know where he lives in Terenure. I could go in the tram as soon as Phyllis gets here to keep you company.'

For of course we had sent for Phyllis. I knew she would put a good appearance on the house in preparation for the coming of Tadek and Laelia. When Tadek would be with us, he would open the door and let in the light. Until then we seemed content to mourn together. Until then we scarcely spoke.

From the beginning Gran had loved the little woman who was now dead exactly as I loved Tadek, never speaking of it but utterly content in living with the warmth of love pressed close inside.

When I was sitting in the tram going to Terenure, I remembered Mr Fay reading to us in Cluny. He read one day from *Wuthering Heights* words I have never forgotten:

> 'Whatever our souls are made of, his and mine are the same . . . My love for Heathcliff resembles the eternal rocks beneath – a source of little visible delight, but necessary . . . he's always, always in my mind – not as a pleasure, any more than I am always a pleasure to myself – but as my own being . . .'

And I loved you, Tadek, as my own being before I ever heard of Mr Fay. Soon you will be here, and this time you must listen. It was not new to talk to Tadek within my imagination, it was constant. The day of his mother's death I felt him very close to me.

Max's father greeted me warmly. His house was spacious, filled with furniture and pictures, for that was his business. Max had often told us that his father travelled the world collecting, that he was famous in his field. When he had seated me, and rung a bell for tea to be brought, he listened to my story.

'Now, I must bring you up-to-date with the boys' whereabouts,' he said. 'Some time ago, it could be eight or nine months, I wrote to Max advising that he leave Vienna. I suggested he should pass on my word to Tadek to leave Germany. Max is now in Paris. Tadek took the hint also, and moved to Budapest. He was working in a military hospital there up to a short while ago. I am sure he moved on before the Invasion. I know Max warned him. His passport is Polish, he might have trouble proving that in fact he is a resident of another country. It has been my experience that to a middle European, there is no such place as Ireland.'

'But why are things so difficult?' I asked. 'There is no war.'

'For the Jew,' he said flatly, 'there is always a war of trouble. For everyone else, soon perhaps, a real war.'

I remembered what Tony had said about labour camps, but I forbore to mention it. This old man, who was handing a dainty teacup to me, would know even more than Tony Lloyd.

I wondered, did military hospitals send on telegrams to labour camps? It seemed doubtful, somehow.

'Do you think they will get the wires I sent?' I asked him.

'Oh, Laelia will. No problem there. Tadek too, but I rather think travel would be more difficult, certainly slower, for him.'

He thought for a while, resting his silvery head on his chest.

'It is Friday now,' he said. 'We cannot delay the funeral beyond Monday. Laelia should be here by then – and with luck, Tadek also. Leave all the arrangements to me. I will find a place for the grave. Write, here, the doctor's name and address, and your own address. I will come for the corpse with the undertaker on Sunday, at midday. Tomorrow we observe the Sabbath, indeed, from sundown today.'

I rose to go. He put his arms around me, kissing both cheeks. Holding me from him, he said, 'I should like to frame you in a silver frame and put you there above the fireplace where we could exchange glances. You are a good and lovely girl. My son, Max, always said you were. You are more lovely now than when we had dinner in the Shelbourne. Quite exquisite. Never cut your hair, my dear.'

Sunday, midday, Max's father came in his limousine. The undertaker and his assistants came in their hearse. They had some difficulty taking the little coffin around the bend of the narrow stairs. I welcomed every delay in the hope that Laelia and Tadek would arrive. Every sound in the street sent me running to the window, to draw aside the blind and peep out.

Saturday had been a long-drawn-out day. We had not gone to bed at all because Gran said it was wrong to leave the poor dead body unattended. Some of the old neighbours, who had grown to know Mrs Vashinsky from seeing her with Gran, came in at intervals to drink tea, and say the rosary. Phyllis, who had always had deep reservations, wondered aloud 'If Catholic Rosaries would do those Jews any good?' Gran said, if there were any such thing as saints in Heaven, then her Mrs V. was there. Phyllis looked doubtful, but she said nothing.

When at last the little dead body was lifted into the coffin, Gran broke down. She kissed Mrs Vashinsky's waxen face and fingers with loving fervour. The sound of an old woman crying is heartbreaking, everyone cried with her, Max's father was mopping his eyes with a large handkerchief as the coffin was carried out to the hearse. I had gone to the flower shop on Saturday. Now I put the bunch of roses on the coffin with a little card which I had waited until the last minute to write: 'With all our love from Laelia and Tadek'.

Gran felt too poorly to go in the limousine to the funeral parlour. We had a neighbour stay with her while Phyllis and I went with Max's father. Afterwards we hurried home. I was afraid Gran would collapse. The death had been a great strain. We sat up late, waiting again for Tadek and Laelia. No message came.

Gran, sick with grief, thought her poor dead friend would feel deserted if she did not go to the funeral. Phyllis's religious principles would not allow her to attend a Jewish funeral, so she returned to work and to Jacques. The limousine was sent and, since we were without scruples of that sort and felt only sorrow, Gran and I went to the cemetery in Dolphin's Barn. Standing by the grave there were only the three of us. Max's father had brought a lovely wreath of irises which was placed

196

beside my roses. As the coffin was lowered, I saw that he, too, had written: 'From Tadek and Laelia with love'. Gran and I waited while Max's father walked slowly across to another grave. There was a marble statue, delicately chiselled, guarding the grave. The old man's face was bent low, his handkerchief pressed to his cheek.

'Old friends of his, I suppose,' murmured Gran.

As we walked back to the car, the old man took my hand in his. 'If there is no word of the children by Thursday,' he said, 'I want you to come and let me know. Could you come in the forenoon?'

I promised to come. Once again we were at home waiting for Tadek and Laelia. That waiting, with the glimmer of hope slowly fading, lives in my memory as a year-long vigil. I was glad to be there with Gran, she needed me. I noticed she was inclined now to wander back into the past at a slight prompting. Philadelphia, Georgio, Aunt Hannah. Her poor old mind rested itself better on distant memories than on more recent sorrows. To her my mother's death was as recent as Mrs Vashinsky's. As time went on, she confused these two in her mind.

All the same, Gran was a resilient woman. By Thursday, she was a calm and comfortable presence again, able to cope with her little chores. Phyllis's younger sister, Peggy, came in on Thursday to help with the cleaning of the range, the washing and polishing the stairs. I went off to Terenure in a reasonably peaceful frame of mind. Maybe Max's father would have news of Tadek.

He was waiting for me.

'Could you come with me to London, and perhaps to Paris? You could? You have an up-to-date address for Laelia? And for Tadek? And you have a passport?'

I was hesitating. I did not have money to take off for London at a moment's notice. And once there, would Tadek be there? I hardly thought so, or he would have come to Dublin, surely.

197

'Do not worry about money,' the old man said, 'that is the least of our worries. I had a telephone conversation with Max. Something he said, or suspected, makes me think it would be better if you saw Laelia – tell her of her mother's death in your own way – that is, when we trace her. Another thing, I no longer travel alone, you would be company for me. And, although I had thought of it myself, it was also Max's suggestion.'

I had already told Laelia, in the wire, of her mother's death, but perhaps she never received the wire. To see her again even if I were to be the bearer of bad news, that would be wonderful. Laelia, in her affection for me, was like the sister I never had. I adored her. I could repeat it a hundred times, she was so exquisitely beautiful it was Heaven to be in the same room with her. She was not only beautiful in face and body, her voice had a deep musical note that set up little echoes. When Laelia chose to speak, everyone listened. Even if I must still wait longer for Tadek, the thrill of going to see Laelia was exciting.

Max's father saw by my face that the idea was pleasing.

'We will go over on the night boat. I have booked sleeping accommodation on the train.' He smiled benignly, 'I could have cancelled if you refused. Meet me at Westland Row at seven-thirty, that is only a step from your Gran's house, yes? Bring an overnight bag, with just one change, if you like. And of course a warm coat for the sea trip. And don't forget your passport.'

I foresaw immediately what clothes I should wear, and the leather valise I should bring. It had been a birthday present from Tony Lloyd. For a fleeting moment, I thought of him. I should have 'phoned. I had been discourteous. Then I pushed the thought out of sight, Tony was not important. Later I could explain.

In London the sun was shining. The streets looked remarkably clean and tidy compared to Dublin's streets. It seemed, on that first glimpse, like an enormous complex city, and Dublin like a village. This was the city in the dream-world of my childhood, where Mama and Dada danced the night away . . . where they explored every toyshop for the little daughter he would never see . . . there perhaps was the plush hotel where they loved each other with a passionate tenderness that Mama never found again. . . . 'Somewhere the sun is shining'. . . . where they lay together planning for a future they were not destined to see.

Max's father usually stayed in a hotel in Kensington, quite convenient, he thought, for the address I had for Laelia. We went into the hotel, telling the taxi to wait. When we were shown to our rooms, the old man gave me money for any expenses I might incur and despatched me to find Laelia. He thought it best to rest awhile after the journey, he had scarcely slept at all. We arranged to meet in the dining-room of the hotel at one o'clock. I did not like to tell him that I felt overwhelmed by this huge city, and I was just a little bit frightened. Quite evidently he thought me a very competent young lady.

The taxi-man noted the address I showed him. He assured me we would be there in 'two shakes', and indeed we were. It was a tall block of apartments with balustraded balconies. I waved goodbye to the friendly taxi.

Inside the glass entrance, a doorman came forward to direct me to an elevator. Soon I stood outside the door numbered forty-six. I pressed the bell. When I heard the lock of the door being drawn, I had my warmest smile ready for Laelia.

It was not Laelia. It was Burton.

'I thought you would come,' he said in that well-remembered voice, deep, unique, full of affection. He drew me into the apartment, held me close, and kissed me linger-ingly. Impressions crowded over me, holding me as if for ever in his arms. The satin-smooth touch of his moustache, the aroma of roses from his body, of cigars from his breath. I was taller now, now the magnificence of his body was not so

199

overwhelming. Not so overwhelming, but more than ever fascinating. The great black marks against him in my memory were difficult to see or feel against his virility. Still within the circle of his arms, I heard myself murmuring, 'How tanned you are!'

We were walking now into a sunny room. Beyond the long window there was a balcony with many colourful plants in exotic urns.

'We went away for a week's sunshine, that is where I got the tan. We got the wire along with our letters late last night. I did not show the wire to Laelia. I guessed you would come. She is still asleep. Shall we make coffee for her?'

She is still asleep. He assumed I knew. Did I know? I have often wondered, did I know? There had been times, oh many times, when I had thought of going to Burton. When I had thought of him with longing. Loving Tadek was different, so different and so supreme it must be kept from taint, loving Tadek was a long-term thing. A lifelong devotion that might take a lifetime to fulfil. It would always be there and maybe never attainable. Burton was a sovereign remedy, a solver of problems both practical and fantastical, a need rooted in that erotic feeling of a girl-child for a father. He was the only father-figure I had known. His formidable person encompassed all the buried emotions of my growing up. Did he, perhaps unknowingly, implant a desire for him in the small body he washed and dried and cradled in 'Sunrise' long ago? I trembled with the sudden memory of him, scooping me into his arms, taking me into his bed after Mama had gone to the shop.

Why had I not gone to London last year, or the year before when my course at the Abbey had seemed futile, and not what I was seeking? Why? Did I know about Laelia? Did I know ever since the night Burton had taken her suitcase and walked beside her on to the mail boat? There was something that had always stopped me. Something deeply hidden. Was it the intuitive knowledge that Burton had taken Laelia, not only on to the mail boat, but into his life?

'Laelia!' I said with well-feigned Abbey Theatre astonishment.

Quite genuinely he appeared surprised, but only for a moment.

'Oh,' he smiled teasingly, 'you came to see me? You did not know Laelia is here? We are just back from Madeira, Laelia and I. Now try this coffee.'

My voice was faint, but I managed, 'I did not know you were here. I came to see Laelia, this was the address.'

'Of course, of course, and you shall see her. The Jews, even worldwide, are a small community. I thought you would have heard. They always know everything about each other. Didn't the mother know?'

If she did, she did not tell us. I remembered how puzzled she looked when she read Laelia's last letter.

'You are married then?' I asked, quite unable to strengthen my voice.

He gave me his full, affectionate gaze. Then he kissed me again very slowly, in a way I remembered from years before.

'You must ask Laelia all about that,' he answered, still in that amused, teasing way.

He had arranged a little tray. As a last detail he took a single flower from a balcony plant, laying it on the dainty plate.

'I will tell her you are here, and that you have news that is not good. I think she is more worried about her brother. You will break the news of the mother in your own gentle way? You will understand when you see her.'

He had gone down a short corridor and into a room, closing the door.

All my life, I have remembered that my instinct was to run away. I could have done so. I should have done so. And all my life, I have known that I did not run away because I wanted to see Burton again, I wanted to stand within the aromatic fragrance of him, I wanted to feel his moustache against my lips, his hands firmly drawing me close. Now that I knew about Laelia and Burton, it seemed my desires had come out

201

of fantasy into reality. I have had time since then to feel bewildered shame. I felt no shame then. I did not run away. I waited like one hypnotized.

The door was opened, Burton's voice called me. In a second I was in the luxurious bedroom, and in Laelia's embrace. I knew at once why she had not come to Dublin. She was largely pregnant. She was also more beautiful than I had remembered.

Burton had left the room. We were crying and laughing, kissing and loving, all at the one time. She guessed what I had come to tell. I had the impression that, in a way, her mother's death was a relief to her, a granting of freedom.

She said a strange thing: 'I could have sent money, Burton always gives me plenty. But if I did, she would suspect. If I had money, she would think I was in a production, then I should be sending the newspaper with my name in print. I was offered several parts, then came this,' she patted her hugely swollen stomach, 'so we decided to give me a year off.' She was half-crying, and yet smiling. 'It was worth it, the year of the baby! We have so enjoyed this time!'

I thought of what Gran had said, that Mrs Vashinsky had starved herself to death.

'But Laelia, if you had told your mother that you were married, and expecting . . .'

'But I am not married,' Laelia said quickly. 'Neither of us believes in marriage. It is too great a tie in the theatre, also it is complicated for a Jewess, or would be if my mother was to be a part of the ceremony. You know Jewish mommas!'

Yes, I thought, I know. They are so credulous and so loving.

'And the baby?' I asked timidly. 'Were you pleased?'

Laelia pouted a little.

'Well, no,' she said. 'Not at first! But of course what could I expect? We have been lovers for so long. It was my fault, really, but he forgave me.'

Laelia was quite happy again.

'Then he took this flat. It is fearfully expensive. Do you like it? We are quite thrilled with it. After the baby, which is in three weeks, I will be going to Rome again, this time for rehearsals. Then my life will really begin!'

'Will Burton go too?' I asked.

'Well,' Laelia replied, 'he is my manager and my agent. You know he is a theatrical agent? A very well-known one, even though he started so late. So he cannot be away from London all the time, but he will be with me a lot.' She caught my hand impulsively. 'You aren't angry, darling, are you? I know you had a bad time, a fright. Burton laughed a lot about that when I upbraided him in the beginning, when I got to know him first. He doesn't remember a thing about it. He says you either made it up, or had a bad dream. Kids do, you know!'

'And will the baby go to Rome?' I had to know although I did not want to ask any more questions. Laelia laughed that musical laugh which sent little echoes through my ears.

'But that would be ridiculous,' she said. 'Burton will have the child fostered or adopted. He will know what to do. Don't look so perplexed, darling, it was all a mistake! Best forgotten.'

Laelia pushed back the bedclothes. She was an enormous size.

'Will you help me, darling? Burton usually runs the bath, and helps me to wash. Isn't he really a gorgeous man? He washes me, it is hard for me to lift my arms,' she laughed at my face, 'don't be shocked, darling! I hear him on the 'phone now, so he is probably very busy, as we have been away for a week in Madeira – lovely place, you should go if ever you get a chance, you would love it.'

So I helped Laelia to bath, helped her to dress, brushed her dark hair. Then I watched her selecting a perfume to suit her mood, which she decided to be a happy one. She chatted easily while she attended to her nails, painting them a delicate lustrous colour like the inside of an oyster shell.

Burton came into the bedroom. He was smiling, a man who has heard news to his advantage.

'So I have two lovely women to take to lunch!' he said. 'And where will it be?'

I stood up. 'I must go,' I said. 'I have to meet Max's father in the hotel for lunch.'

'But we can telephone him, tell him you will be along later,' Burton pleaded, holding my hands.

I knew I should go, I made an effort to be decisive, yet I was powerless. I gave the name of the hotel. Burton got the number quickly. He did not speak to Max's father, but gave the message with a firm instruction that it be delivered. I felt I was acting badly, on several counts. I was totally invaded by the necessity to prolong the time with Burton.

In the elevator, Laelia said, 'Lifts always make me queasy.'

Burton was immediately solicitous.

'You are sure you would like to go to lunch, my dear Laelia? We can have lunch sent in, if you like.'

But Laelia, once out of the lift, was able to smile again. It was as we emerged on to the steps that she clutched my arm. 'Something has gone wrong,' she whispered, 'I seem to have water or something on my legs . . .'

Burton had heard. He was a model of efficiency. Within seconds he had hailed a taxi, most solicitously he got Laelia in. He and I followed. He gave the name of the hospital. Within ten minutes we were there. In the taxi he had held Laelia against him, murmuring words of such fervour that, distraught as she was, her eyes closed in ecstasy.

I suppose it was Burton's appearance that opened doors and dispensed with formalities. He was truly a magnificent specimen of manhood, he expected and was accorded the treatment due to a duke. Added to all his other fascinations for me, I had noticed a new degree of distinction. His grammar was now fastidiously well-bred, where long ago it was colloquial.

Laelia was in her private hospital room, nurses and doctors were hovering over her; Burton and I were in an adjoining waiting room. We were both silent. United in concern for Laelia? Or thinking our own thoughts?

At last a doctor came out to the waiting room. There would be no point in waiting. Everything was under control, the lady was in fine fettle. In fact, she had asked for a case with negligées, slippers, etc, to be brought in the evening. Meanwhile, if the gentleman would leave his 'phone number, he would be contacted with the good news, or sooner if necessary. He was free to ring at any time. We were out in the street again, watching for a cruising taxi.

Burton took my arm in a way that said we were together at last. There was no mistaking the way he looked at me.

'Have you ever been in an English pub?' he asked merrily. 'There is a real beauty just around the square. We could have some lunch, and drink to our reunion.'

I followed Burton into the gleaming, crowded pub. Something made me think for a moment of Gran, of her detestation of Burton. Should I feel contempt for myself because I was thinking only of his immense attractiveness, and not for a moment dwelling in pity on Laelia in the throes of childbirth? Laelia, who had been for me a lodestar of beauty for so many years, had resolved herself into a very distant, dim star now.

Burton settled me into the red banquette, as solicitous for me now as he had been for Laelia a few moments before. He was passing nice little compliments on my appearance, my skin, my hair. The hair especially. He seemed so pleased that I had not cut my hair short as was the fashion. I blossomed under this attention. He was holding my hand in his warm hand for a second or two, then reading to me from the menu, then looking into my eyes, in so unveiled a way that I felt colour coming in my face.

All around me were unaccustomed English voices, an air of drive and smartness unlike the homely Dublin pub of Tony Lloyd's choice. London and Dublin were so many centuries apart that totally different standards would surely obtain. It is hard now to believe that an intelligent girl should have had so many pathetic fallacies. My idea that in London the code of ethics would permit a loss of virtue to go scot-free, was as false as the childish notion that a rose shedding its petals was a special sign to me.

Yet that long-ago day, a loss of virtue became a fixed idea as Burton's lunch proceeded. He gave me the thought that he and I should have a few hours out of time, a little space that would be ours alone, not accountable to anyone in the outside world, not even accountable in my mind to the Recording Angel. I began to see how such a time, spent with Burton in the lovely balconied apartment (to which we must return, he said, for Laelia's suitcase), how such a time would bring together all my past and all my present, and banish forever the nightmare that at times woke me up, panting and longing for I knew not what. I accepted the conveyed idea that Burton would be the one, the legitimate one surely, to show me what awakening means. Momentarily I remembered Chersy telling me that the first time . . . but I quickly forgot Chersy. I did not want to recall advice or warning. I wanted only to bask in the light of Burton's dark-brown eyes, to listen to his lowered voice telling me he would not hurt me, he would not allow any hurt to come to me, he would deal with me so gently. Beneath the table, the pressure of his hand on my thigh assumed an end to resistance. If there had ever been any resistance.

In the late afternoon we returned to the tall apartment block. Going up in the elevator, Burton held me close, his mouth joyously on mine. I felt the hard outline of his body urgently pressing against me. Now there could be no keeping us apart. Trying not to hurry, trying to be outwardly sedate, we walked along the corridor past the numbered doors. My nostrils were full of the aromatic fragrance that Burton's body distilled.

Outside the door numbered forty-six, Max's father was standing in an attitude of one prepared to wait. He looked a little weary. He lifted his hat courteously. His silvery hair glowed like the halo of an angel in stained glass. Urbanely, he acknowledged our approach. Burton was equal to anyone's urbanity. He introduced himself as my stepfather.

'And of course, you are Max's father. I have met your son, a distinguished man indeed. We have come from the hospital. Laelia, whom you know of course, is now confined. Oh, thank you. I feel sure she will be fine – she is in good hands.'

Burton had opened the door, and ushered us into the apartment. The sun was shining through the balcony window, the elegant lounge seemed freshly dusted, the cushions puffed. I took the old man's hat, and stick. He sat down.

Burton was all hospitality.

'A cool drink, perhaps?' he offered, going towards a cabinet. 'Tea? Coffee? So warm today.'

An iced lemonade was accepted, Burton chatted away, quite at ease. I remember little but the shattered feeling of being engulfed in disappointment. It seemed that the old man had come for me because we must take an earlier departure to Paris. Burton agreed that, indeed yes, all times of travel were apt to alter in the last few weeks, he himself had found it so on his recent vacation. Security regulations, he supposed.

'Security regulations?' I repeated faintly.

'Yes, of course, my little dear,' he answered quite casually, 'hadn't you noticed? They are digging up Hyde Park to make air-raid shelters. They seem to think war will come any day now.'

Max's father seemed in agreement that war was inevitable. He was of the opinion that Ireland would declare neutrality.

'Good place to be then,' said Burton, with just the faintest shade of contempt in his voice. 'Laelia's brother would do well to get home. She has been worried about him. Now, would you excuse us? My step-daughter promised to fill a case for Laelia, only take a moment.'

I followed Burton into the bedroom. He did not shut the door, but walked to the far side of the room, stepping into a little dressing room hung around with suits and coats. He took several notes from his wallet and tucked them into my pocket. In a low voice, he said, 'Don't forget who needs you, little one. Ditch the old man on the way back, I will be waiting. Promise.'

207

I nodded. He kissed me very briefly. 'No,' he said loudly, 'this must be the case. Now, I am sure you will know the right things to go into it. Some cosmetics too, perhaps?'

I heard the two men talking desultorily while I packed the case. In a few minutes we had left the apartment. A taxi brought us back to the hotel. Max's father asked for afternoon tea to be sent to his room. 'Do join me, my dear,' he said kindly.

In my own room, I took out the money Burton had put in my pocket. It was a hundred pounds. The waves of hot feeling he engendered deep inside me began to ebb away. I remembered the golden sovereigns he used to give me after a morning in bed in 'Sunrise'. I still had them in a little box among my treasures in Gran's house.

I looked about the room. There was hotel notepaper on a dressing table and in my bag I had a fountain pen. I wrapped the notes into the writing paper, no message was needed. I sealed the envelope with a firm press of my hand. Then I addressed it to Burton. I went down to the hall of the hotel where I had noticed a kiosk for posting. I did not think Burton would be hurt. Amused, perhaps, but not hurt. It was I that was hurt.

As I came back to the bedrooms, the waiter was bringing in the afternoon tea. I tried to find bright social chatter as I poured out the tea. No words would come. Max's father looked at me with friendly concern.

'Burton is a fine-looking man,' he observed. 'How old would he be, I wonder?'

Burton was not old. Burton would never be old. 'Mama was thirty-eight when she died,' I spaced out the words distinctly, 'and Burton was a couple of years older. I was fifteen then, now I am twenty-four.'

'Hitting up to fifty!' the old man said pleasantly. 'Mind you, he looks ten years younger!'

Hitting up to fifty? Suddenly I was in the old man's arms, crying hopelessly, as I always did when nothing else sufficed.

He seemed to understand.

'Do you good. Do you good,' he murmured.

Chapter Thirteen

Max met us at the Gare St Lazare. It was a meeting of immense affection and emotion between the old man and his son into which I entered fully. I became a daughter and a sister and the friend of a lifetime in a loving reunion. The restoration of happiness was in the air as Max drove us through this wonderful city to their house in the suburb of St Cloud. The night-long distressful thought of my failure to resist the glamorous fascination of Burton seemed to vanish for ever when Max murmured, 'Lia, Lia, Lia,' as if his words were a magic spell of disenchantment. In the car, the old man took my hand and, holding it, gave me that warm benevolent gaze which was becoming an essential part of my contentment.

Their house was, and is, a substantial square edifice behind ivy-covered walls in a leafy garden. My first impression of tall windows opening onto sunny lawns has never changed. In recurring memory, the sun is always shining, there is birdsong nearer than the distant hum of passing traffic.

'I hope you can cook a little, Lia?' Max teased. 'The daily woman confines herself to a little light dusting, and I usually eat in St Cloud.'

'Do not ask the little one to cook dinner – not dinner, Max,' his father said. 'Imagine being in Paris, and cooking one's own dinner!'

I assured them I could make an omelette in three languages.

Max hovered around me while I set the table for lunch, obviously he thought I needed help.

'This is quite a change, Max! Long ago, I was always treated as a little slavey, run back to the car, rinse out my togs and don't leave any sand in them!' I smiled up at him. He was such a comfortable friend, like an old teddy bear.

'Wouldn't dare treat you like that now!' he said.

'Why not, Max? I'm only me.'

He came round the table, and turned me towards him.

'Are you trying to tell me that you don't know? I was completely bowled over when I saw you in the station. You were always special, but now – well, I never saw anyone so, so nice as you. I could look at you all day.'

I was astonished. I gave Max a quick hug. 'You were always kind and nice yourself,' I told him. 'My Gran often recalls sitting beside you in Bray, and spinning along through the Devil's Elbow. And the summer that Laelia joined us for the holiday – we had such fun with Laelia there!'

It was his turn to look surprised. 'Laelia! She was there only because she was Tadek's sister.'

The name was out at last. The name that I had been waiting for since the moment I saw him. I had been faithful for so long to Tadek's injunction to reveal nothing; all the years in Cluny, all the holidays that he had been away, all the days I had searched Sandymount Strand for his familiar presence. Even Phyllis Daly could have given me news of Tadek, and I had never asked her. Patiently, I had always waited until Mrs Vashinsky thought to pass on his letters, maybe after she had reread them for weeks. I believed that no one knew of the shrine inside me where daily I knelt and worshipped, and worshipped even more when I sought a warm refuge in Burton's passion. Above all, the very fact that Tadek, while enjoining silence, had never offered anything – that fact had kept me silent.

'Oh Tadek,' I said casually, 'and how is Tadek?'

Max was sad and serious. Then he glanced at his watch.

'It is a long story, and none of it is good. Unfortunately, I have several consultations during the afternoon. Tonight we will go out to a little place I have found. My father loves going out for dinner. I will fill you in on the details while we dine.'

I did not dare to appear other than contented to wait. Waiting for news of Tadek was the same to me as breathing.

The weather was warm, and the garden was pleasant. We sat under a spreading tree, the old man and I. After a while, his silvery head dropped on his chest, and he slept. There was a quality of childhood about his sleep. I fetched a woollen rug from a couch, placing it about him. Then I walked about the garden, admiring the old house from every angle.

I know now that Max's father had bought this house many years before. He loved Paris, he had lived there in his early years. Max had told me the reason he continued to live in Dublin, instead of returning to Paris, was because his wife had died in Dublin during a visit there to Max's grandparents. Like the Vashinskys, they had ended in Dublin. His wife's grave was the old man's precious link with her, she was still in her twenties when she died. I thought of the marble figure in the Jewish cemetery in Dolphin's Barn. Max could not remember his mother.

After a while, I went into the kitchen. Max's father had brought a Bewley's canister of his favourite brand of tea. When I judged he had dozed enough, I prepared a little trolley with tea and biscuits.

He was refreshed, ready to talk and be talked to. 'You are a very quiet little thing,' he said, 'more goes on inside that curly head than you pretend. Don't you believe in communication – this great new word that is bandied around these days?'

'Oh, I do,' I told him, 'but I like best when people talk to me and tell me things I don't know. I like to learn from communication.'

His smile was genial. He was very pleased.

'Ah ha!' he said. 'And I am the very one who likes to impart

211

wisdom. I should have been a professor in a great university! This is the life that would have suited me. Instead, little education. My father had a stall, here on the Quai de Lyons. He sold books, and he could not read them unless they were Hebrew or Russian books, and there were few enough of them. Just think! Without reading he could judge a book! Just think! Without reading he knew the value. I have seen him pitch a big volume, all studded leather, into the Seine. "Pretentious rubbish," he called it. "That man could not write a book!" Equally, I have seen him smooth his hand over the page as if it were a woman's face. "A lovely book," he would call it. And maybe he would not sell it, but hold it by him. And he could not read it. He could never read it. He was a proud man when I could read in French, then in German, then in English. "Read on that page for me," he would say, "louder! Louder! This is my son. He is eight years! He reads in many books from many lands! Look at him! Listen to him!"'

The old man took my hand, a thing he liked to do.

'Maybe he shouted too loudly,' he continued, with a little break in his voice. 'Jews should never shout too loudly, but they do. Ah yes, all over the world. My father was moved on. Moved on – moved on. He had been in Paris since he was a young man. From Zamość also he came, as the Vashinskys. Many pogroms there were in Zamość. But never so bad as now.'

I told the old man that I knew the story of Zamość. Many times I had heard Mr Vashinsky telling the story, I remembered the folk songs. Would he like me to sing the songs I remembered? We sat there, under the trees, my hand in his. I sang softly all the little songs, many of them in Hebrew, words of which I understood nothing. I could see he was lost in thoughts of his childhood. I, too, was back in the days of Little's Terrace when Tadek came in each night from the College of Surgeons.

When Max came across the lawn, he smiled his thanks to see us so happily at ease together.

That night we had dinner in a small hotel in St Cloud. Afterwards, when the old man had retired, Max suggested that we go for a drive to see the city by night. I was very delighted to do this, but also I felt myself becoming impatient. I had come a long way for some word of Tadek. Was I to be disappointed?

I remember very little about that first view of Paris. I am sure it was wonderful. I have no doubt Max was a good and thoughtful guide. Nothing remains but the conversation Max started when we sat on a bench over-looking the river.

'Tadek is in a concentration camp.'

'Oh Max, surely you mean a labour camp?' I implored.

But he shook his head. 'You may have heard, or read, that Jewish doctors are not permitted to enter the military service in Hungary, instead they work in labour camps. I warned Tadek of this when we were in Vienna. I knew he intended going to Budapest. I warned him because I knew the conditions in labour camps to be extremely severe. Few survive.'

'Max, when you left Vienna, you came to Paris. Why did Tadek go to Budapest?'

Max sat hunched in silence. He began to speak several times, changed his mind, fell silent, and began again.

'Tadek charged me to explain to his mother just what he was doing. He gave me a sum of money for her. My father telephoned to say that you had come to tell him of her death, I was just too late. I set up here then months ago, but this I tell you of Tadek is recent.'

'Was he here?' I asked.

'No,' Max answered. 'I went to the border. He joined a Partisan, or resistance, movement. That was why he went to Budapest. Do you understand?'

I thought I could understand that. It was so typical of Tadek. He always had to go to help . . . even to help a lonely child.

'The Partisans infiltrate these ghettos where the Jews are assembled,' Max said. 'The Germans assemble them for

213

months, whole villages of people, into these ghettos. When they are nearly rotted from frustration, they are put in railway trucks, and sent to the concentration camp. There they may be held for another rotting, then the extermination.'

'You mean . . . they kill them?' I whispered.

'The Partisans swear that thousands are marched into gas chambers. Thousands every day.'

'Oh Max, no.' I began to weep weakly against his sleeve.

'Don't cry for him,' Max said almost roughly, 'cry for me. Every day that passes, I have to convince myself that I am not a coward. I have an interminable argument going on inside that says: you did not go to join the Partisans because you believe Hitler is mad and you will not collaborate in his madness and, oh no, you did not go to join the Partisans because you are a coward, you are a moral coward, you did not join the Partisans because you love peace and learning and civilization, because you cannot bear chaos, and oh no you did not join because you are afraid of pain. You are afraid to die . . .'

I pressed closely against Max's arm.

'Do not torture yourself so, darling Max. I would be afraid of pain too. I would be terrified to die. Is it wrong to love life so much? Of course, it is not wrong to want to live. And Tadek wants to live. He will come through. You will see. I am glad you did not go, Max, we are not all the same. We each act as individuals, each must be true to himself.'

'But do you not care so much for Tadek that this news will break your heart?' Max asked this question in a deeply puzzled tone. I longed to say that my heart was breaking at that very moment, but I had discovered from Burton that there was a duality in my heart. It would be scarcely honest to claim eternal loyalty to one man if I ran after Burton yesterday and wept for Tadek today.

'I do care just as you care, Max.'

Max was still puzzled. 'But I thought you and Tadek were special,' he said.

Now I was on firmer ground. This was the very thing Tadek had forbidden.

'We were only kids,' I answered.

'Tadek gave me a message for you when I should go to see his mother. You are to be happy, he said. That is the message.'

I was silent, then. All too well I knew what the message meant. I was to be happy without him. He had said there was always hope. Was I to abandon hope now? Be happy some other way, that was the message.

'Max, do not worry about the argument with yourself any more. Tadek will find a way to save himself, you will see.'

We were walking towards the car, when Max said, 'I know about Laelia.'

'Oh Max, I am sorry,' I put my arm through his, 'I know you thought the world of Laelia.'

We stood still as of one accord. Even in the dim light I could see the sheer surprise in Max's face.

'Laelia!' he repeated, 'I never even noticed her. You were always the one for me. Always. There has never been anyone else since the first day we took old Toozy out to Sandymount strand. Never. You must know that. Of course, you know it!'

All I could whisper to Max was a tender thank you. How could I hurt him by telling him that I had never given him a thought, except when my memory turned to the old happy days in Bray? Too late the realization flooded through me that when I went to Max's father for help with Mrs Vashinsky's funeral I was, in Max's eyes, turning not to the father but to the son. In his eyes, I was using the opportunity of the poor woman's death to bring myself back into his life because of course I knew he cared for me! There was no use in telling him now, that I did not know, and in fact did not believe he had such fond recollection of the child who foisted herself on the Vashinskys. How could I tell him that I had come with his father so that I would see Laelia? The rest of the journey to Paris had been because the old man pleaded need of company.

215

We were walking arm-in-arm along the riverside. There were glass-topped pleasure boats passing on the river. We could hear music, we could see people dancing. I wondered if what Max had just said was simply the result of this starlit night in the romantic city of Paris.

'Oh, Max, I wish there was enough time for you to show me all of this city. In two days, two new overwhelming cities!'

'But London is nothing! Well, nothing compared to Paris. Paris is many cities, one opening out of the other. Even the street names live. Do you remember that writer you had discovered that last summer in Bray? You made us all listen while you read out the story. We were up on Bray Head looking down at the town around the curving bay. Surely you remember? It was a story about a town where, on the ramparts, the citizens kept the great stone statues of their ancient heroes in full battle dress. They were guardians of the city. The citizens had grown lazy and careless because their enemies had long believed those dead heroes would come to life and defeat all invaders. I remember the name of the story, the *Sword of Welleran*.'

'I remember,' I said, '*Tales of Wonder*, by Lord Dunsany.'

'And you told us,' said Max, pressing my arm to show that his recollection was fond, 'that Lord Dunsany had got the inspiration for the story from walking in Paris, noting each boulevard dedicated to a long dead patriot, or valiant soldier.'

'Imagine your remembering that!' I murmured.

'I remember it every time I drive through Paris,' Max laughed, 'and the little actress you were then to act out the story!'

In the house, Max made some coffee. We sat out in the garden, still as warm as it had been in the afternoon. Some flower that scents the air at night-time was giving forth a heady perfume. The wine we had had at dinner, the romantic words by the river, above all the warmth of a special friend, all disposed me to think fondly of Max. I tried, but I could not keep it up. My thoughts were seeking out Tadek in that new and awful place, a concentration camp. If he should be caught with the Partisans . . .

Max had repeated a question: 'You must have quite a crowd of admirers back in Dublin?'

With a mighty effort, I set my mind to the task of being a dutiful guest. I tried to entertain him with a funny description of my double life, of office and theatre, emphasizing how little time I had left over for party-going. He asked a lot of questions about the Peacock. His father had told him how enjoyable his evening of our show had been. He wished he had been there.

'Any special admirers?' Max asked.

I remembered Tony Lloyd. Was he special? Maybe he thought he was.

I smiled affectionately at Max, holding out my hand to him. 'No one,' I said lightly, 'has ever replaced my old friends.'

'And are you fully set then on making acting your career?' his voice was persistent.

'Acting? Oh, Max, I am not so sure as I used to be. Maybe something else in the theatre. Not acting.' There was no need to tell Max that the real career in my life had taken root in my soul on that night Tadek had climbed through Mrs Mayne's window.

We sat there, holding hands, in the perfumed garden. I could hear Max's deep, even breathing. We should have been peacefully communing in the silence. I knew we were not. As quickly as his voice ceased, my thoughts flew to Tadek. As quickly as I recalled my thoughts, I felt that Max had something to say, he was formulating some sort of a speech. I did not want him to say something, I knew not what, that would force any sort of a decision on me. I had waited so long that, although I had learned since yesterday to distrust myself, I was again prepared to wait.

Max was not a psychologist by accident. He was deeply perceptive. At last he spoke.

217

'There will be War soon, European War. Europe will be again as it was in Napoleon's time, destruction everywhere. This time it will be a hundred times worse – modern technology has seen to that. As it happens, a year ago, I accepted a teaching post in an American university. I need that experience. Paris was to fill in the waiting year, and mainly Paris because my father has this house, and I have colleagues here who were with me in Vienna. After America, I plan to come back here – if Paris is still standing.'

I was silent, almost holding my breath. He was coming to his own decision.

'Tadek spoke a lot of your talent. I think you need another while to explore that talent. No one, looking at you, young and lovely, could ask you to give up the chance of a career so rewarding and so satisfying.'

Still I held my breath. Tadek had talked of me to Max, a lot. That was wonderful, that was something to be pondered when I was alone.

'I have decided that I could, for old times' sake, ask you to do one thing for me. Would you, in the kindness of your heart, visit with my father back in Dublin? He has fallen quite in love with you, you know. When he writes or telephones, he seldom gives me a satisfactory account of his health. I am in touch with his doctor in Dublin, of course, but a personal account of him from someone he loves and trusts, I would appreciate that.'

I hoped Max did not see the relief that must have been reflected in my face.

'Of course I will go to see him, Max. I love him very much, I am proud to be his friend. I will write to you regularly, you can rely on that.'

Max's face was sombre. 'When war comes, all communication will be difficult. Travel too – probably out of the question.'

When we parted at the top of the stairs, Max held me in his arms most affectionately, and I was responsive. He pressed

218

his face against my hair. There was no suggestion of restrained passion, no recurrence of romantic words. Max was in full control of his senses, or he had had second thoughts.

I was kissed again at the railway station, and we were bestowed with great care into our compartment. Max had added travelling rugs to our luggage. He bought magazines and bonbons. He fussed a great deal as if we were parting for ever. At the last, he could not find his voice, tears stood in his eyes.

I was sorry indeed to see him so upset. When we were young, he was always so capable, so powerful, always the one who had the money for our little needs, the one who was resourceful and perceptive. To see his bearded face almost in tears from the sorrow of parting with his beloved father caused tears to run down my own face. He kissed me again at the carriage window, and then the train was moving off. I drew up the window. The old man took my hand, he lay back with closed eyes. I knew my hand gave him comfort. I knew he was tired, and would sleep. At last I was alone with my thoughts.

As the weather was so good, the journey was not arduous. We stayed in London overnight. I 'phoned the hospital where Laelia was. She had a baby son, and both were doing fine. The old man had dinner served in his room for both of us. He had slept a good deal on the train, and on the Channel crossing, so he was relaxed and talkative over dinner. There was no better companion in the world. Indeed, he was a citizen of the world, for he had been everywhere, lived everywhere. His memory was retentive of the smallest detail, a colour in a picture, a phrase from a book. There was only one subject to which he never referred in talking about his own long-ago, that was his dead wife. I had my own very special feeling for secret shrines.

We parted at Westland Row Station. I would not allow him to hire a taxi for the short distance I had to walk. His limousine was waiting, and he was driven away. He had handed me an envelope. 'You are to use this as you see fit,' he had said. He was smiling back at me because I had promised to come and see him very soon. On the envelope was written, 'The money from Tadek, why not give it to Gran – Love Max.'

Gran was expecting me. The little house looked bright and neat, as she did herself. The cup of tea was ready to pour out. She greeted me forty times, welcoming me back as if I had been gone a month, instead of only a few days. There has never been so kindly-loving a woman as my Gran. She loved everyone. She loved company, and yet if she was there all alone, she was contentedly happy fixing her little house, setting out a simple meal so correctly, down to the laundered napkin in its bone ring. She managed her meagre money like a little financial genius.

I loved her so much that I had firmly decided I was going to shelter her with a great avalanche of lies. She was too old now to struggle with unsavoury truths.

'Now, don't start talking about your trip to Paris until you have had a cup of tea. No, not a word! And a little piece of toast. Look, I made it at the range. Look, I have it here in the oven keeping hot. Now, isn't that nice? Lots of butter on it! And another drop of tea in your cup. I'm delighted to see you. Do you think you should go to bed? Oh you feel fine. Oh that's good. I'm up since six. I'm delighted you got back safe. The weather kept up? Oh well, we often have summer storms . . . I know that mail boat . . . I remember one time, of course it was in the winter . . .'

At last the little breakfast was finished. Gran poured out the last cup of tea to keep it by her while we talked.

'Now,' she settled herself into her armchair, 'begin about Laelia. Did you find her?'

So I launched into the story of Laelia. She could not come home because – now, a little shock, Gran – she was in a nursing home having her first baby. Oh yes, very happily married to a theatrical agent.

220

'Um,' Gran mused over that, 'wasn't that odd now! Poor Mrs V. had the feeling she must have taken up with someone! But sure, wouldn't the mother have welcomed news like that?'

'Well you see, Gran,' I began more prevarications, 'the husband is not a Jew.'

'Now, that might have worried Mrs V. all right. She had strong feelings about religion, so she had. And how is Laelia, then?'

'She's grand, Gran. She has a baby boy – a little beauty of a baby. A lovely little fellow!'

Gran was very pleased with this, a grandson for her dear dead friend.

'Couldn't we get a little matinée jacket for the poor little thing, and send it to Laelia?'

'Of course, Gran,' I replied loyally, 'we'll get a really nice one down in Henry Street on Monday, I could do that during lunch time.' I knew Gran's fallible memory would assume something had been done as soon as mentioned.

'There is something, though, that troubles me,' said Gran plaintively. 'It would have made poor Mrs V. so happy, she was so independent you know, if Laelia could have sent her some money. It troubles me to think Laelia must be hard-up and now with a baby.'

I took the envelope from my handbag.

'Look, Gran. The money was on its way – from Laelia and from Tadek. It was just too late. Now they want you to have it, you were so good to their mother.'

Now Gran began to cry. I held her in my arms, noticing how she seemed to have got smaller. She put her hands out in a gesture of refusal although she could not speak.

'Gran, love, look at the envelope where Max has written the message. It is for you.'

For the moment, she had forgotten about Max. Now she dried her eyes.

'Ah, tell me about Max,' she said. 'Don't you know he was

always my favourite? A massive build of a young lad! More of a man than the other boy. Always so polite, nothing was ever too much trouble for him. Tell me about Max. Is he married yet? Now begin at the beginning – and about Paris. Wait now, I'll make another pot of tea, I want to hear all about Paris.'

What I had seen of Paris could be told in a moment. But, along with the other lies, what were a few more? Gran got a tourist guide to Paris, pieces of information garnered from many a book I had read. She finally accepted the money which would be lodged in the Dublin Savings Bank on Monday. By some miracle, she managed to save an odd pound here and there, birthdays and Christmasses were eked out of her little account.

One lie I did not have to tell. Gran had given Tadek only a passing mention. I am sure she meant to ask more particularly from interest, and not from any special reason. I had kept my secret well.

Chapter Fourteen

On Monday morning, Chersy saw me crossing Merrion Street, and she waited at the entrance to our offices.

'You are in for a nice row, I can tell you,' and her voice was full of rich anticipation. 'Tony Lloyd nearly went bonkers! What got into you to run out on the party? He must have spent fifty quid on the eats and drinks! No message! When I got back from the hairdresser, the C.O. told me you had taken your holiday leave, but you never said why the sudden decision. God! I'll never forget Tony Lloyd's face. He was fuming mad!'

She went on and on even after we had started our day's work. Every time I opened my mouth to make excuses, she started off again, until finally the C.O. shouted at us to get on with a bit of honest toil. I passed a note to Chersy inviting her to lunch in the Country Shop. In my handbag I had found the money Max's father had given me to visit Laelia. I remembered it was quite a lot.

Chersy, having accepted as an adequate excuse for *her* that there had been a sudden death in my household, did not think it would be a good enough excuse for Tony Lloyd.

'He will be too angry to believe that you ran around to his flat, and up to his office. He made us wait for the first drink, every minute telling us that of course you would turn up. That you had just got delayed! That you were usually a very punctual and considerate person. Francesca made things worse. Every minute she was saying she thought she really ought to go home, she was feeling so tired. Tony had got that

223

friend of his for her, what's his name, Leo something, a nice fellow – he might as well have got the hall porter, she treated him like dirt. . . . Well, she did until the drink started being given out and that was near eleven o'clock. Oh boy, has she a capacity, that Francesca! At one time, I found she was lying across my Denis! I soon put a stop to that! But that was hours later. Once Tony Lloyd started to drink, he poured it out like water. In the beginning it was funny – what times he could forget you had let him down – we played postman's knock like schoolkids. God! That Tony is a tough coort; the drunker he got, the more athletic! He'd have you fighting for your virtue with your back to the wall! Standing up! God! One time Denis had to threaten to give him a puck! How do you handle him at all?'

I never got to telling Chersy that Tony had never treated me roughly, his 'coort' was well within the bounds of restraint, gentle and acceptable. Once Chersy got into a story, particularly one in which she and Denis shone so brilliantly, well, there was no stopping her.

'One time, during the night, Denis told me that your friend Francesca had got Tony in the bed! Oh, Lia – what do you see in him? The effect the drink had on him! He started blowing about his college winning the Leinster Schools Cup. Denis hadn't known about Tony being capped for Ireland. Tony doesn't exactly blow, but we got some famous match in every boring detail – well, it would have been twice as boring if we hadn't all been squiffy by this time. Tony had this fellow, Gladys's fiancé, and himself, and Denis, down in a scrum – that must have been after Tony was bedded with Francesca – and the girls had to throw in a tennis ball. God! Such mullacking and the fellows taking advantage. We were in bits!'

I found my mind was drifting away to the leafy garden in Paris. Through the window of the Country Shop, I could see the leafy foliage of the chestnut trees across the road in Stephen's Green. The weather was superb.

'Chersy, let's go and walk in the Green before we go back to the office.'

'God!' she said, laughing. 'You're not even listening to me. Tony passed out – he was bullifants. (My Dad says Denis holds his jar like a king.) Denis and I got the others out. Then Denis got Tony to bed. We tidied up, put out the lights, and locked the door. I saw Tony down town on the Saturday after, so he's all right. I wasn't speaking to him, I was on a tram.'

That night I wrote a note of apology to Tony, and I posted it to his flat. I had not the courage, nor the desire, to go to his office. For one thing, he might not be alone. I explained in the note about the death of Mrs Vashinsky, and the sub-sequent journey to Paris – hence the delay in getting in touch. I mentioned that I had gone both to his office and to his flat on that day but unfortunately without a pen or paper to leave a note.

I was, actually, extremely sorry for being discourteous; I was quite shocked at the debacle he had made of the party; I did not, purposefully, make mention of any further rendez-vous. When a week passed without acknowledgement of my note, I knew Tony had crossed my name from his book. Although we worked in the same Civil Service department, our offices were located in different wings of the building, and in fact we had scarcely ever seen each other during the nine to five. I observed in myself that, as each day passed, I drew a freer breath of relief.

'I believe your man is spending his lunch hour over in O'Neill's,' Chersy volunteered, 'and every night in Boles. Tom, the barman, told Denis that the poor lad is nursing a broken heart!'

'Chersy, please don't refer to him as my man. He never was.'

'Ah, it's only an expression!' Chersy laughed at my solemn face. 'Cheer up! You are free again. I used to love that hectic feeling of being able to play the field. Game for anything! Of

225

course,' she added staunchly, 'I wouldn't really swop Denis, even if being engaged gets a bit dull.'

Now I devoted myself singlemindedly to Gran, and to the Peacock. The Acting School year was coming to an end. We were putting on an Irish one-acter, 'Spreading the News' by Lady Gregory; the balcony scene from 'Romeo and Juliet'; and a Spanish play, 'Cradle Song', this last because there were more females in the school now than males and 'Cradle Song' called for a convent of nuns. Francesca had been given Juliet, Gladys had the main dialogue in Lady Gregory's play, and I had the young nun's rôle in 'Cradle Song'. It was a sentimental, rather unreal part, but easy to project. Secretly, I would have fancied Juliet. I would have preferred a statement of ecstasy from woman to man, rather than from nun to girl. However, I knew Francesca was a wonderful Juliet. She had learned so much during the years in the School it was almost unbelievable. On stage, she brought everything of acquired art to her part. Off stage, there was no difference. She remained unresponsive as a friend, slow on the uptake, a bit dreary.

Gran had got a handyman from the narrow street to clear out the little back bedroom, which had been Mrs Vashinsky's. Her possessions were few. I kept all her letters and photographs, the balalaika, and the big Hebrew book.

Together Gran and I chose a wallpaper of birds and flowers, with matching curtains. The handyman constructed a narrow wardrobe and corner dressing table. He painted all the wood a pale creamy colour. It was a lovely little room. Gran had recovered a tub chair, one of the pieces that came from Mama's room in 'Sunrise'. A small chest made a bedside table to hold my books, and a small brass candle holder that Burton had bought in an antique shop long ago. The next expense, Gran said, would be to get in the electricity. She did not care to be hurried in acquiring modern improvements. She got far more pleasure from the long slow planning, replanning, and laborious saving. 'Rushing into something you might regret' was a sort of reminder-text we might have hung on the wall. We still took our baths in the long hip bath, sheltered by the Chinese screen.

Sometimes when I spent an evening with Max's father, he referred to Gran's little house.

'Don't let it go,' he warned, 'it could be a valuable property. Sooner or later those old parishes along the river will give way to arterial roads. You see it happening in finer cities than Dublin. The commerce lanes must be open and uncluttered. Dublin is a mediaeval city, it is not geared to modern transport. In the States and in Canada, where the motor is king, already they have five-lane highways. There they have the space in advance of the traffic, here we have sixteenth-century streets waiting for the traffic of the twentieth century. Those old narrow streets must go within the next twenty years. You tell Gran to secure her rights.'

My policy with Gran was to tell her only what would make her happy, and nothing to cause her worry.

'I do not know if she owns the place,' I told the old man, 'or if she has long since stopped paying rent. Maybe her landlord died.'

It seemed that by sheltering one of my old people, I was causing the other to lose sleep. On a later visit, he took up the subject again:

'I have been thinking about Gran's house when I cannot sleep. You know, Dublin Corporation can get an injunction to acquire property. They fulfil the law if they offer the tenants alternative accommodation. Would Gran like to have a Corporation house out in the new estate at Crumlin? They are building thousands of these slum-clearance houses.'

'Crumlin? Where is that? She would die if anything happened to her little house. She loves every brick in it.'

'Find out, little curly head, if Gran pays any rates. Find out anything you can, and let me know. To me the matter is urgent if I am to get a night's sleep.' He was smiling in his benign way, nevertheless it was a command.

So one evening after tea, very casually I asked:

227

'Would you let me pay the rates this year, Gran? I am feeling rich with the rise I got.'

She looked at me over her spectacles, an amused look. 'Sure don't you know the rates are only a shilling a year, honey child? A shilling a year was the fixed rate, some sort of a token payment under some old law. It was something to do with your grandfather serving the Queen in India – you know he was an army man. What is that word, oh yes, in lieu of. In lieu of part pension, they gave us the house at the shilling a year. Of course, they deducted the cost of the house out of his lump sum.'

'What lump sum, Gran?'

'Ah, in those days you got a lump sum coming out of the army, so much for each serving year.'

'And they took the cost of the house out of that?' I queried very gently.

'They did,' said Gran, 'sixty pounds, and the shilling a year. The Corporation man comes to collect it. Sixty pounds was a lot of money fifty years ago, I often told you that story when you were little, how my mother made me marry him, and he fifteen years older than me, and a first cousin of mine as well. I hadn't even to change the name. And you know,' she whispered glancing around to see if perhaps the walls had ears, 'he was a selfish man. Now I never told you that before. He was selfish about everything. He didn't want to make a will to give me the house. It is not nice to live with a selfish person . . .'

I was wondering how to return to the wanted information, so I interrupted her story in an awed tone, 'Oh Gran, I am sure sixty pounds was a huge amount of money then.'

'Ah,' she said smiling, 'and I often got it hard to find the shilling on the due date, long ago.'

'But of course, Grandfather did make the will, didn't he, Gran?'

'Only because my own mother stood over him with a bottle of John Jameson for a reward.'

'Sure I suppose you have mislaid the will, he's dead so long now?' I tried to sound flippant.

Gran was quite indignant. 'Well, I am surprised at you, and you in the Civil Service, and with such a good education. I have not lost the will . . . Certainly not. And it is a proper will too, not like the one poor Marie made for that Burton to put loops in. And what's more, I have the title deeds to the house along with it. And the grave-papers are there too. They are all in the army envelope in a Becker's tea caddy in the picnic basket under the bed. Ah, do you remember the picnics to the Strawberry Beds? Now that's a place I'd like to see again. The Strawberry Beds was the best of all, such a lovely hostelry, a nice Englishman. Watkins, wasn't it? Not too far to travel out along the Conyingham Road, then turn off at Chapelizod, up Knockmaroon. I was there when there was no road, and we followed the river . . .'

Gran had quite forgotten that Cluny was beside the Strawberry Beds, rather where the Strawberry Beds used to be. A change of ownership in the riverside tavern had brought an end to the picnic site long ago.

I told Max's father all that Gran had told me including the location of the papers in the Becker's tea caddy. He pursed his lips. 'And her own will? Did she mention, is that in the tea caddy?'

I scolded him gently. I had no idea if Gran had made a will. As I told him, she was a very independent woman, even in small matters she would not be, as she often said, 'beholden'. He was looking for things to worry about, and he must not, or I should be very vexed with him. Quite obviously he did not believe I could be angry, and he was not content to leave the matter of Gran's house to chance.

'You go on with your theatricals. I have a little plan of my own.'

Everything was forgotten then in preparation for our last big night at the Peacock. We had completed the course. On our night's showing, certificates would be awarded. Perhaps the

Abbey would offer us, or some of us, membership of the Company. That was each one's secret dream. With certificate in hand, we could approach other companies. We could go to England for theatre work, or even to America.

We had been impressed that a certificate from the Abbey was an 'open sesame' to the theatrical world. All we had to do was to get the certificate – not everyone did. We were told ghastly tales of stage fright, blank mind, melting make-up, blinding mascara, sheer nervous clumsiness, toppling wigs, acted tears turning into hysterical weeping, likewise with acted chuckles – beware the asinine bray when you intended a drawing-room ripple. Many actors who look just right, and can act more than adequately, do not have retentive memories. The actor who depends utterly on the prompter is a great trial to others on the stage with him, and is loathed with bitter loathing by all directors.

All of these, and many more strictures, became our daily diet. If we were keyed up, full of dramatic nervous tension, suicidal and heroic, depressed and hilarious – well, it was a wonderful ecstasy to be young with it. Acting is all tension, and it is the relief from all tension. The reward for great acting is great: the actor lives intensely, fully, within himself, and equally intensely outside himself in the rôle. To be paid for doing it is the world's most beautiful bonus.

The entire night was one to live in the memory for ever. Nothing went wrong, and everything went most pro-fessionally. Everyone was congratulating everyone else. I thought Francesca was probably the most heartbreaking Juliet I would ever see. She drew an aching desire from her words, she looked utterly, sweetly nubile. She had long, long silky hair which she cast back from her shoulders to reveal the innocent passion of her childish face.

At the end of the three performances, the Abbey directors made little speeches, and we were called on stage to receive our certificates. As Francesca passed close to me, she whispered urgently, 'I've got to see you after the show!'

230

Gran and Phyllis and Jacques were there, of course. Jacques had thawed, he was smiling, and applauding with the rest. Max's father sat beside them, mopping his eyes, and being pleasant to Aunt Julia. He had issued his invitation for supper in the Shelbourne to include Gladys and Francesca with their escorts, and of course Chersy and Denis. He was very fond of Chersy; 'Quite a character,' he always said, 'a friend for a lifetime.'

Berny and Lucille, the old faithfuls, had come to see the honour of Cluny upheld. Lucille never had a boyfriend, so she came on her own. Berny, serene and comely and deeply immersed in her medical studies, was accompanied by a handsome young doctor. In a year or so she would be qualified.

The old man had made marvellous arrangements for the supper. We had a room all to ourselves, except for a piano-playing lady who had been hired to keep the background filled with soft music. Max's father was especially attentive to Gran, assuring her that nothing would give him greater pleasure than to see her a 'bit tiddly', as she said she would be. I suspected he had some motive in mind. I knew he was still concerned about Gran's will.

I was enjoying myself enormously and the night was nearly over when I saw Berny signalling to me.

'There's someone wants to speak to you urgently – up in the ladies. It is Francesca. I'll go with you.'

Francesca had been crying. This was unusual, to say the least, normally she seemed incapable of showing real feeling, or indeed real interest. All that belonged to the stage.

'I'm in trouble,' she said in a tearful voice. 'And it is all your fault!'

'What kind of trouble,' I asked, very surprised, 'and how is it my fault?'

'You know damn well what "in trouble" means! Acting the innocent! I only went to that party to please you. I never go to parties. I hate men. It's all your fault.'

Berny stepped over beside Francesca. 'How long?' she asked.

Francesca glared at her. 'Who are you?' she asked aggressively.

'I'm a doctor – Berny is my name – friend of Lia's.'

Francesca's manner changed abruptly. Tears fell again. 'For God's sake, help me,' she wept. 'Help me to get rid of it.'

'How long?' repeated Berny.

'I only realized this week that I have skipped the third time, that's June, July and August.'

'Good Heavens!' Berny said. 'Three months is much too late to do something safe and simple. It is even too late for a planned abortion – if people do such things. Why did you wait so long?'

The tears fell faster than ever. They were not tears of sorrow, rather of bitter desperation. She muttered something about 'never being regular.' Then she rounded on me.

'Why didn't you come to your bloody party? It's all your fault. You kept us all sitting there waiting for you, la de da as usual! I thought I would show you something – when you came, I'd be in bed with your fella!'

I felt agonized, horrified. 'So it is . . . it is . . . Tony's baby . . . !

'La de da! Listen to Miss Prissy! I don't go in for telling lies! Yes! Your beloved's baby!'

'But why?' Berny asked in astonishment. 'Why, if it was all only a game to make Lia take notice?'

'Because I wanted it then,' Francesca fairly snapped at her, 'I had got myself worked up. I just plain wanted to know what it is all about. And anyway, it's all your fault. Your marvellous Tony kept pouring drink into me.'

She fell to weeping again. I tried to say I was sorry. I was sorry, but surely I was not to blame? Berny crumpled up some toilet paper, and wetting it, began to clean Francesca's face.

'Come to St Mel's hospital tomorrow at six. You come too,

Lia, bring money. Ask for room eighty. Pull yourself together, Francesca. You don't want the world to know. Show no sign of this to anyone. Come on – the party's over.'

I don't know which party she was talking about, but we went down to join the guests. Soon that party, too, was over.

As I had thought, Max's father had his own way of finishing the night. Outside Gran's house, he sent his driver away with an order to come back in an hour. Gran fussed around unsteadily, making a pot of tea. I sat, heavy-hearted, and waited.

'Did I tell you, Mrs Brabazon, about my son, Max?'

Gran assured him that she knew Max well, a lovely chap, a massive build of a young lad. The old man was very gratified to hear this. But even the best of sons, sons who are doing well in the world, good sons, present problems, problems that have to be faced when we are old, and being old don't want to face problems.

'For instance now, Mrs Brabazon, my death could ruin my beloved son. Could ruin him financially.'

Gran had sat down. Her legs were, she always said, the first thing to go tiddly. She fixed her eyes as best she could on the old man and she set herself to listen.

'I am a very wealthy man. I did not set out to be. Indeed, wealth is a burden. My own needs are few now. But wealth accumulates. Am I to throw it away? All too soon the value of money becomes less. All too soon. Forty years ago, I bought a picture for fifty pounds. That fifty pounds kept a young man in food for a year, he lived to paint more pictures (several of which I bought). Yesterday, I sold that first picture for four thousand pounds. In a few years, the buyer will sell it for double that. I did not want to sell, I had grown fond of the picture. I do not need the money, the buyer pestered me for months. I pitched the price so he would give up. I should be so lucky! He pestered me! He collects.'

Gran was enthralled. She loved a story. And the old man told it so well, his hands gesturing. She knew instinctively

233

that he was going to make a point, she did not dream it would concern her.

'So it is another four thousand pounds for me to put away for Max – along with the monies, the pictures, the antiquities, the houses! And will he ever see a penny, or a picture, when I die? And, Mrs Brabazon, you and I know that we all must die some time. We know, we see it in our fading eyes, our tired limbs.'

Gran did not feel old, but she mopped up a tear for her poor old friend and his destitute son, who would never get a penny or a picture.

'And why, Mrs Brabazon, will our poor Max have not a rag to dust a fiddle when I have passed on to the next life?'

Gran shook her head in puzzlement. She simply could not guess.

'Because of the death duties, Mrs Brabazon. The state will take all. The death duties are excessive and prohibitive. . . . My poor son would have to sell everything to pay the dreadful death duties on his father.'

No one else would have been persuaded, but Gran was. Knowing her so well, I could see her old brain conning the story, applying the moral to herself.

'And what way at all, sir, could a person get over the death duties, and still keep something?'

The old man looked around as if about to confide a secret. In a lowered voice, he told her.

'I had a deed of gift drawn up, giving all my goods to Max. I lodged the deed in Max's name in his bank. I have a good solicitor, he is a cousin of mine, Josh Farbor. From time to time, if I make a sale, the detail is withdrawn from the deed, and the money put to the credit side. I am, in fact, Max's business manager.'

So that was the happy ending of the story! Gran's eyes shone with delight. Max's future was a glorious one, Max's father had outwitted a grasping government.

When the old man was ready to go, he took an envelope from his pocket.

'This is for my little curly head. Buy yourself a trinket in memory of tonight. You were lovely, and a grand little actress.' He gave my hand an extra little press of reassurance.

Gran was still talking about the story as we prepared for bed.

'Such a very clever man. What was the name of that solicitor? Gives you so much to think about!'

In my own room, I opened the envelope. There was a cheque for two hundred pounds, and on a slip of paper he had written: Josh Farbor, Esq., with an address in Dame Street.

Gran went to the solicitor in due course. The title to her little house was investigated. The gift deed was drawn up. Everything was in order. Henceforth the shilling a year was receipted to me.

I went to the hospital the following evening after the Shelbourne party. Francesca was standing on the steps. We went in together, and a porter directed us to room eighty. Berny was there, looking very professional in her white coat and dangling stethoscope. She came to the point immediately.

'Francesca, you told me yesterday you had skipped three periods, but normally you are irregular. Is there any other reason you suspect you are pregnant?'

Francesca pressed her hands against her breasts.

'They feel different,' she said.

'Anything else?' Berny queried.

Francesca stood up, and opened her coat.

'Look,' she indicated, with disgust, the line from her breast to her pelvis. There was the slightest, most delicate curve across her navel. 'I never let myself put on weight. I hate fat.'

'Yes, I see,' Berny responded. 'Do you have any medical history? Such as diabetes, or lung-trouble, or blood-pressure?'

'Never!' Francesca spat out the words almost savagely. 'Never. I was never sick in my life. Never.' She glared at me with loathing.

'What about the irregular periods?' Berny asked.

'What about them?' demanded Francesca.

'Did your mother ever suggest medical advice about the irregular periods? Or didn't you tell her?'

'Yes, I told her,' replied Francesca, resuming her usual listless and apathetic manner, 'and when I told her that sometimes I missed two months, she just said, I could miss nine months so long as I kept away from the fellas.'

There was a small silence, then Francesca continued in the same voice, 'And while we are on the subject, I am not telling my mother. She is not the sort of mother who takes kindly to trouble.'

'Francesca, a mother is always the best one to tell, she's been through it and –'

'Don't bother with the sermon,' interjected Francesca bluntly, 'you don't know my mother!'

Berny stood up, gathering some cards from the table.

'Francesca, I am going to take you over to out patients. We will get you a proper examination, and a pregnancy test. There will not be anyone there now except a doctor, so don't worry. Wait here, Lia, we will not be long.'

I remember so well how badly I felt when they had gone. I had never thought before of the complications of casual sex encounters. I felt no condemnation for Francesca. How could I when I had come so close to this very trap with Burton? I knew the overwhelming sexual tide that rises with desire for a man. It made no difference to my heartfelt sympathy for her plight that she had been caught playing a game, at the last the compulsion was irresistible, the result irrevocable. I walked always within the confines of a prison, my emotions in chains to Tadek's image, chasing phantoms even in my sleep. If Tadek would, were the circumstances to come about, could I be in the position Francesca was in now? I knew I could, gladly, joyfully.

Francesca's face told me at once that, yes, indeed she was pregnant.

Berny sat down at the desk. When she spoke, her voice was businesslike, uninvolved.

'Francesca, don't say any more foolish things. Suicide is a kind of madness, and the only other person to suffer would be the baby, who after all is quite blameless. No one else would suffer, it is not a compensatory revenge as you seem to think. This world is full of nine-day wonders, quickly replaced by more nine-day wonders – none of them remembered in a month. No, Francesca, don't say any more. I know you don't believe in the existence of the baby, you can persuade yourself that it is merely something inside you, eventually to be got rid of – like an appendix. Only time, in the next few months, will dissuade you of that theory.

'Now, here is the situation. You are three months' pregnant. To try to lose the pregnancy at this stage could result in your death, a death of hideous pain. Believe me, when you work in a hospital, your eyes are open as to how fierce pain can be. Moreover, should you be able to find some quick midwife to abort the pregnancy, she would charge – dead or alive – a very large sum of money. Yes, Francesca, I know you have no money just at present. This is what I – and I hesitate for fear you think I order you around – this is my suggestion. You are going to England to find theatre work – your mother, you say, has already agreed to that? Go there, to this address I will give you. They will look after you, free of charge, until the baby is born, and after.'

Francesca looked at the address on the card. 'But this is a convent!' she said. 'I'm not going into any nuns' convent.'

Berny sighed patiently. 'It is only for a few months.'

'But I'll be writing home, my mother made that stipulation – they expect money the minute I'm earning – I can't give this address. A convent!'

'But of course you can, Francesca. The nuns run a hostel for girls who are working. You see by the address that it is quite close to the centre of London. Your mother might be glad you were residing in a safe place.'

'Much she would care!' Francesca retorted. 'She is giving me my fare on the mail boat, and five pounds to keep me going until I can find work. No extra clothes! Nothing! And what I have won't fit me in a month.'

She made a grimace of distaste.

I took the cheque from my handbag. I had written my name on the back, exactly as Max's father had written it on the front. Neatly folded, I handed it to Francesca.

I wanted to express my sympathy and understanding. Something in her face silenced me.

She glanced at the cheque. 'Oh, thanks,' she said off-handedly, and put it in her purse.

Chapter Fifteen

A couple of days later, I took the tram to Terenure. I was worried about the cheque. I knew it would eventually come back with the old man's papers from the bank. Perhaps he never glanced at them, but then perhaps he did. If Francesca cashed it at a bank, I supposed the cheque would look in order. But if her mother cashed it for her through a grocer, to retain some for herself, perhaps, then would that seem strange to the old man? On the other hand, from what I now knew of Francesca's attitude to her mother, was it likely that the cheque would be revealed at all? Francesca would take what the mother grudgingly gave, say nothing about having other money, and cash the two hundred secretly. And that would have to be in a bank. I was worried.

He greeted me with his usual affectionate kiss. I saw at once that he was troubled when he asked, 'Have you had a letter from Max?' I told him no, but I hardly expected one, as I had so recently written there would not be time for a reply. In fact, I had delayed writing in order to appear casual – even indifferent.

'We will see him tomorrow,' the old man said, and his voice was full of worried concern. 'I had thought he would be passing through on his way to America, sailing perhaps from Cork. Now, it is a visit. But what is a visit of two days? What is the hurry if only to Paris he is returning?'

We took tea in the long drawing-room. The silver frame was still there by the wall waiting for my portrait. He talked of it often. The portrait painter he desired to commission lived in Amsterdam. Some day soon we would go there. I took his plans as I took Gran's, best to humour fondly.

'I am worried. I am worried,' he repeated, as he balanced the teacup abstractedly. 'I will not say anything until I see him, but I am worried. The only kind of trouble I want is one that I can settle with a chequebook. These ideas he had when we were in Paris – these ideals – they lead young men into trouble to which there is no end. One ideal manufactures another. Lost causes. Lost causes.'

It was best to defer my secret worry about his two hundred-pound cheque to some less troubled time. I tried to distract him by talking about his beloved Paris.

'You should, perhaps, have stayed in Paris, as Max wanted you to. The holiday would have been of benefit. This year, you had no holiday.'

'Paris! Paris! I love Paris, but I never want to be too long away from Dublin. Besides, this dirty old town has a grip on all who live in her.'

I knew exactly what he meant. When I walked down Grafton Street, approaching Trinity College, I said always in my heart: this is my city. The streets fell away, Trinity stood, not among shops and warehouses, but set in flowering fields down to the banks of the River Liffey. That, I always mused, was its situation in the days of the first Queen Elizabeth. Often in summer time, I walked under the arch into the quadrangle. Slowly pacing across the cobblestones, I mingled with the ghosts of Berkeley and Swift, Goldsmith, Farquhar, poor Oscar Wilde. The Elizabethan Garden Party conjured up for me a hot day of crinolines and lace cravats. I had often walked from Gran's house across to the Liberties, noting all the varied attempts at architecture from Georgian through Venetian, Corinthian columns, Dutch roofs, Germanic turrets. I mentioned this.

'Yes,' he said, quite diverted now, 'uniquely hodge-podge but our own! The City Fathers will continue to build assorted designs over our ancient heritage. Let us hope and pray they will not import the skyscraper design now so popular in America. But of course, we must remember that Dublin was not planned, it was grafted. The Vikings should have been let finish what they began, or the Normans, or the Georgians, or even that Woodward Dean, the Great Venetian. All beginnings only to be swept away. If only someone four hundred years ago had said: this is a University City, a Parliament City, let us build great squares of libraries, art galleries, basilicas, noble campaniles. When they built the squares they filled in the sides with houses. Nothing decays more rapidly than a house. Look at Stephen's Green! Decayed houses turned into shops along one side.'

He could talk happily like that for hours, occasionally taking a book from a bookcase to check, or corroborate, and I was happy to be his admiring audience. When I saw the beginning of fatigue, I would find the right moment to say goodbye until the next time, always the promise exacted to come soon again. I knew he found something in my person, perhaps my hair, or perhaps my face, something that satisfied his need for beauty, for he was, he said, a bond-slave to beauty wherever he perceived it. I was glad to add my living form to all the other forms of beauty with which he surrounded himself. I loved him dearly, for the patrician quality he brought to life and for the constant care he evinced towards me. This old man was exquisitely courteous. Gradually, I was learning from him. Gradually, he shared all the treasures of his knowledge. At first, I was fearful of intruding on the privacy of his rich life, so different from my own. I came to see, with each succeeding visit, that our loving friendship grew apace.

Max was waiting outside the Department the following evening. I was very happy to get into the car, very happy to see him at the wheel.

'Where to, James?' This was the old password of the famous Citroën days. I could see Max remembered but his face was a little sad and serious.

'I have instructions to take you out to dinner, my father says you should put on weight.' He tried to smile. 'You are two ounces heavier than a shrimp – it is too much!'

Foreboding was heavy in the air between us. It was not easy to recapture the mood we had in Paris. Max drove out of the city, taking the road to Rathfarnham. There he turned off the main road, and up the long mountain road to Ticknock. He remembered an old public house, the Lamb Doyle's. We sat in the pub window, drinking, and gazing down at Dublin city in the evening light.

At last I had to ask him, but very gently, 'I think you are not going to America after all. Did you come home to say goodbye to your father?'

He nodded gravely. 'I knew you would guess at once when my father told you I was coming. Lia, I could not resolve my conscience. I joined the Partisans.'

I moved closer to him. He was never so dear to me as at that moment. I knew he was about to enter a life that was utterly repugnant to him, a rough life of sleeping in dug-outs, of wearing filthy clothes; worst of all, of using a gun on another human being.

In a way, it was different for Tadek to join the Partisans. His people had suffered grim poverty because of the oppressor. Perhaps I alone knew how great were the privations Tadek had endured. And in a way, I thought, Tadek was tougher. I was very conscious that Tadek had never offered a commitment to me, he had refused to. Max had offered his heart generously. Tadek had fortitude and endurance to repress even his most tender emotion. He would withstand anything that a concentration camp could do to him.

Max, I feared, would go under. Max did not know the meaning of aggression.

'Have you told your father? Better tell me what you have said, so he will feel free to discuss it with me.'

Max put his arm around my shoulder. I knew he was thanking me for my friendship with the old man.

'It is all right, Max, I enjoy him. He talks to me a lot. He is very good to me. But please tell me.'

Max never had the words ready. He sought around in these long pauses for the right words. I remembered he was always like that. The words aimed at concentrating on the truth. When at last he spoke, his voice was troubled.

'I have told him very little yet. There is no easy way. I want to break it gently. I am afraid that, no matter what I say, he will see it as the end.'

'He has talked about the Partisans,' I told Max. 'He is immensely proud of underground resistance. He knows that since last year or maybe since earlier, the persecution against the Jews has intensified. He sees two immense difficulties for the Jews in Germany. They are easily identifiable, scarcely any merging with the local population either in language or religion. The other difficulty is the apathy of the outside world. He believes the Partisans have sought help from Britain, but to no avail. This, he thinks, is because they are diverse groups, scattered.'

'They have to be diverse,' Max said quickly, 'from region to region the language and customs change. Germany has many dialects. Also it is necessary to know the terrain. And essential to have many skills. I, for example, have just now taken a hospital refresher course in basic medical skill, the alleviation of physical pain may be more necessary for now than the study of mental neuroses. Later that will come.'

After a while, Max continued. 'The Germans see themselves as a self-chosen race also, but with this difference – they are the Master Race. The German State does not see itself as an instrument for securing civil rights for minorities, but rather as an instrument for furthering the high destiny of the German *volk*. I have heard them singing in the beer gardens of the south:

"Erst mussen Juden bluten
Erst dann sind wir befreit."

First they must shed Jewish blood, and then they will be free.'

For a long time, we sat in silence, his arm around my shoulder.

We went for dinner to a little hotel in Enniskerry. We did not talk any more about the sad and tragic fate that we both felt to be near. We pretended we were very young again, laughing softly about 'the old days long ago' – the 'do you remember?' days. Max remembered loads of things that I had almost forgotten. He had seen himself as equally in the picture as Tadek was, whereas I had seen two people with Max as a third. But, strangely, I was not longing for them to change places now. I was glad to be with Max, the glad feeling of being needed, of being loved. The way he looked at me revealed his tenderness.

When we came out into the garden of the hotel, the moon had come fully up. Across the valley, we could see the big Sugarloaf, a mountain stretched against a starry sky. It was like a vast backdrop in an open-air theatre.

'Shall we climb the Sugarloaf like when we were kids?' I begged. 'I told Gran not to worry if I was very late.'

Max drove across the valley road, and onto Callery Bog. By a boreen, the car crept upwards until there was no more path. We got out, and climbed a little way across the heather. The night was warm as day, the moonbeams almost like sunshine. We sat down, hand in hand, to admire the view of stars and dim peaks and far-off twinkling lights.

'We are like Diarmaid and Grainne making our bed on the heather,' I told Max. 'Do you remember the legend – hunted by Finn and the Fianna a thousand years ago?'

Suddenly I was in Max's arms. I could feel the soft bristles of his beard against my cheek, I never thought to struggle. It was a lovely feeling.

'Oh Lia, Lia, Lia. I have been longing to kiss you since the first moment you walked out of that office. How I missed you when you left Paris. I could see you in the garden, hear your soft laugh everywhere. You are a little Irish witch haunting me. All my life, you have been haunting me.'

His kiss was gentle, and searching. I felt that fierce familiar tide of longing within me. Thoughts like hailstones rushed against my closed eyes – thoughts of Burton and Laelia, I wanted what they had. I clung to Max.

'Oh Max, I need you so much!' And in that moment I did, my lips were whispering and kissing all at once. I pleaded for this wonderful act, given to everyone else and so long withheld from me . . . 'Let us be Diarmaid and Grainne, please let us, Max. Please. This is our bed on the wild mountain. Finn will find us. He will hack you to pieces. I will never be with you again after this wonderful night. Max, please now, before you are killed. . . .'

Against my cheek, I could feel his lips smiling, but he held me closer and closer. They used to tease me for being so dramatic, he and Laelia, on our holidays long ago, and I used to do it to make them smile . . . the acted-out joke.

'Don't laugh at me. This is symbolic, Max. This time will never come again and I shall be alone for ever!'

His voice was muted against my hair. 'Are you sure this is what you want, Lia? Are you sure?'

I struggled out of his arms. I wrenched off my jacket, and threw it on the ground.

'Look at me!' I cried out to him. 'You said you loved. Have you forgotten so soon? Do you refuse me?'

He drew me beneath him on the heather. We were loving in a passionate entreaty for more and more. We came near and nearer and nearer. It was wonderful and acceptable. There were only two people in the whole wide world under the brilliant moon. I wanted this coming together to go on for ever, whispering each other's names in an intensity of desire. This violent upward climb of our bodies to a climax was the magical solution to all my seeking now. Suddenly, abruptly, the thrilling spiral ceased.

I was flung down from the highest pinnacle of the temple. Instead of the hot rush of sexual fulfilment, there came a flood of tears. Always tears came when things went wrong.

Max was consolingly contrite. 'Lia, don't cry, darling. Please don't. You know I want you. You know I love you . . . always and always I love you. Don't cry, darling, I want you. I was forgetting everything else when I held you so close.'

Now he took me back into his arms. He was gentle and in full control. Rocking me to and fro, he murmured many tender words. I was rigid with disappointment and slow to respond.

'Lia, let us do this properly.' He kissed my tears, 'I love you, Lia. Will you marry me?'

All I had asked for was the enchanted formula. All I wanted was the total involvement of all my desires with all the desires of a loved and loving man. Marriage was the fulfilment of a future dream, a dream quite apart from the romantic candlelit dinner of tonight, a dream reserved for the secret lover of my very soul.

'Max, have you forgotten that you are going to leave us? That you have come home to say goodbye?'

'But only for a little while, Lia. This will all be over in a few months. I must do my bit, make my contribution. The last time I got so far in this conversation, it was not my future that was in question, but your future in the theatre. So what about that?'

I thought about it, as I had been thinking since the exciting night when we had received our precious certificates from the hand of Mr Lennox Robinson. The excitement had ebbed away, as if that night was the achievement rather than the prelude to a life on the stage.

'What your father said to me has weighed on my mind. He said I have not got the killer instinct.'

'You know what he means by that?'

'Oh yes, I think so. He is right. I should remain an enthusiastic lover of theatre with, as your father says, an informed ability to know what is good. I esteem his judgement, Max.'

246

There was a long, long pause. Max was considering. When he spoke, his voice was diffident.

'Lia, I stopped – I gave up – tonight because I thought suddenly that, well, that this might be, well, would be the . . .'

'It would be the first time, Max. Is that not the best reason for you not to give up?'

'No, darling. The first time, we will not be on the hillside. The first time, there will be garlands on the walls, wine in the glass.'

I thought about that. I wanted to know what being loved was going to taste like, and I wanted to know now. Max was going to Germany to fight for the release of Jews imprisoned. Would he ever come back? Tadek was gone. Would he ever come back? I had heard fearful stories from the old man, stories of young men who were never seen again.

I pressed my face against his coat, and I whispered, 'Max, couldn't we love each other just for tonight?'

But Max shook his head. There was another of his long pauses.

'Lia, tonight we will tell my father it is our intention to marry. You will wear my ring and we will go away for a few days. It will not be exactly as we could have planned. But the important thing is that I must leave you safe, because I must go away. You know that, darling, I could not do less than Tadek is doing for our people.'

Tadek, Tadek, Tadek – the echo spread across the moonlit valley, calling me, reproaching me. The first time. The first time. The first time.

'Lia,' Max whispered, 'tonight is dangerous. I could not go and leave you in possible trouble. Tomorrow I will look after you better. Do you trust me?'

We lay quietly in each other's arms, the safe past tidied away, the uncertain future settled for one more day. Max had not noticed that I did not answer his proposal of marriage. I had not said yes and I had not said no. All I wanted was to give and have

247

my giving taken . . . to love him for the sake of loving.

The windows were all lit up in the house in Terenure, although it was long past the midnight.

In the car, I hesitated. I had remembered what Tadek had once told me: 'You have to be born a Jew.' Wouldn't Max think the same way?

'Lia, please, best come in with me . . . I want you to see his face when we tell him . . . come, he has known my feelings for years, and he has come to share them . . . come, darling.'

The elderly couple who looked after the household were standing in the hall. They appeared agitated.

Pointing to the long drawing-room, the man said, 'He won't go to bed. It's the bad news!'

We went into the drawing-room. The old man rose at once. Holding out his hands to us, he moaned, 'Ah, my children, were you listening to the wireless at six o'clock? England has declared war on Germany.'

So, it was at once decided that Max would go from Dunleary the following morning because, if he delayed, the traffic between Ireland and England might be terminated. That happened very soon.

He brought me home to Gran's house. In the car he held me close for a few moments. We knew that the dream was over. Reality had come into our lives at last. We knew, although neither of us said a word, that all the study and planning which had gone into our lives to give us careers and destinations, had been tentative child's play. Now decisions had been made for us in far places. There would never again be a light-hearted 'see you tomorrow', because our tomorrows had been taken out of our hands.

Perhaps I did not think in those words that night, but the final doom of carefree youth was in our passionate kiss. And I was certain I was saying goodbye to love, in a man with whom I had never fallen in love, a man who had stood briefly in another man's shadow. And I remember, oh how well I remember, the lonely feeling as I closed the door. Each time I had come close to that Particular Friendship for which I longed, each time I had almost come face to face with total giving, a crooked destiny defeated me. I remember standing with my back against the door while futile tears spilled down. There was no one to comfort me in the way I needed comfort. Would there ever be anyone?

Next morning in the office, Chersy was a comfort, an everyday, common-sense, commonplace comfort. The fact that there was a War in Europe had to take its place in importance beside the fact that Guiney's shop in Talbot Street was offering Persian lamb coats for fifteen pounds! She had decided that we should go across town at lunch time. A Persian lamb coat for her winter trousseau was quite the thing.

'Let's fit on every coat in Guiney's!' Chersy said enthusiastically, 'and I'll buy the lamb if you think it suits me. After all, those coats were nearly up to eighteen pounds last week! It is a real sale bargain, my Mum says when it comes to next winter they won't be there, but I'll have mine. And they have squirrelene swagger coats for three pounds nineteen and six! You could have one for this winter!'

'Are they good fur?' I asked dubiously.

'Of course!' replied Chersy, warmly loyal to Dinny Guiney's shop. 'What else would they be?'

I thought of rabbits, or furry rats, but I knew it was best to say nothing like that. 'All Dublin swears by Dinny Guiney for good value!' And Chersy should know, because there was never a week but she and her Mum stocked up another item of household value for Chersy's dowry. My 'bottom drawers are now full to bursting,' Chersy said frequently, enjoying the office laughter.

During the lunch-hour walk downtown to Guiney's, Chersy told me all about the house in Clontarf, in which she and her Denis would settle when they were married.

'You'll have to come out and see it, it is nearly built! My Dad gave us the deposit, a hundred pounds, that's our wedding present from Mum and Dad.'

I watched her happy face as she chatted away. Chersy could come out with such outrageous vulgarity from time to time. She was a great one for uttering blasphemous opinions on men's morals, and for giving grandmotherly advice on that subject. Yet she was a loveable, innocent soul at the back of the brash words. I envied her the carefree secure way she referred to her Mum and Dad, her forthcoming marriage, her loving hold on Denis.

'Wait till you see the kitchen!' Chersy was saying. 'The houses are going to be called Kincora Park, it is off Oulton Road. They are a bit pricey, of course, eight hundred and fifty pounds! But of course you pay for the location, my Mum says, and Clontarf is a very select district. After you put down the hundred pounds, the repayments are twenty-four shillings and ten pence a week. Denis says we can well afford it, and that in a few years it will be very little, with his salary going up, and we'll own our own house before we're fifty!'

Fifty! My heart sank. Did life run away so fast that she could equably, even happily, contemplate fifty?

'Of course, there's furniture!' continued Chersy. 'My Mum has been paying off on a lounge (that's what they are calling the parlour now!), a lounge three-piece, for the past year. Green moquette it is! And Denis's people are giving us an oak dining-room suite. Real oak! My Uncle Harry, you met him at our Christmas party, you said you liked him, he is doing all the lino and the lounge carpet. He's in the flooring business, you know, in Capel Street. And my Granny has all the curtains made. Later on, I intend to get Venetian blinds! They are the very latest fashion, did you know that? They're gorgeous!'

Chersy bought the Persian lamb coat. I wondered how she had managed to save such a large sum as fifteen pounds. She was a thrifty person always. She did not think the squirrelene coat was quite me, which was a relief. I bought a grey woollen frock for twelve shillings and eleven pence. I was glad next day was payday. My weekly pay was a little less than four pounds of which I gave two to Gran.

Gran was greatly concerned about the War. She remembered all too well the hardship endured by fighting men in the Great War, the losses to families of good husbands and sons. Four of her own sons had given their lives for freedom in the War that was to end War. We bought the paper every day during September. We also bought yards of coarse black cloth to hang over our windows at night. This was called 'the blackout'. The papers printed notices of heavy penalties for those not observing the blackout.

Almost immediately, the Irish Government had rules and regulations. The Free State was to remain neutral. Passports and travel permits were obligatory to cross the Irish Sea, or the border into the North of Ireland – although excursions to Belfast were still being advertised at six shillings return. Belfast for a shopping spree was always very popular with Dubliners. Gran had often gone with Aunt Julia in earlier years.

I read in the paper that in England all cinemas, theatres and other places of entertainment would be closed until further notice. I thought immediately of Burton and Laelia. The theatre was his livelihood. I supposed he could join up and fight for his country. I wondered, would he? In London, policemen were wearing steel helmets, and carrying gas masks. Soon gas masks were issued in Dublin.

One day, we saw a picture in the *Independent*. The women of Poland were at war alongside the Polish soldiers who were attempting to stem the German and Soviet invasions of their country. The picture showed tense-faced officers of the Women's Legion at Lwow. One of the women was an exact likeness of Mrs Vashinsky, the small sensitive face made for love but turned to tragedy. Gran cut out the picture, and for many days she had it propped on her little chiffonier.

Poland was the place in the news. For eighteen days Poland held out against invasion, the people in desperate straits. The old man told me that Max had gone to join Tadek's group on the Polish border. The day Warsaw fell, I burned the paper picture of the women officers. Gran wept again for Mrs Vashinsky, and I tried to comfort her. I did not tell her for whom I wept, and for whom, in spite of my tears, I still hoped.

Life was not all sad. Gran and I were knitting little vests and coats to have as a surprise for Phyllis's baby. Phyllis and Jacques and all the Dalys and Gran and I were delighted with this lovely news.

About the middle of September, Phyllis came in the usual way of regular visiting, but her eyes were not shining in the usual way. Phyllis had enjoyed superb health during her pregnancy. She was never happier, never more full of gusto, until that night.

'Jacques has got his papers,' she said the minute she sat down. We knew at once what she meant.

'When must he go?' I asked immediately.

'They are fixing it now, lovey. Now, as soon as the travel permit is issued. And it's only for him. I can't get one. Anyway, he wouldn't take me, on account of the baby. He says the War will be over before Christmas. Madame will keep his job for him.' Phyllis began to heave with helpless, indignant, frustrated tears. 'I don't know what I am going to do without him. What did they want to have their old War for now?'

'How will you be fixed for money, Phyllis?' Gran enquired.

'Well, there's a soldier's allowance for a wife and child, Mrs B. And Madame wants me to continue in the kitchen. I can bring the baby, they have a cradle there upstairs, and she says she will make my duties as light as possible.'

I felt very doubtful about this. I had read in the newspaper about the allowances a soldier got in the Irish army: a wife with one child got twenty-one shillings a week, a wife with four children got twenty-eight shillings, for a fifth child she got an extra three pence. I hoped the French army looked after their men rather better.

'Well,' Gran was saying, 'at least with the Jammets you will not go short of food.'

Phyllis looked woebegone. I stood up.

'I am going to take you to the pictures, Phyllis. Drink up that cup of tea. The flicks will cheer you up.'

Phyllis dearly loved a visit to the cinema. She seldom got a chance with Jacques, he had few words of English .

'Oh lovey, could we go to the Astor? It's Miriam Hopkins, I'm mad about her! She's so aristocratic. She always reminds me of poor Mama.'

I looked at the newspaper's entertainment page. The picture in the Astor was 'Becky Sharp'.

'But Phyllis, there could be wars and bloodshed in that.' I was thinking of the Battle of Waterloo in the book. But so long as it was Miriam Hopkins having a happy ending, Phyllis could put up with Waterloo. Gran always came to the pictures with us. She swore it was all done with mirrors and trick-photography, and she enjoyed it enormously.

Before Jacques went away to France, he brought Phyllis to a great three-day auction in Stephen's Green. The Guiness's had donated to the Nation, Iveagh House, a huge mansion on the south side of Stephen's Green.

It was to become the Department of External Affairs. The auction comprised the contents of the house. The Jammets had been to the sale on the first day, evidently their enthusiasm had spread to Jacques who had a Frenchman's eye for art. Also he wanted to give Phyllis a present for their little apartment, by which she would remember him when he was away. I often wondered what he thought of her choice, from among all the lovely pieces and pictures. For Phyllis wanted one thing only. It was a massive Irish oak chair, whose front legs and arms were carved in the likeness of Irish wolfhounds. When Phyllis told us about it, she was very excited.

'The two of us between us couldn't carry it home. We had to hire an old fellow with a handcart. We walked behind him. I was never so proud in my life. Bold Robert Emmett or even Brian Boru himself might have sat on it! Oh lovey, wait till you see it! It'll look gorgeous with a green velvet cushion! It took us an hour to get it up the stairs! I thought I'd burst! Then Jacques sat in it like a hero!'

Gran clucked over Phyllis for carrying heavy things at six-months pregnant. Phyllis, back to form, only laughed in that irrepressible way so everyone had to join in.

On the last day of September, Jacques sailed away from Dunleary. He had orders to join a contingent of his fellow countrymen in London, and proceed to France. Gran and I went out to wish him well.

All the Dalys' sons, daughters and grandchildren were at the barrier in force, and all in floods of tears. Quite clearly, they had grown very fond of Phyllis's Jacques. Mr Daly shook him by the hand forty times adjuring him to put a bullet in a Hun and come home quick.

Poor Jacques had to tear himself from Phyllis who showered love and kisses on him, the while begging his promise that he would be home soon, safe and sound.

'It puts me in mind of Marie and Will,' moaned poor Gran, 'only twenty-five years ago in that other War.'

And sadly there was a certain similarity. Jacques was killed a month later in a mine explosion. He had gone straight to the Front in charge of a catering operation. A few days after we received that news Phyllis's baby, a boy, was dead-born in Holles Street Hospital. Phyllis, too, was very close to death. But for the skill and knowledge of the devoted doctors, she could not have survived. That great gusto for living, the shining love of life and of everyone in it, had been quenched. The will to live was practically extinct.

Chapter Sixteen

After Phyllis was released from hospital, the little apartment was closed. Phyllis went home to Ringsend. She was painfully thin and wan. One night Mrs Daly came to Gran's to ask, would we take Phyllis for a while? There was so little room in the house in Ringsend.

'Mrs B., I don't know where the years have gone,' said Mrs Daly. 'Overnight they have all come into being men and women! I managed grand when they were boys and girls, but honest to God me husband would want to build an extension as big as Clery's ballroom!'

'And how is Phyllis?' enquired Gran.

'Wound up she is like a mechanical toy. You wouldn't have the bit in your mouth but she is up and washing the delph! Food has no appeal for her, she'll starve to death, so she will! And not a word to say to dog or divil!'

Gran turned to me. 'Would you go over and have a word with her, child? She might listen to you. Would she come over to us, do you think, Mrs Daly?'

'It's not that I'd ask, Mrs B. but since Tricia and her husband moved in with the three kids, we're skint for room. She's pregnant again, and she'll get a Corporation house when she has four. They make you have four childer before they will give you the key of a house – and, of course, you have to be homeless as well. Tricia had two rooms in Barrow Street and she would never get housed out of that, that's why me husband let them move in with us. And Tricia's man is the best in the world, an electrician he is with four pounds eighteen and six a week. Great money! You see, Mrs B., me son Shay and his wife Nora and their three have been with us from the beginning. Nora is trying to get up the spout this past three years to make the fourth babby, but whatever is wrong, they still only have the three. They could borrow kids from one another, but the Corpo man makes you show the birth certificates. And Shay is in the building in good employment and he could well afford a house. Miko went to England, you remember Miko, Miss Lia?'

Mrs Daly took the cup of tea from Gran with a nod of thanks, and without drawing a breath, she was off again.

'Miko did very well in England. He got the trade of motor mechanic, and he made a lot of money on the side playing the saxophone with another fellow on the pianna in a pub at nights. But me husband doesn't like them being in England – they lose the run of themselves, he says. Miko is coming at Christmas and he will look over the prospect of setting himself up here at the mechanics. He saved his money, him and Josie, and they have the four kids so they will get a house after they are homeless for six months, so they will move in with us. By that time, Tricia will have been fixed. Josie is a grand girl, we're all mad about Josie.'

I thought Gran's second offer of tea and cake would be taken as a hint by Mrs Daly that time was moving on. There was no hurrying Mrs Daly.

'Would you believe, Miss Lia, what I am going to tell you? Me husband, a better man never lived, and me have six of the childer in our bedroom? Me husband made three tiers of beds along one wall for them – and a little ladder. They are as snug as a bug in a rug. And he put in a ventilation in the wall so there is plenty of air. He is a very clever man, Mrs B. And you remember Sylvie, me youngest girl? She is nearly finished school now. She is mad about the books and the typewriting is what she wants. So me husband made a little study for her up in the roof at the back, and she sleeps up there as well. There's only room for one, though. Poor Phyllis has a shakedown in the kitchen, but as true as the gospel she won't lie down until that kitchen is cleaned and swept and polished and rearranged to her liking – even the windows, Mrs B.! She'll kill herself! And it's not easy with all those kids around – you can't be nagging them all day. Not that she nags. She never says a word. She just stands up and begins to clean all over again! Me husband said last night in bed that he can see Phyllis fading to a shadda before his eyes.'

I went down to Ringsend. It was not easy to persuade Phyllis that she was needed in Gran's. Without the words to express her feelings, I knew that life had become a pointless exercise for her. I was perhaps something of an expert in this feeling.

No one needed either of us – except Gran.

Too apathetic to put up a reason to resist, she packed a bag and came with me. I gave up my room gladly for Phyllis. Once again I was on the sofa in the little parlour. After a while we got the same old fellow with the handcart to bring Brian Boru's chair. Brightly polished, the carved hounds joined me in the little parlour. Secretly I thought of it as something of a monstrosity. Gran told me that when I was at the office Phyllis often sat and gazed at it. We both felt that perhaps she saw her poor lost husband seated there, as she had said herself, 'like a hero'.

Madame Jammet came often to see Phyllis. She was very fond of her, and had found her invaluable in the kitchen. The Jammets were thinking of returning to France as soon as was feasible. Did I think, would Phyllis go with them? I thought it was a wonderful idea. She would always have a safe home with the Jammets, they were lovely people. Perhaps Phyllis would find a nice husband in France. I used all my powers of persuasion, but to no avail. At last, one evening, Phyllis melted a little. She would go out to work, she said, but not in Jammet's – too many memories. She was feeling strong enough now. She would take the bed in the parlour. She would look after us like she did in 'Sunrise'. She liked to be kept busy. When the time came for Lovey to marry, then new arrangements could be made. Would Mrs Brabazon agree to that, after all it was her home?

I let that slide about the little house being Gran's. It was not important. Phyllis stayed in the parlour with the hero's chair and I went back upstairs. After a while, she got a half-day job in a shop. That suited her, she liked the customers' chat. It was many a long month before I heard her beginning to sing again around the house, and longer still before her voice found strength.

After the first couple of months of War, known in Ireland as the 'Emergency', we no longer bought the paper. After much thought, Gran had bought a wireless. She listened to all the different news readings, 'the different wires', she called them, thinking perhaps in telegraphic terms, to hear differently on each. Slowly, as the first year of the War ticked away, her mind grew confused between a radio drama over the air, and a fresh calamity. It ceased to affect her that Europe was in chaos. We kept her warm, and rested. Although food was rationed, we tried between us not to let her suffer the lack of her cup of tea, or the fresh egg she so enjoyed.

Sometimes, I thought Gran was failing. It showed in little ways. Having Phyllis there to help me was wonderful. Gran liked to see me 'going out to enjoy myself,' as she said. If I did not have a night at the theatre, or the cinema, now and then, she fretted.

'An old person is such a tie, child,' she would say sadly, forgetting that when she was a great deal younger and sturdier, I was often a tie on her activities.

'Gran, it is not because you did something for me that I do something for you . . . it is because you are my nearest and dearest. And, now stop smiling at me, it is because I am happier here in your little house than anywhere else on earth.' I said this so often that she always smiled – a kind of shy smile of pleasure.

'I sometimes wonder, childy, why did you give up that old theatre stuff? I used to love seeing you up on the stage.'

'I think I grew out of it, Gran.'

Sometimes I accepted invitations to the theatre with casual admirers. When the casual turned to steady interest, I refused to go further.

Sometimes I had an evening out with Berny who was attached to St Mel's. Sometimes, I went out to Clontarf to spend time with Chersy and Denis and their baby son. I was godmother to this little baby, and I delighted in watching his progress, and bringing a present to his birthday party; renewing my acquaintance with the ever-growing family of cousins, in-laws, and neighbours which Chersy accumulated as time went on.

I had made a promise to Max to spend time with his father in Terenure.

My special evening in the week was Thursday. I tried to arrive punctually on the dot of five-thirty. The old man was always watching at the window. Each time I approached the big house, running up the stone steps, my heart beat high with hope. Very often, when the evening was over, I returned home sad and depressed.

The old man was always courteously welcoming. We sat by the fire no matter what the season. Tea was brought in, there was always some special type of sandwich, some dainty little cake to please me. He made many enquiries about my life, my health, my Gran. He responded to my enquiries about his health which was reasonably good. At last I would feel able to ask for news.

After the fall of Poland, it was a long time before he had word of our boys . . . he always called Max and Tadek 'our boys'. He did not dare to write to any previous contacts in Germany, or in Austria, or in France. There was a postal censorship operating out of these countries, he had been told.

There were people in London who might help, but he was reluctant to bring reprisal on an innocent person.

All of this filled me with a sense of helpless incredulity.

When we knew for certain that Max and Tadek had escaped from the Polish holocaust, and were in Austria, the old man warned that the news was many weeks old.

'We must wait for more recent news, my dear Lia.'

When the weather was fine, I usually walked home the better to think over any scrap of news. We must wait. We must wait. I had been waiting all my life. I had been bolstering my waiting with the thought that no news is good news, that hope has an eternal spring. In these lonely walks, I would hear myself begging Tadek to take care of himself, to give up whatever idealistic struggle he was fighting in, to go back to doctoring, and stay safe. Max, too. But Max was bigger, stronger, he would know what to do. Then I would remember how Tadek had been born into hardship and he had coped, and hope would rise again.

I did not always convince myself, and there were many times when I was desperately lonely deep inside.

Then, one Thursday morning, a porter brought a message to the office where I was writing the everlasting rent receipts. There was a man waiting down in the front hall who had asked to see me.

I could scarcely get my legs to carry me down the stairs. I was dizzy with expectation. I never thought to comb my hair, or look in a mirror.

With each flying step, I thought: Can it be? Can it be? Can it be? Oh, please God, only let it be. . . . Please God, I will do anything only let it be. . . . Tadek Tadek . . . I need you so very badly . . . Tadek. . . .

It was Burton. Did my painful disappointment show in my face? I could not speak. Unabashed, as if we met in the office hall every day, he gathered me into his arms. Tears of disappointment started to my eyes and I had to hide my face against his shoulder. I was conscious of the hall-porters in their glass office gazing at the phenomenon of this huge man engaged in a prolonged embrace with a clerical assistant. I struggled free.

'My little darling, more beautiful than ever!' And, disregarding my resistance, he held me even closer and kissed my lips with a warmth so satisfying it made naught of my first disappointment.

It shames me to admit it. I did not want to spurn Burton. I wanted to stay within the circle of his arms. I let him kiss me again. I felt the meaning of his kiss. Within the circle of his arms, where the familiar musky fragrance of roses and port-wine was all-powerful, I believed suddenly that I could find freedom from waiting, freedom at last from that nameless longing within me.

In seconds, I had got my coat and we were out in the street, walking along Stephen's Green to Dawson Street. Burton was staying in the Royal Hibernian. Soon we were seated in the luxurious lounge, I was drinking some concoction guaranteed to woo away resistance. He need not have bothered, in that hour I was all his. Was it my imagination or had he grown younger? His hair, always wavy, was now completely silver. The heavy moustache was now very clipped. Everyone looked dowdy beside Burton, and everyone looked dead. His brown eyes, full of interest, twinkled in a tanned face. Was he always just back from Spain? He looked so marvellously young.

He had joined up at the very start of the War. He knew, he said, that entertainment for the troops would be a priority, and he was right. They called it ENSA. He had got his commission right off, and been pipped up twice in the past year.

He was over here to round up entertainers, comedians, singers. Plenty of Irish in the forces to be entertained! They've got this neutral country, you would think they'd stay at home where they would be safe. Oh no, like a hoard of dogs who have heard of a dog-fight in the next street, off they go, trooping over to England to offer their services, they were prepared to die for England but not prepared to work for their own country!

Oh well, he knew the Irish! Load of poufs! Great sense of theatre, though – put over a drama better than the English. Stolid lot, the English. Good guys, though. Proper men!

Irish women! Oh well, that's a nag of another colour! Irish women were better than most at the love game – not as good as the Japanese but the Lord deliver him from American women – they were still out in the covered-wagon days – a lot to learn, had Americans, but he didn't want to be their teacher.

Burton had a way with him. He could put over this offensive conversation like harmless patter and with fascinating charm. He left no gap in which one could query his remarks; his smiles, so warmly intimate, carried the listener along. All his little speeches were punctuated with concern for the listener's thirst, warmth, comfort. To me these tracks were all so familiar, so close and dear, that they carried me deeply into him, like a puppy on sinking sands.

How was it arranged that I should go home for an overnight bag? Come back in evening dress for dinner in the Hibernian; go away with Burton for the weekend; arrange to join ENSA under his guidance; he would look after me in London?

'That is a perfect plan, my darling little Lia. Of course, you must not dream of giving up the theatre. What rubbish! You have the training but much more important – you have the beauty. I always knew it from the first moment. You are a raving beauty, my little pet. Give up the theatre? With those looks? Not blooming likely!'

I adored him and it had nothing to do with his flattery. I tried to remember all the bad things about him. Promising to be back within a couple of hours, I broke away from his kiss and went out into Dawson Street.

What bad things? Perhaps, as he said at the time, it was a child's nightmare. Did I dream all that?

Suddenly, I knew I did not dream it.

A little unsteadily, I crossed Duke Street and Grafton

Street and, passing the Gaiety Theatre, I came to St Mel's. I had remembered that I had an arrangement to meet Berny that night for a visit to the Abbey. Suppose I tell her that I was tempted to fornicate with a man? My legs were very unsteady, but my mind had made itself up.

Since our school days, Berny had had a succession of handsome lovers. She had become a very sophisticated young woman, always elegantly dressed. She wore make-up long before much make-up was used. We were still the closest of friends, we always would be.

'Berny, would you like to go out to dinner in the Hibernian with a fascinating man? Well, a bit fascinating! Not too young, though.'

'Would I! You too?'

'No, I cannot go. Tonight I have to go to Terenure, to see my old friend. I just have to go to see him.'

'Oh, I am filling in for you, is that it?' Berny's friendly face never lost its serenity.

'Would you do that for me? I think he wants to go dancing – you have that gorgeous dress, the one you got for the medical ball?'

'I would be delighted to give it an airing – it cost my mother the bloomin' bank, so she says! And I could do with a good dinner after the fare here! Tell me about this man.'

So I told her that he was an unexpected visitor from England, maybe a very distant relative, I wasn't sure, a bit old but not a mean person, she would get a good dinner. I was beginning to babble, but Berny was too agreeable to see anything amiss. I went off to 'phone the Hibernian and leave the message for Burton.

I went to Terenure. We spent the evening looking at a book of prints which Max's father had lately acquired. There was no news of Max. When the old man fell asleep by the fire, I crept out and went home. To cry myself to sleep would have been a luxury. Alas, that luxury was for Phyllis now. So far as anyone could see, she had more reason to cry than I had.

263

Why did I feel so close to tears? Why did I feel like a child in 'Sunrise' waiting to hear Burton slam the door? I had kept faith, hadn't I? But with whom?

Berny 'phoned me at the office during the week. She was full of the wonderful night she had had with Burton.

'You don't know what you missed, Lia! He is absolutely gorgeous – a bit older than I thought he was going to be! But not old at all, really.'

I was painfully jealous. 'Did he say he was disappointed that I didn't show up?'

'Oh now,' replied Berny, 'he was much too charming to say that to me. He didn't even express surprise! We got on like a house on fire!' she chuckled. 'A touch of the "singing for my supper" though!'

'What?' I gasped incredulously. 'Oh no!'

Berny laughed enjoyably, 'Five o'clock in the morning when he brought me back to St Mel's! I told you, he is a gorgeous man! Oh, I nearly forgot to tell you, he gave me a bracelet. It's a beauty! I am sure it cost a packet! I can't wait to show it to you! I'll be seeing him in London if I get that appointment.'

She had applied to join a medical unit in the British Forces.

I wanted to go on questioning her, and yet I did not want the intimate details. Whatever it had been for her, it would have been different for me – different, different, different. If I had kept the tryst with Burton (and oh! why did I not?), I would now be feeling that I had been set free – feeling that at last I was a woman instead of this eternal green girl. I was full of wonder that to my friend Berny, this Burton was just another playful sexual episode in a string of them – no doubt quite the best to date, when one includes the bracelet. I should have thought that our similar convent upbringing would have put similar barring on our attitudes to . . . was 'free love' the word? Perhaps her medical education had stripped sexual intercourse of the romantic swirling mists. Or perhaps her family background treated love between the sexes as a natural and health-giving rule of life. Or maybe our natures were different. Berny was always serene, and candid. That must mean she had no frustrations and nothing to hide. I knew I was full of secret desires, urgent needs which were self-defeating because they were centred on an unattainable object.

I wanted to be loved in a very special way, just sometimes I lost sight of the fact that only one special person could love me in one special way.

Life in the office was a dull thing after Chersy left. But if Chersy's going left a gap, there was a worse and wider gap to follow.

Phyllis had been working now for some time in the shop in Westland Row. No doubt because of her cheerful manner and utter cleanliness, the shop became a money spinner. Soon Phyllis's employer, Mr Frare, was moving into the publican business in the more salubrious area of Aston Quay. Phyllis regaled us nightly with all the details. She had observed how the ornate, intimate decor of Jammet's had attracted the right sort of customer. Apparently this was an aspect of pub-keeping that had not occurred to Mr Frare, and he took kindly to the suggestions made by Phyllis – kindly, that is, after some persuasion.

'"Wouldn't they spill their pints all over me thick Axminster carpet?" he says to me. Would you rather they spilt it all over your bright green lino, where other bowsies would slip in it and break their noggins, says I to him, and sue you for damages! And when I pointed out to him that stained glass gives more privacy, says he, "But I want people to see in through the windas that me pub is packed." Such a thick! But we got the amber glass with a shell design on it. Lovely it is.'

Finally, Phyllis persuaded him to put in a piano on a little raised platform. He agreed to this when she said she would play and sing for a few nights until he got a professional. He fancied his own voice singing Al Jolson's 'Sonny Boy'. Phyllis had never had a piano lesson in her life, but she could strum out any tune, filling in a few melodic chords in the background. She made light of her musical ability.

'Sure hadn't we always got the old "bananna" in the parlour at home? I saw me Da at it since I could see anything. All the family can do it – it's only child's play.'

Phyllis was thirty-six years of age on the great opening night of Frare's Lounge Bar. I had been roped in to help as a barmaid. Phyllis wanted us there. She had told us so much. Mr Frare was very sweet about it. 'Let your Granny sit in the corner, and give her whatever she wants. Don't you do any dirty work, just circulate. It'll give a good impression. The fellas love a good lookin' girl around the place. Just fend them off, don't tangle with them! It's all free drink, them reporters have hollow legs for it, so have those writers and poets! They're the worst – the poets! Me brother has a place in Crown Alley, I know them!'

The place, unusual for the time, was sumptuously comfortable, abounding with studded leather and polished mahogany. An air of bonhomie was quickly apparent. The piano was not opened until the drinks had gone into their fourth round, which did not take as long as if the customers had been paying.

Phyllis struck a few notes to gain attention, then, as to the manner born, she launched herself into a song popular at the time, 'You Are My Sunshine, My Only Sunshine'. The old familiar sight of her heaving bosom and flashing dark eyes almost made me weep with the memory. But weeping was not the mood that night. Phyllis generated a saucy spirit of naughty cheer. One song led to another with effortless ease, her fingers tinkling the piano and sprinkling out the tunes.

All the Dalys were there, they formed a perfect claque for Phyllis had she needed one. She did not. She was at once an enormous success. Mr Daly gave his rendering of an old ballad, accompanying himself with martial music:

Hannagan's wife was on the floor
And Nick, the auld Divartar
He raised his hump
Once more he cried,
"We'll strike for Gibaraltar!"'

While Mr Frare sang his favourite Al Jolson with all the verses, 'When there are grey skies, I don't mind the grey skies . . .', his audience gradually resumed the normal noise of drinkers. I do not think he noticed, he seemed lost to the world in the tragic song. When Phyllis returned to the platform, clapping and stamping broke out in frenzied acclaim.

The place was so packed that, after a while, I could no longer circulate as instructed. I stood just inside the flap of the counter, dutifully smiling, occasionally taking and replacing a glass. I was aware for some time that I was being studied, but in the many eyes around me I could not recognize a familiar pair. Then I tracked down the intent gaze of a face above an army officer's uniform. I had never seen the face before, and yet it was remotely like someone.

Despite the fact that I tried to avoid the gaze of this unknown, I could see that the uniformed figure was gradually moving through the drinkers. Many more had come than could be seated, the floor space was thronged.

Then he was beside me: 'Hello, Lia.' The voice was unmistakable.

'Why, it's Tony! I didn't know you!'

I had forgotten his very existence.

'Are you here with someone?' he asked. 'Or do you own the place?'

I told him I was with my grandmother and I watched his face thaw, until it was almost as I remembered. He had been handsome before, now with the moustache and the spanking uniform his looks were superlative. I brought him over to Gran's corner, and we found a space to sit down. I indicated my surprise at the uniform.

'I joined the Irish Army for the duration of the Emergency. That's a pal of mine over there, he's a cousin of the Frares. He was coming up for this "do" and I got a lift with him. We're both in the Curragh. I'm in Administration, he's in Signals. My car is out in Foxrock. It is hard to get petrol.'

His conversation went on like that, filling in pauses in the singing and in the general hubbub. He was on four days' leave. His mother in Tunbridge Wells was very concerned about the War, very upset that he hadn't joined the 'real' army. We smiled at that, remembering how we shared a sense of humour about odd things. He had the rank of Captain, yes he quite liked the Army – easy life in a neutral army, a mountain of paperwork but none of it urgent. Of course he wouldn't like it for a lifetime, a bit boring, but this shindig wouldn't last that long. Suddenly he stopped talking.

Standing up very straight and soldierly, he said, 'I am keeping you from the party, I must let you go back to your friends.'

I smiled at Gran, nodding over her hot toddy. 'My friend will be asleep if I don't take her home soon,' I told him.

'Lia, you're married, aren't you?'

'Not yet!' I answered, holding his gaze.

'Engaged then?'

'Not even that,' I replied above the din, 'just an old-fashioned spinster.'

Tony took Gran and me home in his friend's car. He waited in the little parlour, sitting in Brian Boru's chair, while I settled Gran into bed. Then we went back to the singsong. I had never invited Tony to Gran's house when I knew him before. Now, it did not matter to me what he thought of my humble background, one way or the other. I felt free of him.

Tony was always able to persuade me to have a few drinks, although otherwise I did not drink. Of course the drinks went to my head. In the small hours, with Phyllis's father thumping the piano, we were all dancing out in the street, backwards and forwards between the pub and the Liffey wall.

268

Tony and I were cheek to cheek although we were acting as people who had just met. Our past friendship, and its sudden end, was not referred to, neither explanation nor apology was deemed necessary. When Tony's fellow officer came to say that they had better start heading back to the Curragh, Tony very courteously said goodnight and goodbye. Phyllis and I, in very giggly humour, walked the short distance home to the narrow street, and to bed.

The very next day, Phyllis came home in a state of bewilderment. She had met a man (she gave him the Dublin soubriquet of 'yer man') at the party. He seemed to be talking about her singing and piano-playing, but she didn't take much notice of him because, 'from me Da down to the cat, they were all langered! However, didn't yer man come into the shop that morning, luckily Frare was still in his bed, and what did yer man say, only that he had a pub in the Isle of Man – a high-class lounge he called it, and listen to this – yer man wants me to go and sing in his high-class lounge!'

My astonishment must have shown in my face.

'Yes,' added Phyllis, 'you're surprised now, lovey, but wait till you hear! Me singing, yer man said, is a great comedy act and me piana-playing is even funnier. The almighty cheek of him.'

I could visualize Phyllis's struck-dumb face behind the counter of the shop when yer man came out with this bombshell. Suddenly I thought of Tadek's criticism of Phyllis's singing all those years ago. My eyes filled with tears and I hugged Phyllis very tight.

'I love your singing,' I whispered.

'Oh but lovey,' said Phyllis, 'you haven't heard the whole of it yet! Yer man says to me, I'll give you fifty pounds a week!'

Now I really did feel surprise. Fifty pounds a week in the nineteen-forties was a rare wage in Ireland.

'And,' went on Phyllis, 'when I said to yer man, you're a baldy liar – do you know what he said? He said, it's only a pound an hour. Work it out, said yer man. Six days a week –

269

oh yes, I'm to get a day off, probably Monday – six days. Six into fifty, sez yer man, goes eight and a third. That's the number of hours a day I'd be expected to work! Sure that's nothing. I am working now twelve hours a day for Frare and he gives me two pounds and fifteen shillings a week . . . which I thought was good,' Phyllis added loyally.

'Didn't you tell Frare you would sing in the new pub?' I asked.

'Only till he got someone,' Phyllis replied.

'So are you off to the Isle of Man then?' asked Gran.

'I am not!' Phyllis snorted. 'Making a jeer of me singing and then saying he was going to pay fifty pounds to hear me being an eejit! Pure bloody buggery! He can put his fifty pounds where the monkey put the nuts.'

But, in fact, Phyllis did go off to the Isle of Man. We spurred her on, Gran and I, with all the encouragement she needed. She was swayed, too, by the awe of her mother at the mention of fifty pounds. The thought of how much she would be able to help her own family with fifty pounds a week, that was the final deciding factor. Fifty pounds a week for the whole summer!

'But, Lovey, if you ever need me, you have only to say the word and I'll be back on the next boat. You're number one with Phyllis, and don't go forgetting that now! And mind me chair that Brian Boru sat on, and me few pots and crocks. I won't be gone forever, ye know. Yer man says my fare will be paid home at the end of the season – and going too! Is he mad, do you think?'

'It's Frare that's mad,' Gran said wisely. 'Sure if he gave you ten pounds a week, you'd stay forever.'

We knew Phyllis would do well wherever she went. We knew that her own exuberance blossomed through the songs she sang, making people laugh and relax. We missed her sorely.

True to my promise, I polished the huge oak chair, and sent off a picture postcard every week, receiving the odd card in return. Phyllis was having a great time, the customers in the high-class lounge – three floors of it – were easy to please, they seemed to be all gone daft on her, yer man was delighted. Her only problem was no exercise, no polishing or scrubbing, she was putting on weight – talk about makin' butther!

I did not tell Phyllis in my brief cards that I was worried about Gran. Each evening I hurried home to be with her – always fearful that in my absence she had fallen, or injured herself in some way. The summer was passing, we talked of a little holiday but I could see her heart was not in it.

Towards the end of August, I took leave from the office to be with her all the time. The doctor thought I was being over-anxious, she had no organic disease. On the last night of August, she died in her sleep. I had read to her before tucking her up. The reading had lulled her to sleep. When the grip of her hand on mine had slackened, I had kissed her and gone to bed. She never woke again.

Gran had a beautiful funeral. All the old neighbours among whom she had lived since ever she came home from America, they were all there carrying wreaths of flowers. The Dalys were there, sympathetic and helpful as ever. I had asked Mrs Daly not to tell Phyllis yet. She would only try to come home, or break her heart with frustration. I felt she must be given this chance which had come so unexpectedly.

Mr Heiton had arranged the funeral, as instructed by Max's father. There were carriages for the old neighbours, and a meal afterwards. Gran was buried in the grave of my mother as she had wished. Marie was her most beloved child. There seemed to be no one now to make me stand outside the railings, and I stood at the open grave with Max's father. I became aware that a handsome officer had come to stand by my other side. Through a mist of tears, I saw Tony Lloyd. I felt his arm warm across my shoulder, and I was grateful. I must have said goodbye to him, because I went home with Max's father to Terenure.

271

Here I could write all my memories of Gran. I could cover pages trying to recapture the warm, loving woman. There is no need. Long long ago I lost her, yet I carry her presence always within me. Sometimes through the years and far away from Dublin, the narrow street comes into focus in my mind. I see us, walking down in the evening light, we stop at her door, she puts the key in the lock, we go inside closing the door securely. Inside is love of so special a kind. Ah, she understood how to love.

Chapter Seventeen

Max's father wanted to make plans for my future. Come and live with him, give up the old job in the Civil Service, spend my days cataloguing his books, helping him to pass the time, there were so many ways in which I could help him.

I wanted to give in immediately. I needed so much to be needed. I loved the old man, not in the way I loved Gran, but with a sense of reverence. His erudition, his wisdom, his kindly foresight were magical in my life. And more, much more than that, he was my precious link with Tadek. Any hope of news must come from him. He thought I waited always for news of Max. And of course, to some degree, that was also true.

I stayed with him for a week, taking leave of absence from the office. Each day he made a case for my staying on, at least until the War was over. Each day, I knew more clearly that I must be independent. It seemed to me that my independence could be given up for one person only, to fritter it away would be to diminish the gift of myself to that one person when the time came. I could not begin to explain this to the old man, whose constant thought was of Max's future happiness in which he hopefully discerned I was to play a part.

At last I persuaded him that I would return to Gran's little house, which was of course mine, to put the place in order.

'Do not sell it yet,' he advised me, 'the property market will improve after the War, when new development begins. You could let it, of course?'

How different it was to come home in the evening to a cold and empty house, no cheery voice calling from the little kitchen as I came in through the hall; no cosy, affectionate body to hug and kiss; no Phyllis to keep the little house spick and span.

Only when Gran had been gone for many weeks did I write to Phyllis. I knew she would blame herself, she would feel she had deserted me. So when I came to write the letter, I assured her over and over that Gran's going had been just as we would have wished, what Phyllis's mother had called 'a beautiful death'. Gran had such a particular way of living her little life, she would not have liked hospital with all the enforced humiliation of disease. It was true, as Aunt Julia had pointed out, that Gran 'had not had the benefit of priest or vicar, no Holy Unction, no preparation.' I knew that Phyllis, whose ideas of religion and superstition were tightly meshed, would worry about that. So I pointed out to her that we knew, she and I, how all Gran's living had been a preparation. Did we ever know her to do a mean or an unjust thing?

I have the faded letter before me now, and the other letters and postcards carefully kept by Phyllis in a large blue envelope marked: Letters from Lovey. I thought, in the careful writing of that letter, I was consoling poor Phyllis for not being there when I needed her. I thought it was the letter of a mature woman able to face up to life. It is the letter of a desolate child, loneliness cries out of every word. It cannot have helped Phyllis much, but it helps me now to understand the person who lived through the events in the year that followed Gran's going. Maturity is a long time coming.

Many of Gran's old neighbours were old indeed. They sat by their doors or windows, there was little they could now do but observe the passing scene. When I returned from Terenure, they were able to tell me that an army officer 'had the place haunted, knocking on the door every evening, he was, enquiring did we know were you gone away, or left the place altogether. A great big chap in the green uniform.'

I knew it was Tony Lloyd. Any interest I had ever had in him was evaporated long ago. Nevertheless, when he 'phoned me in the office on the day of my return, I found myself agreeing to meet him.

How many weeks or months slipped by before I was back in the old routine? Most evenings we found ourselves sitting in the bar of the familiar pub. Wartime restrictions were in full swing. There were shortages of everything, and early closing everywhere. Tony had been promoted another rank, with a change from the Curragh of Kildare to Dublin's Richmond Hill. He often asked that he accompany me home for supper. I had not invited him in Gran's time, I saw no reason to do so now. He had let his family home in Foxrock once again, he retained the flat in Fitzwilliam Square, but spent many nights in barracks.

My life reminded me of the glass jar, baited with amber-coloured jam, in which Aunt Julia used to catch summer flies.

Sometimes, I regretted that I had not gone to live with the old man in Terenure. My happiest times were spent each week with him, he supplied the security I found so necessary. All that year, he had no direct communication with Max, all he knew for certain was that the two boys were alive, and together. I spent Christmas, a couple of restful days without any celebration, in Terenure. It was enough to be there with him.

I did not see Tony Lloyd for a week. Tony thought to make a big fight about this, he had bought a present which he withheld when we met again in the New Year. My indifference soon cooled his petulant bad humour. He found himself exerting great discipline over his anger, pleading with me to accept the elegant gold chain. When Tony put himself out to be nice, he could be marvellously attractive.

One night in Terenure, I told Max's father that Tony had given hints that he was working himself up to a proposal of marriage. At first, the hint had to do with when the Emergency is over and he is out of the Army. Now, the hint says this darned

Emergency could last too long, a fellow is getting on.

The old man mused awhile on this news. He smiled across at me.

'In the ancient Brehon Laws that held sway in Ireland for centuries,' he said, 'there was great emphasis laid on physical beauty. Did you know that to be elected High King, a man must be perfect in physique? He must have the height, wonder of build and limb, exact symmetry of features, the hair crisp and golden. I am thinking that your friend Tony would make a High King.'

'And what about character?' I asked.

'Ah,' he replied, 'in Brehon Law beauty was not skin-deep. It went right through to the spirit. The total was perfection. The Brehons believed that outward beauty betokened inward grace.'

'I think I do, too,' I said.

'Ah yes, I know you do. But beauty is often a depiction. You must ponder on that. I have observed that you attribute integrity of soul to the artist who can paint a beautiful picture.'

'But of course,' I told him, 'and to a writer who can write a wonderful book.'

The old man shook his silvery head. 'You will find it is not so.' He was sad and serious. 'The writer and the artist are also men in their essential living, a separate thing. It is the writer who gives the world the wonderful book, the man of course uses his brain and his pen, he is the means not the end – he is not the book. These books, these pictures, are creations of art – the painter himself is a creation of flesh. The question of Sacred Writing would take a lot more debate.'

I went over to his couch. Sitting beside him, and linking my arm through his was my way of coming close to him.

'You love beauty in people, too,' I said to him.

'I adore it,' he answered, 'and it has led me astray many times.'

*

276

At the end of the following summer, Phyllis came home for a week's holiday. She stayed with me exactly as if nothing had changed. She cleaned up the house to her idea of clean. We visited Gran's grave and I took a few days' leave so I could settle down to hear all. She had not come home after her first season, but had had her Mam and Dad over for a holiday. The two full seasons she had been offered were now at an end.

'Yer man is talking of a proper contract – and better pay, no point in working for peanuts! But I think I'd like to see other places, like Blackpool or Bournemouth. A woman I met told me I should get an agent, and he'd divide up me time – she said it's more profitable that way. She did three weeks over in the place opposite me – "gigs" she calls moving around – only a slip of a thing but she does it in a man's costume, drag they call it. Terrible vulgar, of course. You'd wonder where she was brought up, the things she says! If you hadda come over, I wouldn't have let you go to see her! Of course she sings and dances as well – very well, I must say. Oh, a lovely man's evening-suit, top hat and all. It's funny, but women go for her in a big way – I hope they all know she's a woman herself! Well anyway, women are mad about her because she makes a real jeer of the men by telling things about them like as if she knew because she was a real man, but real women usually only suspect them things!

'Well, Lovey, you wouldn't know what I mean but honest to God some of the things are a howl.'

Phyllis had other news which she hesitated to tell. She had seen, and spoken to Burton.

'Ye see, the whole place is like a big military camp. Everyone is in a uniform. You'd be dazzled. But this night, I saw this huge fella in a uniform that shone more than anyone else's. Something familiar but I couldn't place it. I forget people get older, and change – not that he looks older – in a way – only the hair, I think he dyes it – anyway it glitters. He comes up to me and, says he, "I must say I do admire your act. You are quite a card!" Of course the minute he spoke I knew who he was – I never heard another voice like that. Lovey, it was Burton! In the uniform! Puffed and perfumed the same as ever! Isn't he in that thing, ENSA, that buys shows for the troops? I wouldn't be surprised but he's the head man in it. As proud as Punch!'

'Was he alone?' I enquired.

'No,' said Phyllis vehemently, 'and that was another thing I meant to tell you. This young wan was clinging to his arm like a leech, all long black hair and Italian-looking. He introduced her as a friend of yours! Francesca something . . . I suppose they are married, they were together in the hotel.'

At least it was not Laelia. That would truly have scandalized Phyllis.

'That is what he is,' I told Phyllis, 'a theatrical agent. Francesca was in the Abbey School – I am sure I mentioned her to you at the time. Didn't he tell you he was in show business?'

'He was flaunting the Francesca one all around the place! She's the star in some London show, and they were filming her in the Isle of Man. Do you think he's her agent as well as her man?'

'He's a good agent, Phyllis, you'll find his name in the book!'

'He couldn't be a good anything,' Phyllis snorted, exactly as she used to at Mrs Mayne long ago.

I have never understood why I burned with painful jealousy when I heard of Burton's association with girls. It did not assuage the pang to think that I could have had him the night I handed him to Berny, whose association with him continued after she went to work in London. No doubt there were hundreds of girls. I told myself he was disgusting. Or was it me? I thought of Francesca and Burton so enviously that I could not sleep.

The next day I brought up the subject again, and I questioned Phyllis: 'Had Francesca got a child with her? Did you see her on the beach, or somewhere like that?'

'A child! Her? She'd be the last one I'd expect to have a child! What put that in your head?'

'Oh, I thought she had got married.'

There had been a rare moment here and there when, catching sight of Tony's handsome face, I had thought of Francesca. Francesca had carried Tony's child, and there was no doubt in my mind but that she had given up the child for adoption. And Laelia's child by Burton? Frustrated pity filled my heart when I thought of those two unwanted babies.

The old man was at the window watching for my weekly visit. I knew at once that he was deeply perturbed. I did not have to ask for news, a letter was spread on his desk.

'Sit by me, sit by me, and read this letter.' Agitatedly he shuffled the pages round. 'It is bad news, the worst news.'

Sometimes, he said things like this. It gave me time to collect all my secrets into a fortress within preparatory to a siege on my emotions. Tadek had enjoined a silence that I had never broken. Equally I could not hurt the old man by seeming indifferent to Max's fate. I was not indifferent, far from it, but my uppermost thought was always: so long as Tadek is safe. That day, I strove to have either mask ready.

I have the letter before me now. Part of it I can no longer read. It was written in pencil, hurriedly, perhaps in near-darkness. I knew the old man had contacts, through the Partisans, to art dealers in Paris and in London. I knew he was spending much money on international detectives. Nothing came directly to Dublin, but to Belfast in devious ways. From Belfast it was not impossible to contact Dublin. It was a slow way, and difficult, in wartime. This letter in Hebrew was many months old. The old man had written the translation. The date is still clear, 'November 1943, Russian Border'.

'We have been able to establish a sanctuary in the woods. We have got some weaponry from Italians fighting on the Russian front, now scattered trying to get back to Italy. Russian Jews were driven hundreds of miles on foot – passed within some miles on road to Sobibor. Many died in desperate conditions. Partisans followed the marchers. Contact was made and infiltration. In September less than two thousand arrived at the concentration camp. All but eighty were immediately gassed. These were put to help build an extension to the crematoriums. Infiltrated Partisans staged a rising, attacked guards with axes, knives, bare hands. Guards killed many but about 400 prisoners and infiltrators escaped, many of these ran into the minefields all around the camp and were killed. Many hunted down and shot, many killed by anti-semitic members of Polish right-wing infiltrators – our constant plague. I searched three days for Tadek, then we returned here. I fear the worst. Take care of yourself. Look after Lia for me. It must end soon.'

I was terrified to trust my voice. That Max was safe must be acknowledged, but no words came. Tears flooded out onto the desk. The old man understood so many things, perhaps he knew the wound not to probe. He held me against his shoulder, murmuring words of comfort for me, and for himself.

'Oh Father Abram, what these Christians are, whose own hard dealings teach them to suspect the thoughts of others.' Quoting Shakespeare was a solace when words of his own might have been lost in tears. *'Hath not a Jew eyes? Hath not a Jew hands, organs, dimensions, senses, affections, passions, hurt with the same weapons, warmed and cooled as a Christian is. If you poison us, do we not die? If you wrong us, shall we not revenge? The villainy you teach me, I will execute: and it shall go hard but I will better the instruction.'*

The growing bitterness in the old man's voice made me shiver, I strove to check my tears, and smile at him.

'You are not Shylock,' I told him. 'You would not banish your daughter if she stole your turquoise ring!'

He tried to respond with the familiar indulgent smile but no smile would come. His voice was full of bitterness and sorrow. 'Shylock. Ah yes, little one, Shakespeare dealt us a vicious hand of cards with Shylock . . . the typical, black-hearted Jew for every scholar in every school for hundreds of years. The Jew will have his pound of flesh, and in return, the Christian is justified to strip the flesh from the Jew's bones.'

I murmured the words of love over and over to the old man. The love was for him and for Max. But most of all, it was for Tadek, lost in some horrible place called Sobibor . . . maybe trampled under the thousands of feet of men and women he was trying to help. Tadek, I love you so much, all the time, every day and every hour of every day. Please don't die out there in that awful place. Please let yourself be found. I love you. I love you.

The old man was holding me close to him. 'And I love you too, child. "Look after Lia," he writes. Even in the terrible extremity of trying to write this letter, the message is there, "Take care of Lia for me."' The old man pointed to the Hebrew words of which I could read only my name.

I made an effort to comfort him, trying to distract him. He loved to be asked questions about history, or art, or language. He did not love me less because my questions showed my ignorance. Perhaps he loved me more because I needed him so much, and because I longed to be needed, to be essential to the one I loved.

'How does it help Hitler to win the War just by persecuting the Jews who live in Germany?'

Sternly, the old man answered me, 'And in Poland, and in Russia, and in Czechoslovakia – and if he does win the War, he will exterminate them in France, and in England, and anywhere else he finds them.'

I remembered what Max had told me on the night we went out to Enniskerry: the Jew remains a Jew no matter what

281

passport he holds. I listened as the old man talked on about the book Hitler had written revealing his hatred of the Jews, and then I began to wonder what Tadek had meant about the impossibility of a Jew and an Irish Catholic ever getting together across some immense barrier that divided them. Why, I pondered, did Max's father not appear to see that great barrier as between his son, Max, and me?

'. . . In the eighteenth century, the one they named the 'Age of Enlightenment', the new thinkers accused the Jews of being the forerunners of Christianity. The Jews had introduced it, you see, in the person of Jesus! This was a new, a novel kind of anti-semitism. Despite the fact that the Jews had rejected the anti-Jew, Jesus, and put him to death. The nineteenth century made great headway in the persecution of Jews, they were executed for every criminal offence, no matter what. Kill them! Kill them!'

I took the old man's hands and held them to my heart. I whispered calming phrases to him, and gradually he ceased the flow of words.

'It will pass,' I told him. 'Max says so in the letter.'

'Ah no, little one, the persecution of Jews will never pass. Persecution is their destiny. And yet, so much of the religion of the world is Judaic. All wisdom is borrowed from the Sacred Writings of the Jewish belief in Yahweh.'

The old man fell silent. I had an idea, and I put it to him: 'Wouldn't it be wonderful if the gates of a country could be opened and all the unwelcome people could walk out? Say to a new country with everything new like laws and opportunities. Like America, for instance?'

This time I got the benevolent smile, filled up with sadness. 'Whatever might have happened before, it cannot happen now. The Great Powers are locked in combat and the alleviation of emigration laws is not on the agenda.'

He took up Max's letter. He gave me the translation and I put it in my handbag. I listened to him attentively. I would have to wait to explore my heart until I was at home, at home

282

in the little house in the narrow street. I would shut the door and I would know that I was alone in the world. Never again could I hope to see Tadek. He had been crushed and killed. He was gone out into eternal blackness, away from me for ever.

I stayed with the old man until his manservant came to help him to bed. Usually I was driven home by Ted. That night I walked, the sooner to be alone. There were no lights anywhere. All windows were blacked out, but no one could black out the moon and it shone down on the paths of Dublin town, glistening like ice.

I walked down Harold's Cross Road as far as the Grand Canal, then along the Canal to Portobello, beyond to Charlemont, and at the next bridge was Leeson Street. I crossed the road here, cutting down Fitzwilliam Street and into the Square. My reason for remembering that little journey was here, and oh, how many times have I wished I had accepted the drive home that night?

Skirting the railings to Pembroke Street, I stood looking up at the windows of Tony Lloyd's flat. There was no chink of light anywhere, no way of knowing if he were at home or in the barracks. It was long after ten o'clock, I seemed to have been walking for hours. I was indescribably lonely. It was, of course, much too late to call, I told myself, but in an unbearable longing for comfort, I rang his bell.

Tony gave me a heart-warming welcome, kisses had long been taken for granted between us, and I felt grateful for his kiss. I was in, and sitting down with a glass in my hand almost as soon as he had opened the hall door. His sitting-room was cosy and elegant, with his mother's chairs, and pictures.

'Wasn't I just this minute thinking about you!' he said in his hearty way. 'Telepathy, that's what it was! I knew this was your night for going to Terenure. I was wondering, were you home yet. I came down near your street on my way from the Knights. We close early on account of the blackout.'

Tony never revealed what took place at the Knights' Meeting. It seemed to be a secret society. It was very important in his life.

'Here, let me fill up your glass! Your hands are cold, let me warm them.'

Tony had switched on an electric fire. I noticed the fine red fireside rug.

'Is that new?' I asked.

In some confusion, he told me he had bought it for the night of the party to which I had not come. 'Just something to make the place look festive,' he said, 'festive for the occasion.'

'I am sorry,' I said and I felt the tears brimming over.

Tony held me close. 'I am the one who is sorry,' he said. 'I let you down when you needed a friend. I was a fool. I thought you were standing me up!'

I sobbed into his shoulder. I knew he thought I was crying over the past, his past. I knew I would regret this useless hour in which I wept to one man for the death of another. Every instinct told me to jump up and run. This awful need for the warmth of a man's arms was betraying me again. I wanted so much to belong to someone, to have someone need me. I wanted to lose myself in someone's need for me, to forget the horror of Max's letter in an engulfing passion that would sweep me away from minefields and crematoriums.

'If you had come that night, darling,' Tony said fondly, 'we would be married by now. You know that?'

It was too late, too late by a few seconds, to jump up and run. Tony was sure I had come to him tonight because I wanted to belong here. He thought my coming staked a special claim, a special claim which I had almost forfeited on the night of his so special party. I knew now what Chersy had suspected then, that party was to have been my betrothal party. In Tony's confidence there was an assured assumption, on my part a wilful blind ignorance – and tonight a thoughtless complicity. It was too late to hurt Tony with a rude awakening. Besides, the fire, the whiskey, the strength of his arms, and his marvellously handsome face, all worked to my undoing. Muzzily I snuggled against him letting the moments drift by, trying, willing myself to forget what I had learned tonight, to forget, even for an hour, the only truly beloved face and form. For that one hour let Tony cast a spell on me, let Tony be the first.

Suddenly, I was on my feet.

'Oh Tony, you are so sweet. I didn't mean to stay. It is late. I must go. Thank you so much for the drink.'

Tony did not demur. He helped me into my coat.

'That is what I admire about you, Lia. You are not cheap. You keep a fellow on the straight and narrow. We'll wait, darling. Now that I know I am the one again, it changes everything!'

Now I had adddded the complication of Tony Lloyd's affections, and intentions, to my grief.

In the small, lonely house I was torn between tears and thoughts. There was nothing to live for, no hope for the particular future I had planned all my life. Why not cross the street, and jump into the Liffey? The Liffey was the least salubrious of rivers, I detested the smell of it. Why not go down to Sandymount Strand? – but even at high tide it would be hard to drown there. I knew nothing of overdoses of sleeping pills. I could not have used a gun, even had I one. Each time I thought of another quick way to die, I was overcome by tears of self-pity.

That pity turned into pity for Tony. I sat down to write a letter to him explaining . . . but explaining what? That I had made use of him to pass the time? That I was really very fond of him, but did not intend to spend my life with him?

All the specious sentences in the world came to mind: I wasn't good enough for him; we were not ideally suited; I was past the marrying stage; I would soon be thirty and on the shelf – a spinster.

But Tony was a very glamorous prop for one soon to be a

spinster. He was a status symbol of that time. Surely a kind providence would allow me have Tony as my boyfriend for a little while longer? Tony was so handsome and devoted. In the Department of Estates, Tony was considered a real 'catch' . . . his West British Old Ascendancy accent, his superb good looks, his stylish expensive clothes, his car when cars were upper-class, and of course his top-grade position.

In the mirror above Gran's little davenport I saw my tear-stained face. I did not love Tony Lloyd, and yet I had turned to him as if I would put him in Tadek's place, in my heart. No one could ever take Tadek's place. I stared at my face in the mirror, the tear-stained face of a child who needed comforting . . . the comforting that Tadek used to bring long ago. I remembered his hands smoothing my nightie down to my heels. I remembered the little cakes he took to me in case I was hungry when I had been sick. 'You could die of malnutrition,' he said. Tadek, I am dying of malnutrition now. I need to be loved and you will never be there to love me ever again. Never, never again. You used to say that crying was the only thing that helped me. But there has to be someone to dry the tears – someone full of loving sympathy. Tears that dried on the face brought no relief.

I tried to stare myself out of countenance, but the accusing eyes stared back. I did not love Tony Lloyd. Why was I leading him on?

Chapter Eighteen

Tony's 'phone call next day was assuredly confident. Our relationship had evidently gone up in his eyes. He had forgotten to mention, he said, that he was going on training to the south, near Kinsale. Had I been to Cork? Would I come down for the weekend? Maybe every weekend? He could promise me a really bright time. Kinsale was marvellous, as old as the hills. He was so pleased, his tones were so tender. I took details of his address, and promised faithfully to arrange to get to Kinsale.

I had a breathing space. One thing I learned again, I could not trust myself. I would not last out a whole weekend in Kinsale with so attractive a man as Tony. My need for an obliteration of memory would betray me once more.

I think it strange now that I was so sure then, so absolutely sure, that sexual fulfilment was the answer to my longing for love. It did not occur to me that perhaps love is the longing for sexual fulfilment. It did not occur to me that there would be no fulfilment without love. Sheer instinct had made me run away from Burton, but it had not finished the piteous longing that arose at the thought of him. Another instinct – was it self-preservation? – had got me out of Tony's flat, but had not blinded me to the fact that perhaps the next time I would go over the brink of desire into a full clamour for knowledge.

I wondered a lot in the following week if I had all the appetites of a bad girl. Perhaps the nuns had known best when they excluded me from their Convent. Deep, deep down was the never-forgotten image of Bonny Kelarr. I decided to go to Confession in Gardiner Street. The Jesuits, I believed, had the right answers.

Kneeling in the queue to examine my conscience, I realized it was almost two years since I had been to Confession.

I had not missed attending Mass on Sundays. Mass was a routine part of living. Was that good enough? I could not think of any lies, or thefts, or calumniations. What then? Had I sinned against the sixth Commandment? The more I tried to formulate words to convey the hot tide of longing for fulfilment, the more amorphous the feeling became. I felt I had detached the lovely wings of a butterfly, the actual body of feeling had fallen to the ground.

The kindly priest was reassuring. It was good that I had not missed Mass on Sundays. Go regularly to Confession and Communion. What about the sixth? Impure acts? Alone or with others? No, Father, never. So you have not committed adultery? Interfered in the sanctity of a marriage? No, Father, never. And do you pay your way as you go through the business of living? Yes, Father.

'Three Hail Marys for your penance, and go in peace.'

I sat in the gloomy church for a long, long time. I prayed for Tadek's soul, telling the Presence in the Tabernacle that Tadek deserved a top place in Heaven among the angels, because Tadek was the best man who ever lived.

There was no comfort in my prayers. The ghost of Tadek did not come to that church.

When I came out of Gardiner Street Church, I walked home by St Mel's. Berny, I knew, was in London, but the secretariat might have news of her. They had. Her engagement had been announced. He was an American, an internationally famous neuro-surgeon. They had heard he was a divorced man, not once but twice. So, they asked, what do you think of that? It was certainly food for thought, as I walked slowly home. Berny was no stranger to playing at love, 'having sex' was what she called it. I wondered, was this the perfect thing for her at last? Had play ceased and real living begun?

In due course, Berny's letter came. She was head over heels in love, she wrote, and he was 'the greatest'. She would not take no for an answer – I was to be bridesmaid, the date was July 31st, in Belfast. Send my measurements immediately – the dress would be waiting.

Despite my daily good intentions of making a clean break, Tony's courtship gathered pace. I avoided going to Kinsale, I avoided calling to his flat, or having him to my house, nevertheless our association built up. He wanted to accompany me to Belfast, he feared I could meet some new gallant (as he termed it) who would turn my head. I hoped I would, but heard myself arguing in a way that was committing me to the very thing I wanted to escape.

'Oh, so you don't trust me, Tony?'

'Of course I trust you, sweetheart. You are the best person in the whole world. It's just that you're so – so fetching, don't you know. If you were wearing a ring now, I'd feel much safer – a fine big plaster of an engagement ring that could be seen by a galloping horse from a mile distant!'

'But sure, Tony, couldn't I take off the ring up in Belfast, only putting it on for the return journey?'

'But you see, Lia, you're not the sort that would do that!'

Poor Tony, you had such faith in me then.

'Now, Tony, you promised! Not a word about engagement rings until Christmas. We said we would give ourselves this six months.'

I think, to me, it must have seemed like an endurance game I was playing with Tony. Another breathing space. Another postponement. If I kept that up long enough, he would get over it, give in, even hate me and go away. When he moaned, 'You don't know how bad I have it,' I had no idea what he actually meant. I, who longed for so much, did not know what Tony meant. I was full of good intentions, I never meant to be a tease, and there were many times when Tony was so desirable.

There had to be a reason why the wedding in Belfast filled me with tingling anticipation. I knew, from the moment I got the invitation, there was a very good chance Burton would be there. Berny had kept up a very hot affair with Burton since the first night in the Royal Hibernian. In a letter not so long back, she had referred to him as 'her darling gorgeous man, you'll never know what you missed! Wish he came round every night, he's mostly away when I have to make do with someone not half as good. . . .'

I hoped, sincerely, this someone was not the forthcoming bridegroom. It would be a poor start.

A darling gorgeous man. I woke up with the thought, and I slept with it. This time I would not run away.

Yes, he was there all right, and looking more like a film star than ever. A wave of contentment broke over me. I have never understood why, I only know it was so.

Berny's family in Belfast was quite clearly what Phyllis used to call 'top-notch'. There were bishops and banks of flowers, clergy and candles and triumphal music. Berny was radiantly happy in trailing white lace, her dark hair gleaming under a coronet of pearls. I had met the bridegroom before the ceremony, a handsome if slightly dissolute-looking American from the Deep South of the United States. He too was resplendent in the full dress uniform of the US Medical Corps. The bridesmaids' dresses were billowy and low-cut in a clear shining green. There were four of us, two of Berny's sisters, and a teenage daughter of the new husband – or third-hand husband as Burton remarked later.

'It's a good job he's rich,' Burton said. 'Second-hand! Third-hand! He'll be a genuine antique husband before he finishes swopping. A richly gilded antique!'

'Don't you think this might be his last? He seems quite crazy about Berny.'

'Well, if he comes out alive!' Burton laughed. 'She's insatiable, your little friend! Eh, I thought Catholics couldn't marry divorced people – in a church, anyway?'

I had thought that, too. There must be a way. Maybe the groom was not married in church before. Berny's father and mother were very imposing people. They gave the impression that to be a well-heeled Catholic in Belfast was akin to royalty.

Gossiping with Burton, laughing with him at his hilarious remarks about everybody, feeling his eyes on me, relishing his outrageous compliments.

'You are easily the most beautiful girl in this whole damned reception. How do you do it? Penned up in that ghastly dusty office! You should have gone on the stage – not legit – the music hall!'

I asked him about Phyllis. He had signed her up. She had a few acts the soldiers would go for.

'It's the brassy innocence of her!' he told me. 'She's been married and all, and it's eyes up to Heaven if you use the wrong tense!'

'Phyllis never approved of you.'

'Oh, that was in my young days. Now I'm a little older, she can't think what improved me!'

The sillier the things he said, the more involved were my emotions. When he asked a serious question it seemed my heart would stop.

'You did not tell Berny that we were closely related?'

To hear him ask that was to feel a depth of intimacy as if he touched me. I was too breathless to speak.

'I am glad,' he said, 'it means we feel the same.'

In the crowded reception, we spoke here and there, drifting apart and meeting again.

'I have received a proposal of marriage,' I said as he pressed my hand in passing.

'For when?' he demanded when the chattering guests placed us together again. I knew then with a sense of peace that he was totally concerned with me. I smiled only, as he passed.

He seemed to know so many people in this gathering

where I knew the bride, and no one else. Was this truly the same Burton who had been married to my mother, the same man who had bought a pedigree puppy for my birthday, against whose naked body I had slept in perfect happiness on lazy summer mornings in 'Sunrise'?

'For when?' he demanded again.

'Not just immediately,' I answered airily.

And at last the reception was over. We had waved away the happy couple, who were chauffeured off in a splendid car to spend their first night in some lord's castle . . . their honeymoon plans were being kept a secret. Guests were breaking into groups to spend the evening together. I made my way to Berny's mother to thank her for a wonderful day. She was talking to a group of whom Burton was one.

'Ah my dear! The loveliest bridesmaid!' She was most gracious, if slightly overpowering. 'Of course you must not disappear! You must come back for dinner! Please do!'

I made my excuses. I intended to return to Dublin on the late train, and now I must go to the hotel to change. I thanked her again. She continued to fuss loudly about her son driving me to the hotel, but finally I convinced her my taxi was waiting.

There was a taxi waiting and Burton was in it. His dark brown eyes were glittering with amusement.

'You should go on the stage,' he said to me. 'The way you unseated her ladyship was a joy! Old whatsisname Fay taught you well!'

Burton waited in the bar while I changed and packed my case. I was trembling with a mixture of fear and excitement. His eyes lit up with admiration when I joined him. He raised his glass to me.

'You are the most beautiful little thing.' He handed me a drink.

'What about my train,' I asked, trying to steady my voice.

'No hurry,' Burton replied. 'Your train doesn't go until tomorrow!'

He gave me that special look, the look of absolute devotion which no doubt he knew would melt icicles. I wanted him to plead, to persuade, to coax. I glanced at my watch.

'Lia, look at me. Don't do what you did the last time. Fate has given us another chance, let's use it. Please. Even if it never happens again, let's make it tonight. Stay over with me. Please . . . don't make it hard for me. Of course you will, say you will.'

The familiar fragrance of his body was so dear to me. I had meant to tease, pretend, procrastinate just for the sheer wonder of being wanted. Moving a little closer, I was nodding my agreement, caught up in the thrilling certainty that this sexual fulfilment was come at last.

Dimly I remember another hotel, Burton's voice proclaiming with delighted conviction that his wife had joined him. Once again I was going up in a lift with Burton smiling into my eyes. It seemed as if the lift was going up, up, forever.

In Burton's room, I went into his arms with every nerve acquiescing.

He was tender. To him I was still a child – his child – I thought. He held back from me, gently slipping my blouse from my shoulders.

'Have you been wanting me for as long as I have been waiting for you? Tell me?' he questioned softly.

I thought I must have. I pressed closer.

'Then, why did you run away the last time?'

Maybe fear. I had been told it was . . . ghastly . . . the first time. . . . I whispered in breathless longing.

'What about this fellow who wants to marry you? Hasn't he had you?'

I shook my head. No. Never.

'And what about the Jew boy who got you the first time?'

I flung away from him, tears splashing down my face. 'He is dead, dead, dead. Dead in a concentration camp. Dead in a minefield.'

Burton had me back in his arms.

'So he was the one?'

'He never touched me. I asked him. He refused.'

That wasn't a lie. Tadek could have loved me had he wanted to.

'Refused?' Burton queried lightly, his manner had changed.

I turned on him savagely. 'Why did you bring me here? You wanted me! You begged me!'

He lit a cigarette. His fingers were shaking. 'Only in the way I want any beautiful woman. Maybe you are special because I actually love you, have done since the first moment I saw you on your mother's knee. Like I own you. I always wanted to believe you were mine, for my use only. Is that wrong? For years, I was your only friend . . . remember? In "Sunrise" in our bed?'

'What's different, then?' I asked. 'No one else has used me. You would be the first.'

'You see, I did not know that,' his voice was regretful yet tender. 'I could not do that deflowering thing to you now – here – in that bed – in this rotten hotel.'

'But isn't that what you wanted to do?' I was truly bewildered.

Burton was angry with me. 'No, I wanted to make love to you like we were both old hands at the game! I couldn't inflict pain on you, Lia.'

'You could, one time,' I retorted.

'You dreamt it,' he said, 'because you wanted to find refuge with those Jews.'

The rocking world came to a standstill. I knew that whether Burton lied, or forgot, what I remembered was what really happened. I knew the truth of that night beyond any shade of doubt. What Burton had inflicted on me was driven into my innermost being, marking me with a hunger that seemed fated never to be satisfied.

I splashed my face at the handbasin. He spoke but I could not hear. With outward composure, I took my case and left the room. He stood at the door, he was smoking a cigar. I turned once, were his brown eyes beseeching? I shall never know. I thought my heart would break, so bitter was the disillusionment of the love I had never been able to renounce.

Woefully, reluctantly, painfully, my mind went on returning to Burton in the months that followed that night. Disillusion brings so bitter a regret for the love given and betrayed, for the precious passion spilled needlessly and unnoticed. The bitter regret of disillusion is wormwood in the soul for a long, long time.

I never saw Burton again. I was to hear of him years afterwards when the devastating War was long over, and frail memory was taking care of the dead. A letter from his London solicitors would find me, far away from Dublin, a letter requesting my presence in their office.

Tony had decided the wedding would take place on the Tuesday after Easter Sunday, in the Chapel in Trinity College. He regarded Trinity, he said, as his Alma Mater. He had taken his degree in Trinity.

He knew very well that, apart from buying a wedding gown, I was not in a position to have a big 'society' wedding with a few hundred guests. I scarcely knew a few hundred people. Nevertheless, that was the way he was planning it. He could be very expansive. The wedding breakfast would be best in a country hotel, in his view. Perhaps the Bel Air in County Wicklow.

And the honeymoon! Well, no need to quibble about that. The Great Southern in Parknasilla! Of course. Good.

'I knew you would agree, Lia, you are so sweet!' The pater and mater had taken their annual holiday there for thirty years – Tony would be an honoured guest there! This he told me forty times.

He spent a lot of time compiling lists of guests, adding rather than deleting.

'Tony, could I get a word in edge-wise, please?'

'Umm, umm, what is it now, Lia?'

'Tony, my friend in Terenure would like to give the wedding reception in his house.'

Tony sat up straight. He looked positively shocked. 'What! The old Jewman? Lia, you cannot be serious. The old Jewman?'

'Tony, don't sound like that. He is my friend for years and years. I . . . I love him.'

'Yes, well that is something else we will have to talk about. He is not a suitable friend.'

I let that pass. 'Yes, but the reception after the wedding, Tony? He has offered –'

'Lia, are you mad! Many of the guests are members of the Knights. A Jewman's house would be – would be – would be an insult to them – and to me. In Terenure! Of all places!'

I was beginning to be exasperated. 'Tony, you have never been in his house. You do not know what you are talking about.'

Tony rounded on me. 'I know he is a Jew and that is enough.'

'Jesus was a Jew!' I shot the words at him.

'Jesus a Jew!' he stuttered. 'A good Irish Catholic saying that! Where do you get your weird ideas? Jesus was the Son of God – He was not a Jew.'

'But . . . but . . .' I began to stammer when Tony interrupted me. 'For Heaven's sake, Lia, did you never learn your catechism? Listen to me: God sent His only begotten Son into the world. Right? Right. The Jews rejected Him. It was the Jews who persecuted Him, and put Him to death! The Jews!'

'But, Tony, can I ask you something?' I had to beg him to let me get a word in. 'How could those Jews have known He was the Son of God, and not one of themselves?'

'There's a perversion,' sneered Tony. 'Of course they knew. It's all in the Old Testament! Foretold by their Prophets – no one knows his Old Testament like your Jew. They know it off by heart.'

'Two thousand years ago?' I asked faintly.

'Yes, certainly,' replied Tony. 'Two thousand years ago they knew He was the Messiah – and they crucified Him.'

I ran away from this conversation. I was beginning to hate Tony Lloyd at times. I did not care what religion Max's father professed. I just knew I loved him best in the whole world. He was my teacher, he was my friend, he was my father in the spiritual sense of the word father. He gave me a love that was warm and tender, yet remained unsullied by a touch or glance remotely earthy. Yet he was full of compassionate under-standing for my misgivings. He had humour of a rare kind, an enjoyment without shades of malice.

I went to Terenure. I should have to tell him that his offer of my wedding reception had not found favour. I hoped he would not be hurt.

He was watching from the window. He came out into the hall. Taking my hands, he led me into the long drawing-room. There was a suppressed excitement in him, unusual for many, many weeks.

'Now first your news, little one. Is it good news?'

I had never discussed Tony's failings with him. I needed a friend to whom I could confide my doubts about Tony, his temper, his bigotry. I knew that loyalty was high on the old man's list of virtues, so I only shook my head sadly.

'I did not think Tony would agree,' the old man said, 'so you will let me pay instead. No, no, Lia, do not worry any more. Let Tony make his plans in peace.'

He was not crestfallen. He was pleased, almost happy.

'You are keeping back some news from me,' I said to him, 'I can tell.'

'A little, a very little as yet,' he smiled in that benign way of his. 'First you must have a cup of tea. You are a little tired. You know, I can always send the car for you – but no, you are such an independent little thing.'

So we had our tea. He did not like to be hurried into revealing any new things, either a book or a picture, or word from abroad. He had been talking lately about the portrait for

297

the silver frame. He had found an artist who had been painting religious pictures. He rather liked his approach. He would give him a commission. All that remained was to tie this artist to a definite number of sittings, spaced over a definite number of weeks.

'I know these fellows! After all, I want to enjoy this picture here in this room, before I . . .'

I would not let him finish that sentence. I wanted him to live for ever. I loved him now with all the love I had once distributed among so many people like Gran and Phyllis . . . and Tony? There was a large black question mark over Tony's name now.

'I have had a letter, or rather a card, from Phyllis,' I told him. 'She will be back in Dublin soon. She is heartbroken not to be here for the wedding. So when the portrait is done, she will be able to see exactly how I looked.'

The portrait was to be a full-length study against the fireplace in the long room. I was to wear my wedding dress, which the old man had chosen and given to me. He had had dresses sent to him from several shops in town. I always remember his pleasure when I modelled the gowns for him in the long room, pirouetting and blowing kisses to him. Some dresses he discarded immediately, some he had me try again, and again. His final choice gave him intense delight.

Truth to tell, I looked a little like a heroine in the last scene of an old-fashioned musical – but if he liked it, that was my reward.

'And someone else may be able to see how lovely you will be that day,' the old man said.

'Who?' I asked.

He drew a letter from the folder on his desk. 'Read that!' he said, and the small note of triumph in his voice made my heart stand still.

There was no date, no address on the sheet of paper, and it was written in English. It was a message, Max's father said, written to someone's dictation and passed from hand to hand

298

until it had come to him: *Of the four doctors recaptured and returned to Auschwitz after the Revolt of the Twelfth Sonderkommando, two were Tadek and Max. Of the four one was ringleader. He was severely tortured.*

'Now it is a little easier to get some information,' the old man said, 'and from an American source, I have this.'

On his desk were spread out some sheets of blue paper embossed with the American Eagle. . . . I searched quickly for a sight of Tadek's name, because of course in my imagination he was the tortured one as well as being the hero. Through blinding tears I could not find his name and I sought refuge in the old man's arms.

'I will tell you about it.' he said, comforting me and drying my tears, 'I have read it so many times. It is the news I knew would come.'

In the middle of January, those left in the camp were aware that the Russian offensive was approaching Auschwitz. Most of the SS guards had fled. Those prisoners who were able to walk grabbed clothes, food, medicine and set out to escape on a freezing night that was ten below zero. There were doctors among them, this is certain. A man carried by friends was a doctor. Thousands left by the Forest of Birkenau in arctic conditions, and thousands perished. The man on the stretcher did not die. He and his friends and a thousand others were loaded into boxcars at Mauthausen and sent to the Melk an der Donau concentration camp, in the hills overlooking the Danube.

The final phases of the Third Reich's collapse were about to be enacted. The prisoners of Melk were taken further, until they reached the Ebensee concentration camp. There the white flag went up. The gates were opened to the American tanks . . . the long captivity was over.

'It is not known how many survived from Auschwitz. There is no record. The Middle-European names were too long and complicated for Americans to record. No man had a passport, nor any identification. The numbers tattooed on their arms may be ascertained on application.

In answer to your specific enquiry, three doctors left Ebensee, two carrying a third. Their destination was Vienna. Their tattoo numbers are appended herewith.'

I had to read this message for myself many times before I could get its meaning into my mind.

I had tried so hard to accept as a fact that Tadek and Max had been killed in Auschwitz. Strangely, I could not pass a church but I must go in and pray for them. I must implore God's mercy on their souls. When all else fails, there is an immense comfort in prayer. I still lit candles. But, deep inside, I knew why I did that. It was only in doing so that I could let my memory dwell on the days long, long ago when Max and Tadek were my beloved brothers, my family. Only in prayer could I use their names. To think of them at any other time would be like an act of infidelity to my approaching marriage. So I prayed – as the nuns had taught us to pray for the dead in the month of November every year. I tried very hard to keep the love and longing out of my prayers, to remember that Tadek was not in need of my love now or ever again.

I held the old man's hands and listened with wonder as he revealed that he had never given up hope. He had tried to renounce all hope, he had tried. And every morning he woke up with that tiny taper still burning in his heart.

'We will go to Vienna,' he said. 'We will apply for permission to travel. Yes, yes I know, it is not the same Europe, not the same Vienna. But there, on the ground, I have contacts – if they are still alive, I have friends – relations even, but perhaps not. The newspapers say that millions of my race have vanished from the face of the earth. But contacts, yes – contacts – I have much business I could do in Vienna.'

'You will take your servant? You could not go alone.'

'No, no, I will take you. You will come with me. If all fails, but it will not, you are the solace of my spirit.'

I looked at him doubtfully. In his new delirium of hope, had he forgotten that I was to be married?

He saw my face. 'No, no, your old friend is not losing his sanity.' He glanced at the clock on the mantel. 'Call your good Tony on the telephone, and I will talk with him. The telephone has its uses, you know.'

I heard him talking to Tony, but I was not listening to the words. There was a blinding fog over my thoughts, a Hell of doubt and a Heaven of delight. I knew the old man would have his persuasive way with Tony. No matter how reluctantly, Tony would let me go.

'I will give this matter much thought,' said the old man, 'it may be that saying they were going to Vienna was a ploy. Jews have learned to trust no one. On the other hand, Max made a plan with me that he would try to indicate his whereabouts.'

I scarcely heard the details of the forlorn plan, or if I listened, I did not comprehend. All I knew was that he was assuming his son was the one who had escaped. His son, out of all the millions, had come through unscathed. His son was not the man on the stretcher, nor yet the man who was tortured. His son was the one who had kept his head through all the fearsome imprisonment, who had brought himself and his two companions gloriously through the havoc of war to safe harbour. All we had to do was find Max and bring him home.

It did not occur to my dear old friend that perhaps Tadek had been the heroic saviour. Nor did he ask why, in more than a year of peace, his son had remained silent. Silent as the grave.

We would travel across Europe. Each day our hopes would multiply. At long last, in some obscure hideaway, we would meet with two or three pathetic men. They would bear tattoo marks on their shrunken arms. We would know they were strangers, we would shake our heads, and move sadly away. At some hideous mass-grave, our tears would flow as if the bitter fountain would never cease.

And even then, Max's father would still hope on.

Chapter Nineteen

It took time for Max's father to get the required permission for us to travel from Dublin, and to take out sufficient currency. Visas would be issued from London. Tony grumbled constantly.

'The way your friend is carrying on, he will be looking for a postponement of the wedding date. He will get his answer, Lia, so perhaps you had better warn him.'

A grumbling Tony was very hard to placate. 'I have to let you go on the eve of the wedding, to please the old goat, and maybe get yourself shot.'

'Oh Tony, stop going on about nothing! The War is over and you can come too. We would be delighted!'

But Tony had made up his mind that while I was away, he would go off on a golfing holiday with his friend, Tom. 'A last fling before the ball and chain!' I had to find that excruciatingly funny to restore his good humour.

'You think more of that old Jew than you do of me.'

'Oh Tony!'

'It's true. You are never done running up to Terenure. It is hardly decent for a good Catholic girl to be carrying on like that.'

'Oh Tony!'

'Yes, well, I know you are innocent enough. Maybe too damned innocent! But is he? I am glad I put my foot down about his proposed wedding present! A car, if you don't mind! A car! So that, when we are married, you can be dashing over to Terenure every day in the week!'

'But, Tony –'

'If you want a car, Lia, I'll be the one to give you a car! Not that old goat!'

'But, Tony, I said –'

'I know you said you didn't want one, all the same, you took driving lessons from that chauffeur. First the old goat, then the old goat's chauffeur!'

There was no use in trying to speak back to Tony. There was a difference in wanting to know how to drive, and actually wanting a car. I had stopped going out for a drink with Tony because there was a difference in enjoying a drink and drinking until the pub closed. There were so many differences between us that it was becoming difficult to find similarities.

All the same, I had become very fond of him. In a certain, rather affable, rather youthful way, he was adorable. His perfect handsome appearance helped his appeal. On the last night before we set out on our separate journeys, we went to dine with friends. Tony set himself to be exceptionally sweet in his ingenuous fashion. He told our friends that I was off tomorrow 'on the works of mercy', that I would be accompanying an old and ailing friend into the heart of war-torn Europe to search for his long-lost son, an internationally eminent physician who had escaped from a concentration camp. That indeed I had known this famous physician since I was a tiny child – I had moved, he said, in a very elite circle when I was young. Naturally, he was sick at heart to let me go on this mission, fraught with danger as it was. But one must be gallant in matters like this, and the little woman herself was as brave as a Turk.

I supposed he had his own reasons for explaining 'elite circle', my bravery, and his gallantry to our friends.

The next morning, Tony was in marvellous form. He was quite unable to conceal his boyish jubilation at the idea of an all-male trip to the south for his golfing holiday. He enthused so much that I was left with the impression that he felt he had evened up with me. I, too, was up very early and ready for my journey but my mood was very different from his. I was fearful and apprehensive for fear of tragic disappointment. In another part of me, there was a dim glow that was like dawn breaking and clouding and lighting again. It was not a glow of hope.

In Gran's little house, we kissed and hugged with much regretful fervour. He enjoined on me to take care of myself, and come home safe and sound. I enjoined on him to have a good time and a good holiday which he assured me was not in any doubt – with a great jovial wink. At last he was in his car and heading off to collect his friend, and soon to be best man, Tom.

I blew kisses to the departing car with an unexpected flood of relief.

Tony would be home in one week, I would be home in two. I had handed in my resignation to the Land Commission. This was the rule when a girl left to get married. The wedding date was now six weeks ahead, on the Tuesday after Easter Sunday as Tony wished.

I was going with the old man because I loved him. I would be there when he collapsed with grief and disappointment at the end of this unlikely journey. I had not the faintest shred of hope that we would find our boys in that wilderness of a world which Europe must surely be after years of incessant war.

I took one last look at the beautiful wedding dress which was hanging in the wardrobe in the room which was Gran's room. Then I phoned Max's father. I told him I was going to Mrs Daly in Ringsend, and I would be back home ready to be collected at 4.00 p.m. In fact I was ready now, my case and overnight bag were here beside me in the hall.

'Then I will send the car for you now,' he insisted. 'Ted will drive you to Ringsend and anywhere else you want to go. I shall expect you for lunch, and in the afternoon we will rest until it is time for us to be driven to the Holyhead boat. We have much travel ahead. I will not have you tired out when we meet Max.'

When we meet Max. Already, his hopes were flying ahead.

In style, then, I was driven to Ringsend.

I saw the Dalys, Mr and Mrs, regularly. They never seemed to grow a day older, although the family had all left home except Sylvie, the youngest girl. She had had the benefit of a better education than the others. Phyllis's money had seen to that. But she was just as the others were, unchangingly warm and interested.

Phyllis would soon be home. I wanted Mrs Daly to explain to her my going with Max's father. I gave her keys for Gran's house, she would keep an eye on it, and (in true Daly fashion) she would have it sparkling on my return.

They were very excited about my wedding, and the grand house I would be living in out in Foxrock. Sylvie, who was only seventeen, wanted to know all about it. To Ringsenders, the suburb of Foxrock was a world away.

'I am sure our Phyllis will be dying to see your magnificent house!'

'It's funny,' I said, thinking aloud, 'I do not think it will ever seem like *my* house. It is Tony's mother's house. There is nothing I could possibly change to make it *my* house. Her portrait hangs over the fireplace in the drawing-room. She is like a young queen in the picture, and she still reigns.'

'Won't you and Tony have to buy anything like new carpets, or curtains?' asked Mrs Daly in wonder.

'The carpets were laid down forty years ago. Tony says they are as new as yesterday. I shall not be able to put my wedding presents to use, there is so much in use already.'

'Wait until you have half a dozen kids!' said Mrs Daly in her hearty way.

Would half a dozen kids make everything right? And loved? And used? And familiar? If only I could order half a dozen from Grafton Street. Half a dozen assorted and guaranteed and sent by post – no other action necessary or required.

I hugged Sylvie and Mrs Daly, slipping some money into her pocket. 'Give my dearest love to Phyllis the minute you see her,' and I was driven away by Ted while Sylvie and her mother stood waving and beaming.

Max's father was worried and on edge until we had collected all our necessary papers in London. Perhaps in normal times that would have taken a few days. In 1947, among a people slowly rising from a confusion of bombed-out buildings, where places of business – previously undisturbed for centuries – had been moved from place to place, where new regulations to cover changed times were changed each passing day, where wartime conditions still prevailed. In London in 1947, the simplest business took days to complete. To obtain visas for Austria, Czechoslovakia, Poland, Italy, and Switzerland, took a month.

'Being a Jew is less of a help than it ever was,' the old man moaned ruefully. 'Now the Zionists want Britain out of Palestine – so a Jew is bad news here in London – and the Arabs do not want the Zionists in. Ah yes, the Arab knows what wealth he has in the Middle East. He will ignore that Palestine is the natural homeland of the Jew. And no doubt Britain will prolong the Arab's resistance. For the Middle East is one of the world's most convenient highways, and one of the world's greatest sources of wealth. Ah yes – if only the Jew of a thousand years ago had stayed at home, and explored his own backyard! But of course, there were so many of them, each cleverer than the next. And, after all, it is the technological advancement of the twentieth century that has turned the eyes of the Great Powers on the barefoot Bedouin. If the Great Powers could buy the desert acre by acre, the way land can be bought in Ireland – ah yes! They would like that! But the Arab does not sell land, nor does the Jew, they die to hold it – who knows what may be in the land?'

There were times when the old man seemed close to

collapse. Great furrows of worry appeared on his brow. He ate little. His concern daily increased for the rapidly approaching date of my wedding day.

One day, I said to him, 'It may seem strange to you, but that date is my least worry.'

'Poor old Tony,' he said sympathetically . . . but smiling a little.

Towards the end of our month in London, Tony sent three lengthy, and very irate telegrams. I tore these into tiny bits, remembering what the old man had said about my being the solace of his spirit. Tony and I had all our lives before us, we could easily make up for this short separation. I wrote to Tony, explaining the circumstances, asking him to be patient. I made the ending of the letter as affectionate as I could to placate his anger. It came into my mind that I was always more ready to placate Tony than to care for him.

There was no time to contemplate my own misgivings. There were so many officials to interview us, so many questionnaires to fill in, that every minute of every day was occupied.

Then, at last, we were on our way. The journey was to be as comfortable as the old man could make it, with his knowledge and resources. I knew he was more relaxed when he settled down in the train from Paris, holding my hand in his, and rambling on about himself, and his family ties – a favourite subject always.

'You know I am a patient man, Lia. Ah yes, you know that – and patience is a monumental virtue. To me it comes from my great-grandmother on my father's side. She was Czech. Among the Slavs, the Czech is the business man, the provider, the repository of commonsense. Oh yes, the Czech can be creative – Dvořák and Smetana among others prove that. My great-grandmother was still alive when I was born, nearly a hundred years between us. Think of that! She was the founder of our enormous fortune – afterwards lost in many pogroms – but great from her early time to my early youth, over a century. My father often told me I got my brains from her laying of her hands on me. I went once to visit her grave in Prague, a sort of thanksgiving. It is the oldest Jewish cemetery in Europe. If we have a thanksgiving, Lia, we will go there. With a young woman named Leah I went before. You will come with me?'

'Of course,' I assented loyally. 'Tell me about this oldest cemetery, please.'

The old man loved to tell tales of antiquity. His memory for names and places never faltered. He rambled on in a vein drawn from many sources. Much of his talk had a dear familiarity. Many asides and stories I have never forgotten, many I felt I had always known. One day, I asked him:

'How is it I am more at home in your tradition, more at ease, than in my own?'

'But what is your own?' he replied. 'Perhaps it is mine. You know of the theory of reincarnation? Maybe, I say maybe, many centuries ago my immortal soul was the father of your immortal soul.'

'Could that be?' I asked. 'I would like that.'

'Who knows for sure, little one? Even I, who see cracks and gaps in that theory, have in a long lifetime found new friends who were as familiar to me as my own face. I remember very clearly the first day I ever saw Rome. I knew it immediately as I knew Paris, every inch and part of the inner and older city. I was able to walk directly to masterpieces in painting and sculpture which had been undisturbed for centuries. You must tell me, little one, if in our travels you think: "I was here before." It is an interesting thing.'

I did not tell him but I thought I knew when my part in his tradition had started. Surely it began the night Tadek climbed in through Mrs Mayne's back-bedroom window to quell the noisy crying of a lonely child. That night Tadek had transplanted the wilting seedling into his own rich earth, his own traditional humus. In a few short years – the only few years of real growth in a lifetime – the little plant had rooted forever.

Vienna was a heartbreak for the old man. He could not speak in his usual easy fluent way of the long-ago time he had spent in Vienna, and of which he had often talked to me. Now his voice was choked with sobs.

I knew he had been in the Ballhausplatz in 1934 when the Nazis had ransacked the building, and murdered Dollfuss. I knew he remembered forever the singing of Lehmann and Jeritza in the Opera. The Opera was razed to the ground; the Burg Theatre, where he had first fallen in love with Shakespeare, was a shell. The roof was gone from St Stephen's Cathedral. We searched for the Café Louvre – the finest coffee and pastry in the world, he said – here he used to meet his journalist friends every evening. There was no trace of it – nor of the journalists who might have information for him.

Everywhere there were American military police, clinkingly uniformed with brilliant scarlet scarves worn around their collars. They paced smartly, in pairs, through the restaurant in which we dined. They eyed everyone in a cold silence.

'There is no doubt they know much of what is going on in this city,' the old man murmured, 'even without the benefit of knowing the language. But I do not think we will seek information from them, little one.'

The destruction in the streets of Vienna was caused by American bombing at the time of Nazi occupation; and later by fierce street fighting when the Red Army drove the Germans out of the city. The seeking for the once-familiar homes of friends, or relatives, was thus inextricably confused by gaps.

'Vienna is like a beautiful woman with all her teeth knocked out,' he commented sadly, 'but we are narrowing down the calls, and there are plenty of taxis – more than in Paris, do you notice? The Russians control the petrol supply, I am told – but some wily Bolshy must be selling concessions to the taxi-men.'

We went to the home of a doctor friend; the house still stood but we were told he, and his wife, had killed themselves when the Nazis came in 1938. Another friend, a political journalist, had been murdered in Buchenwald. Then we sought a sculptor. He had disappeared without trace. Almost without our being aware of it, a week had passed.

'We must find news soon,' the old man said. 'This city is being carved up into five zones. The Americans, Russians, British, French, and a fifth or International Zone held by the other four. This zone is in the Inner Stadt. I can mark that off, it would be too confined, too dangerous for someone hiding out – too closely "cased", if that is the word.'

I was aware that the old man had a method in his search. Gradually, as he realized the extent and location of the city's devastation, his own built-in street map from long ago began to take shape. He knew there was little use in explaining everything to me, because my credibility was sadly stretched by this seemingly endless looking at numbers on doors that led into roofless houses. Often he spoke to workmen, already rebuilding and repairing. He spoke in their own language. By the way they gesticulated, nodding or shaking their heads, I could only guess at his words. I was there to take his hand, to smile in sympathy, to encourage him to eat a little, to rest when his strength was ebbing.

Then one day, he had news of a kind – the breakthrough he was hoping for, he believed.

'The family with whom Max lived in Vienna – you remember when he came here the first time – they were distant relatives of mine. He was a senior professor of pathology in the University. He was a Jew. She was a German, a Lutheran from Berlin. There were two sons, of an age with Max. I have learned that when the Nazis invaded Austria in March 1938, this man and his wife were parted. Many Jews saw the writing on the wall before then – Herr Professor had left it too late. He was put to death in a concentration camp – maybe Auschwitz. Today, I was told she has come back to Vienna.

She is looking for her sons. They were sent to a labour camp, as children of a Jew. Maybe she thinks they are still alive.'

'Have you spoken to this lady?'

'No, that is the point. I am told she has a stall in the open market which is on tomorrow. We will go, and you will buy at each stall. You can think of things to buy, little one? A fish, some bread, perhaps a fifth-hand skirt!'

He was so pleased with himself. He was laughing.

'And you will hold a parley with each stall-holder?' I asked. 'But why not go to the lady's stall directly?'

'Because, my little one, I do not know her. I never saw her. And even if Max described her, which I do not recall, she would surely be aged, and changed. It is nearly ten years ago that he lived in Wien. This one we will play by ear!'

And it came about as the old man had hoped it would. We were going, like tourists, from stall to stall, buying here a useless brooch, there two wine glasses engraved with a Hapsburg monogram, a pastry-tart of jam, a redolent fish. Then a woman beckoned the old man to go behind the stall. I turned over her shabby wares with seeming great interest while I quaked apprehensively at the sight of the two military policemen who were parading solemnly through the aisles of stalls.

When the old man emerged from the stall, I purchased a large black lace brassiere that would have fitted Phyllis in her heyday. We continued from stall to stall, looking or buying, until we had circled back to the entrance. I wanted to drop the bag of bargains into a little bin, but the old man said very sagely that would arouse suspicion. He had no doubt we were observed.

As we walked slowly along the street towards our hotel, it was revealed to me that the stall-holder had given him an address in Budapest. She had recognized both of us from pictures Max always kept on his dressing-table.

'Tell me, little one, have we been talking freely about our problems, in the hotel?' he asked.

I thought for a moment.

'Not here in Vienna,' I answered, 'because we have not had tea sent up to your room, as we did in Paris. In fact, I have not been in your room at all here. We have talked a little, while dining, but very little because of the blaring music. Mostly we have spoken of our problems while resting in the park, or on a street bench.'

He was relieved. The lady in the market had told him that hotel rooms were equipped with recording devices.

'Budapest is safer because it is not yet organized, she said. One of her sons is the third man of the three doctors who left Ebensee. He was a leader in the Partisans. She is on the track of the other son, he was imprisoned for murder.'

'But the other two men? Is she sure?'

'Ah yes,' the old man seemed content, 'the other two are Max and Tadek!'

'Then why . . .' I began in a whisper.

'She thinks it is censorship of the mails. They have moved several times and two needed medical attention. She has not seen them. She cannot get a visa to leave Vienna. We will bring back word for her, yes?'

For three days we stood all day in the station. Everyone in Vienna was going to Budapest, or so it seemed. I was very worried about my old friend, but joyful thoughts kept him going. Each time he pressed my hand, I knew it was to tell me that he felt a surge of new hope in his spirits, that all the worries of the weary years would have been worthwhile, that soon he would be reunited with his beloved son. Nor did I resent this long wait in the station. I was blissfully grateful for my youth and strength. I knew I would have stood there for a year just for the chance to see Tadek once more.

At last we were on our way, crammed into a ramshackle carriage, unable to speak, only able to read the rapture in each other's eyes. Each time our tickets were scrutinized, we trembled with fear. Each time the danger passed, the rapture was back in our eyes.

The old man wept to see the city that, long ago, was his Budapest. At the station there were few taxis. He was always able to find some polyglot jargon to make known his needs to taxi-men or waiters. I saw now that each taxi-man shook his head.

'Every hotel I ask for no longer exists,' he told me. 'I have not forgotten, but they are full of fear to answer a casual question. Freedom in them has been extinguished. The War is all too recent and they are being conquered now by new ideology.'

Everywhere there were brilliant red posters, extolling Communism – promising, exhorting, threatening. And everywhere, pairs of military police paraded the streets, their eyes swivelling in granite faces.

The old man persuaded a cab, with horses, to take us to a nondescript hotel. We sat up all during the night, we were too wrought-up to think of sleeping. In the morning we found the address which the woman in Vienna had given us. It was a cobbler's shop. The old man was instructed to return to the hotel like a sightseer, pointing out churches and other buildings as if we were tourists. We were to eat and drink, and appear in no hurry.

The following morning, a cab would be waiting outside our hotel. We would take luggage, inform the hotel that we were about to go sightseeing in the mountains outside Budapest. Once inside the cab, we would hand over this small card. The watchpoint was that our visas enjoined on us to report to the local office regularly. Not to do so was almost certain imprisonment. We reported on the way back to the hotel.

I had enormous difficulty in concealing my terror. I had not thought of anything like this. Eyes seemed to be every-where, watching every movement. I kept thinking of the market-lady whose son was in some prison for murder. Who did he murder? What crimes did our men commit that they were hiding out – no communication with the outside world?

'Recently, I was reading some poems by a Czech poet, Seifert, and I think, Lia, you would like this one.' The old man murmured in a strange language, and then he translated:

> *'Whoever says goodbye*
> *Waves a white handkerchief*
> *Every day something is ended*
> *Something beautiful is ended . . .*
>
> *Dry your eyes*
> *And smile through your tears*
> *Every day something starts again*
> *Something beautiful starts again.'*

'I remember you told me the story of Lidice,' I said to the old man, 'when the invading Nazis murdered every single person in a village, even the little babies. Surely the Czechs could not now be worse off than they were then? That was so awful.'

He looked very sad at the thought of Lidice. 'I hope they could not. I hope they could not. They are a proud and very special people.'

Early in the morning, the cab came, and we left Budapest. Higher and higher into the wooded mountains we went. We left the wider road, following tracks and turn-offs so many that I was filled with amazement that the driver could go on at such a breakneck speed. It seemed like entrusting oneself to a madman.

'If we were being kidnapped now,' I said to the old man, 'we could never escape, we are miles and miles up into these terrible mountains.'

He pressed my hand. 'We are not being kidnapped, Lia, and I promised to have you home safely, although perhaps not on time, for your wedding.'

314

I had not thought of the wedding for many days, maybe weeks. I took my hand from the old man's hand. There was no magnificent ring on my finger, no reminder of Tony, no place in my heart for him. At that moment, I could not remember his face.

'When your Ted was driving us to the mail boat,' I said, 'I put Tony's engagement ring into its box. I asked Ted to take care of it.'

'A wise precaution,' the old man answered.

And I shall never wear it again, I thought. No matter what this journey brings, I know now that I could never marry Tony Lloyd. If I must go on searching to the end of the world, and to the end of my days, futilely and in vain, then let it be so. I thought again of the words I carried in my heart: *my love is as the eternal rocks beneath . . . always, always in my mind*.

It seemed there was nothing but trees, trees, trees. The forest grew more dense with every mile. Hour after hour after hour there was not a rooftop, not a field, not an animal. The forest would go on forever.

Then, quite suddenly, we were there. There was a powerful gun emplacement trained down the path up which we had driven. There were many huts and cabins glimmering in the twilight.

For a moment after the cab stopped there was a silence, the noise of the engine had ceased abruptly, and we sat, stunned by the end of movement.

Then we were surrounded by people. I was in Max's arms, clinging to him, and kissing his dear bearded cheeks. Tears were running down the old man's face, he could not speak.

I was to come to know this scene in the Partisans' headquarters over the next weeks. Loved ones were found, and sometimes the reunion came too late.

'Come,' Max said to us, 'we will go into my office. There are things you must hear before you see the others. You will need refreshment. Someone will see to it.'

Chapter Twenty

Up to that very moment I must not have believed in a single feeling, a single word, a single fact. I was going along on a written script, a play within a play. My whole life was like that. I had come to this place to please the old man. He was the only real person left. He had taken over the script and I was grateful to pick up his cues.

Now, suddenly, in this strange mountain pass, the static ceased. Life, real and throbbing, took over again. A tide of joy, such as I had never known, rushed into me. Tadek was here, here in this place, here close to me. At last. At last. At last.

My question must have shone out of my eyes as I leaned back in Max's arms and looked up into his face. He said, close to my ear so I could hear above the clamour of welcoming voices, 'He is sleeping.'

It was like a song. It took up a tune in my heart, a tune of a lullaby . . . he is sleeping, merely sleeping, lightly sleeping. Sleeping. Sleeping. And waking after sleeping. The song swelled into a symphony. Sleeping was a great sea of rest, lapping in little waves of peace towards a shore of gentle awakening. Sleep, Tadek. Sleep awhile.

Now the old man was putting his arms around both of us. I could feel his frailty, his ebbing strength. To him, to him alone, I owed this wonderful joyous exultation.

In Max's office we had some cognac and coffee. We settled the old man into the place made ready for him. He was weary. It was good to have Max help take care of him.

Then we were alone. The last time we were alone together, it was out on the mountainside above Enniskerry, far away in Ireland. That night we were to become betrothed. Despite the undoubted love in his embrace, an instinct within me had warned of a change in him.

He looked at me so tenderly. 'When you are tired, you are the most beautiful of all.'

I waited. I remembered how slow he always was to find the words. And it took time while my heart went into a diminuendo rhythm of *Sleep Tadek sleep sleep sleep*.

When Max found the words, his voice was broken with held-back grief.

'In Auschwitz, Tadek told me that he is the one. The chosen one. He told me, not once but many times, when his thoughts were constantly with you. He told me, the first time, after an attempted escape when he was . . . I am sorry, Lia, when he was tortured. I know he thought death was very near that day. He asked me, if I survived, to give you a message. He said you would know what it was. He had given it to you long, long ago when you were six years of age, "in an historic cave" – I was to say that. When he was delirious, he called your name over and over. *Neyn veynen, meyn kleyn* . . . you were his beloved. There was never anyone else.'

But I wept bitterly against Max's shoulder for a long time. I had missed out on a lifetime of love with Tadek. He should have taken me with him. I would have followed him into the concentration camp.

'Do not say these things, Lia. Our paths were made difficult for us. We had no choice. And look, *balibt*, Fate has given you a little prize. You will be with Tadek, you will have time now to love each other.'

Could I hear it in his voice? A desperate finality?

'For all the future? Please, Max, for all the future? Please tell me there are years ahead. I have waited for so long. Please, Max . . .'

He shook his head, great tears glinting in his eyes. At last he found his voice. 'His heart did not stand up to the strain . . . did not withstand the strain of . . . the strain . . . of the things that were done to him.' Then he murmured, very very softly as if to spare the hurt, 'There is no future, *balibt*.'

'Then I do not want to spend another hour away from him.'

'You will not be parted from him,' Max replied, 'I have arranged it so. My room is here. There are some facilities if you wish to change, perhaps leave your things here, and come as you need to. I am seldom here, my office is in the next hut.'

I turned at the door. I wanted to put all the gratitude of the world into my eyes. Max looked back at me with so much loving tenderness in his gaze.

'No, Lia, I never told him that I too have loved you all my life. And he does not know that you are to be married.'

'But I am not!' I cried. 'I am not!'

Max waited for me. 'Lia, let me tell you – just a little – to help you. Tadek has healed, a great deal of healing, in the many, many weeks we have been here. There is no mark or blemish on him now. Lia, the damage done to his heart cannot be healed. In the end, we carried a friend between us from camp to camp looking for help. That final burden was too great, but Tadek would not give up. Even if this place were a great hospital, the damage to Tadek's heart is irreversible.'

Max enfolded me in his arms. I could feel the shudder of tears in his great frame. 'Give him your strength, Lia. The strength he will find for you is the strength of his spirit. Sustain him.'

When Max opened the door into Tadek's room, I had a moment to recognize the scene of my constant yearning

318

dream. There was a room with drawn curtains, a golden glow of a lamp on a table, the leaping flame of a log fire, and Tadek seated in a big armchair as one who awaited a guest. His patterned dressing gown was like that of a prince.

'She has come,' Max said, and he went away.

I remember forever the wonderful smile when Tadek turned and held out his arms and I went into them for the very first time.

'Oh Lia, you are so beautiful!'

I remember forever with love and with tears the first sound of his voice when he spoke my name. Of course we shed tears, both of us, but only for a little while.

To be in his arms after all the years of exile was intoxicating ecstasy. There was delight and wonder and utter contentment in touching his face with my face, in smoothing back his hair.

We whispered against each other the words of love we had never used before, words I did not know I knew and now I knew their inmost meaning. I felt at last the rising joy of desire, and I felt that Tadek shared each leaping pulse when his lips touching mine were not gentle but passionate.

That first evening, we talked hardly at all, and only in whispers. We were exploring all the paths leading to each other, looking into each other's eyes for long moments, holding kisses in utter breathless tenderness, experimenting as lovers do with easy, and easier, caresses.

We laughed a little, too. Tadek said, his lips against my throat, 'Do I remember telling you that you were a shameless little hussy when you demanded long passionate kisses, like in films?'

I nodded. 'I was so mad at you!'

Tadek held me closer. 'Will you be a shameless little hussy and stay with me tonight?'

'And every night for ever and ever. Oh Tadek, I love you so.'

Just as when I was a little girl, loving Tadek poured into

me like a fountain. I was filled with love for him. I would gladly have died that his life might be spared.

Later that first night, Max came with his father. I felt guilt in front of the old man. I had never said to him that Tadek was my beloved. In his presence, I was humbled to think that I could now come to Tadek as a bride because of his son's care for me. Left to my own care, I had come close to disaster.

There was no sign in the old man's demeanour that I had fallen from grace in his eyes. His benevolence covered all three of us. With his usual resourceful foresight, he had brought a special bottle from his cellar in Terenure.

A simple dinner was served in Tadek's room. The old man filled our glasses for the toast:

'To happiness!' he said, and we raised our glasses. 'The most precious gift of the Gods! And, now, Lia, your toast.'

'Let us drink to our boys!' I was so proud of them.

Max and Tadek smiled. They understood our years of anxiety in those words.

Max lifted his glass. 'To all of us here,' he said.

'My turn,' Tadek smiled that wonderful gleaming smile, 'may I offer this toast for Lia, whose gift to our lives has always been her beauty. She has always had my love.'

I thought my heart must break with joy and love and infinite sadness.

They raised their glasses to me. 'And mine,' the old man said. 'And mine,' muttered Max in his throat.

We talked for a time, a short time. . . . The four of us together at last.

Max put logs on the fire, turning to speak a little hesitantly, 'Let us establish a pattern here about this fire. Up here in the mountains, it gets very cold at nights no matter what the season. I will come each night to build the fire, and Lia may like to use our poor facilities at that time. In the morning, the same idea. Around midday, one of the camp doctors will come to see Tadek. Perhaps Lia will walk around the camp with my father at that time?'

It was a long, difficult speech for Max, but it was necessary. The pattern was not about putting logs on the fire, it was an inauguration of our days to follow a life of our own. It was an acknowledgment that Tadek had entered into a special status with Lia. A recognition.

I went to Max's bathroom. I put on the pretty nightgown that Tadek's mother had made for my birthday years before. When I came back to Tadek's room, Max and his father said goodnight.

Tadek and I sat holding hands beside the fire. We knew this was a solemn moment, the real ending of exile.

'Lia, the twenty years are over. This night will be our Wedding Night?'

'Then let me offer myself to you, Tadek.'

I stood up and across the fireplace from him. I slipped off my nightdress. I stepped out of my shoes, and came to him.

I was trembling so much that my voice was only a shaky whisper. 'Will you put on my nightie now, Tadek please, like you used to, all those years ago? And smooth it right down to my heels, just like you used to?'

Tadek took the nightdress from my hands. 'Oh Lia, is it possible I could have forgotten how lovely you are? You are a beautiful child, and yet you are a woman, my woman.' I was in his arms. He was kissing ardently and I was responding, my kisses following his along every curve.

That night, that first night, as Max had said, Tadek found the strength of his spirit.

As volcanoes smoulder, and finally erupt, so it was with Tadek's passion, so long suppressed, so long denied.

There was ecstatic pain for which he wept, and yet he gloried in it. I did not hold back from the exquisite hurt. I was unconscious of fear because I had forgotten that Tadek's strength was ever in question. He came back again and again until, at last, he fell asleep like a child pillowed on my breast, his breathing steady against me.

In that awesome mountain fastness, in that first hour

before daylight, it was hard for me to believe that my life was not beginning. It was ending.

I would not wake up every morning for years to come with Tadek's head on my breast, his arm under my shoulder. It felt so gloriously right and just and perfect to lie with him this way.

He was in a deep, deep sleep. The light was breaking through the curtains. I slipped out of bed to find my nightdress. Then I went over to the window to see this first dawn.

I was gazing out at a graveyard full of small white markers.

I crept back into bed. Tadek stirred and murmured my name. I slipped back into the circle of his arms. Tadek Tadek Tadek. I loved him so.

I determined that every dawn would bring another day of joy. Every minute would be filled with tender giving. Every day would be a Heaven-sent bonus to fill me with profound gratitude.

Tadek and I needed each other in all the ways of lovers. We gave ourselves over to the delights of lovers, discovering ourselves in each other's response. We wondered at the two of us who had so little practice in the art of lovemaking, how very quickly we found out the magical mysteries.

We meandered through long drowsy conversations when, spent with loving, we lay against the pillows on Tadek's bed. Sometimes he drifted into a deep sleep, very deep, very quickly.

I said this to Max . . . perhaps I was . . . perhaps I was too much for Tadek. Would it be better for Tadek if I . . . if I . . .?'

Max's answer was almost stern. 'Give him all your love, Lia. All. All. It cannot make a great deal of difference to his span of life, but all the difference to that life. Sustain him in his response, and in his coming. Do you understand, Lia? Do you understand sustain?'

Yes, I understood.

'We never refer to the future, Max, always we talk of the past. Do you think . . .?'

'Yes, Lia, he knows. He is a doctor, and a very brilliant doctor.'

Tadek never referred to his incarceration in the concentration camp, nor to the rôle he played in the Partisans. All I knew of his time of torture I have learned from Max, and that was years afterwards. Tadek talked of the third man, the man carried by Max and himself. He regarded that man as a great hero. The SS had removed his hands, and later his feet. It was the sheer spirit of that man which had engineered the uprising to liberate them from Auschwitz.

I told Tadek about that man's mother in the market in Vienna, of how she longed to see her sons, but could not get permission to leave Vienna.

'She will meet him in another world,' Tadek said, 'his body lies in the graveyard beyond that window. Oh Lia, how lucky I am to have you here before I join him there.'

Our talk was seldom sad and then only sad when he told me of Laelia. She had renounced Jewry. Max had been able to let her know about Tadek, her answer was silence. Her silence probably included her bearing of Burton's baby. It never seemed appropriate to tell of my visit to London. The thought was swiftly banished.

'Do you remember, Lia, how I tried to explain the word "syndrome" to you, one night in Mrs Mayne's? I always thought afterwards of that room as "our cave".'

'A cold dark cave!' I smiled at him.

'But ours!' he said. 'Where we spent the happiest hours we ever knew. That is so, isn't it, dearest? Anyway, you were always asking me "wouldn't you think?" questions, do you remember? "Wouldn't you think Mama would do such and such a thing?" "Wouldn't you think the teacher would shut her eyes when she is saying her prayers?"'

He was making me laugh by imitating my little girly voice. He enjoyed making me laugh. ' "Wouldn't you think, Tadek?" ' he mimicked. 'I told you that you had a "wouldn't you think" syndrome! You were worried to death for having a "sin" anything! You were an adorable funny little girl. Do you still get syndromes?'

'I have a dreadful one about you!' I told him, laughing. I remember there were days we laughed a lot.

Now and then, I worried about the stupid commitment I had made to Tony Lloyd, far away in Dublin, and no doubt railing angrily at my continued absence. I brought my worry to the old man with whom I walked every day for an hour.

'Lia, do you want to go home immediately?' He was truly concerned.

'Oh no, no, no! I want to stay. I just feel I am being very lacking for someone's feelings. It seems unfair not to show consideration. To leave someone waiting from day to day in the circumstances.'

A letter breaking off the engagement would be the honourable thing to do, but I never wanted to go away by myself to write a letter, or even to enquire about the possibility of posting one.

So the old man made arrangements to have the contact in Vienna contact London to wire Dublin that all was well, simply prolonging an enjoyable trip – indefinitely.

I hoped Tony would not be angry. I felt when he was told the whole truth, well, most of the truth, well, if he . . . it was . . .

After a while, I stopped thinking of Tony. There were times I could not recollect what his face was really like – his image would not come to mind.

In our midday walks around and around the perimeter of the huts, I always linked my arm into the arm of the old man.

'I owe you so much,' I told him, 'I can never hope to repay you.'

He tightened my arm against him. 'You have repaid me over and over again,' he said. 'You have brought youth and beauty back into my life for almost ten years now.'

'Is it ten years?' I asked in wonder.

He smiled down at me. 'Yes, almost ten. Since the first night I went to the little Peacock Theatre to see your play.'

'And you took us all to dinner in the Shelbourne. Did I ever thank you for that night?'

'Of course you did, little one. But I knew you long before that. Max talked of you many times. And your little Silky lived in my house before she died.'

Tears, never very far away, threatened to fall when I remembered Silky. Silky and Toozy.

'Max said you had put a little tombstone over the grave in your garden?'

'Yes, there is a little stone. Their names are on it. Ted, who does so many things for me, has planted heathers all around it.'

I thought about that. The loving kindness of this old man. But was he so old? I would ask.

'We are friends, aren't we?' I asked. 'Do you feel as I do, as I feel – special friends?'

He turned me towards him very gently, and very gently he kissed my head, on the left and then on the right.

'So very special,' he answered gravely, 'despite our ages.' And he smiled at me, as if he read my thought. 'At the end of this year, I shall be sixty.'

Into my memory flashed the day he had said that Burton must be hitting up to fifty. So, in fact, he was not so very much older than Burton.

The thought flashed away as fast as it had come. In this place where I dwelt with Tadek, there was no room for memory of Burton. There was no room for anyone, nor anything, nor any other need. Only Tadek Tadek Tadek.

'You are contented now, little one?'

I tucked my arm closer into his arm. There would always

be room for loving him. There had been room for the loving of him for a long time. Even the very look in his eye, the very style of him, meant loving. I admitted the tender emotion into a closer harbour within.

I watched him as he walked away. Since finding Max, his weary stoop had disappeared. Almost for the first time, I noted his tall ample figure, his benign face, the undoubted elegant cut of his clothes.

And then I forgot him. All of life had concentrated in Tadek's need for me. I could not conceal from myself that each day he was a little weaker. He allowed me to nurse him in a deepening intimacy, to bathe his face and hands and, after a while, his body.

Now, our rôles were indeed reversed. I did for him all the tender, loving things he had done for me in that dismal back bedroom long ago. I brushed his hair with gentle strokes, talking to him as he used to talk to me. Every day, I noted the fragile contours of his handsome face, the narrow wings of his eyebrows above the almost-black depths of his eyes. I memorized each feature.

'What nice thick curly hair you have,' I would say. 'I see a silver hair here and there – worry, and dissipation, I suppose!'

'No, not so much dissipation – just growing old!' And I would hold him close against my breast, weeping in my heart for the fact that he would never grow old.

'Oh Lia, I had such a good life planned for us. We were going to the States just as soon as I had all the experience. A man could have a really good life there, a properly qualified man could do well. Wouldn't you have liked that? In the States, our different religions would not stand out against us as they would in Ireland. I had such a comfortable and happy home planned for you, and for our children, Lia.'

Ah Tadek! We had the same dream which we were not fated to share.

The days went slowly by, and he lost strength, unable

326

now to swallow much sustenance. If we talked at all it was of the distant past. When he could not speak, I remembered aloud for him the merry days in Brittas Bay, how he taught me to swim – and earlier days when we went out on his bike to the Pigeon House Fort, and we brought back fanshells to his mother.

One day, with a great effort, he expressed his gratitude for Gran's kindness to his mother. 'She told me in every letter how you all loved each other in that little house.'

So I told him about those days, and how dear his mother had been to us, how kind to me especially. I described clothes she had made for me. One day, I wore for him a grey silk blouse of her making which was a favoured treasure among my clothes. She had embroidered cherries and green leaves on the small scalloped collar.

'Talk again about learning the alphabet in our cave,' he would whisper, 'and hold me close.'

I always went to see Max in his office at nightfall. There was always something to tell about Tadek, some small worry. I had come to value Max in the same way I valued, and loved, his father. They were my family. Max was the officer in command of the camp where many Partisans looked to him to deliver them back into the world.

'Max, I know you are very busy, but may I ask you something? I may have lost count, but I think I have skipped a period.'

He paused. 'The food here is poor, Lia. If you are worried, there are still several other doctors in camp who . . .'

'Are you angry with me, Max?'

He came around his desk, and took me in his arms. 'Because I suggest another doctor? I have never been angry with you, *balibt*. You are my total concern in this world.'

'Do you think I might be pregnant?'

'It is not very likely but – ' and now he managed a smile, 'miracles do happen. You feel well?'

'I feel wonderful! You would not send me away?'

He lifted me up to sit on the desk. 'Your hair has grown so long since you came here, you are more beautiful than ever. No. I will not send you away, *balibt*. But I think you know that time is running out?'

I nodded, unable to trust my voice.

'Tadek is failing rapidly. You know I promised him you would come. I never told him you were to be married although I knew that, from my father, after we left Auschwitz. He had been tortured so terribly that I could not. In Auschwitz he told me that he was going to marry you after the War. No, Lia, don't cry. You have been so good up to now.'

'He told you,' I sobbed, 'but he never told me. Until now. He always told me never to mention his name. Oh Max, is there no hope?'

'You know there is not, Lia. He just willed himself to live until he could see you once more. If you had not set out with my father, he would be . . . gone.'

Tadek's sleep was often fitful. Many times, I would hear him murmuring my name. I would press my lips to his shoulder, his arm, his hands until his murmurs ceased. Another month began to slip away.

One morning I called Max. Tadek's sleep seemed very deep and unmoving. Max brought another doctor, a Partisan who had been a very famous consultant before the concentration camp.

'Tadek will have recurrent spells of coma,' he said. 'It is a form of ischaemia. The heart has almost given up. The end will come without pain, so you must not be frightened. I give you my word, there will be no pain. You will know when the heart stops, it is not the same as this coma. You will know. The pulse will not come back.'

There was almost another month of glorious life. Tadek was able to sit up in the big armchair. There were little meals prepared for us in the Partisans' kitchen, which we shared at his table. We drank a little wine, toasting each other in all sorts of silly hopes. We slept together in Tadek's bed when we had loved and talked ourselves to sleep.

'Lia, do you remember our very last night together in the "cave"?'

I told him I remembered every second of it. How the candle had guttered out and he had rocked me in his arms in a lonely silence.

'But inside in my mind,' Tadek said, holding me closely, 'I was not silent. I was giving you my promise of love for ever and ever. I could not tell you, you were only a little girl, but I was promising.'

There were hundreds of times when I would have given my life to have known that. And there are thousands of times when I treasure those words now like precious diamonds.

'And I have been utterly and absolutely faithful to that promise.' Tadek gave me that smile of his.

All of his lovemaking was prefaced in that way with a tender retelling of his endless love.

I longed to tell Tadek that I might be pregnant. The hope grew in me each day when the period did not come. But I did not tell him. In his conscious moments, we escaped together back into the distant past. I talked softly to him of those times as I held him to my breast. He scarcely answered, but his eyes filled with adoration and spoke for him. I knew now the special ways in which he needed my love, and the special things he wanted remembered. It was the same day after day. It was truly wonderful.

For almost another month and then . . .

Tadek's heart stopped beating as he lay, loved and cherished, close to my heart. I did not call to Max for help. I waited with my lips against his brow while his body grew cold and a film came over his dark eyes. I whispered my undying love so he would take it with him into another world.

Then Max came and took me away.

When I stood beside Tadek's grave in tears of desolate misery, I had one thought – if only my life could end at this moment. If I could drop down dead on that sheeted body, and we could sleep together for ever and ever. What matter that our arms would be arms of clay so long as there was nothing ever again to keep us apart?

I sat alone in the room we had shared, looking out at the little rocky cemetery where he lay, apart from me. Life is over for me too, Tadek, I whispered. I am there with you, I will always be with you in this cold windswept mountainy place.

Late in the evening, Max came to share my vigil.

'Tomorrow you must go away from the camp, *balibt*. You must go back to Dublin where it is safe and easy. I have told my father.'

'Do you think it will be easy now that I have known the reality . . .'

Max silenced me with his fingertips on my lips. 'Don't, Lia. You have been through a great strain, greater than you realize. I will not rest until I know you are safely home in Dublin.'

'Can you come with us?' I pleaded.

'Not yet,' he answered. 'I have a duty to many people to close down this last camp and get people home. We have friends working for us to retrieve each man's papers. Many now would wish to travel under false names, fear makes cowards. And some are mentally distressed.'

'But when will we see you again?' I begged.

Max shook his head. 'I do not know, little one. I do not know. I have given my father a telephone number. There will be some news, some sort of news, from time to time.'

We stood at the window until the last rays of light had gone, and the shadows of the craggy rocks closed in over the little graveyard.

I buried my head against Max's arm. 'Talk about Tadek just once more,' I whispered.

Max held me tenderly away from him. 'Darling Lia, do you remember the message I brought from Tadek to you?'

'Yes,' I answered. 'I remember – he said I was to be happy.' What had Max's father said: Happiness, the gift of the Gods.

Max hugged me very gently. 'I am giving you the same message now. Go back with my father. Start living your life, Lia, you were made to be happy. There is a man who wants to marry you . . .'

I pulled away from Max. I could not speak for the choking desolation in my heart.

Chapter Twenty One

So we came back to Dublin, the old man and I. The journey was very different now. I was desperately sad and always close to tears. I had to make an enormous effort to accept the old man's comforting hand. When I saw his pleading eyes I felt I had let him down. I was not the prize he had thought to bring to his son. The prize was for another . . . and that other was now . . . and I would weep again.

I could not give coherent thought to my own future. What future? I had handed in my resignation to the Department. Without a job, how would I survive? Only in brief moments did I think of myself. My inward gaze was fixed on the small graveyard in the Matra mountains. Soon I would be hundreds of miles away from that place . . . more poignantly loved than any other place on earth. I knew now why Max's father stayed always close to that grave in Dolphin's Barn where the carved figure kept guard.

When I look back on the old man, I realize what a truly remarkable man he was. Patient and loving and resourceful and knowledgeable. Even now, so many years afterwards, I remember my amazement to find myself in Le Bourget Airport, boarding a plane for Dublin, and being met at Dublin Airport by Ted and the limousine – all accomplished as if we were seasoned 'plane-travellers in the year 1947! My old friend never drew my attention to the deftness of his arrangements, although he liked to be noticed and he accepted gratitude so graciously.

Ted told us that Mr Lloyd had 'phoned every day to

enquire if we were home. He had been told that we were to arrive on this evening. He had said he would call about nine o'clock.

'Are you too tired, Lia? Perhaps I should 'phone and suggest tomorrow?' The old man looked a little apprehensive. We had not discussed, nor mentioned, Tony Lloyd, but my old friend read my change of heart. Who would not? My life had changed its course.

'No,' I said with a firmness of purpose which did not deceive, 'let him come.'

Tony came at nine o'clock, handsomely debonair and nonchalant as ever. He did not attempt to kiss me, nor take my hand. His deep (and justified) displeasure must be made to be felt although that was a little difficult to maintain against his surprise as he took in the splendour of the house: the paintings, the sculptures, the luxurious furniture. The old man indicated the sideboard of glittering decanters. In his dignified courteous style, he asked me to attend to a drink for Tony. With Max's safety assured, my old friend was restored to his former spry elegance, a princely elegance.

'And you will excuse me if I retire, the journey was fatiguing.'

Tony accepted a glass of brandy. I waited for him to speak. I was trembling with the effort to pluck up courage.

'I am a patient man, Lia, but you have really pushed your luck a bit far.'

A gleam of hope shot up that he was going to bow out of our engagement.

'Don't you think you have treated me rather badly?' His voice verged on the truculent.

'I am sorry, Tony.'

'Where were you that you could not 'phone or write or send telegrams in the last ten weeks?'

'It was difficult . . .' I began.

'I refuse to believe that,' his voice had risen, 'I am not accustomed to being treated shabbily.'

'I am sorry, Tony, I wish I –'

'Sorry isn't enough. How much longer do you think I am going to be pushed around in favour of other people? Why are my interests not paramount? Do you expect me to believe you the next time we set the date, and I have all the arrangements. . . .'

I found a strong voice. 'There will not be a next time.'

'What do you mean?' he almost shouted.

I spoke quickly. 'I am returning this beautiful ring, I wish to end our engagement.'

His manner changed swiftly. 'Oh Lia, come on! Don't be silly – can't a fellow blow off steam? I have been hanging around for months!'

I put the ring in its box on the table between us.

'Take the ring, Tony, and forgive me.'

'Lia, don't try my patience. We will set a new date tonight and, this time, you will honour it.'

'Tony, please take the ring and please go away.' I had found the courage.

'What have *I* done?' He spoke in much astonishment. 'You're the one who went off! You're the one . . .' He stood up as if to take hold of me.

'Yes, I am the one,' I said. 'I cannot marry you.'

'Of course you can, Lia! You are only –'

'I cannot! I cannot! I am pregnant!'

Tony Lloyd's face went livid with anger. He made a movement of raising his arm. I was frightened, my fingers went to the electric bell on the table.

'So that is what it is!' Tony flared at me, his expressive glance took in the magnificent room for whose riches I had evidently surrendered my body. 'You bitch! You filthy bitch!'

Ted was at the door. 'Is there something?' he asked.

'Yes, Ted, Mr Lloyd is leaving . . .' the sentence was never finished. Tony had brushed past Ted. He fled down the steps and into his car. He had gone out of my life.

Now the torrent of tears could come at last. In the old man's arms, all the grief spilled over. The loss of a lifetime's dream with the tragic death of Tadek, the loss of Max who had been defrauded, the guilt for Tony who had been shamefully used, the guilt for the little baby who had no name, no father to cherish him.

In a few days I went home to Gran's little house in the city. It was my house now and at least I had a roof if not money or happiness.

I went into each tidy room, opened each window, and collapsed in utter misery on Brian Boru's chair. Suddenly there was a great commotion at the door. It could only be Phyllis. And it was – complete with shopping bags of groceries.

In some way which I had not detected, the old man had arranged for her to come and take care of me. She seemed to have money for all our needs, and very soon her familiar cooking aromas wafted around and the place took on the old remembered shine.

In the weeks that followed, I made endless attempts to find out from Phyllis, what exactly were our resources? Where was the money coming from?

'Will this money run out, Phyllis?' I asked every day.

'Lovey, will you stop the long list of batty questions! You would drive a holy saint into sinful exasperation. And it doesn't matter a continental thrawneen – the money is there every Thursday and that's an end of it!'

I went frequently to Terenure. I never brought up the subject of money. I supposed it was his money, but then it might have been Phyllis's savings. The weeks were passing and slowly I began to be certain I was carrying Tadek's baby.

'Phyllis,' I said for the hundredth time, 'I really am able to look after myself now. You are wasting great chances just hanging around here.'

'Whisha what chances?' she replied. 'Is it the singin'? Sure I

335

had enough of that. Singin' is all very well for its own sake but dressin' up and powderin' yer face and singin' for a load of aul hoors drinkin' their guts out – that's a different kind of singin'! Like a Godforsaken Jezebel!'

'But all the good money you were earning,' I protested many times.

'Well now about the money!' she would reply. 'You spend a lot of money just keepin' yerself earning! Isn't that a quare one for ye? That was something I had to find out for meself – you have to provide your own perks when you're gettin' the fists of money. Like buying gowns to show yourself off in, the same gowns that you can't get five shillings for after you've worn them! A dead loss!'

'You were very good to your mother and Sylvie,' I always said.

'Yes, well they don't need me to be dishin' out so much now. Sylvie is workin'. She gets more for sittin' at a desk typing letters than I used to earn in a month. She doesn't get the perks, though, that Mama used to give me – God be good to her poor soul,' and Phyllis crossed herself piously. 'And me Mam is not in need now, either. Me Da makes more money on oul nixers now that he's retired – puttin' up a shelf or a bit of wallpaper. He has a lot of the oul stock still up in Sandymount that never lets him down.'

Sandymount was still the horizon of my dreams – the great empty strand where I searched for Tadek, or walked long, long ago with Gran while she told me about the emigrant ships, and Aunt Hannah in Philadelphia. I could have gone walking on the strand, it was only a short distance from the city.

I did not go. When tears of forsaken loneliness threatened to build up behind my eyelids, I suggested the 'pictures', and Phyllis was delighted.

'All the same, Phyllis – didn't you ever think of marriage again?' I chanced one evening.

She gave me a long, fond look out of those brilliant eyes.

336

'Well, I did and I didn't,' she replied in her teasing way. 'I did because I liked it, and I didn't because you can't repeat a good thing – Jacques was near-perfect, a proper gent! And anyway I'm gettin' a bit long in the tooth. I had an offer, you know!'

'Please tell me, Phyllis, please!'

'Well, it was oul Frare – the wife died, you know? He asked me again last week. He's makin' pots of oul loot with his two pubs.'

'And would you, Phyllis?'

'No bloody fear!' she said and she crossed herself piously as usual. 'That oul fright! I wouldn't marry an Irishman anyway. If he was a Frenchman, or an Italian – I met a nice one of them in the Isle of Man – he was a waiter. He was doing the waiter to learn English for when he'd open his own hotel somewhere!'

'A waiter,' I just pictured him, 'and how old was he?'

'Oh,' she replied airily, 'in the region of my own age – thereabouts!'

'And what was his name?' I begged.

'Wouldn't ye know,' she said, 'Luigi! I don't remember his surname at the moment. Luigi!'

'Phyllis, begin at the beginning and tell me every little detail about this Italian. Where does he live in Italy? Start by telling me his name again.'

'Luigi! Wait now and I'll get the card for you, Lovey. Here it is. Luigi Martelli. He is gone home to Italy now and he wants me to write to him, he asked me when we were parting in the Isle of Man.'

'Parting, Phyllis?' I asked inquisitively.

'Yes,' she said, 'he came to see me off. He took me out to dinner the night before I left. I told him I'd write if I did not lose his address!' The impish giggle was never far away.

'So he is sending this card to make sure you have his address.' I turned over the picture postcard, his name and address were printed neatly on one side, and on the other

337

side, a picture of a cathedral in Siena. 'I suppose he is a Catholic?' I asked.

'Oh God, yes,' Phyllis said, 'very devout. He has a brother a monk, and two sisters nuns. The monk never comes out, and the nuns teach and nurse. That was the family, two brothers and two sisters. A small family.'

I could see that Phyllis and Luigi had exchanged family histories. That was a good sign.

'Would you like to keep in touch with him?' I asked.

'What do *you* think, Lovey? Would I be demeaning myself to answer a picture postcard?'

Knowing she wanted to, I answered loyally, 'Of course not!'

Phyllis thought about it, smiling at me speculatively. 'He is a lively little fella,' she said, 'a proper gent.'

That was Phyllis's accolade, so I did not let her rest until she had written an inviting letter to Siena, telling Luigi she would meet him in Dublin, 'if at any time he happened to be passing this way!'

'I have me pride, so I have,' she told me, 'it wouldn't do to give him any ideas!'

'Or false hopes?' I enquired.

'You know, Lovey,' said Phyllis with a kind of shy pride, 'I have Jacques's pension. I don't need to go running.'

Unexpectedly, Berny came to stay for a few days.

I was full of apologies for not being in touch. We had always made a point of remembering birthdays, and writing the occasional letter.

'I was away,' I told her. 'But actually, you would have had a letter very soon in answer to the one in which you told me that you would be in Dublin for the Spring Show. Please forgive me, I was not here at all at that time.'

'Where were you, Lia? I 'phoned your office and they said you had resigned to get married. I called here on chance that someone would have your address. In Foxrock, isn't it?'

'Yes, I mean no. I was away on a long holiday with my old friend. In Europe.'

'Long holiday?' Berny echoed. 'But what about your engagement?'

'I have broken it off.'

Berny looked at me thoughtfully. 'Still the same old Lia – full of secrets as always!'

'I am sorry, Berny, I . . .'

'At least,' Berny was smiling a little, 'at least, you didn't go off and get married without letting me know! Wasn't I to be your matron-of-honour? Wasn't that the promise?'

I am sure my answering smile was a doubtful one. My marriage was in the past. And Berny was right as always: it was another secret.

'It doesn't matter now,' Berny said, 'I've come anyway – I guessed you didn't know. If you were not here to see it in the newspapers, who would tell you?'

'What is it, Berny? What?'

'It's Lucille,' and Berny's lips were quivering. 'After all those years and years of horse shows and Spring Shows and winning firsts and the whole damned thing – how the hell does she come to fall and get kicked in the head? How?'

'Lucille? Impossible! When? Out hunting? Is she hurt?'

'If she was hunting, accidents happen hunting, but she wasn't – she was in the dressage competitions in the Spring Show,' Berny's tears were falling, her words became inaudible, 'she was kicked in the head . . . she . . . she was badly hurt . . . she died.'

Then we were both crying together, and we cried for a long time, clinging to each other for consolation.

'I've been wanting to cry for weeks and weeks,' Berny sobbed, 'I wanted to cry ever since, but I had to find you to cry with. No one else would understand. Oh Lia, I was there. I saw her fall, I'll never understand why. I was out of the stand . . . like a flash . . . I raced up the turf . . . horses pounding all around me . . . I held her . . oh Lia, her head was wide open . . . she was gone . . . I know nothing could have saved her . . . but I stood up and started screaming at them to shoot the bloody horse.'

All our memories of Lucille came flooding back and we were crying through our words and laughing through our tears. Lucille had always come to Dublin for a day of shopping at Christmastime. Sometimes, she had come for a meal with Gran and me. Lucille had never changed in the smallest way. In a way, she had never grown up.

'The three brothers were the important thing in Lucille's family,' Berny said, 'there was no room for anyone else.'

'But she was always poking fun at them, wasn't she?'

'I know,' Berny replied, 'but she never talked of anyone else.'

'She used to buy a million of baby presents for their children,' I told Berny, 'she couldn't do enough for them.'

'They were all at the funeral,' Berny began to cry again, 'I hated them for not being more demonstrative.'

'Do you remember the way Lucille tied the pens together to do lines? She was the nicest of the three of us, and yet she never got anyone to love her. She never once mentioned a man to me! And you know, Berny, with her lovely colouring, she was quite beautiful, wasn't she?'

Berny smiled at me through her tears. 'Oh Lia, you were always an idiotic dilly! Didn't you know that Lucille was not the marrying kind?'

When we were getting ready for bed, I asked Berny about her marriage.

'There is nothing much to tell,' she said. 'I do not think I am suited to marriage but we grind along. I am home in Belfast for a month or two because my father has had a heart attack. I don't miss America, or anyone in it. Hey, do you ever hear from Burton?' She held up her wrist to display the bracelet she always wore. 'Souvenir of one hell of a night – and of many a night! Some man! What's the news on him? My God, I adored him!'

'I have never seen him since the day of your wedding, Berny,' I answered steadily and directly. The name of Burton had slipped through a web of words without an after-trace.

'Me neither,' she murmured sleepily.

I took Berny to Terenure. She had fond memories of my old friend from the long-ago dinners in the Shelbourne Hotel.

She was enthralled with the lovely house, the evidence of his great wealth. He was sixty, and old as he was, he could turn on immense charm. We spent a couple of hours in his delightful company.

'That old guy is in love with you, Lia,' Berny said when we were going home, 'he cannot take his eyes off you! Why don't you move in with him? He obviously worships you.'

He worships you. When Berny had gone away, her words recurred again and again. He worships you. I loved him as I would have loved my own father. I was forever promising myself that if he were ever ill, I would spend each day at his bedside. I would nurse him back to health. I would devote the rest of my life to him.

Perhaps my desolate loneliness, now hidden from Phyllis's eyes under a mask of gaiety, could be dissolved in caring for the old man. He was my bridge to my lost brothers.

There my thoughts would stop.

I was not alone. I was carrying Tadek's child within me. That was my true bridge back to Tadek. It was also my link with Max. Each time I thought of the baby, I would hear Max's voice, remember his smile . . . 'Miracles do happen'. And then I would remember how safe and warm it was within Max's arms.

I needed comfort, but no: I should not consider moving from this little house into the palatial residence of Max's father. That was the crux: he was not my father, he was Max's father.

I had nothing to offer the old man. I had not become the actress he had seen in me. I had not accepted his son's love. I was a failure. Self-pity? Well, let it be self-pity.

In the old Dublin phrase, I was 'in trouble'. And I had yet to face all the complications of being a pregnant woman without a husband.

And yet, and yet . . . the old man's loving care of me was very precious. Perhaps for a little while, perhaps for just a little while, perhaps if he should ask me again?

Then one day, I asked him to tell me about the money so readily available. I had begun to worry in case Phyllis, in her generosity of heart, was spending her savings on our household needs.

'Please tell me, if you can, how I come to have money for every day in the week?'

'I did not broach the matter, little one, until you would ask. I wish with all my heart that you will bear with me, and my little arrangements for your wellbeing.' As always, he took my hands in his. 'I have made a settlement for you. No, no, do not protest. It is my pleasure. You know what you mean to me. If you would come and live here, that would be an even greater pleasure. And you could sell your little property very well at this moment.'

I was thinking of Phyllis and her hopes of Luigi. For I knew her hopes, despite her fervent denials.

'Is that what you advise,' I asked him.

He nodded gravely, adjusting his spectacles to study my expression. I smiled for him, and I kissed his fingers very gently. His fingers were always dry as paper.

His face lit up with radiance when I said, 'Then you have my power of attorney – doesn't that sound very important! Go ahead and make what plans you think best. I love you, and I will come to you soon.'

Many times now, I noticed how he looked expectantly for

342

a few words of affection. No longer did he mention the name of Max. The special 'phone number that Max had given him seemed to have been forgotten. There was no future of a family nature indicated to me as there used to be. Nor did I press the name of his beloved son into our lovely conversations.

I had written a long letter of gratitude to Max. There had been no reply.

Why should there be a reply? Was not love dead and buried forever in a shadowy graveyard among makeshift tombstones? Tadek. Tadek ... Far, far away in the terrifying Matra mountains.

'Lia, my dear little Lia, please do not look so sad.'

It was best to be honest with so loving a friend.

'Before you receive me into your house, there is something I must tell you. I was going to go away and hide, but I will not, I am not ashamed.'

He was turned fully towards me, the radiance had not faded from his face. 'Then tell me, Lia, my dear child.'

'Not a child any more,' I told him gently, 'I believe I am to bear a child of my own.'

The joy intensified in his eyes and he folded his arms around me. 'You are carrying our dear Tadek's child. I hoped. I was not sure.'

This old man was truly amazing. 'Then you are not angry with me?' I asked.

'Angry? Angry? I am overjoyed. To Tadek I owe Max's life. Did you not know that? Ah, some day all the story will be told. Our dear Tadek was an heroic soul. A welcome there will be for his child as never has been seen. *Kabolas ponem oyfele sheyn.*'

He kissed me ceremonially on both sides of my head, 'Ah, *mayn lyubenyu!*'

When he allowed his deepest feelings to show through, he was not aware he spoke in Yiddish. Max, too, had this habit. Now my friend was welcoming my beautiful baby, and he was calling me his darling. The words always moved me unbearably because I remembered them from my treasured days in the Vashinskys' kitchen in Ringsend.

The old man rang the bell on his table. When Ted came, he directed him to bring champagne. Ted's wife, Shanlee, brought the glasses. All four of us drank champagne, toasting, in the old man's words: 'The Future!'

Phyllis was bubbling with news when I opened the door into our little shining house.

'Lovey, you'll never believe it! Look what came in the post – would you looka? The registered post!'

She was holding out a letter and a small box. In the box was a really beautiful ring.

'Phyllis, is it from Luigi?'

'The old cod!' She was almost overcome with laughter. 'But wait for the letter. It's half in Italian – it's not English anyway. I can only get bits of it. You read it, lovey.'

'Wait,' I said, just as full of excitement as she was, 'wait. I have a little Italian dictionary somewhere. We'll figure it out together.'

'He has his glue,' laughed Phyllis, 'if he thinks I'm hopping on the next flight to Italy!'

In fact, it was Luigi who came hopping to Dublin. The ring was for their engagement. His letters of freedom followed quickly. He wanted no delay beyond six weeks. They would spend their *mese miele* with his mother in Siena. *Non problema*!

My problem was to keep my weight down until after the wedding. Phyllis was boasting how well I was looking these days: 'Filling out under my management.' If I told her that I was pregnant, her wedding would never take place. Mama's daughter would come before Luigi. It would be unbelievable that I could survive without Phyllis!

But I had never shared the secret of Tadek with Phyllis.

When she was married, and far away, I would feel safe to make my own arrangements. When the baby was born would be time enough to look to Phyllis to help me.

I managed to lose myself in the preparations for Phyllis's wedding. We spent hours in Dublin every day, unable to decide whether the shops on the south side of the Liffey, or the north side, were the better for style or fashion. Better value for money on the north side, in Phyllis's view. I fancied Grafton Street, and she fancied Henry Street, the day usually ended in George's Street where, in Phyllis's opinion, 'the larger lady was better catered.'

Phyllis had brought Luigi to the house in the narrow street, and she introduced him to Brian Boru's chair. She told him all the history, and ancestry, of the chair. Mopping her eyes, she bemoaned that she must part with it, the last memory of her beloved Jacques who had died a hero in that bloody war.

Luigi had a delicate way of patting her heaving bosom, his own eyes glistening in tearful sympathy.

'But no! *Che bellissima sedia* there will be no parting. Contemplate the wood, admire the carving! *La sedia bellissima* will go with us to Siena. So to be admired in the . . . in the . . . is it hallway? *Si, si*, that is the place.'

Now Luigi patted the chair in the same sensitive way he had patted Phyllis's bosom. He was a generous person. '*Olmo Irlandese scultore in legno nei tempe antiche! Cosa antica! Vecchio antico in legno mogano non olmo!*'

It is doubtful if Phyllis understood Luigi's flow of language, any more than she had understood Jacques's French. But Phyllis understood tender feelings with the instant response of love. That day, in Gran's old house, her tears ceased magically. Henceforth Luigi could sit, like a diminutive hero, in the famous chair where had sat Brian Boru who drove the Danes out of Ireland at the Battle of Clontarf; and Bold Robert Emmett in his white plumed hat, he who was the Darling of Ireland and the beloved of Miss Sara Curran; and Phyllis's own heroic husband, Jacques,

345

whose feats of bravery had multiplied since his death for France. Heroes all, and now Luigi had been given the honour.

I have never seen Luigi actually sitting in that chair. Luigi has nothing to fear from the heroes of history, written or unrecorded. He enjoys the love and devotion of a beautiful woman. With Phyllis at his side, he has built up a hotel and *ristorante* unrivalled for excellence.

Glittering like bronze, the chair with the carved wolfhounds stands in the atrium of their hotel as if it embodied the dead heroes still on guard.

A brass plaque describes the chair in three languages: it is an excellent example of ancient Irish wood carving; many earlier owners of this chair were of royal lineage whose names are illustrious in history. Moreover, this chair has magic properties in its own right. You may wish your special wish, once only, while you sit in the chair and count slowly to seven. You may, of course, count in any language of your choice. Your wish will come to pass.

La Sedia Bellissima is also known as The Wishing Chair and it is at least one of the crowning achievements of Phyllis's life.

The wedding was to take place in St Patrick's Church, Ringsend. Phyllis moved back into her mother's house some days before. There were many things to supervise including the decoration with flowers of the church. This was the old man's wedding present to her. Phyllis was astonished and very grateful. Over the years, she had held off from completely accepting my friendship with him. Jews, she held, no matter what you said, Jews were different.

'Spending his money to decorate a Catholic church! Lovey, I can't get over it! You wouldn't know the old church, it's like a cathedral, Ma says! Me Da says it must have cost the bloody Mint!'

On the morning of the wedding Ted brought the old man to my little house so they could drive me to the wedding in style. Of course, my old friend had come to admire.

'You have the look of a bride, Lia. That hat suits you so wonderfully. I am glad you are wearing a full-length dress, it is graceful. It is your colour.'

Sometimes I laughed at his arrant flattery. Mostly I cherished it and rewarded it with a kiss.

'Now, Ted will come to fetch you. Say what time you would like? Shall we end the day with dinner in the Shelbourne? For old time's sake? I shall dress formally in keeping with you. Shall we celebrate?'

'Perhaps we will,' I smiled at him, 'but after the wedding feast, I am going to make a little pilgrimage of my own up to "Sunrise". That, too, is for old time's sake.'

'And the Shelbourne?' he pleaded.

He was so dear. I would never refuse him anything.

'The Shelbourne,' I agreed, 'a little after seven. Please do not worry about sending the car. I will get a taxi.'

Phyllis looked wonderful on her wedding day, with that glorious shining look that only she has ever achieved.

The Dalys threw a party, in Mr Daly's words, 'The like of which the neighbours in Ringsend had never witnessed, a wedding feast that was guaranteed to knock all other wedding feasts into a cocked hat!'

The church, festooned in colourful flowers, was packed with every friend, relative, and neighbour the Dalys had ever had. When we returned to the house, the whole street was overflowing. Within minutes, the piano was going and all the sons and daughters who could add to the music and singing were contributing with true Daly gusto. The gaiety was infectious and hilarious.

Phyllis had told me that it was her singing in the Isle of Man which had made Luigi fall in love with her, and she was singing for him now with all the old exuberance I had known and loved as long as I could remember. He was gazing at her, his glass raised in adoring admiration, a smile of pleasure

347

on his face. I knew Phyllis would make him the happiest man in Italy. I was filled with gladness for them.

As I watched the party swinging along, the loud voices faded into the mist of memory and I was drifting back to that never-forgotten long ago.

Here in the Dalys' front window was the very place I used to watch out for Tadek to pass by. And he watched for me – now I knew that. He used to ruffle his fingers through his hair as he passed the window, and I used to give him what I fondly hoped was a passionate seductive smile. Tadek. Tadek. The eternal study books pressed against his frayed jacket, the old dark trousers just a little short as he grew taller, the glimpse of that gleaming smile as he hurried by.

Tadek, I was less than ten then and now I am almost thirty. For every single moment of all those years, you have been in my mind, and in my heart, and in my dreams. Tadek. Tadek.

Mrs Daly was filling my glass. She was inviting me to partake of the buffet laid out on trestle tables. I could see the guests all joining in the singing. Luigi, too, was singing and his hands were clasped around a big tumbler of stout. I smiled to think of the effect of half a dozen of those! But Phyllis would take good care of him.

She was singing now an old favourite Moore's Melody: the song with which she had competed against Laelia in the Ierne Hall in Parnell Square all those years ago:

> 'She is far from the land
> Where her young hero sleeps
> And lovers around her are sighing
> But sadly she turns from their gaze
> And she weeps
> For her heart in his grave is lying. . . .'

The flood of memories was overwhelming. I went out into the front garden to get away from the haunting, heartbroken melody.

There at the end of South Lotts Road and the corner of Ringsend Road was Mama's shop, now empty and abandoned. There on that turn was Hastings Street, and back to back with it was Little's Terrace.

In all the years, nothing had changed except life itself.

I had told Phyllis that I would be at the airport the next day to say our final goodbyes. Now I stole away to be alone. At the corner, there was a bus for Sandymount. I had been thinking of this little journey for days. I wanted to lay my ghosts in the place where memory began. It was time to begin a new life with no more repinings. I must trust myself to have the courage now to move on into a future that I had never planned.

At Sandymount Tower, I sat on the low stone wall looking out across the great empty strand where I used to search for Tadek. I could almost taste again the childish tears of disappointment when I failed to find him.

You would have come, Tadek, if only you could. I know now, oh how well I know now, that you loved me, and needed me, and longed to comfort me. But, like you told me when you held me close in our marriage bed, I was only a little girl, and there were so many barriers between us.

And long before that time, Burton used to take me walking across this strand with our dog Silky. It used to seem like miles and miles of walking and Burton used to jaunt me up on his shoulders all the way home, twinkling his eyes up at me and whistling some sort of marching tune. I loved him then as children love a sharing, caring father. Burton came back in memory like a Greek god of mythology. Was there ever so magnificent a man? Yes, I loved you, and I went on loving you in a special way – perhaps in the same special way you loved me. I would have given myself to you, and however wrongly, I wanted to. Was it not strange that whenever our paths met, there was always a Guardian Angel on duty? I am grateful to that Angel now. I wonder, all the same, where are you now? It must be somewhere very far away . . . that old bitter disillusion, so troublesomely within me, has been long gone.

I looked back across the Strand Road at the house that was Mama's 'Sunrise'. Poor Mama. If only I had been nicer to you. You were so excited to discover that the sun rose in the east specially so it could fill your bedroom with the morning light. I can still see you standing at the window, holding back the filmy curtains, your fair hair falling down, your so blue eyes wide with expectation, taking my hand: 'Now look, now look, now look – oh Lia, the first golden tip of the sun is just . . . oh look . . . oh look.' Poor Mama. We were worlds apart. I gave all my love to Gran.

I did not have to conjure up Gran's image. She was always there within me. We were secure in each other today and every day, just as secure as when we walked on this strand, going home to tea in 'Sunrise'. We always walked on our bare feet through the shallow water, and Gran always remarked how good the seawater is for the feet. And I always pleaded for more about Georgio, and Aunt Hannah, and Philadelphia.

I left the wall and went down the steps onto the hard-packed strand. The tide was so far out that the silver line of sea was on the horizon. The Head of Howth filled the skyline, glittering in the evening sun like some promised land.

I walked slowly across the rippled sand. I knew I was searching again for Tadek. I was searching for a miracle. Could you come even for one moment, to hold me once more for even a moment? My eyes went on searching. Tadek, please . . . please. . . .

There was no one, not a single person, in all that huge empty strand. And still I searched. I have your child, Tadek, and oh my darling, I rejoice in that. Our child. If only I could share this wonderful burden with you. Just think, the three of us going forward to a new and future life. Will it be a very lonely future for only the two of us, without you? What happens to a woman without a father for her child? Is it terribly sad for the little child? Will people scorn us?

My old friend, on whose kindness I can now depend, he will not be there forever. Oh God, please spare him to the child and to me for another while. I thought then of his invitation to dinner, given for fear I would succumb to sadness after Phyllis's wedding. He would be expecting me to join him in the Shelbourne.

I turned back towards the land. The sun was going down now behind the distant villas. I shaded my eyes with my hand. In the shimmering light I could see one man had come out onto the strand to walk a dog.

Perhaps when the baby was born, and we had a little house near a strand, I could get a little dog for extra company.

I watched the man's dog romping, and running back to the man, and away again. It was only a little puppy. A little puppy with the Blenheim colouring of Silky.

Shading my eyes from the setting sun, I bent down to watch the puppy running towards me. I wanted to pick up the puppy but I hesitated because of the long full dress. Well, at least I could pet the little dog. I bent down low.

'Lia, Lia, Lia!' It was Max's voice. No other voice in the world could say my name in just that way.

Max had come from nowhere out onto the great empty strand to look for me.

I did not think to ask how or why. There were no questions. I knew at once that this little puppy would be a present from Max to me.

And then he gathered me into his arms. I felt the soft wiriness of his beard on my throat, on my face. Then his lips were against my unresisting mouth. I reached up to put my arms around his neck.

It was a luxury beyond price to stand there and to be kissed with tenderness, to be comforted with love, to have the helpless loneliness banished forever.

Not then, nor ever after, did I question the perfect rightness of that moment.

'I have found you at last,' was all Max said.

351